Aljce

in Therapy Land

Lawrence & Gibson Publishing Collective
www.lawrenceandgibson.co.nz

Aljce in Therapy Land
First edition published in Aotearoa/New Zealand by
Lawrence & Gibson.
Copyright © Alice Tawhai, 2021

Printed at Rebel Press, Trades Hall, Te Aro, Wellington

Aljce in Therapy Land / Alice Tawhai
ISBN 978-0-473-59379-7

Cover image: Alice Tawhai
Copy-editor: Johanna Knox
Editorial oversight: Brannavan Gnanalingam
Cover and page design: Murdoch Stephens
Design consultant: Paul Neason

Published with the assistance of a grant from

ARTS COUNCIL OF NEW ZEALAND TOI AOTEAROA

Aljce

in Therapy Land

Alice
Tawhai

For my Jaaneman, Jake Johnson,
cos, yinno; love.

Also dedicated to everyone who has ever been bullied at work. (Or bullied and controlled in any way by anyone.) And also to the person to whom this story belongs to, who learned four things; don't doubt yourself, have courage, never give up, and everything passes.

In order to see a rainbow, you must have your back to the sun.

And those who were seen dancing
were thought to be mad
by those who couldn't hear the music.
- source unknown

DOWN THE RABBIT HOLE

ON HER FIRST day, the sky had a salmon tint to it; after the rain, and before the cloud had entirely cleared, as if it had been put into a washing machine with roses. Someone was probably really annoyed at the way they had run. Aljce parked on the asphalt in the carpark outside the Therapy Hub. She was looking forward to her new job. It would be an exciting adventure with new challenges. That's what she'd told Jillq, her new employer, at the job interview. She'd loved her old job, but she could do it in the dark after all these years. And she was looking forward to working with Jillq, who'd impressed her straight away. Aljce liked what Jillq said, and the way she said it. She even liked the way she smelled – like flowers that had been locked in a wardrobe for years, suddenly bursting free. Jillq She had a pretty name too. The clear glassiness of the I and Ls in the middle were smeared between the jammy apricot of the J and the deep plum of the Q. Aljce couldn't wait to work for her.

And Mrs. Kingi worked here. Aljce had known Mrs. Kingi through work for a few years now. It would be nice to work alongside her, to already know someone here. Even better, Mrs. Kingi hadn't been able to say enough good things about Jillq; persuading Aljce to leave the job where she'd been so comfortable and to take the plunge into something new. Aljce had initially been reluctant to leave a good thing when she had it: flexible hours so she could work longer during the term and take time off during the school holidays, and employers who were generous in their support of her. Hannah had been a great boss. And Aljce was more of a cautious person than a risk taker. But she'd always wanted that counselling qualification.

Mrs. Kingi had reassured her, so she was looking forward to it. A new job AND falling in love. Life couldn't get much better. A good job was crucial, because she needed to work. Someone had to pay the mortgage and buy everything that Pleasance and Liddell needed. It wouldn't be their father; he was long gone. And it wouldn't be her most recent ex, he was in jail. Aljce had to be the person who provided for her daughters. As a single mum, all her bills were on her. Although maybe it would work out with her potential new love. It would be lovely to have a best friend. Someone to always support her and to share the load, someone to care about and laugh with, someone who thought she was special.

And perhaps that would be Lewis. He lived in Wellington. She was still feeling for the edges of his personality. Messaging and calling him was like connecting with a ghost. Neither of them were into FaceTime or photos, so she'd never seen his face. Aljce didn't know why, but it was as if he was somehow tangled up with her brain. She thought of him for no reason at all; without making any choice to do so. Sometimes she wondered if he was thinking of her at the same time. Could it be possible to fall in love so quickly and for it to be real? Perhaps some people just did. Could it be real love if you'd never actually met a person? Two things were possible. He would make her either very unhappy, or very, very happy.

In honour of it being her first day at her new job, Aljce was wearing an Alice in Wonderland themed outfit. She liked to dress up without actually dressing up, and it fitted with her name and her situation today. A mid-blue cotton dress that was printed with the outlines of small white hearts and had a heart-shaped cut-out back, white knee socks, which no one wore, mainly because they weren't in fashion, and shiny black Mary-Janes. The idea was that it should remind people of Alice, even if they couldn't put their finger on why. Time to go inside, she thought. Aljce in Therapy Land!

There was a large topiary tree with dark leaves next to the entrance way. It was cut into the shape of some sort of animal, but Aljce wasn't quite sure what. Possibly a rabbit with floppy ears, but it could have been a Cocker Spaniel, or even a donkey. Aljce put her hand on the metal door handle, ready to start her new life. But as she gripped the handle, an electric shock ran through her body. It didn't really hurt. It was just unpleasant; roughing her sensibilities up the wrong way, like someone rubbing polystyrene on a window pane. She stared at the door handle. She didn't want to touch it again, even though it was likely she'd already discharged the static electricity. So she wound her light cardigan round her hand and tried again. Perfect. Except she pushed the door when she should have pulled. She wished she had a dollar for every time she'd ever done that, but everyone else probably wished the same thing. It was just one of those rules of the universe that the door you were trying to open always opened the other way.

The interior of the building was so pink that it was like entering a womb. Candyfloss pink, little girl pink, vagina pink. A woman was leaving the building with her head down, trying to hide her tears. Perhaps her therapy had been distressing. Jillq came out and spoke to the receptionist. 'You know WHO has been in again,' she said, sounding annoyed. The receptionist looked sympathetic, and murmured something in a low voice. Jillq turned and, seeing Aljce, was at her side immediately.

'Wonderful, my dear,' she said in her husky voice, reminding Aljce of thick, dripping honey. Aljce loved Jillq's voice. 'You've arrived. Let me show you around. This is our reception area, where we receive clients, and this is Chelsea, our Administrative Greeter.' The Administrative Greeter winked at Aljce, and Aljce liked her immediately.

'I'm sure Aljce will be feeling at home in no time,' said Chelsea.

'Time,' said Jillq. 'There's no time to waste! We need to show her around!' Aljce pegged Chelsea as a friend because she scrunched up her nose behind Jillq's back, in a mocking, here-we-go-again sort of way. Chelsea seemed fun. And surely you could trust people who were fun.

'Ooh,' said Aljce, standing on something that moved under her foot. She bent over.

Jillq turned to see why she was no longer following her down the corridor. 'What are you doing down there, Aljce?'

Still scrambling for the golf ball that she'd stood on, which had now run down a rut and into a hole in the wall, Aljce answered from between her legs and through her hair. 'I was just trying to pick up a golf ball.' Jillq looked huge from her upside down perspective.

'One rule you must learn here, my dear,' said Jillq, 'is to leave the things that don't concern you alone.'

'Oh, but I was just trying to help,' said Aljce.

'Best left,' said Jillq. 'We have a lot of ground to cover today.' Aljce stood up. Her head spun several times. 'It really is best not to get disorientated,' said Jillq, patting her kindly. 'Mind on the game, Aljce.'

Jillq led Aljce into another room, at the far end of the building. The morning sun had come out while Aljce had been inside, and it was now pulsing in through the large windows. Jillq and Aljce sat down at a round table with a brown, imitation-wood melamine surface, of the type that had been popular in office staff rooms around the world way back in the '70s. Someone had left a spoon with a tea bag resting on it at the edge of the table. Underneath the curve of the spoon was a rimmed tidemark of dried milky tea. Aljce stood up to clear it. There was a rubbish bin and a sink in plain sight. 'Leave it!' barked Jillq. 'Hattie needs to learn to clean up after herself!'

'I really don't mind,' said Aljce.

'People can't learn unless they're held accountable,' said Jillq. 'That spoon doesn't move until she clears it away.'

Aljce sat down. It seemed unprofessional to be meeting at a dirty table without clearing it, but maybe she just needed to be more in tune with what seemed to be the informal atmosphere of the Therapy Hub.

'So,' said Aljce. 'I'm really excited to be here! But I really need you to sign off my student placement agreement. We talked about it previously, when you asked me to apply for the job, and you told me to bring it with me today.'

'I don't like placement agreements,' said Jillq. 'They tie me down to things.'

'All you have to do is agree to provide the placement,' said Aljce, feeling a little panicky. This was not going well; a bad start to her first day. 'It won't tie you down to anything other than what you've already employed me for. And you can pull out at any time. I'm the one who has to do the work; there's nothing for you to do other than sign it off.'

'I'm not keen,' said Jillq.

'The only reason I took this job,' said Aljce, her voice rising slightly, 'is because you said you would provide me with the practical counselling placement I need to finish my qualification. Otherwise I could have stayed where I was. I was really happy there.'

'Have they already filled your old job?' asked Jillq.

'I'm sure I could still go back to it,' lied Aljce, knowing there was already someone sitting at her old desk, and wishing for a brief moment that it was her. 'I don't think they've advertised it yet.'

'Hmm,' said Jillq. 'Let me have a look at your Placement Agreement. I'll get back to you this afternoon. It's important that I read it through properly and give it due consideration. These things can be full of fish hooks.'

Phew, thought Aljce. Silly her; panicking over nothing. She must be over hyped, and more nervous than she thought. Of course Jillq had to be careful about what she signed and read it through first.

They went down the hallway. The building was like a rabbit warren, with rooms leading off the corridor and all connecting to each other, which in turn led to more rooms and cubby holes. Jillq went on ahead into an office with two people sitting at desks. Aljce wondered why people shared offices when there were so many empty rooms. Perhaps it kept costs down in some way.

'Can we clear space for Aljce in here?' Jillq asked the two people.

'There are only two desks,' one of them pointed out, stating the obvious.

'Why isn't anyone ever helpful?' asked Jillq.

'There's a spare desk next door with Kat,' said one of the two.

Jillq went through the gap in the partition into the adjoining space where there were two identical desks, mirroring the layout of the office they'd just come from. One of the desks had a mirror, some lipstick and an iPhone lying on it alongside a book on childhood trauma; open upside down.

'I need some help in here,' called Jillq to the two people next door. They heard her easily, as the partition between the two spaces didn't reach all the way to the ceiling. Jillq directed them to move the desks around so that the one which was already occupied was now in front of the window. She gestured to the desk against the corridor wall. 'This is your one,' she said to Aljce.

Aljce was pleased. It was a nice big desk, with drawers. She wasn't even sure what she would do with it all. 'Thank you,' she said. Jillq didn't introduce anyone, but Aljce supposed that there was plenty of time for that.

After Jillq's tour, Aljce went out to her car and got her photos of her children to put on her desk. 'Is it possible to get some stationery and a new diary?' she asked Chelsea.

'I'll have to check it out with Jillq,' said Chelsea. 'I'll let you know.'

Aljce put her things on her desk, and went to seek out the toilets. She frowned when she found there was no sanitary pad disposer. 'What are we supposed to do with our sanitary pads?' she whispered to Chelsea, back at reception.

Chelsea shrugged. 'Wrap them up and take them home to burn.'

'You must be kidding!' said Aljce. 'Lots of women work here. Surely they can't all be taking their sanitary pads home to burn.'

'That's what I do,' said Chelsea.

Aljce sighed, making a note to herself to bring it up at her first staff meeting. She went back to the toilets, collected the used sanitary pad that she'd wrapped in toilet paper and hidden in a crack in the wall behind the toilet, and took it back to her office and biffed it in the bin, taking care to crumple some sheets of blank paper on top of it. There was no way she was leaving it to bake in her car for the rest of the day, or carrying it around in her bag.

She had only just finished concealing it when Jillq rushed in, waving her arms. 'We need to move your desk!' she said to Aljce. 'You're in the space Kat wants.'

'But we just moved the desks,' said Aljce. 'You gave her the window. Surely she'd rather be there than facing the wall. And I don't mind facing the wall.'

Jillq opened the door to the hallway. 'Chelsea!' she called. 'Quickly! We need to move Kat's desk. She wants it back the way it was!'

'Aljce is already facing the wall,' said Chelsea, arriving within seconds.

'No, no, Bun,' Jillq said. 'Aljce must have the window corner. Straight away. I don't know what you were all thinking.'

Kat arrived at the door just after Chelsea did. She was a slim woman in her forties with an expressive face. 'It's all being fixed Kat,' said Jillq. 'Come down to my office and have coffee while you wait. I've brought some really lovely smoked fish in for you.'

'That would be nice,' said Kat. 'And I can update you about my Pilot.'

'Surely she'd rather have the window,' said Aljce to Chelsea, as they pushed the desks around, swapping their positions.

Chelsea shrugged. 'What Kat wants, she gets. She's the qualified counsellor around here. If she wanted her desk on the roof, Jillq would put it up there and build a sunroom around it. The light probably gets on the screen or her phone when she's messaging if she has the window desk.'

'Can't wait till I'm properly qualified,' said Aljce, who couldn't believe her luck in getting a window desk. 'Why does she call you Bun?'

Chelsea shrugged. 'Like Chelsea Bun. Sometimes she calls me Bunny. She treats me like a daughter. That's what mothers do. They give nicknames.'

Once the desks were settled, Aljce sat there for a while. There were no instructions yet on what she was to do. The field outside the windows was flush with green clover. It undulated in small mounds every now and then, so that it was possible for a person to be not too far away, and yet be hidden from sight. Some of the space was given over to a neat earth garden, sown with orderly rows of cabbages; knit one, pearl one, cabbage one. Aljce's grandmother had taught her to knit when she was a little girl. Aljce hadn't been very good at it; dropping stitches and getting the pale wool all grimy from the palms of her hands.

Someone called Marj came down to ask her what password she'd like to use for the office computer system. 'Marj, short for Marjharee,' she said.

'I'll use the password I always use,' said Aljce. 'I get confused if I've got different passwords for different things.'

'You should mix it up,' said Marj. 'That's good security.'

'Nah, it's okay,' said Aljce. 'Saggitarius99 hasn't let me down yet.'

'Your call,' said Marj. 'I'll get it done straight away. Things are just starting to come right with the computers. I did an extra three hours last night to get them sorted. I've been working ten-hour days all week.'

'That doesn't sound good for you,' said Aljce.

'Well, I didn't get a weekend,' said Marj. 'Your password will be good to go in ten minutes. Is the S capital?'

Aljce logged into her computer when the ten minutes was up, and was delighted to find that Marj had done her work, and she could get into the system. There were still no instructions from Jillq as to what she would like Aljce to do, so Aljce quickly checked her private messages. At least, she intended to quickly check her messages but, as had been the way of late, she spent quite a lot of time in there. She had met Lewis through an online dating app. In an effort to do something different in order to get a different result, she had decided to change the type of man she was interested in. She had resolved not to hook up with men who hit her, or who were too insecure to let her have an opinion in case it contradicted their own. She was now hoping for someone educated, someone with a job and money of their own who didn't have to sponge off her, and someone who could value women as equals, not chattels.

She got a little thrill of pleasure when Lewis messaged her. It was like a happy secret of her own that no one else knew about. Today he was telling her about his family. A difficult ex-wife who had broken his heart and was now challenging him legally over their financial settlement. (She expected to get more than he did because their teenage son was living with her.) An elderly father who didn't like to be touched, and who still expected Lewis to dress in a suit when he went to dinner with him. Two beagles and a cockatoo called Van who spat seed across the kitchen and who could projectile poo on the walls from the confines of his cage. Lewis was contemplating giving Van to his father for Christmas later that year. Aljce wrote back, hoping that her return message was as amusing as Lewis's, and that he would be as interested in her as she was in him.

LATER THAT AFTERNOON, Jillq gave the student Placement Agreement back to Aljce in a sealed envelope, and Aljce breathed a sigh of relief. This morning, she had sensed a real road block, but it seemed that her instincts had been wrong. 'Is it signed?' she asked.

'Of course it is,' said Jillq, impatiently. But when Aljce got home and opened the envelope, ready to send it off to the university, she found that although Jillq had signed it, she had failed to check the boxes requiring ticks next to the list of things that needed to be agreed to. Aljce sighed. She was not out of the woods yet.

SHE BROUGHT IT up again the next morning. 'I don't need to tick the boxes,' said Jillq. 'I want to leave my options open. I've signed it, haven't I? You just said you needed it signed.'

'Yes, but you need to tick the boxes to indicate that you agree to what you're signing up to,' said Aljce, trying to be patient.

'I haven't decided what that is,' said Jillq. Aljce really didn't want to argue, because she wanted her new job to go well and she sensed she was starting off on the wrong foot. But unfortunately, the Placement Agreement was crucial to the plans she had for the rest of her life.

'Can we go through it together?' she said. 'I'm pretty sure that if you understand what it's asking for, you won't have any problems with putting the ticks in the boxes. It's just stating things like you agreeing to the amount of hours of counselling I will need to do before becoming fully qualified, and that you agree to me arranging and paying for my own external supervision. It's really nothing that will affect you or the way I do my job here at all.'

Jillq looked cross. 'As Hub Manager, I'm a very busy person,' she said. 'However, I am also a generous person. Get Chelsea to book a meeting into the diary.'

Aljce breathed a sigh of relief, and went down to see Chelsea. Of course Jillq was busy. No wonder she was impatient.

Chelsea reached for the book on the desk, which contained a weekly planner. 'Hang on,' she said. 'I've got to open the computer too. Jillq's diary is in there.' Aljce waited. 'Looks like Friday could be free,' said Chelsea, eying her computer. 'Can you check on that white board on the wall?'

'Where?'

'Behind me. What does it say on Friday?'

'Professional development for new staff,' said Aljce, squinting.

'Friday's out, then,' said Chelsea. 'Jillq will be doing that with you and MaryAnn. She's the other new girl. Where's your diary?'

'I haven't got one yet,' said Aljce. 'You were going to get it approved. And some stationery. I'm going to need pens and highlighters, and a stapler, and a hole-punch, and some folders to make up client files.'

'We usually bring our own pens from home,' said Chelsea. 'And we share the stapler and the hole-punch. I've got them here on the front desk.'

Aljce raised her eyebrows. 'Should I buy my own diary then?'

'That's a good idea.'

ALJCE WAITED PATIENTLY outside Jillq's door at 1 o'clock the next day, when Chelsea had managed to squeeze in an appointment for her. The door remained firmly shut, so eventually Aljce knocked. 'I'm here for our meeting,' she said when Jillq came to the door.

'I have no time to meet with you right now Aljce,' said Jillq. 'I'm talking to Marj.'

'But I've booked an appointment,' said Aljce in surprise. 'So that you can tick off those boxes on my student Placement Agreement.'

'Placement Agreement, Placement Agreement,' said Jillq crossly. 'That's all I'm hearing from you Aljce. And you've only just arrived.'

'If you could just tick these boxes,' said Aljce, 'you won't hear about it again, I promise. It will be no trouble to you at all. You won't even know you've signed it. And you may as well tick the boxes, because it is signed.'

'Very well, Aljce,' said Jillq. 'Marj, please pass me a pen.'

'That's a nice pen, Marj,' said Aljce, looking for a distraction from Jillq's irritation.

'Thank you,' said Marj. 'My daughter gave it to me. She works in hospitality, and they have them at reception.' She chattered aimlessly while Jillq gave the boxes angry ticks.

BACK AT HER DESK, Aljce once again contemplated the view, where a white cat with large ginger orange patches was prowling. Aljce had overheard Chelsea calling him Sailor and presumably he had been named to give people the pleasure of saying 'Hello Sailor,' as they arrived. When Sailor smooged Aljce's legs outside on her way into the building, it was possible to see that the blue of his turquoise blue eyes was so pale it was almost white while, in the late afternoon when she left, they had a gold sheen if the sun was in the right place. There were still no instructions as to what she should be doing with herself, but it suited her because she could chat to Lewis again.

She gazed outside, thinking about what to write. There was a big oak tree with new leaves not far away. The garden with the neat rows of perfect cabbages was close to the left side of the building. Something caught Aljce's eye. A rabbit. A big floppy brown one, with white inside its ears. Oh my gosh, she thought. A rabbit! What a perfect omen. And oh my gosh, gosh, there's a whole family of them. Baby ones too! She could hardly believe her luck. She had a window seat to watch rabbits eating fat, juicy clover while she worked! Thank goodness she was her and not Kat and mostly preferred to dream out the window than stare down at her phone screen. When she was in the office and not with clients, Kat was constantly playing on her phone. And what had she been saying earlier? 'Do you know what they said? We don't want Kat coming with her perfect legs and perfect body! So I'm going! And I'm going to slay! Slay!' Still, self-absorption was a relatively small sin. Sailor sniffed the grass, no doubt hoping to come unexpectedly close to a rabbit.

But perhaps Aljce was self-absorbed as well. After all, she was about to talk to Lewis. If there had been something else to do … But there wasn't. She drifted off. Flirting by music, that's what she and Lewis were doing. At least it was what she was doing. Well, not flirting. More like communicating. Falling in love to music. That was what was happening

16

to her, anyway. He sent her the Cults' 'Always Forever,' and Kurt Vile's 'Baby's Arms.' She sent him Chet Faker's 'I'm Into You.' 'I can barely hold my tongue, the shit we do could warm the sun,' the lyrics crooned. She wondered whether to actually tell him how deeply she felt. Perhaps she was mistaken, and he just wanted friendship with a light serving of flirtation. One wrong move and she could lose everything, leaving them both embarrassed. But on the other hand, maybe she would miss an opportunity by being shy, by being scared, by not expressing herself. Other people were so confident. They had no trouble taking moments like this. Aljce did. She avoided rejection where possible.

He had no problem replying immediately to her messages, because he was a self-employed writer, often at his laptop. 'One of the things I like is the different ways of saying things that you have,' he said. 'The way that you use capital letters, or use three dots to let the thought hang in the air ... The way that you p.u.n.c.t.u.a.t.e things. It's pretty fucking brainy.'

'Wow, I AM a bad influence if you're going to start to swear. I'm sure you got that from me. You're a smooth city boy.' Aljce herself said fuck quite a lot when she wasn't at work. And she was delighted by his praise. After all, he was a writer.

THE AA MOBILE mechanic had come around to Aljce's house to fix her car, which was having troubles due to her lack of finance with which to get it serviced. He'd been round a few times before over the past year. They shared a thing, an undercurrent of something that amused them both. He was young and cocky. 'Are you going somewhere?' he said, glancing at what she was wearing; a body hugging grey jersey which had a lower drop of ballet-pink pleats from her mid-thigh to just above her knee.

'Nah, I just got home from work.'

He gave her the form to sign. She didn't have her membership card, of course. 'It's okay, I know you,' he said. She scrawled her signature on an angle to his clipboard.

'That's not even close to how my signature is s'posed to be,' she said laughing.

'It's okay,' he said, 'I believe it's yours.'

'Well, you're easy!' she said.

'Oh, I'm easy,' he told her, and suddenly, she knew it was an invitation. She dropped her eyes and changed the subject. She never had any idea what to do when a man hit on her. Still, it felt nice. Someone physical, who could actually see her, was sending her a message that she wasn't too ugly to be wanted. Afterwards, she mildly regretted not accepting. But it wasn't more than a flicker of a thought. She had Lewis.

She was closing doors, but she couldn't even begin to think about anyone else while her mind was completely full of him. If the universe had wanted her to be with someone else, it would have left space for them at this point in time. It would be what it was. No need to fear making a choice. It was right to delete some options, because choosing one over the others allowed the chosen one to be an intensified experience.

SHE EXPLORED IT with Lewis. Not the mobile mechanic thing. Chance. Destiny. How it all might work. She was interested in those things, and she'd never had anyone she could discuss them with before. 'Do we have free will,' he said, 'or is programmed? Who knows…?? Binary code is made up of ones and zeros, but what it really represents is a yes or a no to any question about information. Binary codes could write every possible world in terms of information. Because every part of every moment can be broken down to a yes/no. Is it this, or isn't it? The question is whether we have randomised free will with which to select a 1 or a 0 or not.'

'Sounds complicated but cool. I'll have to think about it more; get to grips with it.'

'Here's a joke to go with your thoughts. There are only 10 types of people in the world. Those who understand binary code, and those who don't.'

'Oh, gosh. Brainy jokes. I never get told those. Wow. I think I'm in love.' That was forward of me, she thought. But he can take it as irony too, so he can't be sure. Not really sure.

'Binary code can even write what I'm writing,' he said. 'Yes/no, put my finger on the g key. Yes/no, give the character a moustache.' Lewis was a well-known writer, which was why he could afford to be self-employed. A published one, with a few books behind him. Good reviews. He spoke at literary festivals. Someone like him wouldn't want to be with someone like me, she thought. But we get on so well…

'WELCOME, DEAR,' said Mrs. Kingi, kissing Aljce's cheek. She had been away for Aljce's first few days. 'You're going to find this is a wonderful place to work.'

'Aljce in Wonderful,' joked Aljce. Mrs. Kingi looked confused. 'Wonderful to be here,' said Aljce, saving Mrs. Kingi the thought process.

'It's good that you've got the window desk,' she said to Aljce. 'They really take care of you here.'

'Oh,' said Aljce, 'Kat didn't want it. She wanted to be in the corner.'

'I suppose it depends which side the sun comes up,' Mrs. Kingi was saying. 'Some days it might come up on this side.'

'So, the sun rises in the east, and sets in the west. All over the world.'

'I did not know that,' said Mrs. Kingi.

'Cool, huh? You can figure out what way you're facing if you can see the sun moving from one side of the sky to the other.'

'Really? I honestly did not know that.'

DESPITE JILLQ'S ADVICE for Aljce to keep her mind on the game and not get disorientated, Aljce couldn't and Aljce did. I can't find anything, thought Aljce, knowing that soon it would be familiar and enjoying the confusion of not knowing where the stapler was, or which door was her office. She went into the wrong room by mistake; a longer room with office desks set out along the long window. A woman was crying quietly at the nearest one. 'Oh, sorry,' said Aljce, beginning to back out before realizing that she had advertised her presence when she hadn't needed to, and now it was too late to just leave.

The woman sniffed and wiped her eyes with her sleeve. She had dark, pretty freckles, eyes the colour of topazes, and long black dreadlocks pulled together in a band at her brown neck. 'Are you alright?' asked Aljce, wondering whether she should be intruding on someone she'd never met.

'Yes,' said the woman. 'I'm being stupid. I've just decided to leave.'

'Oh, are you sad about it?'

'No, not really. I'll be able to spend more time with my daughter; she's a teenager, and she's got some stuff going on.'

'Oh, okay. Sorry, I didn't mean to interrupt you.'

'Oh, no, it's okay. It's nice to see a friendly face. I AM sad to be leaving. I don't feel I've done what I came to do. I feel like I've let myself down.'

'Oh, but if your daughter needs you, then you're an awesome mum to leave to spend time with her. That's not letting yourself down.'

'I'm pretty sure that I have. But maybe it'll look different once I get some time out. Sorry to be crying on you. First day?'

'Almost. I'm really looking forward to this job. It's a shame that you're leaving though. Just as I'm coming.'

The woman shrugged. 'Yeah, you seem nice. I better go and wash my face though. I'm going to pack up after this.'

Wow, thought Aljce, that was fast. Perhaps her daughter's pregnant. Or sick.

Aljce's own thoughts were upbeat, despite her being a bit disorientated by her new job. All new jobs seem very different at first, she told herself. Until you get used to them.

'I BET YOU'RE GORGEOUS,' said Lewis.

'I don't think so. I mean, I guess I'm not ugly,' she replied. But every day I have to fight against that thought in my head, and sometimes I'm conned into it for a while. Particularly when I see photos. I'm not sure if I'm not photogenic, or if I just interpret what I see in the worst possible way; or, what occurs to me most frequently; that thinking I'm not ugly is the actual illusion, revealed by a photo. It's really hard to explain, other than to say perhaps I don't like the part of me that makes me myself.'

'People aren't beautiful or ugly, they're just possible for you, or not.'

'Well, I'm definitely not beautiful like other people. I'm beautiful like me. And hopefully I have nice energy.'

'You ARE deep,' he said in a pleased way. 'I hope I'm going to be able to keep up.' He sounded only mildly worried, and that pleased her too. Perhaps he sounded curious. She loved curiosity, very much. 'I prefer brainy girls. Intelligence is sexy.'

'I never show men that I have any brains,' she wrote. 'Because if I'm with them for a while, and something accidentally shines through when I'm just being myself, they get angry and defensive with me for having small opinions, and a matching rationale. It's a wonder you haven't run a mile.'

'I prefer brainy girls,' he said again. Aljce felt encouraged.

'So you're going to be a counsellor?' he continued. 'Counselling is so funny… You tell someone who is an absolute blank slate to you all of your deepest secrets. Someone you don't know at all.'

'That's what counselling is. Emptying yourself so that someone else can see themselves more clearly. Becoming a reflective surface. A good counsellor is a mirror. I strive to remember that, and not to get excited by the conversation and forget that I'm there to play my role. And that's listening, and helping to construct their stories. It's hard for me to subdue my personality, but in all the practice sessions I've done at my course I've been oddly good at it. I just try to be kind and genuine. And sometimes I throw them a little scrap of me, but only enough so that they don't feel that I am entirely a blank slate. Because it's hard to connect if you realise that the slate is blank. Not that people commonly notice that the conversation is all about them.'

'I'm sure you're very talented,' he said and, for a moment, she thought she caught a dry tone.

'What, you think my personality's too big to suppress?'

'Not at all,' he said.

'Actually, I'm still myself,' she said. 'It's just my life I keep private about.'

'Good for you. Not everyone deserves to know all about you.'

'I can't wait till I get into doing some counselling for real at work. Any day now, I guess.'

'I've always taken the approach of never getting involved. Stay separate. Observe. Be objective,' he mused.

'What about life? Don't you want to live it?'

'But I'm a writer. That's how I live. By translation.'

'Oh. I couldn't do that. I'm my own raw material.'

ALJCE'S FRIEND STRAUSS sat on the bed wearing a giraffe onesie in apricot and cream tied loosely round her waist, with the giraffe horns hanging past the back of her knees. Aljce had a few friends, but none like Strauss. None at all. Aljce grabbed a bill she couldn't pay yet from off the floor. It may as well make itself useful. She tipped her weed onto it, and got some papers ready. 'I wonder how many other women in their pyjamas are out there tonight rolling a joint?' she asked Strauss.

'There'd be quite a few, I think. Do you think we're better mothers when we're stoned?'

'Definitely I am,' said Aljce, 'I'm more patient, more laid back. Little things like stuff spilled all over the floor don't bother me. Cos I can tell myself that they're just kids and it will all pass, and it's a privilege to have them now; enjoy them while they're young, and they'll grow up soon enough. If I'm straight it's like, pick that mess up, right now! And none of us are better for it.'

'Yeah. I think it makes me more real, I guess, as well. As a person.'

'I liked it first time I smelled it. I thought yes, that's me.'

'YEAH. DEFINITELY.'

'Star drunk,' said Aljce. 'That's what I like to call it.'

'What, being stoned?'

'Yeah.'

They talked about the weather. Small talk with Strauss wasn't like ordinary small talk. She was good at putting up with Aljce's random thoughts. 'It's a weather horoscope,' Aljce said, dismissing the forecast for the next day. 'People need to get that forecasts are a prediction not a truth. Same thing as when a reader predicts your future. They look at all those little clues. White skin ring where your wedding ring used to be... The look in your eyes... Maybe... Maybe not. It's the same as thunder in Jamaica heading our way. Might happen. Might not.'

'You mean that the other way around. The weather is the same as the look in your eyes.'

'Maybe. Sometimes I see echoes of larger systems, like when I look at the moon, and I remember that we're on a planet, and that in another part of the solar system, I might be looking out to Uranus. Or standing in the shadow of Saturn's rings. Black for miles. Icy silver sunlight on the surface of the mountains far in the distance.'

'Cool.'

'Imagine if there were three different coloured moons in the sky.'

'Yeah, normal depends on where you're standing.'

Strauss was eager to hear about Aljce's new job.

'All goods,' she said. 'Got my Placement Agreement signed off, and my desk is by a window, and there's rabbits hopping around on the grass outside... The people are a bit different, but I suppose I just have to get used to them. Everyone's different, in the end...'

'How are they different?'

'Oh, well, hard to say... Like, Jillq's the Hub Manager. And there was this big discussion in the lunch room about scones, and Jillq said she didn't like them, and everyone started to agree with her, and then Marj, who's in charge of computers and finances I think, pointed to Jillq's plate, and there was a half-eaten scone on it. And then, Jillq looked down at it and said, 'unless they have just a smidgeon of jam on them.' And I couldn't stop laughing. And I got in trouble, like I was at school or something. Smidgeon. Sounds like a small pigeon.'

ON FRIDAY, as promised, there was a meeting about the 'Rules of the Hub' for Aljce and MaryAnn, who was also new. Mrs. Kingi was there with a notebook, as was Marj. 'Where is Hattie?' enquired Jillq.

'Um, she said she didn't think she needed to be here,' said Mrs. Kingi, with a look on her face that suggested she knew that the messenger was likely to be shot. 'She had something else that she needed to do.'

'Very unprofessional when we have new people to welcome,' said Jillq. 'Please tell Hattie to come and meet with me later.'

'Will do,' said Mrs. Kingi, making a note in her notebook.

'Where are the others?' enquired Jillq.

'Dulcie had to go out and collect something for you,' said Marj. 'Dinah is leaving. Chelsea will be here soon. Kat is with a client.'

'I think we need to have a meeting about priorities,' said Jillq.

She wrote 'proffessionalism,' on the board.

'Um, I think it's only got one f,' said Aljce.

'Thank you Aljce,' said Jillq, rubbing it out and correcting it. 'It's good to know that you are so good at spelling.'

'So many talents,' said Aljce, joking. MaryAnn snorted. Jillq paused.

'Aljce,' she said. 'Where is your notebook?'

'What for?'

'To take notes in, of course.'

'Oh, I didn't realise I'd need to,' said Aljce. Marj passed her a piece of paper. MaryAnn passed her a pen.

'If you're ready,' said Jillq. 'We need to discuss the Okay Line.' She drew a horizontal line on the board, and put a small line through that to mark the midpoint. Underneath it, she wrote 'OK Line.' 'You will all be familiar with the Okay Line,' she said.

'Um, I'm not,' said Aljce.

'Really, Aljce? I thought you were training to be a counsellor.'

'I am,' said Aljce, 'but we've never covered that. What is it?'

'I don't want to spend time on that now,' said Jillq. 'You must research it in your own time. The thing is that it's the Okay Line.'

'But what's it for?' said Aljce.

'Really, Aljce,' said Jillq crossly. 'I don't have time to catch you up. Please make a note of it for homework.'

'Sure,' said Aljce.

'Any questions?' asked Jillq. No one said anything. 'What's next on the agenda?' Jillq asked Marj.

'Washing your own cups,' said Marj. Aljce sighed. It was going to be a long morning.

LATER IN THE MEETING, she and MaryAnn were given some blank sheets to fill in details for new clients. 'Isn't this my job?' said Chelsea, who had come in about an hour after they started.

'Of course it is Bun,' said Jillq. 'But there might be times when you're not here, and we need Aljce and MaryAnn to be able to fill in.' Marj passed out some example forms, already completed.

Aljce looked at hers. 'Ahh, excuse me,' she said. 'But I know the woman on this form. And there's some quite explicit details about her mental health here too. Is this appropriate for me to be seeing?'

Marj grabbed the form back. 'Perhaps this one wasn't the best one for me to use,' she murmured.

'Is that the sort of thing that gets written on intake forms?' asked Aljce. 'By the admin person?'

'We do not call Chelsea the admin person, Aljce,' said Jillq frostily. Her voice was no longer dripping honey. 'Please be respectful and use people's proper role descriptions. I am very clear about role descriptions.' She wrote 'proper roll desciptons' on the board, and then rubbed it out. Marj had quietly taken MaryAnn's example form back as well.

'It's just common sense really,' she said. 'I'm sure you girls can work out the intake forms.'

'Would we take that level of detail down on an intake form?' said Aljce, sensing that she had lost ground with Jillq, and seeking to recover it by being interested and intelligent.

'Perhaps you should be paying attention, Aljce. As Marj said, it's just common sense. Different situations call for different responses. We need you to be responsive. At all times.'

'What's the Hub's confidentiality policy?' asked Aljce.

'Marj was perfectly entitled to show you those forms,' said Jillq. 'Now that you're an employee here, you will have access to all sorts of confidential information. We expect you to KEEP it confidential. As long as the information doesn't leave the Hub, it is perfectly acceptable to share it. Amongst ourselves. And as Hub Manager, I should be fully informed of everything at all times.'

'Sure,' said Aljce.

'So,' said Jillq. 'Are there any questions?'

'Yes,' said Aljce. 'Can you tell us about opportunities for Professional Development?'

'Professional Development?' said Jillq.

'Yes,' said Aljce. Her last employers had been very generous about paying for training days for her so that she could upskill.

'There's no professional development until you've been here for a least a year,' said Jillq. 'Professional development is earned. It's a privilege, not a right. You do not need professional development in your first year.'

'I would have thought that would have been the most important time,' said Aljce. 'When we're new, and we're learning?'

There was a silence. 'Are you saying you're not willing to abide by our rules?' asked Jillq.

'Of course not,' said Aljce. 'I was just querying the reason behind your Professional Development policy.'

'May I remind you, Aljce, that you're on a three month trial?'

'Am I?'

'Check your contract. In accordance with New Zealand employment law, all new employees are on a ninety-day trial. If you fail to provide satisfaction at that point, your role will be terminated, no questions asked. So I wouldn't be querying our Professional Development policy.'

Aljce blinked. What just happened? she thought.

'I think Aljce was just trying to make a point,' said MaryAnn.

'And I have made my point,' said Jillq. 'I will be very clear about that.' MaryAnn grimaced at Aljce behind Jillq and Marj's back.

THEY ALL HAD morning tea together. 'My sisters,' said Mrs. Kingi chattily, as she unwrapped her sandwiches, 'are really annoying to eat around.'

'Why?'

'Because if you even make a little sound when you're eating, a noise that you don't even notice yourself, they look at you like they're going to murder you. Real evil eyes they give you!'

'That's misophonia,' said Aljce. 'That's what it's called when someone goes crazy angry over the sound of someone else eating.'

'We're glad that you know more than everyone else, Aljce,' said Jillq.

'It really kills the mood when you can't enjoy your food,' continued Mrs. Kingi, cutting off any opening there might have been for Aljce to defend or explain herself, leaving her feeling unfairly accused, and somehow subtly isolated from the others as if it had been pointed out to all of them that she was in a subset of the more intelligent who wanted to rub other people's faces in their own mediocrity. Unfairly. She hadn't given their faces much thought at all before now, but she was beginning to wish that they were more friendly. She would have to keep trying to build an alliance with someone. Mrs. Kingi probably hadn't even noticed what had happened there; she was probably oblivious to those subtleties. Aljce would try to build on her friendship with her.

THERE WERE MORE rules to go over when they returned to the meeting. 'Any questions?' asked Jillq.

'Sorry,' said Aljce, 'but there's just one more thing. I was wondering if we could get a sanitary pad disposal bin for the toilets. Seeing as we're all women here, it just seems essential.'

'We need to be mindful of cost,' said Jillq. 'Those things cost money to be emptied, and they need to be emptied every week. It's not in the budget. Unless you would like to empty it every week Aljce?' Aljce couldn't believe that Jillq was asking her to do that, but she wanted to be helpful, and she wanted to be part of the solution.

'Um, wouldn't I need special chemicals for that? And where would I put what was in it?'

'Exactly,' said Jillq. 'Let's move on.' Aljce hesitated, torn between getting something important addressed, and not wishing to find herself disposing of used sanitary pads. She was already mindful, as Jillq would put it, that they all had to take turns with vacuuming the carpets and corridor and cleaning the toilets. On a Friday. It didn't seem too out of the box that Jillq might actually follow through with the idea that Aljce should dispose of sanitary pads. Perhaps she would organise a lidded bucket or something. Aljce bit her lip, which was what she did when she needed to suppress her thoughts and stop them from coming out her mouth.

When they were finished, Aljce looked at her notes. 'Okay Line,' she'd written. What a waste of time it was taking notes, she thought. The times in her life when she HAD taken notes, she'd never looked at them again, and they had gathered dust until she'd thrown them out. She knew some people who took lots of notes. She had no idea what they did with them. Her theory was that if she didn't remember it, it wasn't worth remembering. She shredded it up little and put it in the bin as she left.

'PERHAPS IT'S JUST a settling-in thing?' said Strauss that evening.

'I hope so,' Aljce said. 'I mean, I never thought I'd come to hate the phrase 'very clear.' Once I would have loved it like a window looking out onto a full moon. But now all I can hear is Jillq saying it. She's always 'very clear' about pretty much everything.'

CURIOUSER AND CURIOUSER

SHE WAS REMINDED again of the pleasures of glass the next morning. The frosted window of her bathroom sparkled gold; like champagne. She opened it a crack further as she stood under the warm water, wondering where the light hitting it was coming from. On the hill directly facing her window she could see that the house with the big clear windows was being struck by the sun at exactly this time on exactly this morning so that it seemed as though God might live there, in the next street. The windows might as well have melted into liquid gold. But unfortunately she had to get ready for work. And it would be gone before she'd finished her shower. Beautiful. But momentary. And she didn't have even a single moment to spare for beauty.

AN OLDER WOMAN sat in the waiting room. 'Hello,' said Aljce. 'Is someone helping you?' The woman looked up from her Sudoku.

'It's okay, I don't need any help,' she said. 'They're making these too easy for me now.'

'Not with the Sudoku,' said Aljce. 'With anything.'

'Oh, no, I don't need any help with anything,' said the woman. Aljce wished she could say the same.

'My daughter's a psychotherapist, you know,' said the woman. 'She gets that from me.'

'Oh, so you're a psychotherapist?' said Aljce. She hadn't realised that the woman was a professional and not a client.

'Her talent. She gets all her talent from me.'

'Wow. A talented psychotherapist. You must be very proud.'

'Oh, I am. There's a lot of envy, you know. A lot of envy of me. I take it in my stride.'

'I'm sure you do,' said Aljce. Perhaps she was a client. Sometimes it was hard to tell who was mad. Her sister had seen a psychiatrist at one stage, and Aljce had realised that there was a fine line between him and her sister.

'I keep my brain sharp by doing Sudoku. Use it or lose it, they say.'

'They do indeed,' said Aljce, peering over her shoulder at the squares made out of squares, where every number filled in to the boxes was a three. Except the few that were rounded capital Es.

She drifted over to the desk. 'What the hell?' she whispered to Chelsea. Maybe if Aljce could just make friends with her… Chelsea looked at her but didn't say anything. 'I was actually just wondering if we should be helping her,' Aljce said, not wanting it to be her fault if a client was left unattended.

'She goes through five books a week,' said Chelsea finally. 'Three, three, three. Over and over.'

'Why?'

'You'd have to ask her. She's not here very often. But Jillq has a terrible time with her. Poor Jillq.'

'Why poor Jillq? Is it her client?'

Chelsea looked furtive, and stayed silent again. Aljce shrugged. If Chelsea wanted to be like that, she would let her. She was the reception-ist. Fuck her. It could be Chelsea's fault if the woman was a client and everyone ignored her. Aljce wasn't going to take the blame. But Chelsea followed Aljce down the hall.

'It's Jillq's mother,' she hissed. 'Poor Jillq. She has a terrible time with her mother.'

That makes sense, thought Aljce. Jillq must be a psychotherapist.

Jillq sailed past in the corridor, seemingly not noticing the presence of her mother. Behind her came a trail of flowery scent. Aljce loved her perfume. It was just what she would have chosen for herself. 'Can I see you in my office, please, Aljce?' she said.

Aljce sighed. 'Sure,' she said, trying to project positive thoughts. It was probably nothing. But it made her uneasy.

'Give me a moment,' said Jillq, as if Aljce had invited herself. 'Come after lunch.'

'Sure,' said Aljce again, hoping her positive thoughts could last till then. Every time she thought about it for the rest of the morning, she had to override her niggle. In fact, she spent most of the morning theorising as to what Jillq might want her for. It wasn't as if she had anything else to do. Perhaps Jillq wanted to give her something to actually do. Perhaps she wanted to discuss Aljce's 'role' again. Or perhaps she wasn't happy with Aljce in some way. No, she had done nothing wrong.

In her personal life, Aljce often felt that she never really belonged anywhere. Although sometimes she pretended to herself that she did, and tried her hardest to fit in by doing everything the other people were doing, only to eventually realise that that wasn't her and never could be, and that she didn't even want it to be. Surely it wasn't going to happen here at work too? It's all in your mind, she told herself. Don't make it a self-fulfilling prophecy.

SHE WASN'T QUITE sure when after lunch was, but at one o'clock, she knocked at Jillq's office door. There was no answer, so she wondered if she'd knocked loud enough. Torn between getting into trouble for knocking too loud and not knocking loud enough, she tried again, firmly but still hesitantly, although surely Jillq couldn't read that into a knock. There was no answer, so Aljce settled into the chair provided for those who awaited Jillq. It looked comfortable, but the longer she sat there, the more she realised that the wire under the thin cushioning dug into her legs, and that the back was tilted slightly forward, making it exhausting to sit in, unless you leaned right forwards as well, with your elbows on your knees and your chin in your hands. That wasn't the look Aljce was going for, so she busied herself trying to balance her posture, ending up sitting on the edge of the chair, which was the only place possible to do so.

She had waited for an hour for Jillq to get back from lunch before Jillq surprised her by opening the office door from the inside. 'There you are Aljce,' she said. 'You're late.'

'I've been waiting out here,' said Aljce.

'I don't think there's any need to challenge everything, Aljce. Come in.'

Aljce sat down. 'How are you?' she asked Jillq, in lieu of anything else to say.

'I am perfectly fine, Aljce. Which is surprising, given how hard I work to keep everything together here.' Aljce nodded, wondering how to turn this interaction into something positive; how to make a connection with Jillq.

'I'm really enjoying my job,' she said politely.

'I'm glad that you are enjoying being a Therapy Hub team member, Aljce. But we need to remember that when we work here, there are certain standards to maintain.'

'I hope I am maintaining all the standards,' said Aljce cautiously.

'Are you aware that we have a dress code?'

'Um...'

'In a professional situation like this, it is absolutely vital that we have a dress code.'

'I guess.'

'So I expect you to keep to the dress code.'

'What is the dress code?'

'There, I expect you to apply your common sense Aljce. It should be perfectly obvious to you what the dress code is.'

'It would help if you could be more specific ... and then I would know if I was breaking it.'

'Aljce, those who aspire to be therapists do not need to be told what the dress code is.' Aljce had that going-in-circles feeling again.

'Sure,' she said. It was always a safe thing to say. And the meeting was probably over, because Jillq had swivelled her chair around and was typing on her laptop, ignoring Aljce completely. 'Should I go?' she asked.

'Are you still here, Aljce?' said Jillq in a tone of exasperation.

'WHAT DOES SHE MEAN?' asked Strauss. 'Does she mean your top's too low? Or your skirt's too short? Are you only allowed to wear neutral colours? Perhaps she doesn't like your outfits? What are you today?'

'Boho Dutch girl.'

'Oh, yeah, I can see it. So what are you going to do?'

'She can get fucked until she tells me exactly what the rules are. And I've got demure nun picked out for tomorrow. Black dress, white collar, long white socks, black Alice shoes. Some plastic white crosses to hang around my neck. She can't complain about that.'

'Oh, good luck with that then. Remember that confidence is the best thing a woman can wear. Makes you look real purrty. When you look in the mirror, you look the way you feel that day. If you're hating on yourself, you'll have a bad hair day for sure. If you're infatuated with you, dammit; you're beautiful. Can't you go back to your old job?'

'Love to. But they've already replaced me,' said Aljce sadly. 'There's a new Aljce.'

'Can't they get rid of her?'

'I don't think that's the done thing under employment law, Strauss.'

ALJCE FELT THAT her entanglement with Lewis WAS making her more confident about herself, as per the very good advice that Strauss was giving her. Outside of work anyway. The problem was that she was never quite sure if he meant what she thought he meant; everything had potential double meanings. She also hedged her bets. Instead of telling him her feelings, she said, 'I'm probably the most loyal person you'll ever meet. And if someone corners my mind, there's no room for anyone else.' She wondered where she was going to go if he pressed her for more, but he didn't. 'Loyal... It's such a blue word, isn't it?' she continued.

'What do you mean?'

'The colour of the word...'

'The words have colours?'

She didn't feel the need to talk about the colours all the time, only when a word particularly struck her. They were just there, of no more note than the air that she breathed, unless there was a particularly pleasant breeze, or the wind was particularly harsh. But it felt good sharing it with him. Perhaps the two of them were actually entangled; like entangled electrons. If electrons were entangled, doing something to one of them caused an instantaneous change in the other one, even if it was on the other side of the world.

She thought of some colours she associated with him. 'So you're forty nine, ay?'

'Yes'

'So forty nine can be words, written down. Or you can say it, and it becomes a sound. Or you can write it down with numbers. Or count it, in an abstract theoretical way, or by laying out forty nine objects. But forty nine is also blush pink and yellow gold, and it's still forty nine, and it's still all those other things, it's just another way of looking at it. As valid as any of those other ways.'

'But how do you know, where is it pink, and where is the yellow gold'

'In some sort of fold or space between imagination and solid reality. Between the inside of my head and the outside of my head. Between my internal perception and my external perception. In the in-between. In the nowhere.' She felt an urgency to explain it, as if this might be her only chance. Her only chance to be asked, and her only chance to make herself understood.

'I have a whole alphabet,' she continued.

He didn't seem bored or disinterested.

'So what do you see for A?'

'I see pink, but I saw a woman on TV who thinks it's pale blue like Alice in Wonderland's dress. Maybe it's your earliest association with that letter. Your early life really shapes you.'

'Do you see all the individual letters in a word?'

'No, just words.'

'Like say, an orange crush for Tuesday?'

'Tuesday is a crimson wine, and Thursday is dark blood red. I used to have trouble telling them apart. I've never had orange crush. Nothing more orange than apricot. I bet it's nice though. It must make for a whole different way of seeing the world if your colours are different.'

'Like that woman with a different colour for A?'

'Yeah. Like, same, same, but different. Someone else might be the same as me, because they see colours. But they're as different as the ones who see nothing at all. We work the same way, but we get different outcomes.'

She sighed. Explaining it felt so futile. 'Colours bring me sensory pleasure. Like dopamine or something. I get this flash of bright pleasure, associated with the colour. It is the colour, and if it's one of the colours that do it for me, one of the ones that give me pleasure, then it'll light up that colour in my brain. Bright in the dark. And weed. It just accentuates that. Just makes it more powerful. Like it does with the other senses. Music. Tasting food. Sex. Perfume. They're colourful too. In a smooth way. Good pleasure should be really smooth. And rich. Maybe colours just represent my emotions. But I only like the pure colours. There's this deadly thing that people often do to colours, I don't know what it is. They make them muddy, and it takes all the joy out of them. You see people wearing muddy-colour clothes all the time. Not brown ones, just muted colour. I find that aw-fucking-ful.'

'Is that your new word?'

'Well, yes, it might be. I'm not sure. I'll see how I go and get back to you. But yes, I might be developing it.' There was a pause. 'Maybe they put more brown, or grey or white in the colours,' she continued. What are people thinking?'

'Well… colourless thoughts, I suppose. Or maybe colour oblivious thoughts. It's not really a flash of colour inside your head though, is it? More like a flash in that other dimension that's not outside your body or inside it, but, perhaps where your thoughts go?'

'Yes, where your thoughts go. I've never met anyone who would have understood that before… It's not on the plane of inside and out of the body. It's on another angle entirely. Wow. And you get that.'

'You have me wondering whether I should try your weed.'

'OMFG, haven't you ever smoked?'

'No, we obviously live in different worlds. My world is one where people stagger about stupidly when they've had half a bottle of wine, and they can insult people and just blame the wine later, and not feel bad about it. They were incapable after all… in the throes of a drug that they chose to take.'

'You should definitely try weed sometime. I'll hook you up.'

'Oh, well that will involve meeting.'

'Why not? Why not meet?'

'I don't know. Maybe we should. Sometime.'

'What do you look like?'

'Oh, not much. Just your average Pakeha New Zealand man.'

'What's that?'

'Written shrug.'

'Anyway it's not about how someone looks. It's about the energy they exude.'

'Not everyone exudes.'

'Haha. But that's what's missing in a virtual connection. No feeling for the other person's energy.'

'Is that your life? Is that how you experience this? Stoned and synaes-thesiac?'

'Pretty much, yeah.'

'Wish I was you.'

'Ahh, well there's some mundane stuff too. Like cleaning toilets. And work. I don't write to you about those things. But I do think then too. And sometimes at home I have a little party for myself. Actually, quite often. I put on some music with a bit of deep bass, and I turn down the lights so that only my white bunny lamp and my blue and my plasma light, you know; the one like a pink and blue brain, are on. And then I smoke some weed while I'm dancing. I think of it as a sacrament.'

'Exactly. Wait, what? Is that what it's for? Communication between dimensions? Making a bridge between realities?'

'Actually, think of it being about delight.'

'And it must be. Because you're spiritually in touch with whatever is beyond.'

'Yeah, it does make it feel as if there's something more beyond the veil of what we can perceive.'

He sent her a picture of an old stone cottage set into the side of a small hillside, with no windows, because three of the walls were banked up with earth. It looked as if it would be safe and warm inside. And when she clicked the gif, smoke puffed endlessly up from the small chimney. 'Who do you think is in there?' she asked him.

'You, Aljce,' he answered. She sat there watching it for a while, imagining them inside together. Their minds alone together in the dark, cosy womb of the cottage. Warm by the fire. Puff, puff went the smoke emerging from the chimney. What was inside was a secret that could never be known.

'What's your house like?' he asked. Her heart skittered to the side. Whether to be her honest self, or whether to say whatever would make him like her more. It's only real if you're real, she told herself.

'Clean, but a bit cluttered,' she typed.

'Perfect,' he said. 'I like a bit of clutter, as long as it's interesting clutter.'

'I've got cats,' she said. 'They're called Steinie and Highsy.'

'You've got a party right there.'

'Oh, yes, I guess. But it's actually accidental. They were called Einstein and Heisenberg before I shortened their names.' What did it mean that he liked clutter? Was he indicating that he'd like HER clutter?

'Is this further than you usually go?' she asked him. 'Like, giving me your address and phone number?'

'Yes.'

'Good, because I have this strange craving to be special to you. I can't explain it.'

'You're definitely out of my comfort zone, yeah.'

She thought about that. She wasn't quite sure that it was the response she was hoping for. On the other hand, it indicated that she was special, and that was what she had been wanting him to say... Perhaps it WAS just a game of double meanings, and who could do it best. She tried to advocate for herself. 'I'm the most interesting person you know. And plus I wanna be friends with you. You can't stop thinking about me even though you want to.'

'True. It feels very intimate.'

'Perhaps I use intimacy as a way of getting people to like me,' she wrote. 'Shed down to my genuine self. Mental undressing. My core self is sexy. But I don't let a lot of people see it. Only when I'm interested. Which is rare.'

'We talk like lovers.'

'We do.'

SHE STARTED TO make up conversations that she might have with Lewis. She imagined herself lying on a blanket at night, listening to music drifting from a stage at the Botanic Gardens. He would sit down beside her. 'What are you doing here?' he would ask. She would show no surprise.

'Waiting for you to get here.' There would be a pause, but it wouldn't be awkward. It would be shared silence. 'I was thinking that I should lie on my back and watching the stars while I'm listening to the band. But then I was worrying about chilling out so much that I might fall asleep. But let's do it. 'Cos you can wake me up if it happens. I don't want to miss anything.' They would lie down, and there would be another pause while they began to drink serenity. Then she would speak again. 'Lewis. Let's be like the stars. Touch my hand here, and touch my foot here. As above so below.'

'Let's try three points touching,' he would say. 'Put your head next to mine.'

'I can't twist that far. I've lost your leg. I can only do two.' They would laugh; softly, gently.

'Never mind. Hey, our heads are so close that we should be able to hear each other's thoughts.'

'Can you hear what I'm thinking?'

'You're thinking how cool it is to be doing this.'

'Haha. Right. You know me so well.'

Part of her worried that she would not be able to tell the difference between the real him, and the him that she wanted him to be. Perhaps it overlapped. Perhaps not. Was this just result of the distance and physical absence between them? Were they just projecting their own versions of reality onto each other and without really knowing each other at all? So would it matter? Should she stop? She didn't want to. Thoughts of him filled her head in happiness.

'I've long since given up on expecting interesting conversation, so I've started having to make my own,' she wrote. 'Between me and me. Both of me are the same, and because I am my own intellectual equal, I really stimulate myself to think.'

'It just doesn't seem the same now, when a day goes by without our exchange of words,' he said.

'I like it too,' she said. 'Don't go away.'

'I have to,' he said. 'I've got writing to do, and I've been spending quite a lot of time when I should have been writing on writing to you.'

'Oh, fine to go and do what you need to do right now,' she said. 'Just don't get bored with me.'

'I won't, I promise,' he said. 'You're stuck with me now.' Her heart gave a stupid, unwise upward lift. It was nice that someone looked forward to her.

SHE DIDN'T HAVE to make up ALL the conversations either. They talked about themselves. 'Of course I'm a poet,' he said. 'Most poets can't put a story to their work, but I can. And I can sustain that the whole way through a novel, when most people writing a novel can't fashion it out of poetry. They either write poems, or they write books. And I write a poem book. Or a book poem.' Aljce didn't reply because she was thoughtful. It sounded exactly like what she wanted to do herself.

They played the favourites game. 'Favourite book?' Aljce said. 'One you would want everyone else to read?'

'Hard. I don't care what they read. Oh, wait. Maybe Dr. Seuss. 'The Lorax.'

'Oh, yes. Good choice. Very relevant right now.'

'And Alice in Wonderland. And Tove Jansson. 'Finn Family Moomintroll.'

'Alice in Wonderland. That book was really something. Maybe it will be the bible of the future. Nothing is impossible, not when you go down the rabbit hole. It was built for quantum physics. It's a way to describe a worm hole and alternative realities. Lewis Carroll loved maths, but he wasn't the best mathematician. His ideas came in words, like mine. But in the end, it is all the same thing. We need the stories to give shape to it all.'

'Best passage in a book then? As a variation on the last theme?'

'Haruki Murakami, in *Norwegian Wood*. Writing about a firefly that's had its light nearly washed out of it. So beautiful that it made me want to cry.'

'Really? I've not read it.'

'Oh, you should.'

'What's on your to do list?' he asked.

'To do list? Design my own tarot card deck. How beautiful would that be? Especially the major arcana. The fool. The magician. The hanged man. The tower. The tarot is just a metaphor for everything. Imagine doing the artwork to that. The universe would be writing itself through you.'

'Sounds ambitious,' said Lewis. 'But very commendable.'

She asked his question back at him.

What's on my to do list? I'd like to write a cult novel and have people love it enough to read it several times in their lifetime, and talk about it with other cool people at parties. And I don't mean rich people, I mean people with ideas. I'd like it to be appreciated as a unique piece of artistic endeavour. Imagine dying and having a story that you had created live on when you're gone.'

'Yeah. That'd be cool. I like all your ideas. I'm sure you could do it. I wouldn't mind doing it myself.' And just like that, his plan became hers.

'If I was writing a novel, what I'd want is for people to wonder whether my characters are real, or whether they're just figments of the main character's imagination,' she said. 'Like the film *A Beautiful Mind*. And to add another layer, I want them to wonder whether that person, or that version of myself is just a figment of my own imagination, or whether it's the real me; a self that they don't know.'

'No good book can be anything other than a memoir of the writer's self,' wrote Lewis.

SHE DIDN'T TELL Strauss about Lewis, because Strauss would te̶͇
that falling in love with someone she'd never physically met was a reall̶
bad idea. But it suited Aljce. She was happy, and she didn't want anyone
spoiling it for her with disapproval. But that didn't mean that she didn't
spark conversations with Strauss with Lewis in mind.

'My to do list…' said Strauss thoughtfully. 'Green flash. When the sun
goes down over the sea. And the whole world goes green and gold just
for one second. If you blink, you'll miss it. And you have to be so lucky
to see it in the first place.'

'What causes that?'

'I don't know actually.'

'Well, I think I'll Google that. 'Cos I have no idea why I haven't already
wondered about it. Isn't it amazing how we don't wonder? Things happen
like magic without us wondering about the science behind it, and how it
all works. I mean, do you even know how your phone works?'

'Waves bounce off cell phone towers,' said Strauss.

'Yeah, but what the fuck? How are they harnessing them? How are
they encoding the information on them? How am I actually hearing
you from Auckland if I ring you from there? And even the geeks that
make it all work… They know the formulas, because they've been passed
along to them and they've even put a few more bits of maths on top of
it. But how do they know that maths actually works, and it's not just an
illusion, designed to distract us from the mysterious source of our ever
expanding technology? How we just build it out of thin air and thought?
When you think of how we just started out with wood and rocks and
other natural things… Look at the colours we can make. Look at the
materials we can make. Listen to the sounds we can make. Look at the
magic we can do. Steel birds hovering in the air. Flowers growing in
winter. Ways to stop ourselves from feeling our own pain. A brain with
invisible tentacles that connects everyone… called the internet. And
those are commonplace things.'

'Well, fuck, I must say that I have trouble even interpreting the instruction manuals. Do you know anyone who's actually read the whole
instruction manual on their phone? Maybe the trouble shooting part, if
you can't figure out which way up the battery goes in.'

'True. It's so much science that it may as well be magic. We've created
our own magic. Humans have magicked up magic out of science. We've

reality... So Strauss,' she continued, 'there's this famous
ed the double slit experiment. Which basically proves
at when we're not watching electrons; that's those things
the nucleus of an atom, that they are waves of probabil-
xed particles. Unless we're actively measuring them. Then
they bec... particles. When we observe things they're real. Until then,
they're only potential.'

'Really?' said Strauss. 'That can't be real.'

'Ha. Yeah, it is.'

'How do you know?'

'Check it out on You Tube. Where you can find it being explained
and discussed by a great many science geeks in simple language. Same
as quantum entanglement. It's not a complicated experiment. But even
though it's been repeated over and over again, most people find that
because it doesn't fit into what they know, they're not interested. It's too
much to comprehend. And nobody knows what it all means for sure,
because it's so mind bending, but it does imply that nothing is actually
real. Unless we pay attention to it.'

'Feels real.'

'Sure does... so to all intents and purposes, it may as well be.'

'So we can't escape it?'

'Pretty much.'

REALITY OF SOME sort was inescapable at work. 'Aljce, when you have a
spare moment, can you fill this out please?' said Mrs. Kingi.

'Sure,' said Aljce. 'What is it?'

'Oh, your profile. Your qualifications and things.'

'What for?'

'I'm redoing our pamphlet. We need profiles of all our staff on it.'

'All of them? It must be going to be a big pamphlet!'

'I've spent a lot of time on it,' said Mrs. Kingi, slightly miffed. 'It folds
out. So it will look small, but there'll be a lot of information on it. We
need to promote ourselves.'

Aljce could hear Jillq talking in Mrs. Kingi's last sentence. She had a
look at the form. 'Name. Qualifications. Modalities. Personal position
in regard to therapy.' It was going to have to fold out a long way. She
scribbled out her answers and dropped it back to Mrs. Kingi's desk. 'Oh,

you're finished already,' said Mrs. Kingi, looking at it as if Aljce must have missed something. Aljce got the impression that she should have spent at least the morning on it.

She passed Jillq in the hall on her way to the toilet.

'I hope you gave your profile some thought Aljce. I hear you finished it very quickly.'

Aljce startled mentally. She wondered how Jillq already knew that she'd completed filling in her profile. Mrs. Kingi must have told her. Clearly they were in very close communication.

'You have a degree,' continued Jillq.

'Yes.'

'I didn't know that.'

'I told you when you employed me.'

'I'm sure I didn't know Aljce. I prefer to employ people who come willing to learn. I'm very clear about that.'

'I'm willing to learn.'

'People who have degrees think they're too good for learning.'

'The fact that I have a degree shows how much I enjoy learning.'

'Hmm. Well, I hope you don't think you're too good for us here. I don't want you flaunting it.'

'You must have known about it. That's why I'm eligible to do a post graduate degree in counselling.'

'That's what I'm talking about Aljce. Always thinking you're right. That's what happens when people have degrees. I'm going to expect a more humble attitude.' Aljce sighed internally. It seemed that no matter what happened, or how the conversation went, she just couldn't get into Jillq's good books. Must try harder, she thought. 'Anyway, I'm very busy,' said Jillq. 'I'm rushed off my feet at the moment. I don't have time to stop here in the hallway with you. So remember Aljce, don't rush through your work. Do a good job.'

'I DO A GOOD JOB,' said Aljce to Strauss. 'EVERY little thing that there is to do, which isn't much, I do well. I've even done some extra stuff, but Jillq didn't like it. It was some ideas I had for a school education campaign. Said it wasn't in my role description.' Aljce changed the subject. 'Cigarette papers are made out of maybe the most beautiful paper ever, don't you think? See-through; like the dust on a white moth's wing. It even has slim dark blue veins, making it look as if it's off to the office. Do you think they're watermarks? And that strip of pale honey-coloured glue that reminds me of childish things.'

'Off to the office?'

'In a pinstripe.'

'Yeah? Yeah, I can see that.'

'Anyway, so then we were talking about someone that Mrs. Kingi mutually thought we knew, and I said, "is she fair?" and she said, "what does that mean? What do you mean is she fair?" And I was like, "it means whitish. Fair-skinned. Dark is the opposite of fair. Black is the opposite of white." And she was like, "ohhh, yeah. Gotcha." I think she thought that I was questioning the person's moral values. We've kept dark in our store of words, but we've lost fair. What sort of random selection is that, when even paired words can lose their mates?'

'Sounds like the state of my sock drawer.'

'Do people even still use pale?'

'What's the opposite of pale? Is it dark? Perhaps that's replaced fair.'

They descended into silence. 'Intense?' asked Aljce.

'Bright,' said Strauss.

Aljce had seen a line on the net that said 'I'm so high, I could eat a star.' Yes, she thought. Yes.

Strauss lifted her nose towards the clear twilight sky and Aljce's Mad Neighbour's fence. He was smoking too, outside his sliding door. 'That smell. It just fucking sings to me, you know.'

'Yeah.'

'Sweet and longing and flowers all in one hit.'

'Yeah. Yeah.'

'Your neighbour looks like Jesus. Hanging out in a white towelling dressing gown. Long unwashed hair. Do you think he can do magic too? Part the seas with his hands? Walk on water? Divide up a few fish and loaves of bread and feed multitudes?'

'I expect he can, Strauss.'

'Perhaps he's undead like Jesus too. A Jesus zombie.'

'Wow, Strauss. We should go over and ask him for a miracle.'

'Yeah, but what?'

'I might ask to escape from the Therapy Hub. It's not going that well. I think I need a new job.'

'I would ask for love and happiness.'

'That's not a miracle.'

'Sometimes it is. I would ask for it for everyone. I would share.'

'Well that's just lovely of you, isn't it Strauss?'

'Must be the weed.'

ALJCE LIKED THE way her Mad Neighbour had projects: the caravan he was doing up, the glasshouses he was building with sheets of glass from the dump. At the moment, he was making a patio lounge on the concrete. He had green Astroturf under a large green sun umbrella, to which he had strapped palm fronds cut from down the back of his section. There were two green and white striped deck chairs and some pink flamingos he'd found at the recycling centre that he thought gave it a tropical ambience. All it needed was a pool. Of course, no one ever reclined on the chairs. But it was a great concept.

She also liked the way he never made anything last forever. Everything was transitory, so that it marked a certain place in time. The year he installed a home-made spa pool in the garden. The year the clothes line stretched between their two houses with a pulley system, so that if it rained, he could just wind them in. The year he washed his clothes in an outside bath, and then stamped grapes from their mutual vine in the same bath to make wine. Soon, the flamingos would be bent, and the palm leaves withered, and perhaps the umbrella would rip in the wind while the Astroturf slowly went mouldy. And still no one would sit there. But they could look back on the year when he'd had a tropical patio in his back yard. 'You'll be able to look out your windows and imagine you're at a resort in Samoa or Fiji this summer,' her Mad Neighbour had told her. 'You can't buy that!' Indeed, thought Aljce.

He lived like that because he just didn't give a fuck. He came and went as he pleased, hung out in his garden, got stoned and had all-nighters with strange, eccentric people whose names he couldn't recall later. He didn't have to worry about anything, except perhaps the Police. But even the straight people had to worry about the Police, like when they were speeding. That was the crime that no one really thought was a crime, and everyone had to be alert to being caught breaking that law, because many people were tempted.

Her Mad Neighbour didn't want to be a straight person, it held no attraction for him, with its rules and conventions and boundaries, and its competition to see who could keep to them the most tightly, because that was how you gained social standing in the straight people group. Although, sometimes, he did say that he wouldn't mind being a landscape gardener. She thought he'd be brilliant at it. But she wondered if he envisaged earning money enough to save, and living in an expensive house and finding someone to share it, or whether he just dreamed of being out in the garden all day, which was what he already did with his time. Who knew?

TWINKLE, TWINKLE LITTLE BAT

It was the next morning and back to work time before she knew it. Aljce heard a noise and looked out into the corridor. She sighed. Jillq was early. Just what she needed. She loved the quiet time in the morning before anyone else got there. 'Good morning, Aljce,' said Jillq. She took her glasses off to rub them, and Aljce was suddenly seized with the urge to make things better, to fix what was broken. Jillq looked more approachable without her glasses on.

'Jillq,' she said, on impulse.

'Yes, Aljce?'

'I know we haven't exactly gotten off to a good start, and I'd like to apologise. I am grateful for the job, and keen to fit in with you and your team. I'm sure you're an awesome Manager.' She didn't know what she expected. Perhaps a rush of relief as they both melted and mutually apologised and made up.

Instead, Jillq stiffened. 'I think,' she said, 'that you need to consider whether you are suited to a career in counselling. Anyone who lacks basic people skills the way you do isn't going to be suited to therapy. Therapy takes a special person. Consider it please, Aljce.'

Aljce had to stiffen her lips to stop them from drooping, because once they did that, she knew that she would cry. She had made herself vulnerable, and in return, Jillq had used that to wound her, not to make mend fences. She really, really wanted to be a good counsellor. That was her dream. It was the sort of work she had always wanted to do, and she would be able to support Pleasance and Liddell without having to stress out about finances. She would be able to buy groceries without wondering if her card would decline if she bought butter that week. She made it to the toilets, as if nothing had happened, before the tears could come. She spent the next twenty minutes splashing her face with cold water so that Jillq would never see her red eyes. She would not try that again.

'HAVE YOU TAKEN the time to consider what I said yesterday morning?' Jillq asked her the next day. 'I did ask you to consider it.' By this time, Aljce had hardened that part of her heart.

'Yes,' she said stubbornly. 'I have, and I believe I am very suited to counselling. I think I will be a very good counsellor.' Jillq looked momentarily disappointed, but she collected herself.

'Please don't say I didn't warn you Aljce,' she said, flowing on by.

Aljce knew that it was likely that soon her team of colleagues would be of the same opinion as Jillq, because they all seemed to hang adoringly off every word she uttered. It seemed so unfair that she, Aljce, wasn't going to be judged on merit, but on the opinion of someone who it was impossible to please, who was determined not to value her. Because no matter what she did, and no matter how good it was, no one would give her any praise for it.

'SO WHO DOES Jillq report to?' she asked Chelsea.

'Jillq is the Manager. She doesn't report to anyone.'

'I mean, there must be someone. A Board, or something.'

'Jillq is the Chairperson.'

'So she reports to herself?'

'She started this place. Why should she report to anyone?' Perhaps, thought Aljce, so that if anyone wanted to complain about her, they'd have someone to go to.

'Oh,' she said, covering her intentions. 'I didn't realise. Gosh, that's pretty good, to get a place like this off the ground by herself.'

'Exactly,' said Chelsea, not realising that Aljce was doing her bit to fit in and be liked.

SHE HASTILY MINIMISED her conversation with Lewis as Jillq came into her office. Sometimes it was convenient to message him on her work computer so that it looked as if she was working. 'It's cold because it's been snowing,' she had written. 'I saw it from my car window today. Fresh and bright and newborn. Snow looks like the sharp white absence of something when the sky is grey; like it did yesterday; but if the sun hits it up there on the top of the ridge, it turns brilliant and incisive. Gold.'

'No snow here in Wellington. Just a lot of wind.'

'Spring, huh?'

She needed to be more alert to external movement or she would be in trouble.

'The Reporter is here, Aljce. To profile your role. And MaryAnn's role. Please remember it's not all about you. It's about the role.' Aljce hadn't known a reporter was coming.

'Did you know he was coming?' she whispered to MaryAnn in the corridor.

'No,' MaryAnn whispered back.

'What's it for?'

'To profile our roles.'

'Do you know what your role is?'

'Not really.'

'It's going to be interesting then.'

They sat in a circle of mismatched chairs in one of the funny little rooms off the main corridor. They all faced the Reporter, who sat nervously with his iPad notebook. He was older, but Aljce could see he was still nervous. 'Shouldn't take long to get from A to B,' he said.

'Unless we start talking about C,' said Aljce, and the Reporter laughed, suddenly at his ease.

'Yip, it takes a lot longer to get from A to Z,' he said. MaryAnn and her boss from the Council laughed too. There was a silence from Jillq and Marj. Perhaps that was their problem. Perhaps they just lacked a sense of humour. Perhaps they had a misunderstanding of Aljce because they just didn't get her.

'Anyway,' said Jillq.

'I'm not quite sure...' said the Reporter.

'MaryAnn and Aljce will profile their new roles here at the Therapy Hub,' said Jillq.

'What are your roles?' asked the Reporter.

'Well, my role is quite new...' said MaryAnn.

'Connecting with the community about the subject of family violence,' said MaryAnn's boss.

'Further extending the professional team here at the Therapy Hub,' said Jillq. There are now ten people on the team, and we are able to offer one-stop professional wrap-around service.'

'Who to?' asked the Reporter.

'Clients,' said Jillq. The Reporter turned to Aljce.

'And what is your role?'

'It fits in with MaryAnn's,' said Aljce. 'I'm going to be working with children and families affected by family violence.'

'Total wrap-around service,' said Jillq. 'One-stop shop. We can provide everything clients need. Therapy, advocacy, support.'

Perhaps, thought Aljce, Jillq was counting Dulcie. Dulcie hardly came in, but it wouldn't surprise Aljce if she was on the pay roll, because she had a desk. What she did was unclear. She was Jillq's daughter. Aljce wasn't sure who else she was counting, but perhaps there were staff she hadn't met yet. Jillq, Marj, Kat, Hattie, Chelsea, Mrs. Kingi, Aljce, MaryAnn, Dulcie. Nine.

Hattie was a psychotherapist who worked there part time. She stood out in a crowd because her curly hair was a misty forget-me-not blue. 'Aljce or Alice??? Isn't that said Alice?' Hattie had said when they'd met.

'No, it's Aljce,' said Aljce.

'Aljce, it sounds just the same,' Hattie had said, sounding suspicious. Aljce shrugged her shoulders. She preferred people to say it properly, because it made a difference to the colour. Alice was whiter, while Aljce had much more of a translucent jelly tint, with a hint of apricot at the end with the c.

'Do you have children of your own?' asked the Reporter.

'Yes, I have two.'

'What do you hope for, for your children?'

'I hope I hear them laughing a lot. I couldn't wish for more than that.'

'Off topic!' said Jillq.

'So how do you get your referrals?' asked the Reporter, speaking directly to Aljce again.

'Through main reception,' said Jillq.

'The Child Protection Agency are going to refer,' said Aljce. 'And I'm quite new, so I'm still in the process of trying to make myself known in the community. I've only spoken to the parents of two potential clients so far.'

Jillq whipped her head around to look at Aljce. 'You have clients already?!'

'Well, I'm trying to connect with them,' said Aljce. 'That's my role.'

'It is very early in the role,' said Jillq. 'We didn't anticipate you taking on clients for a few months. Not until you're ready. 'I'm sure I've been clear about that.' What would I do till then, wondered Aljce, but she sensed that now was not the time to argue. In fact, it was a topic to avoid, or she would be banned from doing any real work.

'Bit of an easy ride for you then,' said the Reporter, winking at Aljce.

'Indeed,' she said dryly.

'I will provide you with the role descriptions,' said Jillq to the Reporter.

'Great,' he said, closing the cover of his iPad. 'Thanks for your time.' He stood up and looked nervously at the ceiling fan wobbling alarmingly in its orbit as it sliced through the air above his head. 'I'm in the right place if I need counselling because this flies loose and hits me!' he said. Aljce liked him.

'Fan-ily violence,' she said. 'We take care of that here.'

'Haha.'

She felt envious of him, about to leave the Hub, and go back to the company of normal people, while she stayed here with mad people.

She found him waiting at the main reception an hour later. 'Oh, are you still here? We'll have to get you a sleeping bag!' she said.

'Yes, haha. Your boss wanted to see me to give me those role descriptions before I left. But I've been waiting for a while!'

'Hopefully soon!' said Aljce encouragingly.

'I keep thinking I should just leave,' he said, not quite sure of whether he should.

'I'm sure she won't be long,' said Aljce, continuing down the hallway to her office, where Kat was checking her messages.

'He says I have nice legs!' she said excitedly to Aljce.

'Who does? The Reporter?'

'My Pilot.'

'Oh.'

'I have to go in to an appointment with a client in a minute. But can you knock on the door if I get a message? It might be him.'

'Sure,' said Aljce, wondering what sort of attention the client was going to get, with Kat focused on the Pilot she was seeing at the moment. She hoped he wasn't texting and flying. Surely Kat wouldn't interrupt her counselling session to receive a Messenger compliment about her legs. But nothing would surprise Aljce here. Fifteen minutes later, Kat popped her head around the door.

'Did you hear my phone go off?' she asked. 'It's in my bag.'

'No, nothing,' said Aljce, fiddling idly with the computer, trying to get a border around her pamphlet.

'Are you sure?' said Kat. 'I must have left it on silent.' And she went to her bag to check it. 'Nothing,' she said disappointedly, and her white smile suddenly disappeared.

'Maybe he's flying or something,' said Aljce.

'Yes,' said Kat, brightening up and letting her smile slowly reappear. 'Maybe he's flying. Yes, I suppose so.'

'Gives you time to do your counselling,' said Aljce helpfully.

'Yes,' said Kat.

PLEASANCE AND LIDDELL were getting ready for bed. 'Damn, Steinie, stop lurking!' Aljce said, nearly tripping over him in the hallway near Liddell's room. Steinie had a bad habit of lying on the girls in bed at night. Aljce always carried him to the door; stroking his soft, vulnerable stomach, and then putting him out, just to teach him. Of course, her teaching never learned him, and every time she went back, there he was feeding off the body heat of one or other of her daughters, and purring happily. In this case, however, both her cats were just lying around like fat caterpillars, waiting to be fed. Later, Steinie would make his advances on the beds.

'Do you want your stars on?' she asked Pleasance. Pleasance and Liddell had glowing lights that threw soft blue stars on the ceiling, as well as a couple of moons. Aljce was unreasonably pleased every time they chose to have them on and the blackness became a universe overhead, full of galaxies and starlight.

'Yes,' said Pleasance. 'Stars on.'

'Yes, what?'

'Yes please.'

And when Aljce turned on the switch, Pleasance's face was soft beneath it. Aljce touched her lips to Pleasance's forehead and her kiss spread like a jam flower. She stroked Liddell's hair. 'Close your eyes,' she said. 'Here comes a lullaby.' Lullaby was one of the most beautiful words in the English language. Amygdala was good. Mushroom. Horse. Lipstick, although that was more for the clicks than the colour. Words were such a pleasure.

Steinie nuzzled up to the nightlight. A sprinkling of small blue stars fell across his black fur. She leaned forward to stroke him, and the stars fell across the back of her hand. Aljce's thoughts were captured by what she saw, and she scratched Steinie's neck absently.

'Do you ever feel like you don't belong in the world?' she asked Lewis. 'Like, no one else has the capacity to understand you? That no one will ever get you, because their minds just aren't complicated enough... And nobody knows what to do with your energy, so they keep their distance? Because they prefer the familiar to the strange.'

'Maybe. Possibly not like you. There are people like me.'

'I've always thought I didn't like hanging out with people much, but the truth is I just don't like hanging out and being bored. I've realised that I'm actually highly social, and I'd like frequent social stimulation, but I just can't find anybody who can give it to me. I'm great at making friends, but they're just not quite on the same planet as me. I'm too strange. I get excited about things I think are cool that don't interest other people. I wanna do stuff outta the box. I want friends on the same planet as me. But I'm not super popular, because I'm from quite a rare planet. An obscure planet.'

'What do you think is more important?' he said. 'To be loved, or to be understood?'

'Well, it seems like the right answer is loved. My problem is that I think such small amounts of attention are love. It feels like that to me cos I've never BEEN loved. But I don't know... I'd be pretty keen on being understood... Wouldn't that be the key to real love anyway? Can anyone truly, really love you if they haven't understood you?'

'And wouldn't that be the hardest and most valuable thing? Because it's so uncommon?'

'So we're in agreement then?' she asked. He didn't reply, and there was a long space. She continued. Perhaps he was busy with something unexpected. 'Yeah, sometimes when I think someone has a hope of understanding me, I throw everything about me at them, in the hope that they'll be the one.' He returned to the conversation.

'The one to understand you?'

'Yeah. I think it could be what I'm doing to you now.'

'Has anyone ever understood you before?'

51

'No. I don't give many people a shot at understanding me. And I'm pretty sure I'm giving you that chance here.'

'You're what makes my life worth living,' he said.

'Really?'

'Really.'

'Okay, so that's the nicest thing ever. Don't go and try and take it away or anything. Say there's been a mistake. Cos I always want to remember that at one point in our lives, this was how you felt.'

'I wouldn't do that Aljce. I think you've just got to trust me. Have some faith in me.' 'Trust me,' he said again.

'I am quite surprisingly trusting,' she said. 'But I can't recall even a single experience where trusting a man has paid off for me. Still. I suppose there's always a first time. And I guess I'm just longing to be proved wrong. Sure I'll trust you.'

And so, she put her heart out for bruising again. But it felt safe. Life was good. How much pleasure was it to stroke her ginger cat lying on her bed? Marmalade fur with a soul, and throbbing with purr. How much would such an experience be worth if she wasn't taking it for granted, and she was experiencing stroking a cat for the very first time? I'm so glad I'm a cat lover, she thought. I'm so glad I'm in love.

ABOUT ELEVEN O'CLOCK the next day, Marj put her head casually around the door. 'Aljce,' she said, 'can I get you to come down to Jillq's office for a minute?' Aljce's adrenalin shot through her body in every possible direction at once. Life was not good. This could not be a good thing. She just knew it.

'What for?' she asked.

'Oh, we just want to speak to you,' said Marj vaguely. Aljce sighed. She did a lot of sighing here.

'Sure,' she said. It will be about that Reporter yesterday, she thought, but she couldn't put her finger on what she would have done wrong.

Jillq could. 'We have called you in Aljce, because of your behaviour with the Reporter yesterday,' she announced.

'What behaviour?' asked Aljce, suddenly feeling very alone.

'Your behaviour,' said Jillq.

'Yes, but what behaviour?' asked Aljce again. Circles. They were going around in circles.

'You were very mean to him,' said Jillq. 'Making jokes at his expense.' Aljce felt exasperated.

'I was just teasing him,' she said.

'Teasing? TEASING?' said Jillq, pouncing on the word. 'So you admit that you were teasing him?'

'Yes,' said Aljce. 'We were just having a bit of fun.'

'Aljce, I'm very disappointed in you. Someone who wants to work as a therapist should know how damaging teasing is. Teasing is bullying.'

'I wasn't bullying him. I meant teasing in the context of joking. Joking is what I meant.'

'Please don't try to change your words now Aljce. Marj heard you admit that you were teasing him. And it even continued out at the reception desk after the interview.'

'For goodness sake,' said Aljce heatedly. 'We were joking together.'

'Teasing,' repeated Jillq, 'is very inappropriate for staff members of a Therapy Hub.'

Aljce was busy considering how Jillq even knew that she had spoken to the Reporter at the reception desk. She didn't see Jillq producing the letter. 'Aljce!' said Jillq. Aljce blinked. 'This is for you.'

'What is it?'

'It's a written warning. For bullying.' Holy fuck, thought Aljce. That escalated quickly.

'You can't give me a warning for something I didn't even do.'

'Marj is my witness Aljce. You have admitted it. Bullies do not make good counsellors. We cannot have bullies working at the Therapy Hub. This is a place where people come to heal from that sort of thing. Your fellow colleagues all agree. You are a nasty, hard person. Everyone else can't be wrong. You are the only person who thinks you are perfect. I think you need to take this warning and reflect.'

'People close their doors so that they don't have to talk to you Aljce,' she continued. 'You're very hard. No one wants that sort of energy around them.'

'I had noticed them closing their doors,' said Aljce in surprise. 'But I'm sure it's because they just want to concentrate on what they're doing.' Goodness, she thought. Am I really hard? And suddenly, her strength and independence seemed cold and mean and left a flat taste in her mouth.

'It's because they don't want to talk to you,' Jillq repeated. 'We only like good energy around here.'

Aljce remembered a boyfriend who'd called her a hard bitch when she called him out about something. She remembered another time when she'd slicked her hair back with gel on a Saturday afternoon, and her friend Bella had said that she didn't really like it, that it made Aljce look hard. Aljce had visions of a prison warden and washed it out when Bella went home. Not that she'd admitted to Bella that her comment had bothered her. Perhaps she WAS hard. She never let anyone know that they'd upset her, and now was no exception. 'Perhaps they should give me more of a go,' she said to Jillq, with defiance in her heart. 'They can't get to know me properly with their doors closed.'

'They're not sure that they want to,' said Jillq.

'Can't do anything about that,' said Aljce, putting away Jillq's comments for reviewing later. She couldn't let Jillq get to her, or she would cry. She didn't want Jillq to know that she'd wounded her, and the best way to stay calm and poker faced was to think about something else. If people knew how they'd hurt you, they knew how to do it again.

She considered refusing to take the paper from Jillq's hand, but that would have made her seem ill tempered. She had to remain super reasonable and show them all how wrong they were. She would take it and consider how to deal with it later. Something so trumped up could surely be overturned. Because Aljce believed justice always came through in the end. 'Am I finished? Are we finished?' she asked.

'I believe we are,' said Jillq. 'Marj, did you want to say anything to Aljce?'

'We're very disappointed in you Aljce,' said Marj.

'For what?' asked Aljce. Marj looked at her blankly. She obviously couldn't articulate what had disappointed her. Perhaps she was just delivering a prearranged message.

'Are we finished?' repeated Aljce.

'Yes, I think we are,' said Marj quickly, pleased to be relieved of Aljce's first question. 'Yes, you can go Aljce.' Aljce went outside. She felt as if she was in shock. The letter fell open. The only thing that Aljce was capable of noticing was that it was signed by Marj. Not Jillq.

Aljce was overcome with self-doubt. Maybe they were right about her, and working here was showing up parts of her personality that she hadn't considered before. Surely everybody couldn't be wrong about her? She tried to see things from Jillq's perspective. Perhaps she was teased when she was younger, she thought. Perhaps it was cruel. Perhaps that's why she has a different definition of teasing. Perhaps that's why we're on a different page. With different definitions. Perhaps she, Aljce, just needed to be more understanding and compassionate.

'JUST LEAVE,' said Strauss.

'Strauss. I've been fascinated by people for as long as I can remember. Of course I'm going to do counselling. This is the job I want to do. It's like breathing.'

'Well, you're going to have to put your skills and experience to work with her, aren't you?'

'Yeah, but if she's got a Narcissistic Personality Disorder, which she possibly could have, there's not much hope for change,' said Aljce, putting her skills to work, as instructed. She'd done some thinking in the last few hours. 'And if that's the case, I could shake her till fairy dust pissed out, and nothing would change. Because she would never, ever see that anything she does is wrong. She wouldn't be able to self-reflect. She would have no empathy. There would only be her, and how she feels. It wouldn't be a choice. That would be how she was wired.'

'Narcissistic. What a pretty word. I think you should leave.'

'Yeah, it's named after a vain man who turned into a flower. The word is pretty. A rich cream pink. Slight blush of peach. Which is no help with Jillq.'

'I thought you were doubting yourself and wondering if it was your fault.'

'I am. This is just an alternative theory I'm considering.'

'You're always trying to figure out how people tick. I reckon you do it to try to keep yourself safe. What causes this Narcissistic thing?'

'Some people say childhood trauma. That it stops that brain development in a critical period. Traps them in a child-like place where the world revolves around them. Like a baby when it cries. The baby doesn't care that you're tired or that you're desperate for sleep. It just wants its milk. Other people say it's just genetics. Inheritable. Jillq could potentially be narcissistic because she doesn't respond to my feelings, and she doesn't seem to think that any of the rules that should apply to her. She's got no ethical boundaries, or personal or professional ones. No regard for process and policy. Unless it's about me that's breaking the rules. Clearly I'm not as wonderful as her, so I need to be censured hard for any transgressions.'

'What a bitch. What's a transgression?'

'Crossing the line, Strauss.'

'Oh. Perhaps it's best not to cross the line then, Aljce.'

'That would be fine if I knew where the lines were.'

Aljce was on her high horse now. 'I do good work, way faster and way above the standard of anyone else, what little they give me to do, that is, and all they can say is that I look unprofessionally sexy?'

'Did she say that?'

'I think it was the implication. Belittling me for being myself instead of looking at the quality of what I do. Women using sexism against their own. And I'm so busy feeling small, that I forget to even feel resentful that they haven't valued my hard work and talent. There was this random moment yesterday when I realised that those things were never going to pay off in this organisation, and that's when I realised I was in the wrong place. Original thinking isn't appreciated or admired by mundane thinkers. They prize the cliché. Plus they hate to think that someone else might have a better thought than them'

'I can't say it strongly enough: leave.'

'Sometimes I just imagine you're there with me, Strauss. And what you would say. I'm a grown-up woman with made-up friends. How cool is that?' Aljce smiled with random glee that was at odds with the way work was troubling her mind. She could put Jillq briefly out of her mind sometimes; covering her with other thoughts.

'How do you know you're not making me up right now?' said Strauss.

'I probably am. I may even be making myself up, I guess.'

SHE OFTEN WONDERED if she was making up Lewis. Sometimes she taunted herself. What if he wasn't real, and she was just mad; dreaming him up in her head? Craaaaazy, she said to herself. Was she still delusional if she queried her delusion? Wasn't the definition of being delusional someone who was deluded but convinced that they weren't? Aljce wasn't convinced.

'Do you ever wonder if your thoughts and feelings are my thoughts and feelings, as if they've bumped into each other somewhere because our brains were focusing on each other simultaneously, and we're sharing a thought? Like a dual thought?' she asked him. That's how fucking delusional I am, she thought. Wide awake deluded.

At the same time, she felt reassured by Lewis. 'I feel as if I can be completely real with you, and that I'm perfect just being myself. I don't have to be someone else,' he said.

'Sometimes I'm not sure who I am. I mean, I'm an introverted extrovert,' said Aljce. 'Or an extroverted introvert. One or the other. When I'm with people, I feel like I'm outgoing and fun. But when I'm at home, I just wanna be by myself.'

'We're quite alike really.'

'So alike!'

'Perhaps we're two halves of the same soul.'

WHEN SHE WAS at home, she felt good. She'd started writing a few things in her phone notes. Recording her descriptions and ideas about things. 'I think my moon is in my retrograde or something,' she said to her friend Bella, between puffs. 'I feel like I'm entering into a real creative space in my life, where everything just drops, perfectly coloured, from the sky, and forms an atmosphere around me. I hope it lasts.' She wondered what Lewis would think about her doing some writing of her own.

There was a divide between her love life and her work life. She hadn't told Lewis anything about work. She wanted to keep that separate, and not ruin the haze she was sharing with him with anything upsetting. She would tell him about her writing, but not about Jillq.

SHE SAW HER old boss Hannah down town. 'How's it going?' said Hannah.

'Oh, you know,' said Aljce, embarrassed.

'Are you coming to the Social Services Networking meeting tomorrow?'

'Ohh,' said Aljce. 'Yes. Where is it?'

'Community Rooms. 10am. See you there!' Hannah was clearly in a rush.

ALJCE WENT TO the meeting, and for the first time since her first day at her new job, she felt happy during work hours. She was slightly late, as for some reason she'd felt the need to leave the Therapy Hub without anyone observing her. Although surely there couldn't be any reason to prevent her from going to a networking meeting. It wasn't as though she had anything else to do. She just felt nervy about everything at the moment. Unfortunately that meant that Hannah was already seated over the other side of the room, but she waved cheerfully to Aljce.

When Aljce returned to the Therapy Hub, she was waylaid by Marj. Don't be silly, she said to herself. You haven't done anything wrong. But apparently she had. 'Where have you been?' said Marj. Aljce explained. 'It's not in your diary!' said Marj.

'Yes it is,' said Aljce, flipping open the new one she'd bought.

'It's not in the desktop diary at reception.'

Aljce congratulated herself on being clever. 'Yes it is.'

'What about the planner on the wall?'

'Um?'

'The planner on the wall. It's not on there.'

'That's because I didn't know about it.'

'The one in the hallway! You must use it! And your Outlook Calendar!' said Marj.

'Well, I will in future. But that's quite a lot of places to have to record where I am. Wouldn't it make sense to collate them into one, plus our personal diaries?'

'This is how we do it up here,' said Marj.

'Sure,' said Aljce.

She walked down the hallway. Sure enough there was a wall planner there. Calendar attempts to simultaneously capture what space she and the others were in at any given time were everywhere. She was sure that the wall planner hadn't been there that morning though. She looked at the sheet underneath. It was for the week before, and crossed through solely in Jillq's handwriting with words like staff meeting and morning tea. No specific person had used it. There was only one entry for the current week, where Mrs. Kingi had written 'lunch' for the hour before now. And it was Thursday. Nothing was on the sheets below those two. Aljce betted that Jillq had put it up there while Aljce was out.

The day stretched on. Aljce looked at the clock. Quarter past 3. She hoped she'd be home before the girls could get there. It was raining, and she'd counted on being able to duck out earlier when it was wet, making it up by working through lunch hours, and coming earlier. But the way things were here, there was no way she had enough good will against her name to be able to do that. If anyone noticed, there would be a staff meeting. Aljce had observed that Mrs. Kingi came in and left for the day whenever she felt like it. But that meant nothing. Double standards were no stranger to the Therapy Hub, and depended on your position of privilege. Oftentimes between 3 o'clock and half past 3 she looked at the clock and wondered if anyone would notice, if anyone was even watching. But she'd got to the stage where even though she didn't believe in psychics, she was impressed by Jillq's ability to know everything about what Aljce had done. So she sat there, watching herself for them, making sure that she didn't step over the line. Keeping herself in a space that couldn't be criticised. Where no one could find fault with her.

'Make sure Pleasance looks before you cross the road,' she had instructed Liddell. 'Be a good big sister.' Perhaps she worried unnecessarily. Lots of people's kids walked to and from school. She had walked to or from school in the rain herself. It had been unpleasantness that had needed to be suffered; the cold wet leaking raincoat that stuck to the top of your legs and the rest of your legs so cold that the rain burned them, and it only came to an end when you got home. But she didn't want her kids to have to go through that. She looked across the corridor to the office where Marj sat.

'I might go home,' said Marj, catching Aljce's eye. 'I've put in a lot of extra hours lately.' Aljce cheered inwardly. Perhaps she could sneak out, because she'd be the last one left. But Marj stood up, and lingered in the doorway to Aljce's office, telling her all about the movie that her daughter was planning to go to. Aljce couldn't even imagine how Marj managed to drag such a trivial one sentence announcement into such a long discussion. Some people processed things so slowly, bogged down by mundane details. She watched in agony as the clock ticked through the minutes, giving Marj only brief responses which shouldn't have encouraged Marj to say to continue, because they were conversation closers. She murmured about needing to finish her work, even though she had absolutely none to do. She murmured about needing to pack up her desk, shut down her computer, go to the toilet. But it wasn't till she stood up that Marj said that she's better go if she was going to be babysitting her grandson. While her daughter went to the movies. Aljce hated her stupid, dumb face. She's just so thick, she thought. Then she stopped herself. Thinking this way was bad for her karma. She mustn't think impatient thoughts about other people. Making herself superior. Maybe this was what Jillq was talking about.

By the time she managed to leave, it was actually quarter to 4 on the clock on her office wall. But she couldn't write it down on the timesheet in Marj's office, because Marj had left and locked it. So she wouldn't even be able to claim 15 minutes off the next day, because she'd never be able to prove she'd earned it. The clock down the hallway said it was 4 o'clock. Was it fast, or was she being done out of time by the one in her office? She checked on the clock in the staff room. 6 o'clock, it said. Perhaps this was the clock Mrs. Kingi had left by earlier in the day. Way to make sure everyone's confused, Aljce thought. She needed to go by the time on her phone.

When she saw Dulcie at the end of the hallway she realised that she hadn't been alone in the building. 'Hi Dulcie,' she called. Perhaps Dulcie could verify what time Aljce had left work if they queried her timesheets. Dulcie didn't even turn around. Jillq was right. Nobody liked her. Aljce heard the door shut behind Dulcie as she left.

Home was a much better place to be. Especially once Pleasance and Liddell were in bed, and her head space was all her own. Not that she was actually on her own. Highsy walked across her face as she lay on her back on the couch for a brief minute, the fur of its stomach brushing across her nose and mouth. Cats had no manners.

Aljce liked being home alone with Lewis.

'Doesn't it scare you that I'm going to steal your words?' he asked. 'Don't you worry that I'll leave you naked? There's nothing you can do about how I use them.'

'It's fine,' said Aljce. 'I like your style of thievery.'

'Good,' he said, obviously pleased from his tone.

'I like words and language because they're the doorway into stories. There couldn't be stories if there weren't any words.'

'I have fallen into the pot of your syrup,' he said. 'I am like a moth, drowning in its sweetness.'

'I'm having a party in my room right now, in between our messages,'

Aljce said. She was long since off the couch. 'And I'm doing some writing too. Do you know how difficult it is to write in your phone notes and dance at the same time?'

'What are you writing?'

'Oh, yinno ... just thoughts and things.'

'I thought I was the writer here.'

'Oh, you are. I guess maybe I hope I will be too. The trick, I think, would be to write a book where it could be seen from different perspectives at different times, different layers, and the reader never really being sure of which layers were true, or which angle to view it from. Like a diamond, flashing in the light, different from every angle, but still the same thing. Same diamond, same light, just different perspective.'

'Or a hologram. That would work.'

'Yeah.'

'Interesting,' he said.

'I'm just writing when I feel like it. When I have something important to say. I couldn't bang out two thousand words after breakfast no matter what. That's surely how you get dross. The mediocre are disciplined, not inspired. And the inspired are erratic.'

'Hmm,' he said. 'When you're a bit more experienced, you'll know that discipline is essential, or you'll never produce more than the occasional short story.'

Aljce wasn't deterred. 'I'm finding that my new angel of writing is very persuasive, and I have to follow it... like a... rapture, I guess. I mean, I don't even want to resist. The closest I could describe it really is that when I CAN write it feels as if I'm in the early stages of tripping. My reality alters, and everything is filtered differently. Sometimes when that rapture is there, everything I think is good enough to write down. It's as if words are just there, waiting for me to harvest them. Not like other times, when the angel is gone, and I try to force it, everything is stilted and awkward and stupid. Although I've got to remember to get the words down when I'm flowing. Hence the writing. I don't like misplacing thoughts. Oh, plus being inspired by you, of course... But I do want to save my thoughts in case I want to go back to them again. If I can't remember my thoughts, I can still look them up.'

'Have you yet?'

'No. I'm too busy having new thoughts. But maybe one day.'

'How do you lose a whole thought?' he asked.

'By having so many, I guess. They crowd each other out. That's the price you pay though. For smoking. Plus it does something funny with memory; I'm not sure what. But unless I write ideas into my phone notes, I don't retain them. I try to give them a name; a name for the thought, (like this one could be 'missing thoughts') but even that's not really helping. I've got to be stricter with the phone notes. But part of me is like, if I didn't remember the thought, I'm not really meant to have it. As if the universe is culling for me. Perhaps I think a lot of nonsense.'

'I like the way you think about your thinking,' he wrote back. 'But real writers write in longhand. They enjoy the flow of the words from the pen to the paper.'

'Oh,' said Aljce.

'You're so interested in my writing. It's really kind of you,' she said. 'How's your writing going? I mean, you are the writer.'

'Oh, it seems to pale into insignificance next to yours...'

'Sorry, have I gone on too much about mine? It's still pretty new to me, and I'm just so excited to have someone to talk about it with...'

'Not at all. My own writing is completely stuck at the moment.'

'I thought you wrote every day?'

'I do, but nothing of any value is emerging. Perhaps I am spending it all on you. Perhaps we should co-write something.'

'Oh. I don't think I would be any good at co-writing. I feel like I know where absolutely every word should be.' A little part of her panicked. She could already see herself caught between wanting to make compromises to please him, and needing to be true to herself. Silly, she thought. He just means sharing ideas.

'Give it some thought,' he said.

SHE'S NOTHING BUT A COMMON WEED

'Surely it can't be that bad?' said her friend Mamae. It was more of a statement than a question.

'It is,' said Aljce. 'I know you probably think I'm exaggerating, but I'm definitely not.' She knew that Mamae's ability to comprehend the situation was limited, as Mamae was a Postie and got to spend most of her work time on a bike, not having to answer to anyone. 'I make sure not to go home before half past three, even when they owe me hours, or when there's no one else in the building; with no one even likely to come back. So I'm watching myself for her. I can't bear to leave myself open to be caught by her in something that might have even a hint of anything less than my own perfect behaviour. To prove her to be corrupt, I have to prove myself to be above rubies. Oh, the rubies are biblical,' she said, seeing Mamae's face. 'A story in the bible. You know what I mean. I've got to be all that.'

They passed the joint, and Aljce tried to keep explaining. 'There's this, well, story, I guess, that this man call Foucault came up with. It's about a prison called the Panoptican. The cell block was shaped like a thick outer band of a big circle, with the cells forming a ring around a single guard tower in the space in the middle. The cell walls were see-through with no curtains on the inner and the outer of the ring, even though the walls between each of them were solid. There were always bright lights on in the prisoner's cell, so anyone in the guard house would be able to see right in at any time, and see the prisoners silhouetted. As a result, the prisoners always behaved in the ways that the guards wanted; because they couldn't hide what they did, and they were fearful of punishment. But the prisoners couldn't see into the guard's tower because the light inside was dim, so they didn't know when there was actually anyone in it, watching them. So what I'm saying is that they behaved themselves super well, even when no one was actually watching them. And that's how I am with Jillq. I'm watching myself, and keeping myself sternly to the rules. Her rules. Whatever they are.'

'Gosh, Aljce, that sounds like hard work.'

'It is,' said Aljce sadly.

THE NEXT DAY was no different. 'Aljce, there is a meeting you need to diary,' said Chelsea.

'What's it about?' said Aljce.

'I'm not sure,' said Chelsea. 'Ask someone else.'

'Is it for everyone?'

'Everyone? Yes.'

'And you don't know what it's about?'

'I expect it's just a process meeting,' said Chelsea. Aljce sighed to herself. More time wasting. No doubt she would be expected to record her intention to attend in multiple places, even though everyone would know where she was. Thankfully, Chelsea had indicated that it was a meeting for everyone, so it wouldn't be one of those uncomfortable meetings about her.

'Are you going to the meeting?' asked Mrs. Kingi.

'I thought it was compulsory,' said Aljce.

'Compulsory?' said Mrs. Kingi.

'Yinno, like we all have to go.'

'Oh, yes, we all have to go.'

'Then I'll have to be there too, won't I?'

'Yes, it's compulsory,' said Mrs. Kingi. 'Are you going?'

'Yes,' said Aljce. 'What's it about?'

'I'm not really sure,' said Mrs. Kingi. 'But we all have to be there.'

Everyone WAS there except MaryAnn and Kat. 'Let's bring our chairs to this table,' said Marj. Hattie's spoon and teabag still sat on the edge of the other table, with brown rings of old tea where it had bled.

'Actually,' said Jillq, 'I think for this meeting, we will just place our chairs in a circle. So that we can fully connect.'

'Chairs in a circle everybody!' said Mrs. Kingi.

'We need to be professional at all times,' said Jillq. Aljce failed to see how putting their chairs in a circle so that their knees were practically touching added professionalism. Perhaps it was a social services thing.

'Alright,' said Jillq. 'We all know why we're at this meeting.'

'I don't,' said Aljce. 'I asked all of you what it was about, and you all said you didn't know.'

'Who wants to go first?' said Jillq. Aljce noticed everyone else staring at the carpet. This was not going to be good after all. She had a feeling. 'We will all go round the circle and tell Aljce what we are thinking,' said Jillq. 'Dulcie, you can go first.'

'I didn't want to be first,' said Dulcie. 'I'm still thinking about what to say. Marj can go first.'

'I think you were asked to go first,' said Marj.

'Dulcie, you have been asked to go first,' said Jillq. 'I am not only the Manager of this Hub, I am also your Mother.'

'Um,' said Dulcie, 'um, well I mean, you're not really fitting in, Aljce.'

'Not really fitting in,' said Marj, possibly hoping that her echo would count as her turn.

'What do you mean?' asked Aljce, with a wobble in her voice. 'I've done my best to be friendly to you all. But to be honest, I'm finding some of you a bit funny sometimes.'

'And that is exactly what we mean Aljce. That is a very good example of the sort of remark you make,' said Jillq. 'What's been happening is that people have been experiencing you as a very hard person who says sharp things to others. And that hardness shows because you always have your guard up. You never let other people in. And you can't work with abuse when you're like that. You're showing us that you're exactly the wrong sort of person for this job.'

'It's hard to let anyone else in when people say this sort of thing to me,' said Aljce, wanting to cry.

'That's what we mean,' said Hattie. 'Try not to be so defensive. We're just trying to help you.'

'I'm not feeling helped,' said Aljce.

'You come across as very hard,' said Chelsea.

'I did try to say hello to you yesterday,' she said to Dulcie, hoping to prove her friendly intentions.

'No you didn't,' said Dulcie. 'I didn't see you yesterday.'

'But you did,' said Aljce, shocked. Dulcie looked highly offended.

'I'm not lying you know.'

Aljce pulled her head in. 'I didn't mean to suggest you were lying,' she said carefully. 'Just mistaken.'

'I don't think so,' said Dulcie. 'I don't get mistaken.' Aljce looked at her. Could she be for real?

Aljce started crying. Nasty and hard. The same words kept on coming around and around again from everybody. Jillq regarded Aljce across her glasses. 'That's what you need to do,' she said delightedly. 'We like you a lot better now that you're crying. What you don't understand is that we just want to see some vulnerability to reassure us that you will be able to cope with being a therapist.' Aljce was almost grateful to her. Jillq was now the one kind person in a circle of attackers, because everyone else, suddenly wrong footed, stayed quiet. Everything was going to be alright.

THAT NIGHT, Aljce searched her soul. She liked to reflect on what people had said about her, and take responsibility for things. They had all said she was a hard person, or at least not disagreed with Chelsea. Surely every person at that meeting couldn't be wrong. Jillq had said it previously, but that was only one person. Now everyone else was agreeing. Was that really how she came across? She looked at a photo of herself on the wall by her bed. Her lips were smiling faintly, but she could see something wary in her own eyes, something defensive. No doubt it had been there since she was young. She'd learned to hide being hurt, and not to show any emotion on her face. Not to give anyone the satisfaction, because then that let them know that she was vulnerable, and they could hurt her further. That could lead people to think she lacked emotion, when that wasn't actually the case.

But surely she was entitled to hold something back until she was sure that she could trust someone? All she wanted to do was to avoid being hurt. Which wasn't working out for her at the moment. She felt hurt right now. She felt that her soul had been assessed as being cold and dry and brittle, and she liked to think it was full of flowers; blooming wildly and throwing out scent until people got dizzy. She didn't like to think that it was unwelcoming to others. She really wanted to be a good counsellor. She was going to have to start opening up to other people at her work more. And cut out the secretly amused remarks. She knew she made them. She needed to be more friendly. Smile more. Although smiling wasn't really her thing, and she hated fake smiles. If she was comfortable with people, she laughed out loud a lot. She needed to get comfortable with them.

Being criticised brought out the worst in her. In the meeting, she had felt herself reverting to that sulky kid, who WAS angry and hard. So that her hurt wouldn't show. She felt annoyed that she had cried, although in the end, it seemed to have been the right thing to do. Perhaps crying was watering her flowers. Perhaps she hadn't tended to them lately. Perhaps they were right. Perhaps she was too hard. Perhaps it was her face. Hard felt ugly. She felt as if they'd called her ugly. That was what had made her cry. They'd pushed her triggers. She was ugly and unloveable and nobody liked her.

SHE WENT TO her happy place, which was hanging out with Lewis. 'I like it here with you,' she said. 'I know so much about you, you know so much about me. And when I'm here, I feel so good about myself…

'I can see you are sky high, across the sky. I can tell when you're stoned. You get into those honey moods.'

'Honey moods. That's actually quite an appropriate description.'

'How so?'

'You know how usually we move through air? Well, being stoned is pleasantly heavier than that. It's more like moving through honey, all golden and sweet, while the blues play exquisitely slow.'

'Sounds good.'

'It is.'

'I'll always be interested in you, yinno. Your mind is just so… intricate. I'm like a drunk in a winery, with so many bottles to try that I've become intoxicated. And I love all of them.'

'I believe in love. But it has to be epic and infinite. Like having a best friend and lover all in one. It has to transcend everything. Even my unloveableness.'

'Perhaps we're the same. Perhaps we both want love, but it has to be something startling, something big. A love story for all time. And at the same time, we don't really want to give up being alone, because we like it too much.'

'Perhaps,' she said. 'But perhaps we could change.'

CHANGE WASN'T IN the air at work. Things were not alright as she had thought they might be after she'd cried. The next day, Jillq stopped her in the hallway. 'I hear you went to the Social Services Networking meeting, Aljce. Where are the notes you made?'

'What notes?'

'The notes you made at the meeting.'

'I didn't take notes.'

'How do you know what happened?'

'I was there.'

'You can't remember without notes.'

'I have a good verbal memory.'

'Please don't be arrogant Aljce. I want to see notes.'

'There's no need. I'm happy to report on what happened at staff meeting.'

'Aljce, you are being disrespectful. And I hear that you didn't diary it either. Nothing happens without it being in your diary.'

'It was in my diary.'

'I can't see YOUR diary.'

'Sure,' said Aljce, agreeing to nothing in particular as usual.

'NARCISSISTS GET TO you because they act so lovely towards you when you first meet them,' she read. 'And then you trust them. If they weren't nice at first, they couldn't suck you into their swamp.' Damn, she thought. She threw her memory back to Pleasance and Liddell's father. Jillq wafted through her mind. Repeating patterns in her life. Jillq was not a lover, but she was a narcissist. Aljce had thought Jillq was wonderful; couldn't wait to work for her, with her lovely liquid voice, articulating all of Aljce's values and beliefs. And somehow or other, she'd never turned out like that. She had been cold and ruthless and empty. Blank. There was nothing for Aljce's heart to connect to. It was difficult to understand how Jillq could have been so convincing. Perhaps she had just been throwing out words that she knew were socially persuasive to people like Aljce. Aljce doubted that Jillq did genuinely care for the wounded or vulnerable, it was more likely that she just liked to think that she did. Because she had no empathy, no awareness of the need to be kind to other souls.

She gained my trust, thought Aljce, and then she found my weaknesses. Perfectionism. A need to be excellent at everything I do. And most of all, my desire to be liked and accepted by other people. And she's making sure to tell me that my work is shit and that nobody likes me. Well, fuck her. I'm good at my job. I've got initiative. I can handle complex work. And actually, I don't need other people to like me, because I like myself. Mostly.

LUCKILY THERE WAS more in Aljce's life than just work. 'You're good for my new writing hobby,' she told Lewis. 'The words are just flowing.'

'Tell me some.'

'No, too embarrassing. You can see them later, when it's a book. Hopefully one day.' He seemed fascinated, even though he was the real writer. 'It's so nice of you to humour me,' she wrote.

'One day, I will know where all your freckles are,' he said. 'So why wouldn't I?'

It crossed Aljce's mind that sometimes you let people in, and then all of a sudden you were completely vulnerable. Perhaps she shouldn't. And then it made her laugh; thinking about it like it was even a choice.

SOMETIMES HE DID honour her by talking about his own writing. 'I feel insecure, because I put everything I had, good and bad, into my last novel, and it was everything I wanted it to be. But now I feel like I've got nothing left; that it's over.'

'Perhaps you just need to wait until you think more thoughts?'

'But that took a lifetime...'

'Perhaps you should just use the same ones again then, and put them in a different order? Maybe the story they make will be different; a new way for you to look at things?'

'Hmm. Sounds logical. I hope it's true.' There was a pause, in which he must have been reflecting. 'Is publishing my mind the ultimate vanity? A desperate attempt to get noticed, or a bid to be understood...? Knowing that while some people will appreciate it, a lot of people will never get it?'

'You'll get it. And surely it's yourself that you're writing for?'

'It'll have to be called *Bread of the Dawn Fish* or something. If it's going to sell.'

'Is that what it's going to be about then?'

'No. But I'll slip some little connector in on page 33 or something.' He sounded tired. 'Sometimes I'm just writing for finished product, rather than because I enjoy writing. I don't even know if I do enjoy writing. The process of writing. It's always a relief when it's finished.'

'Hey, look at this quote,' said Aljce. '"If a writer falls in love with you, you will never die."'

'True. You can't help stealing from yourself and your own life, and that means stealing from the people who share that life with you.'

'So we'll be keeping each other alive in words...'

'Funny. People will be able to read our story from different perspectives.'

'Ha. Yeah.'

Perhaps people hoped for life partners to define and record their lives; an observer. But no one was there all the time, no one was forever. In the end, only the self took the whole journey. And being remembered externally was someone else's experience. Still. 'I feel like I'm going to be famous,' she told him. 'Although it doesn't bother me if I'm not. If I'm wrong. I've just always thought that. And why would I think that if it wasn't going to happen?'

'Perhaps it's just a delusion...'

'Perhaps. But like I said, I'm not invested in it. So it won't matter if it is.'

'A delusion of grandeur.'

'Maybe. That makes me think of a big, beautiful hallucination. A grand hallucination, with colours so clear and pure that they blind you. Ultra violet everything. A delusion of grandeur. An illusion of grandeur. Do delusions ever need to end? That's not a rule, is it?'

'If you're going to go mad, I'm a good person to go mad with,' he said. 'Because I'm a writer. A published one, at that.'

'Do you ever wonder if I'm a dream?' she asked him.

'No. You're as real as I am.'

'See, I wonder if you're real. But then again, on a different level, I believe that all of reality is an illusion, no more real than a dream anyway. And you're just another layer of that. I suppose it's like the wave/particle electron duality that I was telling my friend Strauss about. Things are both actual and they're not, depending on whether we're watching. The observer changes everything. And we're the observer. In this case, we're observing ourselves together. Observing together. Observing us together.'

'So we're saying that reality is both real and not...'

'Pretty much, yeah. The illusion is persuasive, though, so it may as well be real. The question is: who is making the other one up?' she mused. 'I feel like I'm real, but then you probably do too.'

'So if you're making me up, and creating your own reality, that means I can be anything. I can be nothing, or everything. All the decisions are yours.'

'It could be the other way around. But you'd have to have a strange mind to dream me up.'

'So much strangeness,' he said.

'Co-creating,' she said, 'we're co-creating.'

She'd never met anyone who connected with her on so many wave lengths at once. He liked quantum physics, he was concerned about planetary destruction and he was witty. He liked music. He could discuss art. And ideas. Play games with her and keep up. She didn't think it was sinful to love someone's mind, or wrong to fall in love with someone whose mind matched her own. It was only natural really. She might never meet such a mind again. 'You make me realise that all I've ever really wanted in life is to love and be loved,' she told him.

No MATTER WHAT was happening in her private life, Aljce had no intention of being vulnerable at work. The next day she wore leopard print and a fake black fur with knee length black boots. She knew it added to the impression of hardness, but she felt perverse, and it made her feel braver. She felt as if she was underwater with turbulent schools of dark fish; one shoal going that way, another shoal going this way, another smacking right into her. How was she supposed to know what they were going to do next? They were unpredictable. When she had thought things were going well, they weren't.

She was surprised when Hattie approached her. 'You seemed a bit blindsided at that meeting,' Hattie said. 'I hadn't realised that you all felt that way about me,' said Aljce stiffly.

'Don't take it to heart,' said Hattie. 'It can be hard fitting in when you're new.'

'Perhaps it's because things were difficult for me when I was young,' offered Aljce, caught off guard by Hattie's surprise kindness. 'I have a hard time trusting people.' Mentally, she congratulated herself. She was opening up. Perhaps vulnerability was the way forward after all.

'Did you have a difficult birth?' asked Hattie.

'Yeah, I think so,' said Aljce. 'I was born upside down with the cord around my neck. But I don't think that's it.'

'Oh, it affects everything,' said Hattie. 'Especially the bonding.'

'I suppose,' said Aljce.

'It can be difficult,' said Hattie. 'And I won't say there's no problems here. I invited a trouble shooter to meet with us all a few years ago, but it doesn't seem to have made any difference.'

'Really?' said Aljce.

'Yes,' said Hattie. 'But it doesn't seem to have helped. The problem is that everyone has to buy into the solutions and not everyone did.'

'Really? What were the problems? What were the solutions?'

'Oh, same old same old,' said Hattie vaguely, refusing to be drawn any further. Aljce was delighted. That was where opening up to someone had gotten her. Hattie was a potential ally. This was the first time that anyone had acknowledged that something might be wrong here, other than herself. 'I encourage you to open up to people and tell us a bit about yourself,' said Hattie.

'What do you want to know?' asked Aljce. And she told Hattie about how all her bills had come in at once this week, and how hard it was to manage financially when you swapped from one job to another and you were a single mother.

'It isn't easy,' said Hattie. 'I'm a single mother too. That's why I work.'

'Do you really shut your door to avoid me?' Aljce said to Mrs. Kingi.

'Of course not,' said Mrs. Kingi.

'Then why do you shut your door?'

'Oh,' said Mrs. Kingi vaguely. 'So that I can concentrate. I find it easier to concentrate when the noise level is down.' Aljce wondered what she was concentrating on. Mrs. Kingi didn't seem to have many clients, if any. Perhaps, like Aljce, Mrs. Kingi didn't want Jillq checking on what she was doing. Perhaps even Mrs. Kingi wasn't immune to being micromanaged. And Jillq was definitely a control freak. Aljce felt slightly better.

At quarter past 3, Aljce packed up to leave. 'Where are you going?' asked Jillq, unexpectedly coming in the front door as Aljce left. She was hardly ever present at the Hub after 2 o'clock. No one was, except Aljce and Marj.

'I did fifteen minutes extra the other day,' Aljce explained.

'Is it on your timesheet?' asked Jillq.

'No, because Marj had already left and locked her office,' explained Aljce. 'But Dulcie saw me.'

'We don't do time in lieu,' said Jillq.

'Oh,' said Aljce innocently. 'Chelsea said she took some yesterday.'

'Not for new employees,' said Jillq. Aljce felt as if she was in a reality with a constantly shifting set of rules. Like the real Alice.

'Is that fair?' she asked.

'Only children talk about fair,' said Jillq. 'We require more maturity here.' Aljce sat down again. Clearly there was another fifteen minutes to go.

'STRAUSS, DO YOU KNOW, like, when you've been in love...?' Aljce asked. She'd managed to get home eventually, and now they were outside in her shed.

'Yeah?'

'Well, have you ever had the same love twice?'

'Hell, Aljce, I don't even love Jimsy the same every year, let alone every week.'

'Yeah, but have you ever had the same love with different people?'

'That's a long fucking time to think back. We've been together for so long.'

'Well, we'll go with my experience then. I've never had exactly the same relationship with any two men. It's always the first time I've done it that way. It's always a mystery to me. And I've never loved any of them in the same way. Young love, possessive love, submissive love, violent love, wanting better love... No, it's never the same love twice. Who knows what new types of love are coming our way?'

'Mmm, yeah,' said Strauss thoughtfully.

But Aljce was off on a new track. 'I don't even love my children in the same way. Pleasance is more golden, and comfortable and soft, and Liddell is quick and precise, bright white, with shadows, really. The difference between peaches and pears. Peaches are soft and juicy and sweet, but sometimes you just want a pear. Or a peach if you have a lot of pears.'

'Yeah,' said Strauss. 'Sometimes it can be difficult to decide who you love the most out of two different people.'

'Indeed.'

Strauss shivered. 'This coldness almost makes me think about going inside before I've smoked and toked enough,' she said. 'Not quite, but almost. I'm not meant for this winteriness. I'm meant for balmy summer nights. And stars. I'm meant for stars. They bring me happiness. As if I'm connected to somewhere beautiful.'

'Ahh. That's longing.'

'Yeah. Wish we were there.'

'Are you wasted?'

'No, not really. Just politely stoned.'

'So. Do you ever think wrong thoughts, you know; when you think something, and then you evaluate it and think, no, that doesn't fit? Or are all your thoughts that pop into your head correct thoughts, you know, and they're all fully formed, and you wouldn't have thought them if they weren't right?'

'Shit, I don't know.'

'So, do you have freedom of choice with thought, to critically analyse it, just like anyone else's thoughts that they try to sell you? And are people who just believe everything they think just stupid, or are they wise, because thoughts don't need to be analysed? And who are those people anyway ... I analyse some thoughts and throw them away. Reluctantly; because it's MY thought. And I'm quite sentimental.'

'I don't know, I can't think whether I analyse mine or not. Can't remember thinking, 'wrong thought' at any moment. But maybe I'm just more relaxed about discarding thoughts than you.'

'Ha, yeah. I should watch myself in case I turn into a wrong thought collector. But that could be good. Because then I can look at where I went wrong with my previous wrong thoughts. And learn something.'

'Aljce, I have no idea what you are talking about.'

'Damn. I thought I was making heaps of sense. It sounded right when I said it. But maybe this whole conversation is a wrong thought.'

'Do you know what you remind me of Aljce? This picture of a polar bear in my Facebook feed, swinging her head and half smiling, half grimacing. And do you know what the meme is? Above the bear it's saying, 'I hate being bipolar,' and underneath it's saying, 'it's awesome.' That's you. You have conversations with yourself, where you argue with yourself. And you switch from one side of the argument to the other, always trying to outdo your other self.'

'Oh, yeah, probably. Debate makes me think.'

'Sad that you have to debate yourself...'

'Well, I'm very argumentative Strauss.'

'Haha. So tell me about one of your wrong thoughts.'

'I can't. I'm ashamed. It could ruin my brainy girl rep.'

SHE AND LEWIS discussed meeting. Aljce thought it was a natural progression. 'I imagine that eventually, I'll risk losing you for the chance that you might make love to me; yes.'

'Losing me?'

'We'll never be able to go back to before that moment of seeing each other for the first time, to being each other's illusions. Not once we make ourselves real. We're having a honeymoon of illusions.'

'I like it.'

'I want it to last forever, but I suppose honeymoons never do... I used to think that I would rather hold the cards I have, and not risk meeting you, in case that happens.'

'Losing me?' he repeated.

'Yeah. Like, how when something's really good; and you just wish that that moment would last forever. But of course that's not possible. There's no stopping the illusion of time; we can't just stay in one place. If we could stay in a moment forever, we'd miss out on lots of different moments; some of them wonderful. And it's got to the stage where there would be no point in feeling the way that I do if it's not real; if who I feel this way about isn't real; if you don't exist the way I think you do. I'm the sort of person who can't praise God every Sunday if the church is empty of any God. I've got to meet you, and trust the universe that it's gonna be okay and that MY you is gonna overlap with YOUR you; the you that you actually are. And if not, I can stop worshipping a false deity. As much as I will feel the pain of empty space if that happens...'

'I have a lot of friends,' he said. 'I hope you're going to fit in. My friends are very important to me.'

'Mmm. Around other people you'll probably be the charismatic one, while I'll be the shy, private one.'

'Shy and private? Haha.'

'Around other people, I said ... Yeah, I've got a frown mark,' she said, suddenly worried that she wouldn't be beautiful enough. 'It's right between my eyebrows. Well, not right between. More to one side. The left side. I don't think of it as frown mark, cos I've had it since I was little. I think of it as more of a birthmark.'

'Everything's beautiful. Blue's beautiful. Pink's beautiful.'

'Unless you don't like pink.'

'Honestly fuck your insecurities,' he had said, and Aljce raised her eyebrows. 'It doesn't matter what you look like. I don't care. You could be fat or ugly, I wouldn't care. I love the person you are.'

'You must have a type though,' she said. 'What's your type?'

'Type? I've never had a type.'

'Think back to the common denominators of past girlfriends,' she said. 'All women,' he replied.

'Picture me fat with crooked teeth,' she said. 'I'll feel better if you do that.'

'Come on,' he said. 'Show me a photo.' And she began to consider whether that would be possible.

The camera lens hated her. It filtered out everything beautiful and soft about her, and just left the hard, harsh residue. As soon as I think it's true, then it is, she scolded herself. Self-hatred. It makes me ugly, she said to herself. Self-love makes me beautiful. I thought I actually didn't care what other people think, but clearly I do. I care about whether they think I'm physically attractive or not. I care about whether Lewis will find me attractive or not. I'm just the same as other people who care about whether other people think they have money or not, or whether other people approve of what they wear. And I'm so happy not worrying about those things. Maybe I could be happy not worrying about what I look like too. But another part of her told her that she could only be happy not worrying when and if there was nothing to worry about.

How can I doubt that he will love me when he sees me, when the entire universe has conspired to bring us together, she thought. Why would the universe waste its own time? Why am I panicking? And isn't that what real love is anyway? Blind?

But still she worried. 'It'll be like when you see a movie, and you've already read the book, and they get the main character all wrong; and you think: they're not supposed to look like that,' she said to him.

'Completely ruins it, yes.'

'Do you think it will completely ruin us?'

'Hope not.'

'Perhaps it WOULD be a good idea to exchange photos; to give ourselves time to get used to each other's look and come to terms with it before we meet.'

'Good idea, I will find one. Looking forward to seeing yours...'

She bit her lip and stared at her screen. She regretted saying that it was a good idea to exchange photos, even though it was. She felt as if she was in an awkward position. If she said she'd changed her mind, it was like an admission of ugliness, and where it would lead to was not having the courage to meet him. Because he just felt so out of her league. Well known author. Older. Educated. Witty and charming. And he was confident about a photo swap. Did she want to be the one who dropped her cake? But producing a photo of her own scared her to death. There would be an agony of moments while she waited for his verdict. And she didn't handle rejection well either, if that's what came back. She was sure it hurt her way more than it ever hurt anyone else.

'Sure,' she saw herself type, aware that she was shooting herself in the foot. Still if that was all he was about, he wasn't worthy of her anyway. Real love saw past exteriors. But that was what was in her mind, not her heart. She just hoped that she could hold that thought in her mind if and when he expressed revulsion for how she looked, or just left without saying anything. Fuck this. Was she creating her own reality by assuming the worst, on the understanding that if it happened, it wouldn't hurt so badly because she had already practiced feeling as if it had arrived?

We're all insecure, she told herself. There's no one who isn't. Unless they're a narcissist, and they're a worse type of insecure than being simply insecure. In order to cope with their insecurities, they project them on to other people, and then attack them for those reflected faults. And that's an elaborate form of self-harm involving harming someone else.

HE SENT HER a photo of himself. Smiling, reclining against a doorframe, with a shadow falling across much of his face. Perhaps it was a publicity photo, although she hadn't found any on Google. Aljce considered his bone structure, or what she could see of it in the portion of the photo that she could make out clearly. Gosh, he's handsome, she thought. Which was good in one way, as it made her want him more. But it was also daunting. Now the bar had been set high. 'Why didn't you send me a photo of your whole face?' she wrote back. Are you worried about how you look?'

'Sorry,' he said. 'Is that the pot calling the kettle black?'

'Me and rejection have complicated status,' she wrote. 'I act irrationally in response to it; like, not at all like myself. I couldn't predict what I might do off the basis of my usual self, because that is temporarily cancelled. I'm the proudest person I know. If I think someone is losing interest in me, or that they don't wanna message me back or something, I'll always give them an out. I'll make out that it's not important to me. Pretend I don't care. But I do. I just don't want them to know.'

'Why?'

'Oh. Dunno. Maybe so that they can't use my vulnerability to hurt me. If they don't know that they hurt me, they score no points, I guess. I avoid humiliation.'

'But is it humiliation to care for someone? Why should you be ashamed of someone else's bad behaviour towards you?'

'I don't know. Yinno what? It's so nice to be able to talk to someone about these things without the risk of being hurt. Like, it's nice to be able to trust someone. Thank you.'

'Just being a human being. This is how it should be. We should be able to be honest about how we feel.'

'Still, I just can't tell you how wonderful it is to be able to share who I am like this, with someone who's interested; who cares. I've never had this before.'

'Someone must have used your vulnerability against you in the past, and made you feel that it was because you were worthless that they'd treated you that way. All your fault. For not being good enough. And you were ashamed to be treated that way, because it meant that everyone would know how worthless you were.'

'Ha. Don't give away all my secrets.'

'I'm not going to reject you,' he said. 'Bring on that photo…'

Aljce was usually a good sleeper. After she'd talked to Lewis, provided that there was time after he went to bed, (because sometimes they talked till the early hours of the morning,) she went on Facebook, where she'd managed to avoid posting personal photos of herself, or read a book until she'd fallen asleep over whatever she was doing and jolted herself awake a few times. But tonight, she just couldn't sleep, because her thoughts were agitated. Not only was there her worry about how to take a photo of herself that would pass with Lewis, but there was also work. Thoughts of work had come flooding back as soon as Lewis was gone. What was she going to do? She couldn't go back to her old job, because there was already a new Aljce. Although she wasn't called Aljce.

She couldn't leave, because then she'd have no job. If she didn't have a job, she wouldn't be able to keep paying off her house. Maybe she wouldn't be able to feed the kids. If she didn't have this job, she wouldn't have a Student Placement for her counselling training. One person shouldn't be able to take all that from her. There must be a way to make her current situation work. She just needed the right strategy. But what was the right strategy? Her thoughts raced around in her head like horses racing around a track without a finish line. Fat streams of tears rolled down her face. She was never going to get anywhere feeling sorry for herself, but there it was. She WAS feeling sorry for herself. She moved her arm to wipe the tears away. Static electricity rippled down her sleeve and through the darkness so that she saw a trail of wet golden sparks.

ALJCE NEEDED FIRM ALLIES, and she wasn't at all sure that she could depend on Hattie. So the next day, she casually waited for MaryAnn to be by herself. She shared an office with Dulcie, who hadn't come in that day, so it wasn't too hard. 'How's the job going?' she asked.

'Oh, yinno,' said MaryAnn. 'Head down, bum up. Do as much as possible. Get outta here as fast as possible.'

'I feel like that too. Can't wait to leave.'

'I know, right? Can't put my finger on it, but... tight atmosphere.'

'I think I'm being bullied,' said Aljce. She and MaryAnn seemed to be on the same page. She'd found someone who would support her. There was hope.

She took a deep breath and started to tell MaryAnn what had been happening to her. 'Oh,' said MaryAnn. 'I don't really want to get involved in that. I just wanna do my job and go home. I don't wanna get involved in this place at all.'

'Sure,' said Aljce, feeling like she'd been kicked in the stomach. She couldn't even comprehend how MaryAnn wasn't interested in what was happening to Aljce as long as she was okay herself. She knew that if she was in MaryAnn's situation and MaryAnn was in hers, she wouldn't even think twice. MaryAnn was safe because the Therapy Hub were only providing her office. Her actual Manager was off site, and nothing to do with the organization. If Jillq were to do anything to MaryAnn, there would be people making a fuss. There would be no twisting things with no right of reply.

'Well,' said Aljce brightly, 'I'd better let you get on with your work again. Just thought I'd pop in and say hi.'

'Yeah,' said MaryAnn. 'I have got a lot to get on with.' The relief in her voice was visible in her facial expression. Back at her desk, Aljce could only try to breathe through the tears that wanted to come.

She opened her inbox. There was an email from Jillq. That could not be good. She considered opening it. If she opened it, it would upset her. If she didn't open it, it would make her anxious until she did, and then it would upset her. She opened it. Some of it was in capital letters. Aljce had no idea why it had been sent. SOME PEOPLE ARE NOT BIENG MINDFUL!!!!! It started off. Spelling was not Jillq's strong point. Aljce had made the mistake of correcting Jillq's spelling on the white board once. Come to think of it, that had been on the first day. Perhaps it marked the starting point for Jillq's dislike of her. Aljce couldn't tell if it was a group email with other people bcc'd or not. Although presumably it was. It continued on through expectations; that people should be positive about what they were asked to do, and not talk amongst themselves. Tidy desks. Taking turns to clean the toilets. To shut the staff room door when in there. I WILL NOTTTT STAND 4 IT!!!!! TAME PLAYERS ONLY!!!!!!!! It finished. It wasn't signed, but it was headed with Jillq's email address. Aljce decided not to take it personally. She opened a folder for correspondence from Jillq. You never knew what might be helpful in the end.

'Did you get that email?' asked Hattie, poking her head into Aljce and Kat's office. Her hair was now a snowy platinum blonde mass of curls. 'Jillq must be under stress.'

'She works so hard,' said Mrs. Kingi, passing in the hallway. 'Did you see that it was sent well after hours?'

'All the same,' said Hattie. 'I don't know if there was any call for that.' Aljce smiled at Hattie. She felt sure she had room to work with Hattie.

Hattie was like a big heap of soft, white marshmallows: her hips, her hair; her breasts all higgledy piggledy. And marshmallow had to be one of Aljce's favourite words. She wasn't sure how she liked to spell it best, marshmallow or marshmellow. Aljce liked being mellow. She liked it a lot. And that's how she used to spell it. But then she'd found out it was a mallow like the swamp flower, which fitted in with the marsh part. She had no idea how this applied to a sweet pillow of sticky-foamy air cut into pink or white shapes. Or the powdery vanilla smell that she had to sniff twice. But she liked it. There were monsters in marshes. Mellow monsters. Lying on pink and white pillows. Aljce felt positive.

SHE WENT TO a music festival with Strauss and Mamae. Mamae brought her Sister. Why did I enjoy that so much, wondered Aljce as they walked back towards their cars with the crowd. She thought it was probably because she had been so totally herself. Wet straggly hair and not caring. Dressed in a totally shapeless plastic poncho to keep the rain off her clothes and being so pleased to stay dry and not giving a shit about whether she looked cool or not. Singing, probably not in tune and not worried about whether anyone heard. No worries about makeup running because the skin on her face that the rain was sliding down was bare. And the people around her had been so totally themselves. No barriers. Just very safe. She wished she could feel like that all the time. Not that it would do to be like that at work.

'Who's your ultimate fantasy man?' asked Strauss as they walked towards the car, clearly mulling the question over herself.

'Ahh, gee, ultimate fantasy man? Joseph Gordon Levitt. Love his smile. Comes out of blank nowhere, and twists your heart.'

'What about Lenny Kravitz? He's smooth.'

'Hi,' said Mamae's Sister brightly, coming up behind Aljce and Strauss. 'I danced to every song that last band played!' A man struck up conversation with Aljce as he walked alongside them.

'Hi!' said Mamae's Sister for the second time, speaking across Aljce. 'What's your name? Oh, what's happening to your hair, Aljce? I can see right through it. It's so thin. Oh, my gosh.'

'She's so up in her own cloud. What were we talking about?' said Strauss to Aljce as she dropped behind to move away from Mamae's sister and the man, taking Aljce with her.

'Can't remember,' said Aljce, annoyed.

'Well damn it,' Strauss frowned. 'I was interested myself. Oh, ultimate fantasy man?'

'One that would put Mamae's flirty Sister in her place. Can't bear to see a man talking to anyone else without cutting in to tell him about herself. And at that point, we bow out because it's beneath us to compete.'

'Did we want to compete?' said Strauss, lighting a cigarette.

'No,' said Aljce, 'not specially. He's just some sleazy married man. How can you smoke that shit?'

'It calms me down,' said Strauss. 'I'm easily addicted to anything, you know.'

'Yes, you're a drug slut,' agreed Aljce. 'You have no taste. You just don't care as long as it buzzes.'

'And you're a drug snob,' said Strauss. 'Not interested if it's not weed.'

'You gotta admit,' said Aljce, 'that it's your favourite too.'

'Yeah,' said Strauss, 'but variety is the spice of life.'

'Doncha love that deep purple vibe that weed's got though? Totally laid back and cruisy. A slow hazy drift. And everything is so delightful.'

'Mmm,' said Strauss, 'but add a sort of metallic, buzzy vibe from the cigarette.'

'No, too nauseating,' said Aljce. 'That would do my head in. Fuck we talk shit. Are we talking shit Strauss? I feel like I know what I'm saying.'

'Yeah, it seems to work,' said Strauss.

'Anyways, what do you think?' Aljce said, gesturing to Mamae's Sister. 'She thinks she's prettier than us. Always got to be the centre of attention. She just thinks she's pretty cos she's so photogenic. How to tell her that she's not as pretty as her photos without being a bad friend and earning shitloads of bad karma?'

'I don't think there is a way, Aljce,' said Strauss thoughtfully. 'Because as soon as we do that, we're worse people than her.'

'Yeah, but I hate vain-ness. My whole values system is based on being humble.'

'But you also don't want your values based on mean-ness do you?'

'True, but when she keeps going on about how everyone says how young she looks, and you know it's just because she's got pimples at our age?'

'Shit Aljce. Fuck loads of bad karma.'

'Fuck off, you know you think the same.'

'I'm not gon' let it into my head.'

'I'd like to get it out of mine.'

'Sshh, Mamae's catching up to us,' said Strauss.

ALJCE'S MAD NEIGHBOUR came over to her house to help her with digging a hole for her tree. They had a joint. 'Do you know what an epileptic shock is?' he asked her.

'Like an epileptic fit?' she asked.

'No, a full on shock. Ninety nine out of a hundred people don't survive it. I'm number one hundred. Last week.' She wondered, as she had many times before, where the edge between facts he knew and stuff he made up was. 'I had to go to the hospital and when the doctors figured it out, they said to me, 'you must be so fit.' And I think I am. I mean, I'm outside a lot, and I don't smoke.' Aljce cleared her throat.

'You're smoking now.'

'Oh, that,' he said dismissively. 'That's different. One's a resin. The other one's a tar. Resin gets coughed up. Tar goes straight down.' That sounded reasonable to Aljce, but for all she knew, it could be a complete fiction. Her Mad Neighbour went back to his story. 'It's an electric shock that passes all the way through the body.'

'Epilepsy's an electrical malfunction in the brain,' said Aljce. 'And you haven't been on that synthetic shit have you? That'll do it to you. That stuff's made out of horse tranquiliser and whatever shit they put in fly spray.'

'No, no,' he said. 'I don't do that. I've got standards.'

'Anyway,' he said, 'I've stopped drinking alcohol, and I feel, so …'

'… sober?' asked Aljce.

'Well, I suppose so, but mainly I feel really good, because I feel like my blood's been purified, because it's been heated when that shock went through me. I feel like a new man.'

'What's that got to do with the alcohol?' she asked, deciding that they were now at the edge she'd been wondering about, and past it.

'I'm pure now,' he answered, 'so why would I go back to the pickling pit?' '

True. It's amazing how alcohol and cigarettes are legal when they're so damn bad for you and cause so much harm, and yet, cannabis, which is scientifically known to be safe and healthy and which causes no harm, is illegal. The world is mad.'

She wondered if she'd be attracted to him if he was handsome. Wasn't every man bearing some sort of double talk? And at least he was interesting in a mad way. Perhaps if he was handsome, she would have collected him. But because froth collected at the corners of his mouth, she couldn't even think about it. He was mad. But wasn't she also?

ALL WAYS ARE MY WAYS

'Here are your referrals,' said Chelsea.

'Referrals?' said Aljce. Perhaps she was going to be allowed to do some real work after all. Chelsea gave her some letters. But when Aljce looked at them, she realised that they weren't referrals at all. They were copies of letters from the Child Protection Agency. To people who had recent Police call outs for family violence, suggesting that they got in touch with Aljce and the Therapy Hub to avoid investigation by their service. 'What do I do?' said Aljce.

'Nothing,' said Chelsea. 'You wait for them to get in touch with us.'

'Nothing?' said Aljce. 'What's the point of that?'

'You can make up files,' said Chelsea.

'Chelsea,' said Aljce, suddenly thinking of something, 'can I talk to you about the system for my filing cabinet?'

'I thought Jillq and I went over that at your induction meetings,' said Chelsea. 'What's the problem?'

'The system you described is going to unbalance my drawer when I open it,' said Aljce. 'And those filing cabinets have a tendency to tip when both drawers are open at once. I know, because we had them at my last job too.'

'Why would that happen?' asked Chelsea. 'Everyone here uses the same system.' Aljce sighed, but only internally. She had seen Kat's filing cabinet tip that morning, bruising Kat's toe and causing her to shriek. And everyone else's was probably empty.

'It would probably be easiest for me to actually show you,' said Aljce. 'Come down to my office.' Chelsea sighed. Unlike Aljce's sigh, her sigh was external, like someone shaking out a sheet in order to air it.

'It would probably have been easiest if you had listened at the meeting,' she said.

They stood in front of the two drawer filing cabinet, which was finished in cold war gun metal grey. 'So,' said Chelsea, 'you put the first ten files,

001 to 010 into the first drop file, and the next ten, 011 to 020, into the next drop file and so on.'

'Well, that's what I thought you said,' said Aljce. 'But I'm wondering if it would be better to do it alphabetically, by client surnames, because it would spread the files across the drawer of the filing cabinet, instead of having them all squashed up at the front for the first year or so, and then having them all squashed up at the back later on when the earlier ones are closed. It just makes more sense.'

Chelsea stiffened. 'This is how Jillq wants us to do it,' she said, as if Aljce had personally set out to offend her.

'And that's fine,' said Aljce. 'I'll do it that way if I have to, but I'm just wondering if there could be an easier way.'

Chelsea turned on her heel and left the room without saying anything. Aljce shrugged to herself. Everyone here was touchy. It didn't matter what she did. She couldn't see how it would help to dwell on Chelsea stalking off. And in the absence of a firm direction from her to continue with the original system, Aljce decided to order her filing cabinet as she pleased, and spent a happy ten minutes making up files according to the client letters she'd been given. After that, of course, there was nothing to do.

So she opened up her computer and checked her work emails. There was another presumably group email from Jillq telling everyone that it was everyone's job to clean the toilets (although surely not Jillq's job! Aljce thought), and an email from Marj with a new time sheet attached (which differed from the old one in that each column was now about two millimetres wider than it had been before). Aljce opened her desk top to her 'personal statement' where she was supposed to be creating another profile of herself – her likes and dislikes, and what she did in her spare time. She fiddled around with a bolder heading and a bit of underlining, and then brought up her Facebook page, keeping one eye on the door in case she needed to minimise it suddenly. She didn't feel bad. If she'd had something to actually do, she wouldn't have been tempted.

She needed to see if Lewis had replied to her last message. Because she'd sent a photo. 'If you don't like me, fuck you,' she'd written underneath. Looking at the photo, she thought she looked sad, even though her lips were curved slightly upwards. Perhaps sadness has left such a deep stain on my soul that I'll never get it out, she thought. What would Lewis think? I have the heart of a shy little girl, she thought.

She need not have worried. 'Very nice,' he said, apparently approvingly. Aljce might have hoped for a more enthusiastic reaction, but at least it was positive.

'I've got a sore finger,' she typed, changing the subject. She didn't want to dwell on herself.

'So I've done quite a bit of writing today already,' he said.

'I cut it on a guillotine at work earlier this morning. Trying to mock up a brochure.'

'There's one character I can't quite get to function on her own.'

'It's a really deep cut.'

'What I want is for her to have a personality that comes naturally. I don't want her to be wooden.'

'It hurts when I type.'

'Oh.' He paused briefly. 'Bad.' She waited for more, but he continued to talk about his writing. 'I want her to arise naturally from the vectors I'm creating. I set the mathematical parameters, and she should exist naturally from that.' Aljce sighed. Clearly her finger was not of interest.

'So you believe that you're creating in the same way that reality is created from the mathematical DNA of the universe? But on a parallel fictional level?'

'Exactly.'

'Don't worry about my finger. I can still type, I guess.'

She looked at it. She'd wondered at the time if it needed stitches, because she'd been unable to stop it bleeding for ages. She'd had to keep it from Jillq, of course. She didn't want to be accused of being a health and safety risk. It didn't hurt now, except when she typed, although that probably wouldn't be noticed here at work, given that there was so little to do. Perhaps she should be grateful. They could have piled her with masses of work, and treated her like a slave. Perhaps it hadn't occurred to anyone to do so.

'I might write a novel,' she wrote to Lewis, seeing that they were talking about writing.

'Nothing about you suggests to me that you would be able to do that,' said Lewis. 'I mean, you might be able to, but I'd be surprised.'

'Why?' said Aljce.

'You just haven't given me that impression,' said Lewis. She would have been crestfallen, but she remembered her rapture in writing, and it elevated her self-belief in her own creativity.

'Oh well,' she said. 'Time will tell, I guess.' She wasn't disappointed by his reaction. She felt more as if she had something she could surprise him with later on.

'Should I ask what you are writing?' he said.

'You should not.'

'Why not?'

'I don't know. Only that it would be spoiled if I let it go too early. It belongs in me until it's finished, and then I won't need it anymore, and you can have it. Hopefully you'll love it.' Of course, she said to herself. Of course he reacted like that. Everyone wants to write a novel. And only a very few, talented people like Lewis, actually did, let alone getting it published.

'Perhaps I could give you some guidance. Have you thought any more about the co-writing?' he asked.

'Mmm,' she said. 'I'm not sure it's me.'

'Aljce,' can you come to a meeting please,' said Marj.

'I don't have a meeting in my diary?'

'We've just called it now,' said Marj. Clearly the diary system was not for everyone. 'I think I heard you saying that you found it upsetting that last time we had a meeting, you had to wait to find out what it was about. So this time, we will talk to you straight away.' Not good, not good, sang Aljce in her head.

'First of all,' said Jillq when Aljce got there, 'what you're wearing today is not appropriate.' Not good, not good, sang Aljce's brain, more loudly than before. The word first implied that there was a list.

'Why not?' she asked. She was having a cancan dancer day.

'Your top's a bit low,' said Marj.

'It's not very professional,' said Jillq. 'When you're out and about, you're representing us. We can't have you rubbing off the wrong way.' Aljce would have liked to have said that it seemed that they didn't like her out and about, but she bit her lip, because that would only have led to a ban on leaving the Hub. She was conscious that she needed to monitor everything she said, in case it was used against her.

'I don't think my top's too low,' she said instead.

'You wouldn't,' said Jillq. Aljce felt hurt. What she wore expressed her. Criticising that was like criticising her. She felt as if she was being called slutty. As if she was a little girl, and being told that she was unloveable because of who she was. She didn't want to say anything in case she cried. Lower cut tops suited her better, it was as simple as that.

'We need to be mindful of what we wear,' said Jillq.

'Jillq looks lovely,' said Mrs. Kingi. 'It's a pity that you don't want to wear one of these nice Therapy Hub jackets, Aljce.' Aljce looked at the poorly cut black jackets with the logo on the breast pocket in badly matching colours. Mrs. Kingi had one on, as did Jillq.

'I don't like uniforms,' said Aljce.

'At least when you leave the Hub,' said Marj. 'We hang our jackets up behind the door where you come in. Please wear one of those next time.'

'You want me to wear one of your jackets?' said Aljce.

'What's wrong with that?' asked Jillq.

'Nothing,' said Aljce. She knew that pointing out that they were all several sizes bigger than her would not go down well. She would probably receive a written warning for disrespecting her colleagues.

'Secondly,' said Jillq, looking at Chelsea. 'You have disrespected Chelsea. Explain to Aljce please.'

'When I was showing you how to put the files in the filing cabinet, you were very disobliging,' said Chelsea. 'And that's what we mean when we say you are constantly refusing to do what we ask.'

'I was not disobliging!' said Aljce, indignantly. 'I was just discussing options with you.'

'You said you would do it our way if you HAD to,' said Chelsea, with special emphasis on the word had. 'But you wanted to do it your way. As if you thought you knew better than Jillq.'

'And that's what we call arrogance, Bun,' said Jillq.

'You're putting tone into my voice that I didn't use,' said Aljce. 'You made me sound sarcastic, and I didn't say it that way at all. And I just thought there might be a better way.'

'All ways here are my ways,' said Jillq. 'I don't know what they let you get away with at your last job, but we won't tolerate this sort of behaviour here at the Hub.' Aljce felt as if she was in a tidal undertow. A potential ally had just been lost. She had thought that perhaps

Chelsea... because she was fun... but that obviously wasn't the way things were going to go.

'I'm sorry if you thought that I was being disobliging, Chelsea,' said Aljce carefully. It didn't pay to burn bridges.

'I told you that Chelsea would show you our filing procedure,' said Jillq. 'I was very clear about that. What she told you was what you needed to do.'

'Sorry,' said Aljce, 'I was just trying to see if there was an easier way.'

'I hope that you didn't think that because Chelsea isn't the Hub Manager, that you didn't have to listen to her.'

'That's not my way at all. I think the role of Receptionist is one of the most important roles in any organisation.'

'Excuse me? Receptionist?'

'Administrator, sorry.'

'Chelsea is our Clinical Administrator.' Aljce tried to remember what Jillq had called Chelsea when she, Aljce, had first arrived. Administrative Greeter?

'Is that what the role has always been called?'

'We had a meeting on Wednesday and decided that was the most appropriate title, given that Chelsea needs to fill in the intake forms when clients first present.'

Meeting?, thought Aljce. 'Sure,' said Aljce.

'I won't have you belittling other people's roles, Aljce.'

'There was no belittling intended.'

'Clearly there was.'

'I'm afraid we're going to have to agree to disagree,' said Aljce, close to tears. 'I'm very sorry Chelsea. I appreciate you and your role.'

'That's okay,' said Chelsea. 'Just as long as you follow Hub procedures.'

'I'm afraid you're going to have to think about yourself very carefully, Aljce,' said Jillq. 'We will meet again next week, to see how you are going with that.'

'Who will meet?'

'You, Marj and I.'

'And what will we meet about?'

'About what you have reflected on. We will talk about whether you have learned anything about yourself.' Holy fuck, thought Aljce. What on earth would she say? What on earth could she say?

'I'm not sure that it's me at fault,' said Aljce. She looked imploringly at Hattie, who had been very quiet.

'What do you think Hattie?'

'Oh,' said Hattie, squirming a bit. 'I think it's always good to self-reflect. Very good for self-improvement.' Aljce could not believe it.

'See, Aljce,' said Jillq. 'We are all in agreement.'

AFTERWARDS, ALJCE SAID to Hattie, 'I thought you told me that you understood the problems around working here?'

'Oh,' said Hattie again. 'I was probably just having a bad day. Just do what everyone says, Aljce, and you will find people very supportive. I've found Jillq very supportive of me.' And what does that look like? thought Aljce. There was no one here that she could trust.

Was Hattie just a narcissist as well, happy to moan and plot against Jillq, but also happy to turn coat with the right threats or inducements? But then again, perhaps she was bait. To lure Aljce to speak against Jillq, so Jillq would know what Aljce thought. She had been so charming and sympathetic to Aljce, and then she'd turned the other way, showing no emotion towards Aljce at all. She could not be trusted. It was very confusing for Aljce, who desperately wanted to be able to find an ally, if not a friend, and who kept trying to see that in those around her.

Narcissists all around me, she thought. What is that telling me, if I'm creating my own reality? That I don't love myself? But perhaps the universe is trying to teach me something. The lesson I'm learning is: let go of the ego of needing to be appreciated and valued. Make approval something that comes from within, not without. Jillq's never going to be happy with what I do, no matter what I do. So I can give up and take on her opinion of me, or I can define myself.

She'd read about a man who wrote about language defining everything. It was certainly true that the language used by people about themselves and about others defined their worlds. She had seized on that when she'd looked into narrative counselling. The narrative was the thing. There was a difference between believing you were an angry person, and believing that you were a person affected by anger. If you were the latter, you could explore why, and look for strategies against it. If you were just angry, all you could do was suffer that energy. Life was the stories you told yourself.

And it was as if everyone at work was so busy altering and modifying themselves to fit in that they were no longer capable of any moral compass, because they were so orientated to fit in with the thoughts and opinions of the majority. Belonging was what was important to them; not values and courage. They couldn't see outside what they were being told. They had accepted the eyes and the filters of those around them, and couldn't evaluate the world independently of that. Just like in Nazi Germany and in Trump's version of America.

SHE WANTED TO talk about it. What good was. What evil was. Whether it could be manipulated. 'So where do you sit on the scale of goodness, Lewis?' she asked. 'Because I try so hard to be good. Good in my heart and in my words and in my actions. To me, goodness is a golden light that I aim for. A pureness. Even though I allow the dark as well. I understand that that is why goodness burns so brightly, because darkness exists. I hate violence, cruelty, meanness, wanton destruction and hopeless addiction. But it fascinates me too, because it has its own beauty. Darkness is attractive. A yin to the yang of goodness. I think I'm confused…'

'Answer to your question. Good I think. Darkness scares me. I wouldn't want to go there. I would be afraid of getting hurt. Which would make me anxious… And I resist anything that might cause me anxiety.'

'Gosh.' She thought about how the act of loving someone had the potential to cause anxiety because something you could never control was another person's choices, and that meant that everything was a risk. 'All you need is love, they say. And if love is the ultimate representation of good, can you get there if you can't make yourself vulnerable?'

'I've never thought about it like that,' he answered. 'I'm not sure that I know what good is anyway. I sneak around my garden with a jug of boiling water, pouring it down into the burrows of crickets. I can't get to sleep at all on summer nights with their rrurp, rrurp, rrurp.'

'Wow. I think that's darkness. Now you're getting interesting.'

'I think of it more as neutrality.' He sounded bored.

'Gosh. I love the sound of crickets. It's like summer music. I don't know how you can kill them. Definitely on the dark side.'

'It's not my favourite part of myself.'

'Anyway, you're in luck to be hanging with ME,' she said jokingly, intending to discuss her ideas from earlier that day about people who could change from one moment to the next. 'At least I'm aiming for goodness. There are a lot of people who aren't.'

'I think you'll find it's the other way around, and if you don't know that, you really should gtfo,' he replied.

'Oh,' she said, but not to him. Perhaps it would have come off differently if he'd said it out loud to her. People said that it was easy to misinterpret texts and posts because the emotion that they would have been said with was missing. Perhaps he'd intended a jokey tone. Or perhaps he'd missed the jokey tone in hers. Misinterpreted her. She re-read her words. She could see how that could have happened. Things suddenly seemed to be getting hard. It was like living on the jagged edge of a knife. If she moved her words the wrong way, or moved them too suddenly, it would rip her; tear her. Maybe getting hurt was a precondition of love.

'So are we still in love?' she asked anxiously.

'I could only speak for myself.'

'Well, speak for yourself.'

'Haha, clever.' He sent her a wink emoticon. She waited, but that was all that came.

'What, not gonna declare?' she asked, bold in the moment.

'Do the daisy... He loves me... He loves me not.' Her heart went down. She could see the almond shaped white petals falling from their yellow Hub, and they were sad. 'He loves me, he loves me not,' he typed again, ambiguously.

'He loves me, he loves me not,' she typed back. 'He loves me.' She paused. 'Can I just rest there please?' she said.

'Yes, rest there.' That was something, she thought. It wasn't a 'no.' If things had been more certain at that moment, she would have typed, 'Shhh, while I read your subtext.' But she was too busy carefully reading it. Perhaps she was expecting too much. He couldn't be constantly expected to declare his love for her, and disagreements happened between lovers all the time. It was best not to expect anything from anything, but to flow instead, and appreciate what came.

'Fuck's sake, I'm lucky to be loved by you,' she said, emphasising her feelings. 'I'm sorry if I didn't convey that.'

'Do you only say fuck when you're stoned?' he asked.

'I do it when I'm really comfortable with someone' she explained, hoping they were back to their previous level of intimacy. 'Occasionally

I do it when I've just met someone, and I feel a good connection. Not consciously though, you know. It just happens. I've got to watch myself at work. Not that I'm not feeling a connection with anyone there, so I'll probably be fine,' she hinted. Perhaps it WAS something she wanted to share.

'I'd better turn in now,' he said. Aljce stared numbly at her screen. They'd only just started talking for the night. And they always connected for hours.

Had he met another woman? Did he just not care enough to want to spend time with her? And what did either of these possibilities say about her level of commitment in relation to his, and should she be worried about that? Perhaps he really was just tired. Was she making excuses?

SHE FLASHED BACK to something Strauss had said to her. 'You only do serious. You care too much, too soon, before they've had to prove themselves. Plus you don't show them that you value yourself, cos you're so keen to do and be anything they want. You treat yourself like shit, so they think they can too.'

'Hey, hey, hey. I'm just being a nice person. I'm not treating myself bad, they are.'

'So how come you let them? Isn't that treating yourself like shit?'

'Wa-ah. I haven't thought of it like that. I've only thought of it, like me being a good person.'

'Yeah, but not to you.'

'And then there's the Exam of Me,' Strauss had continued. 'And fuck Jimsy if he gets it wrong. Like, which tit is the biggest: left or right? And which side is the big freckle on my inner elbow, close to my waist? Do I even have one?'

'Aah. Tricky questions.'

'He should know them.'

'I suppose. I actually found a freckle on my inner arm the other day that even I didn't know that I had. And I only found it because I saw it in the side mirror of the car when I was waiting for Liddell to come out of the shop, and she took ages.'

'Still, fuck him if he gets it wrong. I might give it to him tonight. See if he's been paying attention.'

'Sounds like a fun night for him.'

94

Strauss had been doing her best air guitar. 'Do you do this in front of Jimsy?' said Aljce, suddenly curious. Strauss air guitared in a circle around Aljce.

'If he doesn't like me as I am, he can fuck off. I'm not going to let him make me normal by manipulating me with his disapproval. I love my energy too much to let anyone fuck it up with any negativity.' Aljce wished that she could be more like Strauss. She had a bad habit of letting men shape her to their idea of who she should be. And then when they got her there, the thing they'd fallen in love with in the first place was no longer there. Some miserable-walk-on-eggshells-down-the-thin-line-of-their-expectations thing was there instead. It would be better to be more like Strauss. She tried to commit it to memory. 'I love my energy too much to let anyone fuck it up with any negativity.' And she made a mental note to rehearse it frequently. She believed that too, but she'd never thought to consider it first, above other things.

'If Jimsy said something mean about me,' said Strauss, 'I'd tell him that if he ever said anything mean about me again, it would be over. And then I'd invite him to say it again straight away. Cos if he was going to, I wouldn't want him. I wouldn't want to be in that sort of dynamic. It would be bad for me.'

'Holy,' said Aljce. 'I've never thought of it that way.'

'Yeah, well you're so nice, and look where it's got you. So nice so that they'll stay with you for ages, and all they end up giving you is a very unhealthy dynamic. Better without. Let them go. Tell them to fuck off. They'll stay, they'll just be nicer.'

'Thank you Strauss, thank you for that advice.' Privately, she was miffed she had been so transparent; so that Strauss could see right through her like a window. The draft had been cold. Because Strauss was describing an unhealthy desperation. That she didn't value herself, so neither did her men. Had they chosen her because of that? Because they wanted someone that they could treat badly?

But then she was curious too. Probably more curious than miffed. What the fuck? she thought. 'I guess they're just what I'm used to.'

'Well, Aljce,' said Strauss, pulling her air guitar up to her ear and shutting her eyes, 'if a man can hurt you and instead of being angry, you say to your friend, "I'm used to it," that's really fucking sad.'

'You should have told me this ages ago.'

95

'Firstly, I couldn't, because you never talk about men. And what would have been the point? You're really fucking determined to let men fuck you over because it's always some big love story. So nice… always giving them chances that you've rubbed against your halo. Fuck the love story. If he can't treat you right, you don't need the love story, because your energy is gonna be fucked. Better to be single, Aljce. Not caught up in that sugary shit.'

'Mmm,' said Aljce. 'But I like being in love.'

'That is a problem then. Watch out for defective men.'

'Well, Strauss, remind me why we're friends? Is it cos you swear a lot too?'

'No doubt about it. It shows I'm comfortable with you.'

'Yeah exactly.'

What Strauss didn't know was that she didn't know everything. And not anything about Lewis. Why don't I ever tell anyone anything to do with my heart? she wondered. Why do I always keep everything inside, and never let anyone know what's happening with me? Other people talk these things through with their friends, and that might well help, but oh, no, not me. Perhaps it's because I'm expecting to be left, and I don't want that humiliation to be public. I don't talk about the start, because I don't want to admit to yet another end. Wouldn't it be so nice to meet a man who called me darling, and beautiful; not so much because I'm beautiful, but because he wanted me to feel that way?

Now that Lewis had signed off, Aljce was left alone with her thoughts about her day at work. She'd told Strauss earlier how every now and then she thought that some particular person at work might be good to confide in. But every time she'd tried that, she'd found herself learning the hard way that they were loyal to Jillq. Chelsea. Hattie. MaryAnn. Well, perhaps not MaryAnn. The closest she'd come to success was with MaryAnn, but MaryAnn didn't want the personal hassle of getting involved. She just wanted to do her job and go home.

'I guess she doesn't want to speak up for someone she's just met, particularly since if she does, things might get nasty for her too, and surely she's seen what that looks like with me,' she'd said to Strauss.

'What did she actually say?' asked Strauss. 'Said she just wants to be head down, bum up. I couldn't be like that, you know. If I saw someone else being treated like me, I'd stand up for them.'

'Well she's got no courage, ay?' said Strauss. 'Don't let it piss you off.'

'At least she's one of the few that doesn't actively participate in the meetings where they go round in a circle and tell me one at a time why they don't like me.'

'No!' said Strauss. 'Do they really?'

'Yes,' said Aljce. 'But don't go there. I don't even know if I can talk about it without crying today. I should be good tomorrow.'

THE NEXT MORNING, she looked at herself in the mirror, to see if she had her outfit right. Sometimes things that looked great together laid out on the bed were not so harmonious when they were all worn together. Sometimes there was one thing too many, or the shape was wrong, or she had just plain misjudged. Her outfit was okay, but her hair seemed fine and lifeless, like Mamae's Sister had said. The light was coming right through it, as if it wasn't there. It must be the glare of the mirror, she decided. When she thought about it, even the colours of her words were getting more and more dim the longer she worked there. Submerged in unhappiness, beneath a veil of translucent blue underwaterness. They were wet and soggy and sad. Her colours were drowning.

WHEN MARJ POPPED across the corridor that morning to give Aljce the latest on her daughter's struggle with her neighbours, who had left their rubbish bags in the middle of the entrance to their shared driveway, meaning Marj's daughter had had to get out of the car to shift them, Aljce couldn't believe her eyes. Marj was wearing a lower cut t-shirt than the one Aljce had worn yesterday, and it easily showed off her ample cleavage. The criticism about Aljce's clothing had clearly been something that she'd taken on board from someone else. Typical Jillq, planting things with other people, so that she seemed less of a bully herself.

LATER THAT SAME MORNING, Aljce accidentally came across Jillq. 'You're wearing that to work?' she said, pointing at Aljce's black motorbike jacket, the smooth leather offset by old fashioned MC patches and a black tutu skirt underneath, which hung straight down rather than jutting out. Had Aljce gone too far? Maybe Jillq hates creativity because she can't control it, Aljce thought. For some people, anything that they can't control is scary.

'Is there a problem?' said Aljce? 'You asked me to wear something less revealing of my chest.'

'We will have to review the rules,' said Jillq. Aljce could see her trying to formulate new rules as she spoke.

'Where are the rules?' asked Aljce. 'I would like to check them too.' She could see Jillq thinking hard now. There were of course no rules in written form, but Jillq would pretend that there were, and attempt to distract Aljce for long enough that she could write them up and insist that they had already existed prior to Aljce's question.

'They might be in the back office. Ask Marj to have a look. And I will look in my cupboards.'

'I'll help you look,' said Aljce.

'Marj needs to look first,' Jillq said quickly. 'You can't expect me to look before Marj looks. I might just be needlessly looking for nothing.'

'Exactly,' said Aljce. Jillq looked at her suspiciously.

ALJCE DREW HER breath in as she walked into the lunch room later that day. She was seeing double. Two Dulcies were sitting side by side at the table. She hoped it wasn't some sort of flash back. She did not need that to happen at work. One Dulcie stood up and the other stayed sitting down. So she wasn't having double vision, at least. Mrs. Kingi stopped as she came through the door past Aljce. She was in her nice friendly mood. 'Two peas in a pod,' she said. That was good. Aljce wasn't the only one who saw two. 'I always wanted twins,' Mrs. Kingi said. 'But of course, I'm not like Jillq.'

'Anyone can have twins,' said Aljce, her mind busy processing the incident from last week. Of course it hadn't been Dulcie. It would have been the other one. But Dulcie would have known what Aljce's mistake would have been. So she really had been telling the truth, while at the same time purposefully allowing Aljce to be under a misapprehension. Kidding herself that she was the innocent one, and feeling all offended. While she manipulated the situation. It was hard to believe that the Dulcie with the little tinkling laugh was such a bitch. But perhaps Dulcie saw it differently. Perhaps she thought that since she didn't plan it, she'd done nothing wrong. She was the victim of Aljce's mistake.

'Actually, Jillq said it takes special genes,' said Mrs. Kingi.

Neither of the Dulcies said hi to Aljce. 'The secret is in the sauce,' added Mrs. Kingi added randomly.

'What's that about a secret sauce?' asked Chelsea, and Mrs. Kingi began talking about a cooking programme. Chelsea's thick black framed glasses reminded Aljce of the old Wonder Woman TV programme that her mother had used to watch on afternoon repeats. The difference was that Wonder Woman was dark, and Chelsea was fair. The glasses intensified Chelsea's perfectly blushed strawberries and cream complexion and her sparse soft blond hairs, so fine that they were almost invisible on her jaw line, unless you were up close. Aljce had never understood how no one on TV had ever realised who Wonder Woman was once she removed her glasses, given that she still looked exactly the same, apart from her Wonder Woman costume. Aljce would have recognised her.

ALJCE SAW HANNAH down town again, on a Saturday. 'How's it going?' said Hannah. 'I've been worrying about you, up there. You didn't look happy last time I saw you.' All the horrors of her recent work place experience began to come tumbling out of Aljce's mouth. Hannah's own mouth got tight.

'They don't like what I wear,' said Aljce, 'but it's the same as what I used to wear to work when I was working for you.'

'Of course they don't like it,' said Hannah. 'Can't have any whiff of people thinking for themselves. Can't have people failing to conform.'

'Do you think it looks unprofessional?' asked Aljce. 'They said my top was cut too low.'

'Pff,' said Hannah. 'Describe.' Aljce described. 'Bullshit,' said Hannah. 'Sounds like the sort of thing you wear all the time. I love what you wear. It's so original... so you. Keep being yourself. Don't let the micromanagers extinguish your sense of self.'

'Hard, when they are so determined to kill it off,' said Aljce. 'Perhaps I'd be okay if I didn't have a personality. Perhaps they would "like me better", as they put it.'

WORK CONTINUED DESPITE Hannah's words of encouragement. 'Where have you been?' asked Jillq, materialising from a side room. Aljce jumped. She wasn't wearing the Therapy Hub jacket, but Jillq didn't seem to notice.

'To the Families and Communities Support meeting,' said Aljce.

'Was it in your diary Aljce?'

'Yes, and in my Outlook Calendar too.'

'What about the schedule book at the desk?'

'Yes, it was.'

'Is it on the weekly wall planner diary on the wall in the hallway?'

'What weekly hall planner?'

'Wall planner. The one on the wall.'

'I didn't know there was one,' lied Aljce. She specifically hadn't filled it out in case someone tried to stop her from going anywhere. Marj had probably forgotten that she'd told her about it.

'It is your responsibility to know about our procedures and follow them.'

'How can I know about them if no one tells me about them?'

'This is what I mean about you, Aljce.'

'So I have to record where I'm going to be in four different places? Isn't that a bit pointless?'

'The point is that we need to know where you are.' Jillq paused. 'Until you can be trusted.' Aljce sighed. She knew that would be never. And perhaps she didn't deserve to be. She had just lied about not knowing about the wall planner. Perhaps she was no better than they said she was.

'I hope you took notes.'

'Of course,' said Aljce, lying once again. 'I have them somewhere.' She hoped that she was not going to have to spend the next hour or two making up notes from her recall.

'Please put them on my desk,' said Jillq. She was going to have to, damn it.

'Soon as I find them,' she said, buying herself time. If Jillq could do that when it suited her, then so could she. And it wasn't like there was anything else to do. 'I'm very busy,' she added for good measure, knowing that she shouldn't press their buttons, because it would do her no good, but doing it anyway.

'I'm rushed off my feet too,' said Marj, walking past with Dulcie. Or the other one. 'I've been crawling under the building trying to get all these computers up to speed. I did ten hours on Saturday!'

'Well, I've been working very late at home,' said Jillq. 'I've been burning the midnight oil for months, haven't I Dulcie?' Dulcie laughed her tinkling laugh. Aljce was reminded of a nursery rhyme.

'I'm exhausted,' said Marj.

'I think you'll find that everyone is doing their bit, Marj,' said Jillq stiffly. 'It's not just you.'

'Um, I was just wondering if I could organise my external supervision for next week?' Aljce asked, knowing that there would never be a good time to ask, and thinking that while Jillq and Marj were slightly at odds might be as good a time as any.

'Aljce, you haven't even had internal line-management supervision yet.' Aljce knew what the answer would be, but she had to ask anyway. Perhaps she was wrong.

'Who would I have that with?'

'I am the Manager, Aljce. Why have you not booked line-management with me?'

'I didn't know I had to,' said Aljce.

'That's very thoughtless of someone who wants to be a counsellor,' said Jillq. Aljce's mind scrambled. She had to avoid being told what to do by someone who had no clue, and whose main agenda was to sabotage her. 'It's very unprofessional of you not to arrange it,' said Jillq.

'You didn't ask me about it,' said Aljce.

'It is your responsibility Aljce. Do you have your diary with you?'

'Ahh, no,' lied Aljce, knowing it was about fifteen seconds from her grasp if she chose to go and get it. She felt as if lying was coming more easily to her with each moment. 'I'm not sure where it is.'

'Bring it to me when you find it,' announced Jillq, before wheeling around on the ball of her front foot and stalking off down the corridor, kicking stray golf balls away from her feet to both the left and the right.

Aljce hoped she could mislay her diary until Jillq forgot to book the line-management. Surely she couldn't want it any more than Aljce did; surely she was afraid that if they engaged that they would both see a big hole where Jillq's competency and knowledge should have been. If only Jillq knew how generous Aljce naturally was, allowing others to cover their deficiencies, and helping them to gloss over them. Noticing and magnifying their strengths instead. Because that was what was kind. She never wanted other people to feel bad because of her. If Jillq hadn't chosen to attack her, Aljce would have been kind to her; making her feel good about what she already knew and sharing things that could have added to that.

The unfortunate thing was that now she couldn't bring up external supervision again, in case Jillq remembered that Aljce should be booking line-management. She was having line-management over her dead body. One thing Aljce hated was to be micro-managed. It felt like a type of bullying. Micro-managers always wanted you to do every little thing their way. There was no space for individuality or creativity. And nothing ever got any better than the level that the micro-manager was at. There was no rising above. And definitely no positive feedback or appreciation for doing so.

Well, she thought, Jillq didn't say she couldn't have external supervision. Luckily she was still booked in with the supervisor that she'd utilised at her previous job, but unfortunately, the time was during work time. And she'd found that she couldn't change it to an after school time, which would also have been an after work time. She felt that she desperately needed supervision; it would be a place to talk through and process what was happening to her in her new job. She'd have to go ahead with it anyway. She could maybe use her lunch break to cover part of it, and pretend to be somewhere work related for the other half hour.

'Do THEY SAY you can't leave the building?' Strauss had asked.

'No, they just make out that I've done it in some sort of sinful way. But surely attending social service meetings is part of my role. And supervision is essential to counselling. And, I mean, it's a student requirement as well. And she ticked it off with my Placement Agreement.'

'Perhaps you should just stay up there and not go out.'

'Nah, fuck her. It's such a big relief to get out amongst normal people, even if it's just for an hour. It's like I can breathe. And it hardly ever happens. It's what she wants, to stop me from going. I'm not going to let her control me.'

'Maybe it would be easier though. Just do what she wants. She's the boss.'

'I know. But I tried that. Even when I do exactly what she wants, she just makes sure that I get it wrong. And do you know what fucking happened? I was in the car,' continued Aljce, 'driving, and my handbag was over on the floor by the passenger seat, and I was taking this woman, Hattie, home from work home to her house, 'cos her car was at the garage. And my phone got a message, in my open handbag, and she grabbed it and said, "you drive. I'll read it out and answer it for you. I can't stand people texting while they drive." And I tried to say something, but she was already, like, reading my message. Out loud. Cos it was up on my lock screen. And it was Mamae, saying "do you wanna come over for a puff tonight?" And my work lady is just staring at it. And she says, "what does that mean?" And I say, "it's a sort of profiterole thing that my friend makes. With that chocolate sauce icing. A puff. They're very nice. And I don't need to answer right now, thanks. I'm not sure if I can go or not. Depends on the babysitting situation." And she puts it back in my bag, and she has no idea that I'm freaking out. Or maybe I just have no idea that she does, and secretly she's noting my secret. For further use. Maybe she's just storing it up for when we disagree about something.'

'Wouldn't she forget it after a while, if she didn't think about it because nothing else matched that evidence, so she came to think that it must be a false memory, and let it go?'

'Not at this place. They are just looking for evil to spread. No little nuance goes unused. Everything can be turned into something. Jillq's trying to infect me with her own self-hatred. I don't even want tonight to end. Because then it will be tomorrow, and I'll have to go to work.'

'Geez Aljce, you must hate the place.'

'I do. I'm so tired that I just want to fall into a bowlful of dreams, but tomorrow is where that will unfortunately lead.'

TOMORROW DID ARRIVE, and with it another day of marking time at the Therapy Hub with nothing to do. She went into the lunch room to get herself a glass of water. The new Dulcie and the old Dulcie were both in there, laughing their beautiful, tinkling laughs, and the sound was like happiness falling over itself. It was hard for Aljce to understand how such a pretty sound could come from such mean people. I don't suppose beauty is the prerogative of kindness, she thought to herself. It would have been nice to have someone to share her thought with, but she had to keep it to herself, and sent a mental note to Strauss instead. The old Dulcie looked up and saw Aljce. Purple hiki bruises circled her throat like a necklet of raw roses. She said something under her breath to Deidra, because that was the new Dulcie's name, and the two of them laughed again and then stopped abruptly and looked down at the surface of the staff lunch table. 'Hi,' said Aljce.

'Hi Aljce,' said Deidra looking up with the amusement still dancing in her eyes.

Aljce went back to her office, and was surprised to find that there was a girl under her desk, cowering. 'What are you doing under there?' said Aljce softly. Perhaps it was a client child who didn't want to do counselling, or even the child of an adult client who had lost her way in the rabbit warren of corridors. 'You can come out, you're not in trouble.' The little girl quivered, and tears welled up in her eyes. 'Would you like to do a drawing?' The girl said nothing, but she inched her way up. 'What's your name?' said Aljce, in the same voice that she used to calm distressed animals.

'Pepper,' said the little girl. Aljce gave her a red pen and some paper to draw with, and the little girl began to edge closer and closer.

'How old are you?' said Aljce.

'Six,' said the girl.

'I've got girls around the same age as you,' said Aljce. She carried on with her work. The girl seemed happy to sit quietly, and someone would come looking for her soon. Aljce quite liked having her there.

'Pepper!' said Jillq in a sharp voice. 'We have been looking everywhere! Get away from Aljce's desk!' Aljce felt protective. She could feel the girl shrinking like a sea anemone.

'She's been very well behaved,' she said. 'She's been fine.'

'We're leaving now,' said Jillq stiffly. Aljce looked again at the girl. She did have the same blue eyes as Jillq, although her hair was more brown than red. Subdued, like the rest of her. Deidra and Dulcie joined them. It was clearly a family outing. Aljce took note. Anything that took Jillq away from the Therapy Hub was a happy occasion.

'Pepper! I don't want to have to tell you more than once!' Pepper scuttled away from Aljce's desk, and came to rest in Jillq's shadow. Sometimes Aljce saw shadows out of the corner of her eyes. Unattached, or attached to the wrong thing. Giraffe, unicorn. She often fancied that Jillq had the shadow of a small pig attached to her skirt. And now it was a pool of piglet with Pepper in it.

'We need to thank Aljce for looking after you, Pepper.'

'Thank you,' said a little voice.

'Of course, Aljce had work to be getting on with, but that's neither here nor there.'

'She was so good that she didn't interrupt at all,' said Aljce. It was one thing to be wary of Jillq, but to leave a child to her displeasure was something else entirely, and Aljce couldn't do it, no matter what the consequences. Jillq contented herself with a look, and swept Pepper out of the room in the same motion as her own leaving, with Deidra and Dulcie trailing in her wake.

'Why didn't you say that Pepper was with you?' said Chelsea.

'I thought someone would come looking for her,' said Aljce. 'I wasn't sure who she was.'

'Well, Jillq's daughter, duh!' said Chelsea.

'I thought it would be better for her to just wait quietly. She seemed a bit scared.'

'There's no reason for her to be scared,' said Chelsea. 'You should have let us know.'

'I couldn't hear any commotion of anyone looking for anyone, or I would have been out straight away. How did she get here? I don't remember her being here this morning.'

'Her father Jack dropped her off,' said Chelsea. 'He had to work.'

'Jillq doesn't seem very pleased.'

'Why would she be? She has to work too.'

'I thought she was going out?'

'She can't be expected to work all day!' Aljce remembered Pepper's scared eyes.

'Poor little Pepper,' she said.

'She's so lucky to have a mother like Jillq,' said Chelsea.

'What's that?' said Mrs. Kingi walking past.

'Pepper. Lucky to be Jillq's daughter.'

'Yes, she's a very lucky little girl,' said Mrs. Kingi. 'To have a mother like Jillq.'

'YOU SHOULD LEAVE,' said Mamae, when Aljce was telling her about her troubles and how sorry she was for Pepper.

'I can't. How'm I gonna pay the mortgage if I do that? I'm not giving up my house for her. That's for Pleasance and Liddell.'

'Maybe if you stopped talking about their shit, and you stopped paying it any attention, it would stop affecting you like this,' said Strauss. Aljce knew that was true, but their impact was so powerful. There was this knot inside her body, filled with queasy feelings. And when she focused on that knot, she knew that it was work that was feeding it. 'You always like to say that you create your own reality,' said Strauss.

'Ha,' said Aljce. Mamae drifted off.

'Maybe deciding to write it into a book was a bad idea,' said Strauss. Aljce had told Strauss that she was ticking cult novel off to do list.

'It's therapy,' said Aljce, who'd spent two and a half hours on it the previous night, consumed with writing as if it was burning up all her oxygen and she had to write more to get more. 'And you know I believe in therapy Strauss.'

'I have a therapist,' said Strauss, 'and her name is Music.'

'What do you need therapy about?' said Aljce.

'Ahh, there you go, you little counsellor,' said Strauss. 'Nothing much, just sick of Jimsy and wondering if he's actually adding to my life.'

'Go on, you've been together forever,' said Aljce.

'Do you know what he said to me yesterday? I was talking about something, and he said 'why don't you shut the fuck up?' And I was too hurt to even think of something to say back to him.'

'And you're usually so good at that,' agreed Aljce, remembering how sure of herself and her relationship Strauss had been only a few days ago. Clearly even people with strong relationships had their moments. 'That was hurtful,' she said sympathetically.

'It just came out of nowhere,' said Strauss. 'And when I think about it, we haven't been that great lately. And not just lately. For a while. I don't even know when it started. It's like I irritate him, and he just can't be fucked with me. And I don't like the way it's making me feel about myself.'

'So half of you is hating on Jimsy for being an arsehole, but the other half is feeling like shit?'

'Pretty much,' said Strauss. 'I hope you aren't charging for this.'

'I'm actually not counselling you,' said Aljce. 'Just being a friend.'

'Sounds like counselling,' Strauss said. 'But it's cool. I need counselling.'

'So do I,' said Aljce.

Then she realised she was about to turn the conversation around to Jillq and work, and make it all about herself again, and Strauss had listened to a lot of that, so she wouldn't be a very good counsellor if she couldn't even make time for listening skills in her own personal life. But why should she? If she wasn't a listener, should she be someone she wasn't? And if she wasn't naturally a good listener, could she ever be a good counsellor? Could she be different in her work place skills, and still be her true self? Could she ever talk to her friends again, and not be counselling them? If you wanted to help, you put your best self for that purpose forward, right? She definitely needed therapy herself. 'So do I,' she said again. 'And my services are free. You get a freebie for being my chickee babe.'

'Aw, special!' said Strauss.

She ripped the cardboard tube apart and loaded the twelve sealed shots on to the table. 'What do you want?'

'What is there?' asked Aljce.

'Um, B52s, Sambucas, Honey Shots... no, hang on... Money Shots, QFs...'

'What's a QF?'

'Quick Fucks.'

'No, really.'

'It is really.'

'Where does it say that?'

'They're not allowed to write it on the packaging. So they just write QF.'

'Did you just make that up, or it that real? What would happen if they wrote it on the packaging?'

'True as far as I know.'

'Surely they'd still be able to sell it? What about adult movies? They sell those, although I guess there's not much market now there's the internet? Must be an urban myth.'

'Yeah, I don't know... So what are you having?'

'I don't know. What is there?'

'Fuck sake, we've just been there.'

'What's that one on the end?'

'Don't know, but it's got a star on it.' Strauss turned it on its side. 'Texas Ranger. It's got butterscotch in it.'

'I don't know,' said Aljce, unable to get into it. 'You choose.'

'You choose,' said Strauss. 'Here, close your eyes, and you run your hands over them, until you get a feeling for one.' And she began to shuffle the shots around the table, mixing them up. Aljce got a Texas Ranger. Strauss got a QF. 'That'd be nice,' she said. 'I need one of those. Oh, look, it's green and cream. Down yours Aljce, you need to cheer up and stop thinking about work.' They tipped it down their throats. 'Shit,' said Strauss. 'Beam me a black man!' And she laughed and laughed, but Aljce wasn't sure she could be bothered. She supposed it was funny, but it didn't really touch her. She shouldn't have bothered with the shot. She wasn't really a drinker anyway. 'Holy fuck,' said Strauss, standing up. 'You really need to get out of the space you're in.' She wandered away from Aljce. 'Bella, your beer fridge is filled with jelly shots.'

'That's the kid's,' said Bella. 'They're having pre drinks later before they go out. Have a few if you want.'

Aljce decided to leave the party while Strauss was in the toilet. 'What's that noise?' Mamae had said in the hallway.

'It's me,' said Strauss. 'I know I'm a bad girl, but I'm eating a carrot in the toilet.'

'Oh, my God, you dirty bitch. That's disgusting!' said Mamae's Sister.

'I'm a dirty bitch?' said Strauss. 'Mirror please! You're a dirty bitch!' And she laughed in such a way that Mamae's Sister couldn't possibly take offence, because it was the kind of laugh that didn't expect you to take offence to it. Aljce felt a shiver of envy that Strauss had handled it so confidently because she didn't care at all whether Mamae's Sister liked her or not. Strauss knew she would like her, because Mamae's sister couldn't afford not to. If Mamae's Sister had said that to Aljce, she would have brazened it out, and maybe no one would have known, but underneath, Aljce would have been hurt. Shaken with self-doubt about the way she was in the world. She hadn't heard any self-doubt in Strauss. And that was what kept her safe. Mamae's Sister laughed too, and repeated herself with less conviction and more tolerance.

'Dirty bitch.'

'Come here and say that,' laughed Strauss from the toilet. I care too much about what other people think, thought Aljce.

She was going to walk herself home, but Mamae insisted that she'd walk her. Aljce had meant to say goodbye to everyone, but she'd gone outside looking for her jandals, and Mamae had thought she was leaving without an escort and followed her out, bustling her along the road. She felt a bit bad about not saying good bye to Strauss, but she didn't have the energy to go back in, and anyway, Strauss had drunk so many shots she wouldn't really remember later. Aljce preferred her; preferred everyone when they weren't drunk. Drunk people were quicksand. All the previously stable ground of their personalities sank away, and she didn't know where she was with them anymore. Later, she worried that Strauss WOULD remember, and be offended. The worry got tied up with the sick feeling in her stomach about work, and lasted several hours. 'Worry is a misuse of the imagination,' Strauss would have said. Aljce wondered what Lewis would say.

HE CALLED HER that night, telling her a story about a friend of his. 'We haven't even known each other very long, and yet it feels as if I've known you forever,' she said. 'As if we have so much history between us.'

'Why are you so damn perfect?'

'Well, clearly you don't know my fatal flaws. One of them is to always be attracted to the wrong men. Cocky men. I am just so attracted to men who have that amused by the universe thing down...'

His answer was one word. 'Fatal?'

She couldn't tell if he was interested in a grammatical malfunction or in why. 'Almost. Sometimes. It takes me quite a while to recover. After I find out that they're careless of my heart and not at all worried about hurting me.' She changed the subject. 'Do you think that worry is a misuse of the imagination?'

'Actually, if we're going to talk about worries, I'm worried that I don't have time for this,' he said.

'For what?'

'For spending all this time with you.'

'Why not?' she said, suddenly alarmed. 'You don't have to disclose any fatal flaws of your own, if you don't want to...'

'I'm just saying that I might not have much time for this in the near future,' he said. 'My publisher's given me some deadlines to hit, and I'm at their mercy. I'm not doing enough writing. And I need to. It IS how I earn my living after all.' It's okay, she told herself. He said you were so damn perfect less than a minute ago.

'It must only take you half an hour tops to knock out a written reply, if it's a really long one. A couple of minutes, usually,' she said, trying to make him see the logic.

'It's not that,' he answered. 'The thing is that I can't concentrate on my writing. Because I'm too busy wondering what you're really like and what I'm going to say to you next. I thought you'd understand.' Aljce was torn between understanding; wanting to understand, and not understanding. She'd pictured them doing what they were doing forever, until they could be together.

'I'll try not to interrupt your concentration,' she said.

'I'm sure it will all work out,' he said. But somehow, she sensed he was angry. Angry that she didn't understand.

'WHAT ARE YOUR fatal flaws" she asked Mamae. 'In relation to men.'

'Hell,' said Mamae. 'Plenty. I'm quite fussy.'

'Sometimes I don't like other people's flaws,' said Strauss, descending on them. 'There's no way I could ever be attracted to someone with large moles.'

'Shallow,' said Aljce.

'No, it's not like I think they're ugly or anything; I just couldn't be sexually attracted to them. Especially when they have that pure pink in their skin. Other people might like them, just not me.'

'Ahh, perhaps that's evolution. Perhaps if you got together with them, your children would get skin cancer. Your genes don't mix well with their genes.'

'Maybe.'

'Jimsy's got flaws,' Mamae said to Strauss.

'Yeah, but they're my flaws. The ones I can live with. Like his crooked nose.'

LEWIS DIDN'T RESPOND to Aljce's messages for a few days, and she tried to relax about it. He probably just needed some space to think and calm down about his writing stress. Surely it was just a short rough patch. If he thought of her as he said he did, he couldn't possibly let something so small divide them for long. She tried to be understanding.

For a while, their messages had been getting longer and longer, with the questions separating like rivers at a delta: one short message could yield three questions, which would necessitate three long answers, each with three points that needed to be commented on in turn. But once the tide had turned back again, the waters had withdrawn. Somehow, she sensed that he was still angry.

Aljce tried to think about how she might be conciliatory without being intrusive. How to make a move that would show she understood and cared, while making light of the situation so that they could laugh it away. But her thoughts piled over each other like heavy pancakes, each one crushing the one below it. It didn't matter what you did, men were full of misunderstandings. Mishearings, miscommunications, misconnections. And suddenly everything went wrong. Like dropping a stitch in knitting, only to find the whole garment unravelling, when really it shouldn't be, yet finding there's nothing you can do about it. Men could say that they loved her. Anyone could. But she knew from experience that that might not be true; that next time she looked to check on what she thought she had, their mind could well have changed. You couldn't depend on people to love you.

Love shouldn't be about being in a state of high anxiety, she said to herself. It shouldn't be about feeling stressed or sick in the centre of your rib cage about whether love stays or goes. If it's real, it should just feel right. It should feel like you can trust it not to leave. It shouldn't make your brain dizzy with worst-scenario thoughts. It shouldn't cause constant second guessing. Perhaps that's why she'd often tried to avoid it, despite the fact that she loved being in love. She couldn't take the state of anxiety that it drove her into. Perhaps that's what all love turned to, and what most love started with. Perhaps that was why they called it butterflies in the tummy. Perhaps love was just anxiety about another a person. And romantic love combined that with sexual connection, or the potential of sexual connection.

What was the purpose of being anxious? Was she just in hyper drive to protect herself against rejection? If she was this anxious, she might as well let it go and not worry if it went. Cos it was wrong if that was how it made it feel… so what was there to worry about? A side thought struck her. Would letting go of the anxiety about love make love beautiful again? Maybe and maybe not. But changing her attitude might shift the dynamics of the world.

It was hard to be positive. And suddenly, she wasn't sure that she had the stomach for the love that she craved so much. It was delightfully wonderful in some moments, but its doubts and anxieties made her sick inside, and she didn't know if she could bear them. She felt like she had so much else to bear already.

LATE FOR A VERY IMPORTANT DATE

SAILOR LAY IN the shade of the topiary. Chelsea and Marj were standing on the hot asphalt, smoking cigarettes. No one seemed rushed; no one ever seemed to have anything to actually do. It was as if they were all existing in the illusion of a Therapy Hub. Outsiders thought there was a functioning service, but actually it was just a sham. Oh well, thought Aljce, it was in good company because quantum physics showed that even time and space were illusions. So the Therapy Hub was an illusion within an illusion. Any clients who arrived at the Hub were treated as aberrations. A great deal of fuss was made while they were present, but a great deal of moaning was done about them afterwards, about how they'd interrupted the real work, and how they didn't even want to help themselves.

Kat was the exception to the complaining. Kat had several actual clients, but she never referred to them in conversation, she just talked about Kat. The concert she would be singing at in three weeks' time. Who would be coming? Everybody who mattered. The exact name for the shade of blue of her eyes. Sky or forget-me-not? The cotton thread count in her Egyptian sheets. Aljce was unsure whether more or less thread was better or worse. No doubt more was more. She wondered how Kat's clients found it, but perhaps Kat was different with them. Perhaps she only bubbled over because she had to suppress herself with her clients, and listen to them. Or perhaps she was exactly like this, and they just thought that that was how counsellors were. Aljce sometimes wondered about asking Kat for support for her own situation, but there seemed little point. Kat really only had time for Kat.

'UNFORTUNATELY JILLQ CAN'T make it today,' said Mrs. Kingi, putting her head around Aljce's door ten minutes later. 'She's stuck over in Hastings. We're all going to have to pull together without her, and make it work.'

'How do you know?' asked Aljce, hardly able to believe her luck. But perhaps there'd been a mistake, and she'd misunderstood.

'Jillq told me.'

'But she's not here today?'

'Oh,' said Mrs. Kingi. 'I ring her every morning. Just to make sure she's okay. She works so hard.'

'Really?' asked Aljce. 'Every morning of every day?' She was trying to be super nice, so that people would like her. And when they saw the true her, surely they would like her enough be empathetic. To see how things were for her here at work. Perhaps they would realise that a mistake had been made, and warm to her.

'Every day,' said Mrs. Kingi. 'Someone has to look after her.' Aljce couldn't think of anyone less likely to need looking after than Jillq. No wonder, she thought, that Jillq was good to Mrs. Kingi. She was so adoring; adoration without question. Her mind was so easily tuned. And so grateful for even small gestures. Like being able to sit next to Jillq. Like having her three-day course in Working with People recognised as equal to a social work degree. No, wait; that was a big gesture. Having her tummy tickled with importance, and rolling over. Being valued. Perhaps no one had ever valued Mrs. Kingi before. 'I hope we'll be okay without her,' said Mrs. Kingi. Aljce thought they would be completely okay, and she wasn't wrong.

THE NEXT DAY, Jillq was back with a vengeance. 'There's rabbits in the cabbage patch again,' she screamed from the meeting room. 'Marj, get the spade!' Marj rushed backwards and forwards up and down the hallway for a minute or two, before finally coming to rest at the front desk. She got down on her knees and scrabbled underneath; coming up empty handed before looking behind the door and finally securing a garden spade. 'Marj, where are you?' shrieked Jillq. 'I can see at least three of them!' Chelsea opened the double doors leading onto the cabbage patch, and beyond that, the field.

Marj tottered off over the grass in her high heels. She veered towards the cabbages, and the rabbits lolloped lazily away. 'Why isn't anyone doing anything about those rabbits!' screamed Jillq.

'Marj's gone out there,' Chelsea called from the other end of the corridor. Jillq emerged from the meeting room.

'Did she get any?' she asked hopefully.

'I'm not sure,' said Chelsea. 'You could ask her when she comes in.'

'Why is it always my job to do everything around here?' wailed Jillq.

'Why are we growing cabbages, anyway?' Aljce asked Chelsea. Jillq had been moving away down the corridor again, but she overheard Aljce's question and swept back down towards her, regarding her frostily.

'For the poor people, of course,' she said. 'You can never have too much cabbage when you're poor. Don't you care about the poor people, Aljce?' The correct answer was obviously that she did, but Aljce might as well have not made it, because Jillq entirely disregarded it. 'Anyone who works with abuse must care about the poor people,' said Jillq grandly. 'All therapists must care about poor people and their families. And if you can't do that, Aljce, you may as well go home now and not come back.'

Despite the fact that Aljce cared about the poor people; and border-line considered herself to be one of them, Aljce would have loved to follow that advice. But she didn't dare. It had become a competition between herself and Jillq to last to the bitter end, although Aljce in particular was not declaring the battle. She had more chance of winning if Jillq didn't know she had engaged, and even if she did, she couldn't prove it. Going home was out of the question, because that would have been a permanent win to Jillq, right there. Game, set and match. And even if Aljce lost, she wasn't going to make it easy for Jillq to win.

'Where are they even coming up?' asked Mrs. Kingi, joining them.

'Good point. Good point!' said Jillq. 'We need to find the rabbit hole, and put poison down into it.'

'That would kill all the rabbits,' said Aljce, horrified. Being out there with a spade was one thing; the rabbits were never going to wait around to be hit with it. But putting poison down the rabbit hole was another. She pictured the rabbits trustingly licking tiny white cyanide crystals, glittering like stars scattered on the dark earth. It seemed that the com-pulsory caring didn't extend to the rabbits.

'Exactly the point!' said Jillq. 'Kill all the rabbits! We will all go out and look for the hole!'

'Perhaps they hop for miles to get here,' said Aljce.

'Nonsense!' said Jillq. 'Chelsea, Marj, order some poison. We will all meet here after lunch to find the hole!'

'We will take sections,' said Jillq when they had dutifully assembled. 'In pairs. Aljce, I see you are an odd one out. You will have to search on your own.'

'That's fine,' said Aljce, hardly able to believe her luck. She preferred to be in a group of Aljce. If she found the hole first, she would cover it. It felt so good to be outside in the sun and the clean air. She hated all that false indoor fluorescent lighting that they insisted on having on inside the building; no matter how bright the day was, and she hated the vaguely threatening pink tone it brought to the corridor and the air of the rooms flanking it.

She walked slowly, scanning the ground with her eyes. She blinked, and blinked again before sinking to her knees in wonder. The entire field seemed to be made of four leaf clovers. Dark chlorophyllic green; and still clung with the tiny crystal beads of rainwater from a small shower about an hour before. 'Stand up Aljce,' called Jillq from across the clover. 'Unless you have found the hole?'

'No,' said Aljce hastily. Mrs. Kingi seemed to have gone home. Hattie had not arrived. She hoped the odds of finding it were low. Although she wouldn't have minded Jillq finding an old, disused one by getting her foot caught in it. Aljce caught herself. Imagining Jillq in pain wasn't good for her karma. She tucked a few four leaf clover leaves into her sock. She would retrieve them later.

'We are not looking hard enough!' screamed Jillq.

Aljce saw a rabbit a few metres in front of her. Seeing her, it lazily flopped further ahead. Aljce moved softly towards it. Perhaps it would lead her back to its burrow so that she could conceal it.

She followed it behind of one of the bigger mounds, only to find it had disappeared. She couldn't see a hole, so maybe it had hopped around the front before she got to the back. And when she came back around, the others were gone.

Back inside, Jillq was standing at reception with a woman that Aljce had only seen across the room at social services meetings. Her gaze was frosty as she advanced on Aljce. 'Did you forget we are hosting the woman from Infinite Horizons?' she hissed in Aljce's ear. 'Out going for a walk while the rest of us work! Please take her to the meeting room to wait for me since you have so much time on your hands. She's one of our MAJOR stakeholders.' Aljce raised her eyebrows to herself. So much nonsense was spoken here. 'How nice of you to offer to take care of our guest, Aljce,' said Jillq loudly, beaming at the woman.

'Smile,' said the woman from Infinite Horizons as she accepted Aljce's offer of a coffee while they walked down the corridor.

'Not much to smile about here,' said Aljce. The woman looked taken aback. Aljce was surprised. Surely they knew on the outside that this was a mad house. Although she couldn't say that she'd known before she'd come to work here. But this woman seemed to have had quite a lot to do with them. Aljce wondered how much she could say. She tested the water. 'I'm not really enjoying my new job here,' she said. The woman shrank back imperceptibly, but as surely as a spider confronted with a flame.

'Well, chin up,' she said, turning away to go into the meeting room.

'Thanks,' said Aljce, disappointed. Even an outside ally would have been something. She got the woman a coffee, and then left her to wait for Jillq by herself.

'WHERE'S OUR CLIENT BOOK?' asked Hattie. Her hair was a stark raving blue today.

'Oh, I think I have it,' said Aljce. 'I saw it open on the counter, and I just wanted to ask who all these clients with my name next to them are?'

'Your clients, of course,' said Hattie. 'But I've never met them,' said Aljce. 'I don't know who these people are.'

'Aljce. I gave you those referrals,' said Chelsea.

'But you said to do nothing.'

'Aljce, what is the problem?' Jillq always impressed Aljce with her ability to materialise. Presumably the woman from Infinite Horizons had left, happy with the wool that had been pulled over her eyes.

'Are we counting those people as clients to claim for contracts? Because I just need to point out that I've never actually met them, and I think it could lead to trouble later on, if we claim money for people I haven't met. I feel nervous having my name next to them.' Jillq frowned.

'Aljce. Are you being difficult again?'

'I don't think so,' said Aljce, conscious that even saying that in reply made her difficult.

'We record clients here,' said Jillq. 'Everything in its place.'

'But they're not actually clients,' said Aljce.

'No, but they could be.'

'I think we need to be careful in case we're audited,' said Aljce. Jillq sniffed crossly.

'Everyone just needs to be mindful,' she said. Aljce was surprised at how easily Jillq had allowed her to win. 'We will just pencil them in moving forward,' Jillq said. Aljce sighed. Somehow she felt sure that the pencil would eventually become pen whether the people on the list became clients of hers or not. 'Something to remember,' said Jillq, 'is that we need to get permission from Chelsea to take the client book out of main reception. Did you have permission, Aljce? I am very clear that it is everyone's responsibility to ask permission at all times. Aljce.'

'Of course,' said Alce obediently, but thinking blah. Naturally it was way too much to expect that she could have access to a book listing clients allocated to her. How would that possibly be her business?

'Aljce,' said Jillq, 'have you done your brochure?'

'Ages ago,' said Aljce.

'Why have I not seen it?'

'I didn't know you wanted to,' said Aljce, 'but I'm happy to show you.' She felt secure in the knowledge that she had done an excellent job of creating a brochure introducing herself, and her 'role,' as they liked to call it. It seemed unlikely, but perhaps Jillq would realise that she had a talent for creating and organising, and treat her better. Perhaps she would come to understand that Aljce was an asset, and all that needed to happen for Aljce to put all her focus and creativity into the Therapy Hub was to feel safe there. Safe and valued. Like Kat.

But when she took it down to Jillq, Jillq was critical. 'I don't like the colours,' she said. Aljce loved the colours. 'Can we squash that up to put a map in?' asked Jillq. Aljce flinched. She had spent hours getting that layout perfect.

'I like it the way it is,' she said, aware that she was sounding stubborn and sulky. 'Maybe I can do a bit more work on it,' she said to mitigate things.

'I think that's wise,' said Jillq. It should take you at least six weeks to get this brochure right. I don't know why you thought you could do it in only a few days.' Aljce sighed. How could a brochure take six weeks? No wonder nothing got done. 'Should we complain because the rose bushes have thorns or rejoice because the thorn bushes have roses?' asked Jillq rhetorically, no doubt repeating a quote she'd read elsewhere.

The mention of roses reminded Aljce of a conversation she'd had with her Mad Neighbour. Her spinning clothesline had toppled over. She had been worried that it was spoiling her garden with its upside down umbrella grey metal aesthetic, until the dark pink geraniums and the lilies had started coming up through it last summer, and then she realised that it and the metal pole beside it were contemporary garden sculpture, and with that change of attitude, it no longer bothered her that she had no way to get it to the dump. 'You don't need a clothesline,' her Mad Neighbour had said. 'Just hang out your washing on the jasmine hedge like me, and you will always have shirts that smell like flowers.' She thought about how visitors to the house might enjoy seeing her undies on the hedge as they came down the driveway, or what the postie might think when they delivered the letters. But it did sound delightful; jasmine smelling, sun dried laundry. 'And put your socks on the roses,' he said. 'As long as it's not a windy day. You don't want them ripped to bits.'

In the end, she just asked Lewis how he was. Nothing fancy, nothing complicated; just a genuine enquiry.

'I've been lunching with ladies,' he said.

'Cool,' said Aljce.

'Beautiful ladies,' said Lewis.

'Oh?'

'Ladies who are both gorgeous and interesting.'

'Is that work?'

'Why, is that jealousy you're displaying Aljce?'

Aljce thought. 'Yeah, perhaps I am jealous when you have lunch with other women.'

'Why? They're just people I'm in contact with.'

'Perhaps it's because I haven't really connected with you much lately, and I wish I was them. I'd love to have lunch with you.'

'Well, it's unattractive. I should be able to have lunch with other people.'

'Of course. Sorry.'

She couldn't believe her karma had gotten so ruffled. She was allowing fear and anxiety in through the doors of her soul, and uncharacteristically, she couldn't out-think it. Because it wasn't just about thinking, it was about feeling. She couldn't out-feel it by out-thinking it. That was a more accurate description. And now that the surface of her karma was ruffled, she was vulnerable.

She didn't even know what her own motives were anymore. She was creating a narrative, but how would Lewis look at it from his point of view, if he wasn't selecting and sorting and collecting the same things that she chose to give attention to? Of course he could ascribe different motives to her choices without all the information in her heart. The problem was that no one could be really sure of the truth or what it was, let alone other people's motives, because it was not even possible to be sure of your own. Other people are just screens that we project our thoughts on to, she mused. Our thoughts about who they might be, or should be, or could be. And that included her ideas about who she was herself.

Was she in love? Perhaps she was just clinging to him because she wanted to be loved? Was she, in fact, clingy and suffocating? Or was she just being made to feel that way? There had been nights where he'd talked of the things they would do when they could be together as a couple. If I know that love is just the stories that we tell ourselves, she thought, then why can't I stop telling myself stories full of love about him?

'Maybe my insecure feelings are hurt,' she said. 'My stupid, insecure feelings.'

'My God,' he said. 'If there's an eye of a needle, you'll find it.' Maybe, she thought, maybe I'm misreading things. Do I construct everything to be worse than it is? Do I exaggerate everything and always believe the worst?

'Perhaps I am,' she said. 'I'm sorry. I probably have a tendency to do that. Something to do with how others have treated me in the past, no doubt. My bad.'

'So you're saying that I have to have contact with you every day so that you can avoid your insecurities?'

Uh? she thought. She had expected a different response to her apology. It was beginning to feel a lot like her interactions with Jillq. But maybe she was just reading hostility into it because she was insecure. 'No, no,' she replied quickly. 'I'm not trying to manipulate you into giving me attention. I'm just trying to explain how I tick. I thought we were interested in understanding how we function as people? I am. I guess I just realised this about myself and wanted to share it with you.'

'Well, I almost wish you hadn't. It's put a lot of pressure on me.'

She could feel the silent tears welling up inside her, blurring things. 'Ahh,' she said. 'Not intended. Sorry about that. I was just trying to explain myself. It's my issue, not yours. Something for me to work on. Don't think about it again.'

'It's as if you're purposefully misreading what I write,' he said. Maybe it had been a vicious cycle, she thought to herself. Maybe she had seen the worst possible meaning in his words, and he had gotten angry at being misrepresented, and she had taken the worst from that again, and gotten more and more upset, while he got angrier and angrier. Reality was about what you chose to pay attention to. Other people may have chosen to construe his words differently. Perhaps things could have been different. If she had been different.

Her own words were becoming extremely frantic in her attempts to reinstate their former emotional intimacy, while his answers were coming in shorter and shorter bursts.

'I feel as if messaging is taking over my life,' he said. She was still thinking about how to reply when he continued. 'I don't want you to become an obligation,' he wrote.

'Please don't hang out with me unless you want to,' she wrote stiffly, because she was hurt. Surely he'd created the obligation by being so committed to replying to her, and so keen to arrive every night, at the same time, to talk to her? Never missing a day? Her habit of him had been forged over long hours of sleep deprivation which he had professed to enjoy as much as she did. She felt conditioned; hypnotised. And now he was saying it was an unpleasant chore. She felt as if she was being punished for something, although she didn't know what. Perhaps for not being enough.

'I'm not sure that we're physically suited anyway,' he said. Something in her withered.

'What do you mean?' she asked carefully. 'Is there something about the way I look that you don't like?'

'I wouldn't worry about it,' he said.

'What is it? What exactly don't you like about me?'

'If I told you that, you'd just torture yourself about it,' he said, ensuring that she would actually get to be insecure about everything. Every single thing about herself, she thought. There were so many things she could say, so many things she could throw at him. But she didn't believe in summaries. Everything that had been said was said, and everything unsaid had been said just as much. And that was how it lay. There was no need to try and arrange it. That would be clumsy, and not how she wanted to remember things.

'All good,' she said, and put in a smiley face for good measure. She would be the one who exited with dignity.

It was secret, private pain that nobody knew about inside her, not even Strauss. It was a dull feeling, not even sadness, more like loss, like ache.

She watched from her window as her Mad Neighbour whistled to what he liked to call his birds. He had four white poles just above the height of his head; perhaps the remains of a fence, although they didn't seem to line up with each other. Each pole had a flat top, and her Mad Neighbour placed a slice of white bread on each, whistling though his teeth as he always did. The birds knew that whistle so well that they flocked to him as if he was a bird whisperer. He was convinced he had special talents. Aljce just thought the birds were well trained. He was singing as he threw extra crumbs around his yard. 'I'm Captain Jenks of the horse marines... I get high on corn and beans...'

He'd put up green netting so that random visitors – the Mormons, the Jehovahs, and perhaps the Police – wouldn't see his weed plants, which had bushed up in a healthy uncared-for fashion. Although it had to be said that he'd provided them with shelter underneath a loose pane of clear glass when they were tiny seedlings. 'It's not that I don't want those people here. It's just the plants. But I don't want to blaspheme. At all, at all,' said her Mad Neighbour. 'Me and God are getting on pretty good at the moment. And I don't want to ruin that.'

'You should always try to work on relationships,' agreed Aljce. Not that it was doing her any good, at home or at work. Her usual skills were failing her. I give everyone else such very good advice.., she thought. But I don't seem to be able to follow it.

THERE WAS ANOTHER shouty email from Jillq. What I should do, she thought, is save all these emails somewhere where Jillq can't get at them and have them erased. Somewhere where she won't know I'm even collecting them. She checked herself for paranoia, but couldn't tell. Perhaps she was over reacting. Who saved their work emails? Perhaps it was because the only way to survive when she was growing up was to be subversive. She hadn't started out that way, but she'd quickly learned that the only way to be able to have the life she wanted to live was to be undetected. And as hard as it was for her to believe that her perception of her situation was real, and as much as she periodically doubted herself, and whether it really was THAT bad, she decided that she still needed to protect herself. Better safe than sorry was a good rule to live by.

From then on, she forwarded everything Jillq sent her, as well as her own replies from her sent box, to her home email. Her paranoia kicked in again: could Jillq see where she sent emails to? After all, Marj was the author of the whole system, and they had her password. In case she fell under a bus and someone had to carry on with her work, theoretically. If indeed she had done any real work by then. No doubt someone could do something interesting with her brochure. Maybe include that map of where to find the Therapy Hub. Two maps. One mustard, one lime green. The question was, would Jillq think to look to check on Aljce? Would she expect that level of subversion? If she did, she would look. But perhaps she wasn't bright enough to understand that Aljce was.

Aljce upped the adrenalin level by printing off the emails for a physical file. She didn't have her own printer at home. She would check to see if anyone was near the work printer, and if they weren't, she would click print, and run and wait for the email to be pumped out into the tray. Waiting for the paper to squeeze itself out of the machine was like having monkeys partying in her stomach. Would everything be okay? Maybe it wouldn't. Still, every time, she seemed to survive, and take her printed paper back to her office, hiding it in her car at the first opportunity, unloading it into a manila folder as soon as she got home. When she forwarded an email to herself, she had a sense of imminently being about to be caught. Her heart raced, and she looked over her shoulder, only to find that there was nothing but guilt there.

From time to time she found Pepper under her desk. She didn't know why Pepper wasn't at school. Perhaps she was sick. Pepper would sit there quietly, with felt tips and paper, drawing. No one looked for her, but she cringed away from Aljce's feet when her mother walked past, and got as close to the wall as she could. Jillq was always trailing instructions or comment as she went, and Pepper could hear her coming, as could everyone else. Aljce would also have liked to cringe as far away from Jillq's energy as possible, like cell in a petri dish, confronted with a toxin. Some people, however, seemed to welcome her, and there were happy snorts of laughter from the others as they interacted with Jillq. Perhaps Jillq was right. Perhaps it was just Aljce. When Aljce could overhear Jillq, she even agreed with some of the things Jillq said.

For instance, she told Hattie that if there were passengers, the driver of a car should spin the car so that they themselves took the full impact of the collision in an accident. If Aljce had her children in the car that was exactly what she would do if she was in an accident. Who knew if Jillq meant it or not? Was it all part of the game, to say what she thought should be said, or did she genuinely believe that? Would she die for Pepper, or for Deidra or Dulcie? Was Aljce misjudging her? Could it be that she WAS unselfish, and that with Aljce, Jillq just had an agenda that only made sense if you viewed it from the right direction? Even if not from the direction that Aljce was looking from?

Aljce never spoke to Pepper about her mother, but she let her know by her tone of voice and the warmth of her energy as she gave her paper clips to make a chain out of, or scissors to cut paper snowflakes with, that it was safe to be where she was. The wall between the corridor and her office was glass from waist height; no doubt so that Jillq could survey everything. But down low by Aljce's legs was hidden space.

HOME WAS A better place, and Aljce longed for the weekends, when she felt free of Jillq's gaze being on her all day. Her Mad Neighbour had an old church organ in the shed where he lived, and today he was playing it. Teaching himself to play, at least. It was full of special effect pedals, and it had probably been making trippy music long before keyboards were invented. She wandered around her garden amongst the flowers, tuned into the notes and pretending she was in a science fiction landscape.

Her Front Neighbour, her Mad Neighbour's brother, was out in his back silk kimono, with the custard yellow dragon stitching matching his custard yellow nail polish but clashing with his cherry red lipstick.

She wondered how someone who dressed so femininely could coexist in the same body as someone who let his dark chest hair grow so long and wild. It looked like a curly toddler's head. There was something quite decadent about it; being so feminine while at the same time being so masculine. It was so sensual that it was almost sexual, but not in any way that attracted Aljce. 'Ya got a light, Aljce?' he asked.

'You should give up that shit,' she said, hunting for a lighter in her pocket. 'It kills you.'

'Oh, you do not know what you are missing,' he said, inhaling deeply. 'Now I feel like myself. I can't wake up until I've had a cigarette. And there's a lot of shit that kills you. You've just got to choose how you want to die.'

THAT NIGHT, there was a rare blood moon, and it seemed as if the moon had been stabbed and was bleeding out; saturating the blackness of the night. After a while, Aljce went inside and lay in bed, getting stoned and watching old footage of Fleetwood Mac on YouTube. Her mother had played Fleetwood Mac a lot while Aljce was growing up. Gratitude was second nature to Aljce, and she gave a quick thanks for living single. Some things wouldn't be possible if she was coupled up. But she didn't want to open her Facebook account. She didn't want to open it and be there without Lewis. It was stupid, but she wanted to search to see what he had been doing, to see what he'd posted. To search for clues that would show he still loved her. Not by checking his page, because that would be chasing him, and if it was meant to be, she wouldn't have to do that, but just by scrolling down to see what the universe wanted to share with her. If he'd been active and he hadn't bothered to message her, it twisted her gut. She'd done it once or twice, but she hadn't called out to him, even when he was there. If he didn't want her, he wasn't worthy of her.

If he's going to be that angry with me and I haven't done anything other than make myself vulnerable to him, then he's just another angry man that I don't need in my life, she thought. I've had enough of them. But she was torn between protecting her heart so that he couldn't hurt it, and just wanting to relax right into him.

Keep off Facebook, she told herself. Put down your phone. It's over, you'll heal. But another part of her told her that it wasn't over till it was over. Stupid, stupid to hope that he might have made a mistake, that there might be some reason for him to avoid her, for him to have been angry. It was over, and she had ended it well from her own perspective. There was no reason for her not to go to familiar places if they were where she wanted to be. He didn't own them. There IS a reason not to go there, she said to herself, if the only reason you're going there is because you hope that he'll be there.

But Facebook belonged to her as well. It did. She knew she shouldn't, but she logged in anyway, even as she counselled herself not to. Her heart skipped a beat. He had messaged her. Love and anxiety swooped around in her heart like twin pigeons. Could it be good? Could he want to mend things? Hope, she said to herself. Hope, and maybe you will create the universe. She missed him; she missed his mind. She missed being special to him. Their own little in-club, with their own way of doing things. She missed the little gestures, like how happy she had felt when he sent her a love song. She missed all of that. Surely it had meant something to him too. How could it have meant so much to her and nothing to him? What sort of person would have shared that intimacy with her and now not feel anything?

But tonight he had messaged her. It had all been a mistake, and he wanted to talk to her again. She felt a rush of adrenalin. Things were going to be okay. She opened his message. It was brief. 'Please don't ever contact me again,' it read.

Her heart stopped. She wasn't sure how long it took her to find its beat again. All she knew is that there was definitely a space where she didn't breathe, and when she did, it was painful to suck the air in past her heart. He had messaged her as if she was stalking him. As if even the thought of her burned him unpleasantly. And that spoiled everything in her mind. Everything that she'd taken pleasure in was no longer real. Because in her memory, she had meant something to him too, and clearly she didn't. People didn't discard what they loved. And if he had, he never did.

She felt physically sick and completely overwhelmed. What the fuck, she thought, hanging onto the side of her mattress for stability, because she felt as if she was riding a huge, unstable energy. She willed it to pass, without any real hope that it would. Even when she tried to do deep breathing to calm herself, it seemed as if she was only able to fill her lungs to a very shallow depth. Perhaps she would be sick. This was too big. How could she cope with it? How could she live feeling like this? She felt sorry for all the times she hadn't realised what other people who felt this way were going through when their relationships had ended. It was too big for her body, too big for her to be able to live with this sick emotion flooding through her.

She shook herself. There was no way she was able to absorb this. She needed all of her energy to stay safe at work; to protect herself. She couldn't allow herself to feel this because it would devastate her, and then she would be weak. She would put it aside. She probably couldn't stop herself thinking about him, but she could stop herself from feeling anything. She would deaden herself inside; numbing her heart with mental anaesthetic. One day, she might have time to feel for this, but not now. She was crying. She had to let herself have ten minutes. That was all she could spare. There was a bigger fight to fight. Sleep would be difficult, but until it came, her mind would be full of Jillq, and how she could plan to out strategise her.

Ten minutes of cold, bitter salt came to an end. That is all you can afford, she told herself. You can't spend any more. She lit another joint, and turned Stevie Nicks up louder. I hope my bed doesn't catch alight, she thought, while Stevie Nicks crooned 'well maybe I'm just thinking that the rooms are all on fire...'

EAT ME, DRINK ME

IT WAS DIFFICULT to keep up the mental anaesthetic. I have no time for this, she thought. I need to concentrate on my situation with Jillq. If I think about Lewis, I'll drown. She could refuse to let herself indulge in self-pity, but she couldn't erase the memories which sometimes bubbled up, because knowing him was currently intertwined with her self; her soul. It would have been good if she'd been busier at work, because then work would have been a distraction, but so far only two of the mothers, the ones that Aljce had connected with herself, had agreed to let their children work with Aljce. And they hadn't come in yet.

Jillq, of course, found something for them all to do, although it wasn't client related. 'Where are you all?' she bellowed down the hallway. 'Why isn't this meeting in everybody's diary?' Meeting? Meeting? Aljce thought hard, casting wildly around her memory for a clue. Was there a meeting about her again? 'Everyone,' shouted Jillq. Aljce could feel her heart racing. It was another meeting about her.

'Come on,' said Mrs. Kingi, putting her head around the door. 'Jillq said everyone. We're keeping her waiting.' Aljce wondered how anyone could enjoy having someone so obviously slavish at their beck and call. Unfortunately there was no one to raise her eyebrows to, which is the only thing that would have made it bearable. She thought of Strauss and raised them mentally at her. She drifted reluctantly out into the hall. It wasn't as if she was doing anything, so she had no excuses. But she didn't want to go, and she could feel her body getting warmer as she walked up the corridor. Sweat mixed with her rapidly beating heart. Don't be stupid, she told herself. It's not you, it's them. A part of her observed herself from the outside. Fascinating, said that part. You are truly stressed, and nothing has happened yet, but you're in fear overdrive. Calm down... But she seemed to be unable to pay enough attention to herself to take control of her adrenalin.

'Sit,' said Jillq, waving her hand majestically to them all. The meeting was clearly a surprise to the others as well.

'Can I ask how long this will take?' said Hattie. 'I've got a lot of work on, you know.'

'How long is a piece of string?' asked Jillq grandly. 'We need to talk about the conference in Auckland. It's very important. We need to make arrangements.' Aljce hadn't heard of a conference in Auckland. Her mind flapped like washing in the wind as it processed the idea that the meeting wasn't about her.

'I'm worried about the arrangements,' said Jillq. And she did look stressed; fiddling mindlessly with whatever was in reach as she perambulated around the room. Clearly the command 'sit' hadn't applied to her. 'Very worried. The logistics.'

'I think it's really inconsiderate that people aren't keeping you in the loop,' said Mrs. Kingi.

'Oh,' said Chelsea. 'All the bookings are done. I've sent out the plane tickets and the itinerary to everyone's email.'

'Did you okay that with Jillq?'

'It's okay,' said Jillq. 'I'm used to being treated as unimportant around here.'

'Oh, we'd be nothing without you, esteemed leader!' Aljce wondered if Marj had really said that. It seemed an unlikely thing for one grown up to say to another, but the words still hung in her ears, and their sound was in Marj's voice.

'Jillq asked me to make the reservations,' said Chelsea brightly to Mrs. Kingi.

'What reservations?' asked Aljce.

'The Auckland Conference,' said Jillq. 'We are all going of course.'

'But it's not compulsory, is it?' asked Aljce. She had no idea what the conference was, but the thought of travelling anywhere with her colleagues was not appealing to her. For a starters, how would she be able to smoke weed?

'Compulsory?' said Mrs. Kingi. 'We're very lucky to be going to Auckland at no cost to ourselves.'

'Of course everyone will go,' said Jillq. 'We travel as a team. I hope you are a team player, Aljce.' Aljce could see the trap coming. If she didn't go, she'd be singled out even more as the person who couldn't gel with the team, the awkward one who thought she was too good to do what they did. But if she went, she'd be relentlessly exposed to their energy. Why Jillq wanted her to go, she didn't know. She would have thought that Jillq would have preferred not to have someone, such as she thought Aljce was, around.

'How long is it for?' she asked; heartsick, but academically fascinated by this train wreck.

'Two days and two nights,' said Marj.

'Haven't you been paying attention?' asked Jillq, sounding exasperated.

'Good to know,' said Hattie, who obviously hadn't known either. 'How are we getting there?'

'I've booked plane tickets,' said Chelsea.

'We need to be there the airport at least an hour beforehand,' said Jillq.

'What time?' asked Hattie.

'We will meet out there at half past four in the morning.'

Fucking hell, thought Aljce.

'I WISH WE didn't have to go,' she said to MaryAnn.

'I don't,' said MaryAnn. 'My boss says it's not part of my role. My role is making sure that the community is aware of family violence. I can't do that from Auckland.'

'Lucky you,' said Aljce. 'What did Jillq say?'

'Not much she can say, is there? I just work from here, she isn't MY boss. The Therapy Hub is only providing the venue, and creaming off money for office space. They're just my umbrella organization. They have the money, keep some, and give the rest to my boss to manage me and pay me. And to pay for my resources of course.'

'You're so lucky,' said Aljce again. 'No wonder she leaves you alone. I bet she'd love to make you go.'

'Probably,' said MaryAnn cheerfully. 'But I'm not going to.'

KAT WASN'T GOING either. She was a counsellor anyway, not a social worker, and she had another overseas holiday booked, where she would sing at some concert in Italy. Jillq wasn't exactly fine with it, Chelsea told Aljce; seemingly unaware that Aljce couldn't stand her at all after Chelsea's deliberate contributions to getting her into trouble with Jillq. Jillq had wanted Kat to go to Auckland, but Kat had qualifications, and could pretty much do what she wanted to. Aljce knew that Kat didn't dream for a moment that she would give up her concert in Italy; where the women would wear diamonds and the men would wear dark and handsome, just so that she could go to some social work conference in Auckland. Such things weren't for Kat to worry about.

But they were for Aljce to worry about. The plane was leaving at half past 5. That meant that Aljce would have to take the children to Mamae's the night before, and get up before 4 o'clock in the morning in order to have breakfast and a shower before she drove to the airport. She saw no need to get there an hour before. Half an hour beforehand would be fine. The flight time neatly avoided the Therapy Hub needing to pay for an extra night's accommodation, because they would all be in place for the 9am start. Even if they needed to leave their suitcases in a little office at the motel, until the rooms were cleared and cleaned.

She dreamed of Lewis that night. They were in the clean white snow together, dancing around a huge Xmas tree. And as she watched them both moving as one, she noticed that their feet were leaving no prints. Then she saw that it was because they were lifting, spinning up into the air; twirling around and around the beautiful glittering, sparkling tree as they danced. Gliding through space, their lips came together, and she was happy... until she woke feeling empty, as if something had been stolen from her.

It was said that everyone you saw in our dreams, you'd seen at least once in real life. It clearly wasn't true. Sometimes things went beyond what you saw with your eyes.

In the end, Aljce nearly missed the plane. She got there at 5:20am, having struggled through her shower and trying to drag her suitcases out the door. Aljce never left home without a shower. It relaxed her. On the final leg of the drive there, she could hear the plane landing. Adrenalin flooded through her body as she freaked out about whether she'd get there in time or not. Luckily it was a small airport, and they were leaving on a small plane. Only she and the Therapy Hub staff were checking in. They were already there, in a group, lips pursed when they saw Aljce. Aljce wasn't sure whether Jillq was pleased she'd made it or not, but she was sure there would have been trouble if she hadn't.

Once on the plane, Jillq was clearly distracted by the fact that flying made her nervous, and Mrs. Kingi was in the seat next to her, administering Rescue Remedy on a piece of cotton wool. 'Just don't think about it,' she was saying.

'How can I not think about it,' wailed Jillq. 'I don't even know how they stay up in the air!' She smelt of gin. Aljce slunk to her seat, which was right down the back. She enjoyed flying; that feeling of lifting off into the air the belly of a metal bird. She wished that they could fly forever, and not arrive in Auckland, but it was a relatively short flight.

Ten minutes in, she could hear Jillq snoring from several rows back; her breath gently ebbing and flowing. The Rescue Remedy was clearly kicking in. Or something was. There was no way that Aljce could sleep. She couldn't relax while she was surrounded by people that she couldn't afford to be vulnerable to.

PERHAPS AS A sign of things to come, Aljce got an electric shock from the handrail leading down to the tarmac. It was a weak shock; more of a fright than a sting, but still, Aljce felt it was a bad omen. Think positive, she told herself. Collect your karma.

It was a long, cramped shuttle ride to the motel, and Aljce had to fight sleep as the motion of the van tried to seduce her. Finally, they got off, and walked past a pool as they carried their suitcases into the motel, where the conference would also be. The gate was shut, but Aljce could see Astroturf and plastic pink flamingos next to the cold glassy water. Deck chairs in long slabs of silver metal. She thought of her Mad Neighbour. He would have loved it. On a sunny day, it could have been nice in an Alice does Disney way. 'We must go for a swim later,' enthused Hattie. Aljce shuddered. It was overcast and chilly. The pool didn't attract her.

'Looks like it's you and me,' said Aljce, turning to Mrs. Kingi at the reception desk.

'What do you mean?'

'We're rooming together.'

'No,' said Mrs. Kingi, 'no, that can't be right.'

'Why not?'

'What number am I in, please?' said Mrs. Kingi, leaning over the desk to the receptionist.

'Name please?'

'Mrs. Kingi.'

'You are in the room with the key I have just given out.' Aljce waved her key at Mrs. Kingi. Better Mrs. Kingi than some of the others.

'Come on,' she said, 'let's go.' Mrs. Kingi followed reluctantly.

Once they got to the room, Aljce put her things inside. Mrs. Kingi left hers by the door. 'I'll be back soon,' she said.

HALF AN HOUR LATER, she returned. 'I'm actually supposed to be rooming with Jillq,' she said, picking up her suitcases. Aljce was torn between being happy that she was going to have the room to herself, and feeling unwanted. Both won. But when Mrs. Kingi left, Aljce was happier. It felt safer. She was rooming on her own. She could lock the door and all the unpleasant energy was still on the outside of that barrier.

She glanced at herself in the large motel mirror. She felt top heavy. Then she remembered. She had body dysmorphia. She had come across this before in her life. It was ridiculous to imagine herself with a head too big for her body, when she had no evidence for this, other than a vague feeling left over from looking in the mirror. At least she could catch herself indulging in it when it happened nowadays. What sort of stupid mental health joke was that; that her head should be ginormous in comparison to her body? Once you started examining it intellectually, it was obvious that it didn't make sense, any more than it made sense that Alice should grow when she ate the mushroom in Wonderland. Eat me, drink me, she thought.

She had spent years believing that her jawline was too thick, that her eyebrows, which she didn't pluck, were too sparse, and that her hair was too fine. When she was a teenager, she had believed that her face was the ugliest face in the world, and that people were disgusted with her. That she was lucky when they interacted with her. But she hadn't let anyone know that it hurt her. She pretended that it couldn't touch her. Although even when she'd found out about body dysmorphia, and realised that she had it, and dismissed those ideas, one by one, as wrong, it didn't take long for new ideas of how her body was distorted to move in to her head and take over. Like viruses, they lived in there undetected until somehow, her immune cells recognised those thoughts and attacked them. She was glad that she had gotten on to this one so quickly. Perhaps she was improving. More alert to the attack. More self-analytical. More caring of herself; more able to say, that idea can't be right.

DAMN IT, she thought, sitting in the airless conference room a short time later, and realising she was at serious risk of going to sleep. How were other people staying awake? Perhaps they'd slept on the plane like Jillq. Or perhaps they were morning people. She tried yawning. She tried mentally shaking herself. She poured herself a glass of water from the jug on the table and that helped, but only briefly. Perhaps, if she just leaned forward and put her head on her arms, and just rested a bit, Jillq wouldn't know that she was having difficulty keeping her eyes open. No, she thought, that's a recipe for sleep. She tried to concentrate on the speaker. Something about daffodils, although that seemed unlikely; surreal. Things were clear and bright and slipping away.

Her head jerked her as it fell, giving her a fright. Shit, she thought. My eyes closed on their own, without my permission. Hope no one saw me falling asleep. Hattie tapped her. 'You were falling asleep,' she said.

'I'm okay,' said Aljce, irritated and deprived of her sleep, which seemed so sweet right at that moment. This is what happens when I get up early, she thought. What a stupid idea. Flying up on the day of the conference, just to save money on accommodation. They should have gone up the night before, and sent less people to even out the cost. Did Chelsea, the receptionist-greeter-data collector really need to be there? Did any of them? Other organizations had only sent one or two people. No other organization had brought all their staff with them.

A husband and wife team seemed to be in charge: Wally and Pen. Wally put his notes up on the projector. He had used the heart border that Jillq was so fond of. Aljce sighed. Clearly there was little imagination amongst social workers. Perhaps they all thought the same way.

'Everyone in a circle!' said Pen excitedly. 'Everyone join hands! Fabulous!' Pen had a habit of saying 'fabulous!' every time she spoke. Aljce sighed. She didn't want to hold hands. Fake togetherness was never a good sign, and she hated it. Chairs were pushed aside and cardigans draped. Somebody clicked play on their laptop screen and suddenly they were all singing the words 'I believe the children are our future.' Aljce didn't want to sing. She couldn't buy into such low level shit. It was like wandering into someone's Pinterest boards, and finding them full of recipes, wedding dresses and neutral interiors. Why did so many social workers have to be so earnest, so full of good deeds, and so lacking in a sense of irony? Where was their mischief, their fun?

'Teach them well, and let them lead the way,' the others sang with their eyes shining, grasping each other's hands zealously. Of course the children were the future. That was how biology worked. There was no need to believe in children being the future; it was going to happen, no matter what. And then those children's children would be their future. If humanity hadn't fucked the planet over by that time. Aljce knew that she didn't belong here with these singers. 'Show them all the beauty they possess inside.' Well that wasn't restricted to children. She was clearly too querying, too troublesome, too challenging. She felt bored by cliché, mundanity, failure of originality, triteness. She wondered if any of them could sense it in her, a holding back; a scorn even. She thought they could. They may not have understood it, but they knew there was something dark and potentially unreachable inside her. It was foreign to them. They were earnest and gullible. They didn't discern. But Aljce did.

MORNING TEA CAME. 'Would you like a coffee Jillq?' asked Marj.

'I'm already getting her a coffee!' said Mrs. Kingi.

'No you're not,' said Marj. But Mrs. Kingi had already gone off in the direction of the espresso machine.

'I'll get biscuits!' said Marj, heading in the opposite direction to the buffet table.

'It's nice to be waited on,' said Jillq. 'I have been working very hard. Harder than the rest of you. Planning this conference for a start.' Aljce wondered what she'd done. The Auckland based organisers seemed to have everything in hand. Perhaps Jillq meant telling Chelsea to book the flights.

'Here,' said Mrs. Kingi. 'There was only one espresso cup left, but I made sure you got it. I'm happy to just have hot water anyway.'

'I'll get it!' said Marj, returning with the biscuits.

'I've already gotten it for her,' said Mrs. Kingi. Aljce was glad not to be competing.

She turned to the other people in the room. She hated most people's small talk; it was talk for no reason at all; well, with no outcome but to fill in time, but clearly no one she knew from the Therapy Hub was going to talk to her during the break. She couldn't stand there motionless and quiet, and that's what small talk was for: to fill the silences between people who didn't know each other. The woman facing her had a pounamu round her neck. It was impressively carved, and the grain of the greenstone had some blue in it.

'I love your pounamu,' she said.

'Thank you,' said the woman. 'It is special. My late husband gave it to me.'

'I love it,' repeated Aljce. 'I can see an angel and a cloud whale.'

'I like your one too,' said the woman.

'Oh,' said Aljce. 'Mine is from the $2 shop. It's actually plastic. A dark green plastic tiki.' The woman laughed.

'It looks real,' she said.

'Well,' said Aljce,' if you like it, they actually have them in lots of colours. I have a red one and a purple one too. They're really bright, but they look good.'

'I must check it out,' said the woman smiling.

Jillq had appeared at Aljce's side. 'Hello,' she said to the woman. 'I'm Jillq. Manager of the Therapy Hub.'

'Nice to meet you,' said the woman. 'There seems to be quite a few of you here.' Aljce melted away. She did not want to be anywhere near Jillq. Aljce couldn't stand her falseness, and she felt Jillq's energy like a toxic acid corroding hers. It was so unpleasant to be around, it made her skin prickle. If only the people here knew how horrible Jillq was; but she presented a confident, warm illusion to them all. There was no way any of them would believe that she was anything but sugar.

THE HOTEL POOL came up again over lunch. 'Who wants to go for a swim?' said Hattie brightly.

'I wouldn't mind,' said Mrs. Kingi. Aljce couldn't bring herself to.

'I haven't got my togs,' she said.

'Bra and undies,' said Chelsea.

'We all stick together,' said Jillq. 'Either we all go, or no one goes.' Aljce felt pressured. Everyone else clearly wanted to go, but just the thought sent chills over her body.

'Sure,' she said. No one would know if she turned up or not. She didn't

135

want to share the intimate experience of swimming in her undies with them. It would be like letting them inside herself.

'Straight after we've eaten then,' said Mrs. Kingi. 'Everyone meet at the pool gate. I'll get the key. We don't start again till two thirty.'

AT 1 O'CLOCK, someone knocked on Aljce's door. The door was locked. She hoped that they would think she was asleep, although the urge to do so had now strangely passed. Thank goodness she hadn't shared with Mrs. Kingi. She waited until they would all be in the pool, leaving plenty of time to spare. If she could sneak out through the gate, she could go for a walk. There was a park across the road, with big, leafy trees and soft grass underneath, and Aljce longed to escape to it. Although she wouldn't dare to smoke weed. When they saw her again, they would surely know. She remembered that she hadn't been able to bring any on the plane anyway, and sighed.

Opening the door, she turned in the opposite direction to the pool, and drew her shoulders low. 'Aljce!' said Hattie delightedly. Flight, fight or freeze jostled in Aljce's mid. Freeze won.

'I thought you were going for a swim,' she said.

'Jillq decided that there would be a team meeting instead.'

'Oh. Do we have to go?'

'I'm not going. I'm going for a swim. Come with me.'

'Are we allowed to?' asked Aljce, reluctantly. If there was one thing she wanted to do less than going for a swim, it was having a team meeting with Jillq.

'I'm sure no one will mind,' said Hattie. 'It was the original plan.'

'I haven't got my togs,' said Aljce.

'Did you bring them at all?'

'No.'

'I always bring mine to motels.'

'I don't go to motels.'

'Oh. Well, come and watch me swim.'

'Sure,' said Aljce.

Aljce tried to get comfortable on one of the deck chairs. They seemed to be made of light weight tin. Some of them had blown over. Hattie dipped her toe in the water. She wore a lime green and pink floral bikini. Hibiscuses, perhaps. Her hair was a similar soft pink to the flowers. Aljce hoped she wouldn't be long. At least if she was with Hattie, she could say that she hadn't known about the team meeting, and that she was at the swimming pool as instructed. Unless Hattie said that she'd told Aljce about the meeting. Perhaps she could say that she hadn't heard her. Hattie shrieked as she got in. The water was confirmed as cold. 'Coldish,' Hattie said. Of course it is, thought Aljce. The day is grey. The water's the colour of chilly air. I'm cold, and I'm nowhere near the water. Hattie breast stroked to the other side. Despite being leisurely, it took her only thirty seconds. She breast stroked back. Her own breasts floated on the water in front of her like a floaty ring of green and pink plastic.

Hattie pulled herself out and wrapped herself in a big fluffy towel. Aljce might have hoped they were leaving, but Hattie lay down on the deck chair next to Aljce. Aljce felt not at all in the spirit of things as she perched on the rim edge of hers. Hugging her knees made her feel warmer. Perhaps it was the water that made her feel cold. It was still spring. No wonder the wind was chill.

Hattie was in a friendly mood. She was like a big, soft white rabbit; all bosom and trembling nose. 'How are you getting on, Aljce?' she asked.

'Alright,' said Aljce guardedly.

'I get a bit worried about you,' said Hattie. Caution, thought Aljce. Hattie's let you down before. 'I found it really hard when I first started,' said Hattie. And she began to talk about herself. Aljce put in some encouragement. She didn't want to burn her bridges. Even though she couldn't trust Hattie, she might need her someday. 'I have to work, of course,' said Hattie. 'I'm a single mummy.' Aljce remembered that Hattie had said this before.

'I'm a single mother too,' she said. 'I have two children. Girls. Pleasance and Liddell.'

'What nice names,' said Hattie. 'My daughter is called Florabelle. We mainly just call her Belle.' And suddenly, they were talking just like mothers. Hattie was older than Aljce, and her daughter was older than Aljce's daughters, but they had motherhood in common.

All the same, Aljce couldn't wait to get back to her room, even if it was only for a short time. She still wasn't warm, and she was thankful when Hattie eventually stood up. And as she walked back to her room with Hattie still chatting alongside her, she wondered if maybe she might have said too much about herself. Everything you said could be used in evidence against you, she'd surely learned that. She cursed her own trusting nature.

'Don't forget the dinner,' said Hattie.

'Right,' said Aljce. And then, 'what dinner?'

'The Young Dream dinner. They're going to launch the posters.' Aljce's brain flailed like a duck's legs under water, and her face retained its goodbye smile by the skin of its teeth.

'We wouldn't have to go, would we?' she said. 'Dinner is out of work hours.'

'Aljce,' said Hattie with a horrified smile. 'This is what we've come up to Auckland for!'

'Aljce and Hattie. Where have you been?' inquired Jillq; placing her words with precision. Aljce looked at Hattie.

'We went for a swim,' said Hattie happily.

'Hattie went for a swim,' said Aljce.

'Please don't try and blame Hattie,' said Jillq. 'She at least is taking responsibility for herself.'

'We were expecting you there too,' said Aljce.

'Meeting!' said Jillq in a louder, more forceful version of her already rich voice. 'We were meeting! Together as a team! We must stand together.'

'Oh,' said Aljce. She wasn't quite sure what to say.

'When I call a meeting,' said Jillq, 'we meet.'

'I don't remember you saying,' said Aljce.

'I am saying now!' said Jillq.

'How was I supposed to know before?'

'You may not want to come to our meetings,' said Jillq, 'but it is expected.' Aljce felt an inward sigh. She felt as if she was slipping around in an infinity symbol.

'The water was lovely!' said Hattie brightly.

Aljce was too scared not to go to the dinner. There had been enough meetings about her. Perhaps she had been mentioned at the one after lunch. But the dinner was as awful as she had thought it would be. Hattie was late and had to push her way into the seating arrangement. 'Move down, move down!' she said, pouring water into what should have been Aljce's glass and taking Aljce's place at the end of the table, leaving her blocked in. Everyone was served the same meal. Rare steak. Aljce politely declined hers. I'm a vegetarian, she told the waitress. The waitress was sympathetic. 'I'll get them to find something for you,' she said. Jillq radiated disapproval from a few places down the table. Even in her quest not to put a foot out of line, Aljce was not eating meat to appease Jillq, but she was okay with not having another meal cooked for her.

'I'll be fine,' she assured the waitress. She wasn't fine. She sat there awkwardly, the only person with nothing to eat, in a roomful of people eating. She tried not to watch them; trying to shut out their plates full of slaughtered animals. Aljce had never been comfortable eating flesh. She could imagine what it would be like if aliens arrived on Earth, and sent her and her children off to be killed and cooked for an alien banquet.

The waitress reappeared with another plate. 'The chef had this in the fridge in case of vegetarians,' she said, clearly pleased to be so helpful. Aljce gazed at the plate in horrified fascination.

'What is it?' she asked.

'A vegetable terrine.' Aljce had never seen a vegetable terrine, or any terrine before. It seemed to be composed of the clear, pinkish jelly that was found in tinned cat meat and cheap pies, with vegetables encased inside it. Asparagus stuck out the ends of it. Aljce hated asparagus. What to do? People had gone out of her way to present her with this. Jillq was watching her with one eyebrow politely raised.

'Thank you very much,' she said to the waitress. 'That was nice of you to think of me.'

Once the waitress had left, Aljce had no idea what to do. She cut some of it up and mixed it around. There was no way she could eat it. She brought her empty fork to her mouth and pretended to chew. She cut up some more. She squashed bits. Eventually she secreted bits of it into the paper napkin on her knee, which she had placed there for that purpose. This was her idea of hell. Around her, people chatted happily to each other.

She left a goodly part of the terrine on her plate. 'If I'd had something made specially for me, I would have eaten it all,' said Jillq. Aljce knew that if Jillq were her, she would know what Aljce had done with the rest of the terrine, so it was lucky that she wasn't. Worse yet, Aljce had had to sit through several speeches about saving children by giving them dreams to follow, while the asparagus smell penetrated everything she had in her bag. There were posters, which were duly launched. Aljce didn't think the issue was really about needing to encourage children to dream big about being vets or forestry workers or teachers. Especially when no one was putting any money into actually facilitating this; they were just launching a handful of posters. Aljce thought that the issue was really about making sure that children had enough to eat, and got to school, and that they had no one hurting their feelings or their bodies. All kids had dreams. It was about making sure that they could achieve them if they chose to. She wondered how well-meaning people could go so wrong; and waste so much money in the wrong direction.

SHE DITCHED THE terrine in the bushes afterwards, and hoped that no one would find it in the morning. Surely it was biodegradable. She couldn't have stood the smell of asparagus in her room. Perhaps the birds would like it.

AT THE END of the next day, they had to go around the room and say what they'd particularly enjoyed about the conference. Aljce had appreciated the soft pillows on her motel bed at night. But she managed to say something about children being the future. She was not entirely sure what the conference had been supposed to achieve, but that seemed to be a general theme. Several people after her said the same thing. The woman with the beautiful pounamu came over to say goodbye to her. She was in charge of all the people across the country who were employed in the same role as Aljce, although none of the others were present. It was a regional position. She gave Aljce her card, which had her email address on it. 'Please get in touch if you need anything,' she said. Aljce tucked it away in case she needed it as a last resort.

'HUDDLE,' SAID JILLQ, halting suddenly, and causing everyone else to collide like dominos or cards, knocking against each other as they hurried in single file across the busy airport waiting room. Everyone gathered around her, sitting on their suitcases, or balancing them on their feet. 'We need to talk about Wally,' said Jillq. 'I'm really disappointed in him.' Aljce was surprised, and a little cheered, that this impromptu meeting was not about her. 'He knew that heart border was ours, and yet he used it on his proposal,' continued Jillq.

Aljce knew she shouldn't, but she couldn't help herself. 'Jillq, that's just a border available on Windows Publisher,' she said. 'He probably doesn't even know which borders we use in our agency. And there's also probably not many agencies that would consider themselves to have a signature border anyway. Perhaps he just thought it was appropriate for his project. It IS about healing child abuse.'

There was a dead silence.

Then Jillq recovered herself. 'Once again, Aljce, you are showing that you are not a team player,' she hissed. 'We will need to discuss this further when we get back to the Hub. I don't think it is too much to ask that you would support us! Plus, you were late getting on the plane on the way here too!' And she stomped off in the direction of the baggage check in signs. The others followed at a slight remove, taking care not to exhibit any body language which might indicate that they knew Aljce existed. Aljce followed a few metres behind all of them, and scored a seat all by herself on the airplane, for which she was entirely thankful.

In an instant of clarity Aljce knew that Jillq drew her power from her squad, her team. They were her protective barrier, between her and the world. She was brave from within her kingdom, and a coward without it. A small person. And that was why everyone had had to go to Auckland for a conference where most other organisations had sent a single representative. To make Jillq look big. Her organization so dedicated to supporting her that they could all afford to down tools and go to Auckland with her. Little did the other attendees know that their organisation did very little, and that no one was likely to realise that they were gone. Ahhh, the beauty of government contracts and being able to fudge those numbers. And being able to pencil things in.

Aljce's refusing to be a part of Jillq's protective covering was very disloyal in her eyes. People with entourages were not to be envied, Aljce thought. They needed adoration. They preferred to be surrounded by sycophants than to be in the company of equals. And equals would not agree to be followers. Aljce couldn't stand sycophants. She didn't know what was worse: to be surrounded by them, or to be one; always letting another person define what was cool and what to aspire to. She preferred to define her own reality, and she didn't need an audience to applaud it to make it real. Sycophants gave up that right to express themselves in exchange for the hope that they could mirror flashes of someone else and consider themselves coloured.

Jillq was content to have an entourage, and Mrs. Kingi, Marj, and Chelsea were sycophants. Perhaps they had moments when they were away from the majority and the strong will of Jillq, where they thought, what is happening, what am I doing? But when they were back in the fold, it was as if they were hypnotised, and they acted as if they were not themselves, but as if they were Jillq; carrying out her will. Was this how religious faith worked? Were they all doubters, who recovered their faith? Was Hattie? Faith, after all, didn't require evidence. It only required itself. Or were they just empty cavities, with no thoughts of their own, because they weren't bright enough to think for themselves? Were they just waiting to be filled with the thoughts of someone more dominant, or perhaps with promises of privileges and power?

Something in me has always marked me out as a target to some people, Aljce thought. People like Jillq. Perhaps it's because I can't just accept things without questioning them. Because I can't accept things on faith. Because I can't worship. Or perhaps people like her just have a nose for people like me, who have something vulnerable inside.

IT TAKES ALL THE RUNNING YOU CAN DO
TO KEEP IN THE SAME PLACE

Who am I going to be today? Aljce thought. Maybe the red skirt with the red and white striped socks. And the candy striped clutch purse with the blackened silver chain that meant she could sling it across her shoulder and balance the purse on her hip. Black Alice shoes. Red t-shirt with a black star and yellow yolk hammer and sickle. She could channel pirate. Russian pirate. She didn't need a black eye patch. That would be going too far. It was just the essence that she needed.

'Sailor, you're my only friend here,' said Aljce, giving him a smooge before she unlocked the door. 'Hello, building,' she said, as she walked down the corridors and through the rooms, pulling curtains and letting the sunlight in. It wasn't the building's fault that the people that used it were toxic, spreading their bad energy all across its interior. She felt kinship with the building. Right now, it had a light, clear energy; calm and still before anybody else came. The sunlight felt new and well intentioned. Clean.

Aljce sat at her desk, enjoying the building's emptiness. It felt nice. Eventually though, Marj came in. 'I put so much work into this place,' she said. 'I was crawling around underneath the building trying to sort out our internet until late last night.'

'That's very dedicated of you,' said Aljce carefully. She rather thought she'd heard about Marj crawling underneath the building before.

'Yes,' said Marj. 'I do a lot for this place. I hope it's appreciated.'

'I'm sure it is,' said Aljce, who was wondering if 'this place' was capable of appreciation. The building was. But the people didn't seem capable of much.

'It's been a terrible morning,' said Marj. 'I had to ring the Police on my neighbours.' Aljce sighed. She allowed Marj's voice to weave its mundane rings around her, like smoke, but not so much fun, and not so beautiful. Or perhaps the experience of Marj talking was less like smoke drifting, and more like concrete seeping. Inescapable and slow to set.

Aljce felt irritated and drained; trapped in her own boredom. What she really wanted to do was enjoy the sunshine of the empty building a little bit longer while it still lasted, and Marj was spoiling her opportunity to do so, without a thought in her head that Aljce might not be interested. Thankfully the pace was so slow that Aljce found she was able to lift her mind and think thoughts above the level of Marj's conversation and her responses. People like Marj didn't appreciate the different tones of sunshine, or realise that morning sunlight was like early season new potatoes with butter.

'So, what I think is that only boring people can hook up with boring people,' she had said to Strauss. 'They drive everyone else mad, even if they empathise with them and WANT to like them... It's just too dreary and soul destroying. And then they have boring children. But the children are even more boring, because the genetics of boring are converging on themselves. With every generation the DNA gets stronger. And that's Marj. A culmination of boring people making children together.'

As usual, Marj was completely unaware of her dullness. The irony that this morning Marj expected Aljce to sympathise with her as the protagonist in a story where Marj was totally unconscious of her lack of sympathy for others wasn't lost on Aljce. What Marj wanted from Aljce right now was what she herself didn't reciprocate to Aljce, which was even more galling given that Aljce's own need for support was genuine, and didn't exist within a context brought about by ignorant ego, as Marj's did. It was all about Marj, and her narrow, concrete life. There was a difference between Marj and Jillq though. Aljce judged Marj to be more stupid than mean. Perhaps she actually believed what Jillq said. Because she was too stupid to expect Jillq to lie.

LATER, AN OLD MAN appeared outside, apparently delegated to do the mowing, perhaps by the landlord or lady. He had tanned skin, the kind of brown that only a Pakeha out in the sun all the time can go. What Aljce liked about him was the thick hair on his chest, back and arms. It was all snowy white against the tan, and he looked like a space fox. Sometimes he came close to the Therapy Hub with his ride on mower, and Jillq would hurry out, and try and wave him down, presumably about the rabbits. As soon as he saw her, the space fox changed course, seemingly on a pre-planned track that had been decided long before she came out. Each time Aljce saw Jillq go out, her body language was more and more frustrated, and her stomp back to the building more pronounced.

Aljce walked down to the kitchen to find a place to be that wasn't her office. If she took less of a lunch break, she could at least justify going home sooner if someone caught her leaving five minutes early, and staying on site was easiest. Plus, with everyone competing to work so hard, she couldn't afford to be singled out as the one who didn't. As soon as she opened the door, she realised she'd made a mistake. What she had hoped would have been an empty refuge was full of her co-workers, sitting around the cheap wooden table that was way too big for the space. Usually they would have been eating outside in the sun. Perhaps the noise from the space fox's mower was responsible.

Talking stopped, leaving an immediate vacuum. 'Well, I must get back to work,' said Hattie standing up, her newly bright hair bobbing like one of Liddell's My Little Pony toys.

'Me too,' said Dulcie. Deidra giggled. Their food didn't seem finished, displayed like cards left on the table, mid hand.

'You don't have to go,' said Aljce. 'I can find somewhere else.'

'Why would you do that?' said Mrs. Kingi. 'There's room at the table now.' Aljce's thoughts collided at midpoint. It was nice to be welcomed. But she couldn't trust them. It was like being welcomed into a nest of something not quite right and not quite comfortable.

'Don't mind us,' said Dulcie. 'We've finished our break.' The words 'nobody likes you' echoed in Aljce's mind. She was sure that they were leaving because of her.

'I'm only getting a hot drink,' she said, squeezing awkwardly past Mrs. Kingi.

'Don't you eat?' asked Deidra, who was still lingering.

'Of course,' said Aljce. 'Just not right now.'

And while she was facing the zip on the wall to fill her cup with hot water, the room emptied itself.

ON HER WAY back to her office, she found someone sitting in the waiting area. They turned and smiled. 'Hi, Aljce,' they said. Aljce stopped.

'Hi,' she said, and then she saw it was Billie, whom she vaguely knew. Billie was a youth worker.

'Oh, I'm so glad to see a friendly face,' said Aljce, using her low tone of voice and hugging Billie.

'You said to come and network with you anytime,' said Billie.

'Oh, I did, and I'm so glad you came,' said Aljce, vaguely remembering that she had. 'Wait, I'll get us a room. Chelsea!' she called. 'Which room can I use?' Chelsea pulled the desk book towards her and poured over it.

'Hattie should be finished with the big room,' she said.

'So I can use that?' said Aljce.

'Yip. She'll only just be finished, but she should be out by now.'

'Cool,' said Aljce.

'So how's the new job?' Billie said as they walked down the corridor together.

'Um,' Aljce had started to say, intending to indicate that Billie should wait until they were in the room before she'd answer, but the words left her mind when Hattie pushed past them from behind just as they started to go into the room; like a rabbit sprinting for its burrow.

'No, no, no,' she was saying. 'You can't come in here.'

'Why not,' said Aljce, confused and still trying to get in, even though Hattie was obviously blocking the door with her body. Surely Hattie was joking around with her. No other theory came to her mind, even though she found it slightly annoying. Until Hattie's voice rose a notch and became shrill. And she pushed Aljce.

'What's wrong?' said Aljce still confused.

'I have this room,' said Hattie. 'I have it booked.'

'Chelsea said you'd finished with your client,' said Aljce.

'The notes,' shrieked Hattie. 'The notes are still on the board!' Aljce looked. Some stuff was written on the white board, although it appeared not to make any sense. Hattie moved in front of Aljce's line of sight. 'Stop looking at them! They're confidential!'

'Oh. Sorry. Chelsea said we could use this room.'

'Chelsea knows that I have the room booked for a half hour after I finish an appointment,' hissed Hattie.

'Look, can we still use the room?' said Aljce. 'After all, I work here, and Billie's a youth worker. We will be very confidential.'

Hattie almost pushed her again as she manoeuvred Aljce out into the corridor. 'No problem,' said Aljce. 'I'll ask Chelsea for another room.' She was embarrassed to have Billie see this fuss. Hattie swished back down the corridor with them.

'Aljce was trying to use my room,' she said to Chelsea.

'Oh,' said Chelsea. 'Didn't you know about the half hour waiting rule?'

146

'But you said I could use the room,' said Aljce.

'Oh, not immediately though,' said Chelsea.

'But you knew I needed it immediately.'

'But there's a half hour waiting time.'

'Why didn't you say anything about it?'

'I thought you knew.'

'You knew I was going to need it straight away!'

'What is the problem?' said Jillq.

Hattie turned around, still vibrating outrage. 'Aljce has been trying to get into my session room and look at my client notes on the board.'

'I'm not interested in your client notes!' said Aljce. 'I thought I could use the room to network with Billie!'

'I think I'd better go,' said Billie.

'I'll find us a different room,' said Aljce. 'There must be one that isn't booked.'

'I only had half an hour anyway,' said Billie. 'I shot up here in my car, and by the time I've gotten back again, it'll be nearly gone. Next time, Aljce!' Aljce watched her melting away.

'So Aljce, you have been causing trouble again,' said Jillq from her left.

'There has been a misunderstanding,' said Aljce. 'Chelsea said we could use the room.'

'You tried to push past me,' said Hattie. Aljce sighed in exasperation. 'I thought you were just kidding around,' she said.

'You saw the client notes behind me.'

'I didn't even realise what they were. AND I work here. When I did that first training, and we used those actual client forms to practice on, Jillq said that as long as we all worked here, confidentiality between ourselves didn't matter. Not sure that you were there.'

'We all just have to be mindful,' said Jillq. 'Aljce, you have broken confidentiality. We have no idea who that was that you had with you.'

'Billie from Youth Services,' said Aljce. 'She came up to network. She never saw the notes. And even if she had, no one would have been able to decipher them.'

'I am going back to the room to transcribe them and remove them immediately!' said Hattie.

So much for having an ally, thought Aljce. Surely Hattie knew that there had just been a misunderstanding. She couldn't have thought otherwise. And why hadn't Chelsea told her that she had to wait half an hour? Why didn't she give her another room? There were other smaller rooms which were empty. 'We will deal with this another time,' said Jillq. 'And is that cat hair on your clothes? How unprofessional, Aljce.'

'Why didn't you tell me to wait?' Aljce asked Chelsea when Jillq had retired. Chelsea smiled like sugar.

'I thought you knew,' she said.

'I thought you knew I didn't,' said Aljce.

'You'll probably have to learn the rules,' said Chelsea. Aljce forced a smile onto her face. She couldn't afford to actually alienate anyone for real. The rules are that there are no rules and that you make them up to suit yourselves, she thought.

'Sure,' she said aloud. 'Is there a copy of the rules anywhere?'

'No,' said Chelsea. 'You just have to learn them.' Aljce gritted her teeth behind her smile. She needed to fight the subversive war. Having a meltdown would only give them the opportunity to say she was crazy.

'Next time, I will book a room,' she said as sweetly as she could.

'As long as you know that Hattie always has the big room, and she requires it to be free for half an hour afterwards,' said Chelsea. So why did you give it to me, thought Aljce. Surely Chelsea was a willing participant in this game, no matter how friendly she seemed.

Later, she wondered if Hattie's favoured room status was the reason that Hattie hadn't supported her earlier, when she'd indicated that she would. Hattie seemed to get a lot of special treatment, and Jillq seemed to like her.

'She ran past me like a white rabbit,' Aljce said to Mamae.

'What was even her problem?' said Mamae.

'Who knows,' said Aljce, exhaling smoke into the darkness. 'I can't get her at all. She knows what's happening, and she moans about it, but then she's happy to be part of it. It's as if her moral ground keeps shifting. But how can you have a moral ground if it shifts? That's the anti-definition of moral ground.'

'I dunno Aljce, but it sounds good,' said Mamae, laughing. 'I'm too stoned to contemplate.'

'This is the best time for contemplating.'

'Give me that joint back again then. Maybe a bit more and my contemplating will catch up to yours.'

'If it hasn't overshot.'

'That's very unhostess of you, Aljce. And there's moth dust in my hot water.'

'It's stoner dust. It's in my curtains and on the clothes, and lying on the floor.'

'What, like kif in the carpet?' 'Nah, it's more indefinable than that. Although that is part of it; weed in my laptop keyboard. It's a heavy, sweet scent that gets stirred up when I walk. Oily air. You must have it...'

'Smoking's only one thing to do in a day, ay? But you can do it while you're doing all the other things, and they're even better.'

'Yeah, like, look at us now, listening to music. We can listen better.'

'I like it while I do the housework as well. Get rid of that moth dust.'

'Why would you?'

But on this particular night, Aljce was filled with the sort of energy that even smoking couldn't cut into, and when Mamae left, she drifted into vaguely threatening melancholy. She realised through blurry eyes that the trapped air bubbles in the bright yellow wax globules in her lava lamp made them look like cratered moons. Tears. They provided a new perspective. Perhaps I just enjoy a bit of self-pity, she thought. Although why I allow myself to, I don't know. Self-pity is unproductive and destructive.

THERE WAS A small flicker of hope at work. 'I'm doing up last year's minutes for the Board,' said Chelsea importantly, as Aljce walked past on her way to the toilet.

'What's that for?'

'The Board AGM. We're all expected to go.' Aljce blinked. More expectations. She made a conscious effort to think of an excuse she could keep in reserve. Then she had another thought.

'Oh. Is that the Board of here? This organisation? Who's on the Board?' said Aljce, attempting to sound casual, even though her mind was racing. Perhaps there could be an avenue for her salvation. Perhaps there were people she could complain to about Jillq. People who would be in their rational minds, who would support her.

'Well, we all are,' said Chelsea. Plus Rose from the Council. And Pansy. And Queenie Marama. She represents a club. Jillq's always trying to get new people on to the Board. It's hard. No one shows any commitment.'

Aljce sighed. 'We all are' wasn't promising. Still, there was Rose from the Council. And Pansy. And someone called Queenie. She needed to go, to see if any of them were receptive to hearing her story.

'So Aljce.' Jillq spoke from somewhere behind her. Aljce waited. She had known that Jillq would catch up with her, and wasn't going to give her anything to hang anything off. But inside she could feel her adrenalin diffusing throughout her gut. Disappointed, Jillq continued. 'We need to discuss confidentiality.' Aljce had a conversation in her own head. Will it still be confidential if there's a discussion?' she asked herself. Unsurprisingly, Jillq didn't hear her. 'You brought a person here, and took them to a room with case notes on the board. That is an unforgivable breach of confidentiality. We should not have anyone who doesn't work here in the rooms.'

'Unless they're clients,' put in Mrs. Kingi cheerfully as she went past.

'Clients will not be in rooms where the boards haven't been cleared,' announced Jillq grandly. 'It is our responsibility to wait until client work has been wiped off the board before we take clients into rooms.'

'I didn't know there was anything on the board,' said Aljce, forgetting her resolution to say as little as possible.

'And we certainly don't take guests into our offices!' said Jillq, with the air of someone playing a trump card. 'Loose files on desks. Confidential information on computer screens. Who knows what they might see?' Aljce's mind flashed back. She had given Billie a peak into her office on their way along the corridor. What the hell, and who had noticed, or was Jillq merely making it up as she went along, on the assumption that if it was said, it became the story?

'Why is Deidra allowed in the offices then?'

'Deidra is family!' said Jillq, sounding scandalised that Aljce could query Deidra's presence anywhere at the Therapy Hub. 'I think we all know that we can trust Deidra.' Deidra was not a nice person, but Aljce knew that she needed not to follow this line any further, or Jillq would say that she was accusing Deidra of being untrustworthy. Of being a liar, a thief or a sneak. And then Aljce would be the traitor, the betrayer, not Deidra. Jillq had played it well.

But she didn't rest. 'You should not be looking at another worker's notes!' she declared regally. 'Confidentiality is foundational!'

'So how come, when I first came here, we practiced filling in the forms with forms with real client notes on them?' asked Aljce.

'That was an oversight,' said Jillq, 'and quickly rectified. It is most uncharitable of you to even bring it up, Aljce. We don't want further non confidential disclosures! I hope you will not put those clients at risk. You have already put Hattie's client at risk. Confidentiality is unavoidably foundational, and I am very clear about our need to be mindful of it!'

I'm on a losing game here, thought Aljce. She had to admire how Jillq could turn absolutely everything against her, despite the fact that what she said was fucked up fabrication.

'But that isn't the worst thing,' said Jillq. 'You have embarrassed us all. You were seen sleeping at the conference.'

'I nodded off for, like, ten seconds!' said Aljce. 'Because we'd had to get up early to catch the plane!'

'Everyone was up early,' said Jillq. 'You are the only one who embarrassed us.' Aljce decided to go back to carrying on the conversation on in her head. Because I didn't fall into an alcohol-induced sleep on the plane, she thought. 'Furthermore, you cheapened a woman's taonga!' said Jillq. 'Telling her that it looked as if she'd bought it at the two dollar shop!'

'Oh, hey, there's been a misunderstanding,' said Aljce. 'I admired hers, she admired mine in return, and I told her that I got it at the two dollar shop. She was perfectly okay with the conversation.'

'You always have your own version of the story, don't you Aljce?'

There was a pause. They were still standing in the corridor. Jillq sighed. 'It's so hard to get through to you Aljce,' she said. 'I find it very frustrating.' Spare a thought for me, said Aljce to herself. There was little point in talking to anyone else when she was the only one who made any sense. 'So we are putting you on notice. We will know where you are at all times. There should be no need for you to leave the building without express permission. I will create a list of tasks for you to work through. It's clear that you need more focus. You don't display any ability to self-manage.' Aljce considered the semantics and decided not to argue. It was not a written warning. The possibility was open that she might need to leave the building without express permission. And Jillq's stated 'knowing' of where Aljce was didn't place any responsibility on Aljce. I'm becoming devious like her, she thought.

Who had been standing behind her, listening in on her conversation with the woman with the beautiful taonga? Aljce couldn't remember.

Stress was messing with her mind. Had whoever misunderstood her words, or had they deliberately misreported them? Jillq could have purposefully misinterpreted them, but Aljce knew that the others weren't above participating in that.

MARJ WAS THE one who gave her the list. Create a second pamphlet. Research the history of her role, nationally. Create a power point. Vacuum the entire building. Update all the files. What did that mean? If you hadn't seen a client, how could you add to a file? The two who had agreed to come had been no shows. Maybe they'd heard things about the Therapy Hub from other people. Who knew? Perhaps she could ring them. She had no client contact hours yet. But 'NO CLIENT CONTACT until ALL tasks are complete!!!' was underlined at the bottom. Aljce considered her options. She could disobey. Or she could rush through the tasks so quickly that they would have no idea that they were completed, and do what she pleased. That was probably the smartest choice, given that Mrs. Kingi had been working on some pamphlet or other since Aljce had been there, and had apparently been working on it for the best part of a year. She only went out to see a client every week or so. They would never dream that Aljce could knock the list off in about a week. She would date the files and update each of them with the sentence 'no contact since the last entry.' They would never guess she was finished and free to do actual client work again. She gave herself a dark internal smile. Stupid games that shouldn't have to be played, she thought.

'So are you clear on it all?' asked Marj. 'We don't want any misunderstandings.'

'Of course not,' said Aljce. 'Thank you, Marj.' And even that could be misread. She hoped that Marj wasn't aware of semantics.

'That's good,' said Marj. 'If you need any help with anything, just come and see me. Although I AM so busy that I nearly didn't get home at all last night!'

'What are you doing?' asked Aljce. There was no harm in keeping Marj as much on side as possible.

'Oh, just updating the computer files,' said Marj.

'How do you do that?'

'Oh, I check to make sure that everything has been entered, and if it has, I sign it off.'

'How do you know it's all been entered?' Marj sighed, but didn't elaborate.

'It's a lot of work, Aljce. I give a lot of myself to my work. I'm here till all hours! Not sure if the place could run without me!'

'I'm sure it wouldn't be the same,' said Aljce.

'I'VE SAID IT before, and I'll say it again. Why don't you leave?' said Strauss.

'Fuck, I wish. Just can't afford it. Plus there's not many places that I can get a Student Placement to get my contact hours. And they're probably not hiring. I can't afford to do an unpaid one. If I wanna achieve my goals, this is the price.'

'Seems a bit high. If it was me, I'd just say fuck you.'

'Yeah, but you're not trying to get somewhere. Not this somewhere, anyway. I can't burn my forward facing bridge.'

'Maybe you're supposed to go somewhere else, across some other bridge.'

'That'd be nice, but I don't see one. That's why I'm so determined.'

'As long as they don't blow your bridge up from under you.'

'Yeah.'

ALJCE WAS REALLY looking forward to her external supervision session, but not only would she have to sneak out, which she was nervous about, but she also wasn't sure how to approach the subject of her employer. Would Edyth, her supervisor, believe her? Edyth was fond of self-reflection, and Aljce approved of self-reflection too. Perhaps Aljce could approach it from the point of view of how she herself could respond to them; what she could do better. So that no one would see her leave, she parked her car down the road from the Therapy Hub on the morning of her appointment, went to the toilet later, and didn't come back from there.

'Not much actual client work yet,' said Edyth. 'I suppose you are still a student, and they're right to ease you in to it.'

'I have five hundred hours of direct client time to collect before I can apply for my provisional registration,' said Aljce. 'I wish they'd let me get on with doing some.' Edyth frowned.

'Yes. So what are your options? How can you show them that you're competent?'

'Well,' said Aljce, 'they do have a list of admin tasks for me. Perhaps if I show I can do that…'

'Good,' said Edyth. 'Perhaps they're waiting for you to prove yourself.'

'Could we do our next session actually at the Therapy Hub please?' asked Aljce. 'They're a bit funny about me leaving the building. They say that they don't know what I'm doing.' Edyth frowned.

'Difficult for an organisation to function if they can't trust their own employees,' she observed. 'Have you done anything to justify their mistrust?'

'I don't think so,' said Aljce. 'Although it doesn't seem as if I can do anything right from their point of view. I'm still in my ninety day trial period, and I feel like I'm walking on egg shells. Because if they decide I'm not up to the job at the end of that time, they can discontinue me.'

'They'd have to be able to justify it,' said Edyth.

'I just don't want to give them any reasons,' said Aljce. 'I've heard that it's hard to win in Employment Court, and I don't want to have to go through that. I'd prefer to just move straight into day ninety one without any fuss. Financially, I can't afford to lose my job. That's why it would be good if you could come to me. I mean there's no real reason why I shouldn't come here; but I don't want to upset them if I can avoid it.'

'Supervision is a core component of counselling,' said Edyth. 'Whether you're a student or an experienced practitioner. Surely they understand that?'

'I rather think Jillq sees herself as being all that me or anyone else needs,' said Aljce.

'Well, I'm happy to come to you. But I find it rather strange.'

'Me too.'

ALJCE DIDN'T WANT to remind Jillq about the line management by having Edyth come, but Jillq had never mentioned it after that first time, and Aljce was hopeful that she preferred her interactions with Aljce to be witnessed and strengthened by her accomplices. It would be just Jillq and Aljce in line management. And Jillq HAD ticked off external supervision on Aljce's Placement contract. But what if Edyth came to the Therapy Hub, and Jillq tried to dazzle her with her loveliness? Jillq did good dazzle. Until she turned it off. Of course she made out that it saddened her to say the things she said to Aljce, but she excused herself by letting everyone know that it was all provoked by Aljce. Perhaps she was just projecting her own mean self onto Aljce. Perhaps Aljce was part of Jillq's own illusion. A villain to make herself a saint.

Surely, some level, Jillq must know her behaviour was wrong. Because she took steps to cover it up. But on another level, she believed she could justify it. She came from an entirely self-centred perspective, and you could justify anything from that angle, because all angles were your angle. The quantum wave/particle duality again. It was wrong and it wasn't, and it only became one thing or another from the observer's point of view. Perhaps Jillq simultaneously perceived that it was both wrong and that it wasn't, but because her mind was so disorganised, those two things never faced each other full on.

CHELSEA LOOKED UP when Aljce came back in. Aljce cursed. She'd thought Chelsea would be on a lunch break, and that she'd be able to sneak back into the building. She hoped that she didn't know that she'd been told that she wasn't supposed to leave without express permission. 'Where have you been?' she asked. Aljce didn't feel like justifying herself to Chelsea. Who knew whether she might present it wrapped up in different paper later, when she was reporting to Jillq. Perhaps she kept notes.

'Community meeting,' she said.

'What for?'

'Networking. Telling other people what my role is. Finding out what they do in case I get clients that might benefit from their services.'

'We're a one-stop wrap-around service shop,' said Chelsea. 'We don't need to refer out.' Aljce felt as if she could hear Jillq speaking through Chelsea's mouth.

'Surely if a client needs specialist services ... or they could benefit from a programme we're not running ourselves...' she said.

'We're a one-stop therapy shop,' repeated Chelsea. She clearly didn't know that Aljce was grounded, and not allowed out at all, or she would be tittle tattling right now.

'Sure,' said Aljce dryly. 'One-stop shop.' No point in arguing with people who'd already made up their minds and didn't intend to change them. Especially if they were the Administrative Greeter or the Clinical Administrator. Who was Aljce to argue with them?

Can I be a good person if I'm a liar? she wondered. If I lie about where I've been and what I've done, am I not exactly who they say I am?

Perhaps I have done something to justify their mistrust. She countered her first thought. I wouldn't have to lie if they weren't so unreasonable. True, but what is it doing to my karma to be behaving exactly as they said I would just so that I can do things that no one should have to lie about? Is this how people start off here? Is this how to become like them? Aren't liars on the side of darkness rather than on the side of light? Can there be a case for lying in the service of what's right and good? Corruption by confusion, she thought.

'HELLO PEPPER,' she said, arriving back at her office.

'I'm not allowed to talk to you,' said Pepper, continuing to play under Aljce's desk with some fake diamonds that had come from off her kiddie bracelet. 'Mum said you're not a very nice person.'

'Oh,' said Aljce. 'I suppose you'd better do what Mum says. I don't want to get you into trouble.'

'Why aren't you very nice?' said Pepper.

'I don't know,' said Aljce.

'I don't know either,' said Pepper. 'But Mum says that nobody likes you.'

'She might be right,' said Aljce sadly. There were no friends her for her here. No safe place anywhere. She wished she had a safe person place to go to. Actually, that was what she wanted in life. A safe person place, where she could feel absolute trust that they would never purposefully hurt her, and whether she stayed or went mattered to them as much as breathing did. Where they were thrilled that she had chosen them, because they thought she was so special. Sometimes it seemed that there was no one for her, not even a friendly face.

Pepper clambered out from under and scuttered away down the corridor.

ALJCE HAD HER own children to worry about. 'Of course they will know we smoke weed,' said Strauss. 'Mothers who burn incense always like weed. And when they realise that, they will just know. Without any fuss.'

'Well, hopefully.'

'Think about it when you get there. Don't stress out about it now. Pointless.'

'Hopefully it won't be illegal by then.'

They sat on peeling vinyl chairs, in the mouth of the garage, on the event horizon between darkness and light. It wasn't really that cold, but the air was wet with the thick rain.

'Part of me is freaking out that I've got big fat raindrops just sitting on my eyelids; fat, yinno,' said Strauss. 'But I'm too stoned to bother to get them off because they really don't matter. And other parts of me are appreciating that I've never had exactly this experience before. So I should just enjoy it.'

'Yes, you should. Appreciation.'

The light slap of Steinie's tongue against his fur gave competition to the patting slosh of the rain. Aljce ran her hand lightly over his black, slightly damp back. She wanted the real time feeling of murky cat on her hands. She wanted to rub the smell through her hair. He began to purr. The sound of that and the soft splat of rain arrived into her same ears at the same time. Did they mix? How did she filter them into separate streams?

The droplets trapped in the dense forks of the rose bush off to the side of Aljce were clouds of diamonds, shimmering each other loose. Aljce thought about something Lewis had said. 'Rain makes me ache.'

'Where?'

'In my joints and in my bones. My knees and in my shoulders I suppose. Sort of everywhere.'

'Why?'

'I've got no idea. It's just come over me slowly. There was a time when I didn't ache at all, and now there isn't,' he had said.

'I honestly don't know what I'd do without you to talk to Strauss,' said Aljce.

THE NEXT MORNING, Aljce's early sunshine was interrupted by the ringing of the phone. On one hand, it was actual work. On the other hand, she just loved this time before anyone else came in, and she could just be, without worrying about how she was being. Conscientiousness got the best of her. She must remember to record the call in the message book, she thought as she walked out of her office to answer the phone at Chelsea's empty desk. She had been told off by Marj for not recording the calls in the message book. 'Even if they don't want to leave a message?' she'd asked in surprise.

'Yes, that's very important!' said Marj, and once again Aljce could hear Jillq in someone else's mouth.

'Kia ora, Therapy Hub,' she said, picking up the phone.

'So you've finally answered!' said the other person.

'Sorry,' said Aljce, 'I had to walk down the hallway to get here. The main phone isn't connected to my desk phone, and our receptionist, our Clinical Administrator, she's not here at the moment.'

'That's not what I mean,' said the woman. 'I've left message after message, and no one gets back to me. No one picks up the phone.'

'Oh,' said Aljce. 'I'm sorry about that. But here I am. Can I help?'

'I'm looking for Mrs. Kingi,' said the woman.

'She's not in,' said Aljce.

'Of course she's not. When is she ever in? That's what I'm ringing to complain about.'

'Oh.'

'I was told that she was a Whanau Social Worker. That she would work with my daughter.'

'Oh. Yes, that is her role.'

'Well, she's not doing it!'

'Um,' said Aljce, fascinated.

'She said she would work on a suicide safety plan for my daughter. She was going to meet with us about how we could keep her safe. When we came in, she told us that we didn't need to worry. You were a one-stop wrap-around therapy shop, and everything would be sorted. She was supposed to see my daughter every week!'

'And didn't she?'

'Hell no. We haven't seen her once.'

'We've been away at a conference in Auckland...'

'For the last six months?'

'Um. No.'

'Well, you can tell her that my daughter tried to kill herself last night, and nearly succeeded. She's in intensive care.'

'Oh, my gosh, I'm so sorry.'

'Are you? Well, you can tell Mrs. Kingi that she and her service are rubbish, and that from now on we'll be working with the proper mental health service and that I hope that one day she has to go through something like our family's been through, and not get the help that she's been promised, and then she'll know what it's like!'

'Um, yes. I can tell her. Can I say who is calling when I tell her?' said Aljce, mindful of the message book in front of her.

'Pretty sure she'd know. But then, maybe she treats all her clients just the same. Perhaps she'll have no idea. The Mental Health Social Worker says your service's process is very unsafe. I'll spell my name, it's an unusual one.' Aljce copied it down. What would she write in the message book? She could detail the woman's complaint, but would that come back to her? Would they say she encouraged it? It would be satisfying to see it written down in the book in matter of fact language. 'Call for Mrs. Kingi from a client. Wishes to discontinue services as no work has been done with the family for the last six months, and messages have been ignored. Due to the recent suicide attempt of the client's daughter, the family wishes to discontinue Therapy Hub service, under advice from the mental health services that it's unsafe.' She held it in her head as a little fantasy for a few seconds, but then she let it go. 'Client rang for Mrs. Kingi. Wishes to discontinue service,' she contented herself with.

'I'm sorry that this has happened to you and your daughter and your family,' she told the woman. 'I hope things go well with Mental Health Services.'

'Thank you,' said the woman. 'Are you sure you work there? You should leave.'

'Aljce,' said Mrs. Kingi, 'what's this phone message? Chelsea showed me as soon as I came in!' Aljce stirred reluctantly. She eyed the clock. It was nearly half past ten. It was a nice life for some.

'The lady rang earlier this morning,' she said warily.

'What's this?' said Jillq, appearing behind Mrs. Kingi.

'What did she want?' said Mrs. Kingi.

'She wants to discontinue service,' said Aljce.

'What? After all we've done for her?' said Mrs. Kingi.

'Who is it?' said Jillq.

'You remember her,' said Mrs. Kingi to Jillq. 'Her daughter was raped.'

'Oh, yes,' said Jillq. 'We've done quite a lot. Pushy woman. Difficult to deal with. Wanted immediate service.'

Didn't get that, thought Aljce.

'Yes, that's the one,' said Mrs. Kingi. 'Always leaving messages on my phone. She's got no idea how busy I am!'

'We're all busy here,' said Jillq. 'I don't know what she expects.'

'Well, that's one less to worry about anyway,' said Mrs. Kingi.

'Her daughter made a suicide attempt. She's in intensive care,' said Aljce.

'Well, I hope they don't just expect us to jump for their little crisis,' said Jillq.

'No, I think they're with Mental Health Services now,' said Aljce.

'Well, that's something,' said Mrs. Kingi. 'That woman was really pushy. No wonder her daughter's so messed up! Some people should really look at themselves.'

'Exactly,' said Jillq.

At least, thought Aljce, they were so busy justifying themselves that it didn't come back on me. Although they could save it up for later if they get short of other material. Why didn't anyone else at work see how awful they were?

HANNAH RANG ALJCE after work hours. 'How are you getting on?' she said.

'Not good,' said Aljce, telling her a little bit about it. Well, it was only a fraction of what had occurred, but it took a long time.

'Hmm. Do you know Toti who works at the other counselling service?'

'Yeah. Sort of.'

'Well,' said Hannah. 'He worked for Jillq. And he left suddenly. People say he says she's a bully.'

'Why did he say that?'

'I don't know. This is just a rumour.'

'Pity I didn't know that before I left you and came to work at the Therapy Hub.'

'I know. I'll see what else I can find out.'

'I should have done more research before I left.'

'You couldn't know that she would turn out to be such a bitch. Don't blame yourself.' Thank goodness for Hannah, thought Aljce.

CONTRARIWISE

AlJCE WENT ACROSS the hallway into Marj's office to borrow a stapler. It didn't seem as if one would be purchased for her, and she hadn't yet had the money to buy the larger stationery items for herself. Marj was in there, staring at her computer screen, and oblivious to Aljce noticing a grid record of her own arrival and leaving times lying on Marj's desk. She knew it referred to her because her name was underlined at the top. 'Oh,' she said. 'How do you know what time I get here in the morning when I arrive before all of you?'

'Aljce!' said Marj. 'You shouldn't be looking on my desk!'

'I came in to get the stapler, and caught sight of my name.'

'Jillq wanted me to keep a record.'

'Of course she did.'

'Well, she needs to know what's happening...'

'Of course she does.'

'I wouldn't have kept a record, but Jillq asked me to. Oh, gosh. I hope she won't be angry.' Gosh, thought Aljce. I'm the one who should be angry.

'Why should she be angry with you?'

'She didn't want you to know ... are you going to tell her?' Telling Jillq was the last thing on Aljce's mind. Telling tales would make her no better than the rest of them, and she didn't wish any of what had been happening to her on Marj.

'I'm sure that there's lots of employers who ask their employees to spy on another employee, Marj. Don't worry about it,' said Aljce, aware of the irony that she was the one reassuring Marj; even if it was laced with sarcasm, which went over Marj's head.

'Thanks, Aljce,' Marj said gratefully, shuffling the piece of paper out of sight.

Perhaps that was how everything ticked. People got points for tell-tal-ing on each other, and that was how you became Jillq's favourite and redirected her bullying on to someone else.

Is THAT WHY it's always me? she thought idly as she watched the rabbits. There was so much time to think at work. Some of Jillq's words from the meeting earlier in the week still sang sour notes in her head. 'It's not me, it's you, Aljce. Everyone else here and I get on perfectly well. You might want to wonder why you are not fitting in.' Because Jillq's words were factually correct. It WAS Aljce who wasn't fitting in. Everyone else got on perfectly well. No one else's words and actions were being twisted in unfavourable ways. No one else was walking on egg shells and wondering what would go wrong next. But maybe no one else ever queried Jillq. Maybe no one else ever pointed out how bizarre things were. Maybe everyone was happy to gloss over things for an easy ride. Aljce couldn't imagine being fake for an easy ride. Particularly if someone else was being bullied.

Maybe all the good people had left, and what remained at the Therapy Hub was a collection of sycophants. People who were happy to ignore other people's distress; happy even to participate in it if it was ultimately good for them in some way. People who probably wouldn't be bullies if left to themselves, but when someone else led them into it, were quite happy to comply. People who played nice until they became enablers for the bully, and then their self-centred narcissism became apparent. Apaths. It was going to make Aljce's strategy of winning people over with her friendly and kind personality very difficult to say the least, because these were people whose only real loyalty was to themselves and whoever else was convenient. And Aljce was not convenient or expedient.

She had learned on Pinterest, where she had created a special board, that there were two types of narcissists: the sociopath type, who enjoyed hurting others, and went out of their way to do so, and the ones that really only showed themselves when someone crossed them or when they needed benefit for themselves. Dormant narcissists, who only bloomed when the rains came. Jillq was a sociopath who had surrounded herself with dormant narcissists, and she had rained on them. Feeding and watering them what they needed for their egos, in return for letting her destroy any fresh prey. And they were happy to watch her do that. Symbiosis, they'd called it at school. The others were safe. They fitted in.

And there would always have to be prey. Jillq required it. She fed off it. Preferably the person who might not always buy the party line, or the okay line, and who was likely to challenge it. That person wouldn't keep silent while someone else was bullied, so it might as well be them rather

162

than the someone else. Someone who would self-reflect and doubt themselves was also a good choice of target. Someone who couldn't be fake. She centred on herself again. Plus, I'm super good at my job. Hold up... sounds like narcissism, she thought. Was she a narcissist too? But she knew from her previous work that she was good with people, and good at helping them heal their emotional pain. It was okay to acknowledge your strengths, as long as you were always working to improve by noticing where you needed to do that. And remembered that there were things you weren't good at. Aljce was no good at running fast or restraining herself from asking questions.

But being at the Therapy Hub had taught her that she was great at making pamphlets too. Plus she had a university degree and was studying counselling. If Jillq had to hate on someone, why not the somewhat competent person who queried Jillq's therapy techniques; the one she was scared might choose to expose her as an empress with no clothes? A queen with a fake crown?

And perhaps it helped bond her team around her to share a common enemy.

THERE WAS A man in a blue suit vaping in the staff kitchen area. Jillq would not have approved. And even though it smelled like bubble-gum, Aljce wasn't sure that she approved herself. She tried to back out again. She didn't want to be associated with any wrong doing. The man looked accusingly at her. 'Another one of you treating me like a leper,' he said. 'I feel as if I'm in quarantine! Who are you?' He spoke in a clipped way, as if every word was its own sentence. 'Who. Are. You?'

'I was going to ask you the same thing,' said Aljce. You had to be careful. You could never be sure where anyone else stood. The man huffed out an annoyed smoke ring which drifted right up to the top of the hot water zip before unravelling.

'Your Manager has left me in here for nearly two hours, and you can say what you like: that's rude.'

'It IS rude,' said Aljce, sensing a potential ally, by still wary. The man gave her a suspicious squint with his sky blue eyes.

'Going to tell her what I say, are you?'

'Other people might tell Jillq,' said Aljce, 'but I would not be one of them. In fact, I am probably the only one here who wouldn't.'

'Why don't you leave if you don't like her?' the man asked. His long fingers twirled his vaping pipe in and out between themselves.

'Paying the mortgage. Feeding the kids. It can be hard to get another job in a town like this, especially if your last employer says bad things about you. Employers are biased towards the words of other employers. They don't care about the employee's side of things. Plus, if I'm honest, I suppose I just don't like to fail.' The man blew some more smoke rings, and they drifted across the table. He looked at his watch.

'Why don't you leave if you don't like her?' asked Aljce, turning his own question back on him.

'Right,' said the man. 'I guess I don't like to fail either.'

And then Aljce realised what a lovely energy he had. Calm and encouraging. Underneath what he said. 'Did you have a happy childhood?' she said. He didn't regard the question as unusual.

'My mother and father stayed together,' he said, 'and I suppose everybody loved each other. Treated each other with kindness and respect. So yes, I'd say I had a pretty happy childhood.'

'Perhaps that accounts for your energy,' she said. He gave no sign that he found this bizarre, and he lifted his cup and finished his coffee.

'If she's not here,' he said, 'I am going to go.' Aljce frowned. She felt that she needed him to stay. But she could think of no reason that she could use for asking him too. She considered what she could say for so long that it was too long.

I SHOULD HAVE seen him out, she thought; considering further considerations. I could have kept talking to him if I'd done that. But if she left now, she'd be running after him into the car park. Mad. And she couldn't have kept talking to him. Someone would have seen and reported it.

She opened the windows to let out the vape smoke. The man in the blue suit had left half a pink cupcake uneaten on his plate, and she picked the cherry off and ate it before throwing the rest of it in the bin. She didn't want to get blamed for an untidy staff table. She was just finishing her hot drink when Jillq put her head around the door. 'Who are you looking for?' said Aljce, forcing herself to attempt conversation to show that she wasn't paralysed by Jillq, even though it felt surreal to be friendly to someone she knew was her fiercest enemy.

'I thought I left a man here,' said Jillq, every bit as cross as the man himself had been.

'There was a man here, but he said he had to go,' said Aljce.

'I hope it isn't your rudeness that's driven him away, Aljce, said Jillq. 'What did you say to him?' Aljce sighed. She could almost predict another meeting being called to discuss her imaginary sins. 'I think we need to have another meeting,' said Jillq. She sniffed the air. 'I hope you haven't been smoking in here, Aljce. We don't smoke inside.'

'I don't smoke cigarettes,' said Aljce.

'So you say,' said Jillq. 'Can you prove it?'

THERE WAS MADNESS everywhere. Aljce was sitting inside looking outside through a section of wall that her Mad Neighbour had removed floor to ceiling from his house in honour of the good weather. The garden was a wild fairy wonderland of coriander and fennel and huge poppies in lilac and apricot and soft pink. Rambling roses sprawling over trees. Dragon flies and nearly summer afternoon sun.

Her Mad Neighbour looked furtively over his shoulder. 'I'm having trouble with the greys,' he said, in a loud confidential whisper.

'Who are they?' asked Aljce.

'The greys. Presenting themselves as human when we all know that they came here on ships surfing the currents of space. Trying to confuse and bamboozle us. Taking us away and returning us with new memories. Well, they can forget it. I can remember everything.' She wondered if he'd been smoking too much. Or whether he just enjoyed the drama.

'Some weird things have been happening lately,' he said.

'Like what?'

'Well, I was walking down the road, and this woman popped out. And she said , "I know you're good at fixing cars. Can you come down to my place and have a look at mine?"'

'So I said, "yes okay." And then when I looked at it, it was a wreck. I said, "This car's a fucking wreck!" Half the dash board was gone, and one of the doors was hanging off, and the windscreen was cracked.'

'Did she want you to fix that?'

'Yes, that's what I thought. But then I said to myself, she just wants me to get it going. So I turned over the ignition, and I saw the indicator light didn't come on, and that wasn't promising. The battery was probably fucked too. So I went inside to tell them, because the door was open, and I knew they were in there, and I was going from one room to the next, and I was calling, "hello? Hello?"'

'Can I get some attention here?'

'Exactly, exactly. And then I heard them down in the back room, so I went into the hallway, and I called out "hello!" And they said, hang on, and I heard them coming out. So I took some steps backwards, because it wasn't MY house. And then she came out. And then about thirty seconds later, her girlfriend came out, the one that she had been visiting earlier, that had driven us down the road to her place. And then a guy came out. What do you think they were doing in there?'

'I'm trying not to think.'

'They all had their clothes on.'

'Oh, I thought you meant they were having a threesome.'

'No, not that. And I said to her, "This is just wishful thinking. This car's a fucking wreck."'

'This is where you started the story, Neighbour. It's a circular story, starts at one point and ends up back there.'

'You see, I knew you'd like that. So when we got there, they just left me out there with the car. And they just all headed for the house. No explanation of what was working or not working. Didn't even leave me the keys.'

'I see what you're doing. You're adding more detail in each cycle. Thought you turned over the ignition though?'

'I had to call out to her for them, and she just turned around and threw them. Didn't even stop to say anything, and they all carried on into the house. And when I found out it was a wreck in the engine as well as the body, I went into the house to tell them that it was a waste of time.'

'Sounds like it would cost more to fix than to buy a new car.'

'Exactly. And then I couldn't find them. Because that's how it is. It's the sort of thing that you have to do down in the back room. Even if you do it in your own home. Not like coffee or something. You can just do that in the kitchen.'

'I don't drink coffee. It's bitter. And it can't be good for you either. It's soooooo bitter. And every time something is bitter in nature, it's always poisonous.'

'That's true.'

'And coffee is fucking bitter. Without that sugar and that froth.'

'And that cream. That's what they put with it, isn't it? And anyway, what was she asking me to fix her car for? She can't even fucking drive.'

Aljce laughed.

'What about pears and lemon and honey?' said her Mad Neighbour.

'What about them?'

'And maybe the juice of two oranges. Coffee. Or am I thinking of tea?'

'Must be tea. I think your tea would be better without the oranges. You've got quite a lot going on there. Maybe you'd need them for sweetness if you didn't have the honey. You can get too much honey though.'

'Oh, only one teaspoon per person.'

'What are we having, recipe night?'

'I suppose we could be.'

'Why not?' she said, realising that this would be a new experience. She egged him on. 'What about horse radish? What would you put with that?'

'What is it?'

'Don't you know horse radish? It's a vegetable. Hot and stinging, but sort of cooling at the same time.'

'Sounds like radishes that my mum used to grow.'

'That's what I said. Radish.'

'Oh, horse radish, radish. Same thing. I see. I think I'd put them with some salt, and a little bit of oil. And then maybe a little bit of nutmeg.'

'Can you put that on roasted vegetables?'

'Roasted veges?'

'Nutmeg. Is that something you've actually tried on roasted veges, or are you just theorizing that it would be nice?'

'I'm not roasting veges. I'm making a pickle.'

'Oh, I see. Are you sure you're not making a relish? Pickles are full of vinegar and sugar, freaking your taste buds out on both ends of the spectrum.'

'Yes, you're right. I'm making a relish. That's the one where it's spicy and sour and a little bit sweet, and a lot more cloudy.'

'Yeah. Milder. All crushed up like a spread.'

'So I am making horse radish relish.'

'I would maybe put some lime juice with horse radish. And some ginger. What do you think of that?'

'I think it could work. But you would still need something sweet. What about banana?'

'Not if I wanted it to keep.'

'True.'

Her Mad Neighbour returned to his former subject. 'So I know three more houses now, just from that one experience. The house she popped out of, where her girlfriend lives, her house two doors down, where we got into her boyfriend's little black car, and this other house that we drove around to. Perhaps that one's hers, and the other one's her boyfriend's. Who knows…'

'Who, the same woman?'

'I should start up my own network. Show crackheads how to get from one house to another.'

'Join the dots between the houses.'

'I can draw more than the dots, I can show them how they can just jump from house to house; they're so close.'

'It's everywhere, isn't it?'

'Yeah, it is.'

'Mmm. First stage, once their body and mind really get to like it and they've made a decision towards it, is that their head sort of reduces to their skull. You know, like their skin is really thin on their bones. Then they go that grey, blue, dead blood colour. Like they fading from colour vision into black and white vision. And then they start picking at their skin and making those sores. Before their teeth start falling out.'

'It feels like spiders crawling on their skin.' And he made crawling motions on his cheeks with his fingertips. 'I know about spiders.'

'Why, have you been on it?'

'Hell no. Hell no. I'm so glad I didn't get into that stuff with other people, when I had the opportunity. I'm so glad I didn't waste my life on that shit.'

'I hear it's beautiful, but I'm not willing to give up what I have here, or turn my back on my obligations. That wouldn't be worth the price. Not for me.'

'What price joy?'

'And can I buy it elsewhere?'

They sat and contemplated. 'Which house?' asked Aljce.

'Oh, the one a few doors down.'

'What, that way?'

'Yeah.'

'That's Amber.'

'Like the traffic light?'

'That's the one.'

'As long as you're talking about the one with a little boy. Always out the front playing on the grass by the road. When there's no one else on the street. They've busted her before, and they took away some men, but they left her there. But I reckon it's her, cooking it. They just assume that it would be the men. But it's her.'

'You said there was a man there.'

'Yeah, but she just replaces them. She can get any man she likes. She's a fry cook. Well, not any man, but there's a lot of them, and there's always the potential to get new recruits.'

'So she's all go, hey, Amber?'

'It's her, she's the cook, not the boyfriends. Hang on, what colour is amber? No, not red. It's the orange.'

'It's not really. It's really the colour of beer, I think. Have you seen those pictures of pieces of amber, with whole dragon flies, and beetles that don't even exist anymore, because they're extinct? Like they're still flying; they hang inside the amber so perfectly.'

'Oh, you mean real amber.'

'Yeah, not that traffic light shit. That's some sort of orange. I don't know why they call it amber.'

'It's not right anyway. Because there were kids there. Do you think that they have much chance growing up without becoming addicts? Hey, do you know, when I was fifteen, and I had my first operation then ... And they gave me too much, what's the word? What is it?'

'Anaesthetic?'

'Morphine. Opiates.'

'Is that how you say it?'

'Opiates, yes. Opiates. They gave me too much. And I was seeing metal spiders coming at me, and I was freaking out. They had all the psychiatrists in there. And do you know what they were doing? They were drawing me in to what they wanted me to think by coming into my world.'

'That is the right way to do it. But not a lot of people know that. Not even ones who work in mental health.'

'They were placing themselves there with me, and then they changed the story. And they told me that the spiders wouldn't hurt me, they were just there to dance for me. And I started laughing. And they had to wean me off it. And they were sure I was going to grow up to be a drug addict.'

Aljce waved the joint in the air. 'And here you are.'

He threw his hands up in delight. 'And here I am.' He thought a little bit more. 'But it's not the same. It hardly counts. It alters reality, but it doesn't enslave you. It's more of a thinking tool, really.' He paused. 'People think the mind can't hurt you. But it can.'

'Fuck yeah. It's all in your head. That's where all the evil is.'

'Your mind can turn on you just like that.'

'That's what I don't really like about trips either. Not enough control and the mind can attack you. Hard to escape when it's your own mind. It's just like bad dreams. You get better at avoiding them. You've got to be in a good space. Anxiety will make monsters.'

'Yes.'

'The sights and colours when you're tripping are amazing. But you don't really know what you're going to come back to. What you might have done in this reality. With weed, I'm still in control. In both realms.'

It was Aljce's turn to pause and start again. 'You know meth heads? Do you think that they all see the same reality, inside their big crystal world of transparent glass?'

'Well, they're all experiencing the same thing. But it also depends on what angle they're on to each fracture, because that's going to affect exactly what they see. Angle is everything… And do you know what that woman said? She said, 'oh, okay then. See you.' Just like that.'

'She was just off her nut, wasn't she?'

'She was.'

'They're just living in a parallel universe, meth freaks. Like looking through a mirror to an opposite world, but in some not quite right land that shimmers slightly crookedly.'

'It's an underneath world, that the top dwellers don't see. Only the crack heads can see it, and sometimes, if the Police dig in the right place, they find it.'

'What are they digging through?'

'The rest of us. It's like a needle in a haystack. But digging is all they do, and sometimes they're successful.'

'Well they have special powers to be able to find out information that we don't. So they should be.'

'What? Successful sometimes?'

'Yeah.'

'They won't be, because they're not cracked like the looking glass freaks. Crystal freaks. They're in their own reality.'

'I suppose that's why straight people treat the addicts bad. Because they don't know that other universe. Don't know it, and without knowledge they think it's evil rather than destructive. Because all they can see is how that world interacts with theirs, and they feel it makes them unsafe. They have no idea what it's like to be there, and how the people there came to decide that the sacrifices are worth it.'

They paused to inhale. 'They weren't aggressive with you then,' she said.

'Hell, no. They were just strange. They made me look normal.' He seemed offended at the thought.

'Cos that's where I thought you'd be going with this, since we are having a meth freak conversation. Or maybe we were having a convo about lil grey men ...'

'No, not at all. They don't bother me.'

'Well, thank you for the conversation. I wasn't feeling like talking, but that was ...' And she realised that when he wasn't actually mad and obsessive, and not listening at all, that he was actually quite interesting, because he wasn't bound by any conventions, and he was quite happy to go anywhere his thoughts took him. What had he said about smoking? It was more of a thinking tool.

ALJCE BEGAN TO wonder if her cleverness in avoiding Jillq wasn't just down to luck, and that in fact, there might be another reason why she hadn't seen Jillq for a few days. The place felt quiet; almost restful, and Aljce speculated that it could have been quite a nice place to work if it wasn't for the existence of Jillq. She would only ever have encountered the outer illusions of the others, and have been none the wiser as to what lay inside of them. Dulcie said hello in the hallway. Hattie offered to lend her some books on counselling technique. Aljce couldn't relax completely, because Jillq might be lying low somewhere, planning something to destroy her. She wasn't sure whether to ask where Jillq was or not.

A friendly Mrs. Kingi told her. 'If you can just sign this card, please Aljce. You know Jillq's mother is in hospital, of course. If it's not one thing, it's another. As if she doesn't have enough to cope with already!'

'Ahh,' said Aljce, eyeing the card, not knowing what to write. She didn't want to be false. She could see that the others had written things like 'hoping and praying for you,' 'sending you special love' and 'always in my thoughts during this difficult time.' Aljce wasn't sure if she could genuinely send Jillq special love, and when Jillq was in her thoughts, it was never pleasant, although it was frequent. Sometimes she could think of little else.

'What's wrong with her mother?'

'Oh, going a bit senile, I think. And she's had a fall. Poor Jillq. She's so kind and good to her mother.'

'That's good.'

'And her mother has been nothing but a bully to her. There's a lot of issues there.' Aljce blinked, she hadn't seen that one coming.

'Really?'

'Oh, yes, Jillq has had a lot to put up with. She gets very nervous when her mother's around.' Aljce ran that around and around in her head. Was Jillq a bully because she'd been bullied, and because that was the only way she'd learned how to be? Or had she just twisted it up in her head to make out that she was a victim, so that people felt sorry for her, and so that she could manipulate people against her mother while she did her wrong? Either was possible. If Jillq had actually been bullied, it might explain her sensitivity to the word 'teasing.' On the other hand, perhaps she was just narcissistic by nature, and her anti bullying stance was just her way of casting an illusion that she was on the side of good rather than on the side of evil. Perhaps it was heritable, and she and her mother were the same. If that was true, perhaps she'd learned it from a mother who taught her well. Who knew?

'I think Jillq is a saint, the way she looks after her mother,' said Mrs. Kingi. 'She's been up all night every night at the hospital. Those nurses don't even answer the buzzers these days. People could die! It's lucky that there's good people like Jillq in this world. She's been looking after her mother up at the hospital practically single handedly.'

'She's so lucky that you're so supportive,' murmured Aljce. Mrs. Kingi looked pleased.

'She's such a saint. I wish I could support her more,' she said.

'Hope your mother recovers well,' wrote Aljce.

WHEN JILLQ RETURNED, things were almost peaceful for a few days. Perhaps she has just been under stress, thought Aljce, beginning to doubt herself again. Perhaps she had contributed, coming to this job all cocky and querying. Perhaps it had been too challenging for Jillq. After all, no one else challenged her. Perhaps things had settled down now. But it seemed that Jillq enjoyed allowing ebb and flow. She allowed people to relax; to forget about what had been done to them, so that when she struck again, they weren't expecting it, and she could get triple damage points. Aljce was called to Jillq's room.

'There is a new rule,' she said. 'And unfortunately it has had to be created for you Aljce.'

'External supervision will now be done on site.' Aljce blinked. She hadn't mentioned her external supervision. Was the woman psychic?

'External supervision is a Student Placement requirement,' she said. 'I've got to have it.'

'We need you here on site,' said Jillq. 'Who is thinking about that? Who is considering the needs of our busy service? It's incredibly thoughtless of you, Aljce.' Aljce remembered that she held a trump card.

'Yes, I thought that would be what you would want, for me to have it on site, so I've already organised that,' she said sweetly. Jillq looked at Aljce as if she was a particularly disgusting smell.

'You've already organised that,' she repeated.

'Yes,' said Aljce. 'I always keep what you would want in mind.' Jillq looked at her very carefully, squinting as if she wasn't quite sure whether she'd detected sarcasm or not.

Unable to decide, she said, 'I expect you to keep to this new rule Aljce.'

'Of course,' said Aljce, as if she wouldn't dream of breaking any of Jillq's rules. My gosh, she thought to herself, I'm as deceitful as she is. Perhaps I'm no better than her.

'You're always so reasonable,' said Jillq accusingly.

'That's because I think it's the best way to be,' said Aljce.

MARJ CAME IN through the front door; spoiling Aljce's morning again. Aljce hurriedly put down the mini putter she was using. She'd been trying to hit the golf balls that were lying in random pockets of unused energy in the hallways through cracks in the plaster walls. No one knew where they disappeared to, but there were always more that were being found lying near the building, and others; particularly Marj and Chelsea, brought them inside. Somewhere, there was a factory that churned out hard little white balls with pits in their surface. Somewhere else there was a zone where they all disappeared, making room in the world for all the new ones that the factory was making. A zone where the world just tucked them in underneath itself and no one thought of them anymore.

Everyone picked the putters up to have a go, although technically they all belonged to Jillq. She thought it was funny to have some joke putters mixed up with the real ones, where the club bent if somebody attempted to hit the ball, or retracted entirely. Aljce didn't find it funny, and she'd once gotten a quick shock from touching a normal metal one which had been lying in the sun by a window, but the others always did. Aljce only occasionally partook of the game, mostly when no one else was in the building. She couldn't afford to be accused of playing when she should be working. And she had to consciously block out the thought that the putters could have the dual purpose of also being for clubbing rabbits to death outside. She hoped it hadn't occurred to Jillq, and wouldn't in the future.

'So what are Jillq's qualifications?' said Aljce to Marj, thinking that if she did have to talk to Marj, she may as well put the time to good use and do some research.

'Jillq,' said Marj frowning. 'What do you mean?'

'Well, her practice qualifications. Like, she was telling everyone about how to do the Okay Line the other day. And talking about when she was trained in it. What has she trained as?'

'I don't know,' said Marj. 'What's the top one? It'll be that. Psychologist I think.'

'If there was a pile, the psychiatrists would think they were on the top,' said Aljce.

'Perhaps she's that. I get confused.'

'She's not a psychiatrist,' said Aljce. 'We would have heard all about that.'

'What do you mean?'

'Well, if Jillq was a psychiatrist, we would all have to call her Dr. Jillq,' said Aljce.

'True,' said Marj. 'Good thinking Aljce.'

Aljce couldn't imagine Jillq as a psychologist or a psychotherapist. She could barely spell, and seemed to know very little about best practice or mental health. Marj was no help, and Aljce wouldn't dare ask anyone else because they might report back to Jillq. Marj seemed as unaware of Jillq's games as she was of Aljce's. Jillq didn't need to share the game plan; Marj was just so easy to manipulate that she played the game exactly as she was intended to.

'I THINK MARJ genuinely thinks that she's really giving service to the community, like she's some sort of charitable saviour,' she said to Strauss. 'Coming out of nowhere to mix it with the people who she thinks matter. When really she just does some basic computer bookkeeping, and wriggles around under the building plugging in computer wires. Most of the time she just sits in her office doing nothing and looking at her computer screen. Once I went in and she was trying to minimise Solitaire.'

'You've got to give it to her, she could be just sitting around on her arse eating Tim Tams and getting stoned like other little old ladies.'

'Ha. You make it sound so cool. I hope we're little old ladies like that.'

'Me too.'

'As long as we're not Marj. Although she's not even old. More middle aged. I'd never want to be Marj. In particular.' Uncharitable, she thought. I am becoming uncharitable. Perhaps I always was.

TURNING UP THERE the next evening for the AGM was really the last thing Aljce wanted to do. Night time was her time, where she could be herself and remember what that was. She entered the room with dread. This was over and beyond the call of duty; having to come back after she'd gone home for the day, and spend precious time with people more dangerous than snakes. Any of them could coil and bite her at any time, lashing out suddenly from some unexpected angle. Still, Rose from the Council would be there. Aljce had met her once or twice, and she seemed like a nice lady – privileged, but interested in the arts and social justice from her particular corner of the universe. She saw it as her duty to foster them. No mention was ever made about her luck at being in a position to do so. It was framed as being all about her goodness. All the same, Rose seemed to be a fair playing person, keeping to the rules which had been formed in her corner of the universe, and which she believed were for the good of all.

Things didn't start well, with Jillq fawning on Rose, offering her the special expensive orange juice and breathing down her sleeve with tales of the Hub's good works and the people who had been personally rescued from oblivion by Jillq. But once the actual meeting got started, Aljce breathed a sigh of relief when Rose told Jillq that she couldn't be Chair if she was also the Hub Manager, as it was a conflict of interests. Jillq blustered a bit, letting air escape her in all directions, and said that she didn't see how it mattered. 'Process,' said Rose crisply, and Aljce rejoiced inwardly. Not everything would be Jillq's way tonight, and that felt safer for her, particularly when Rose announced that she didn't mind being acting Chair, unless anyone minded. No one came forward to mind, and Aljce supposed that they were too confused by seeing someone tell Jillq what to do.

The meeting itself went smoothly, if somewhat boringly, up until it was time to present the financial report. Aljce was making sure that she didn't say anything, or move or second anything, in case it could be held against her later. With the added catch that it was in the minutes. Jillq was also saying little, still sulking from not being the Chair. 'Who is presenting the Financial Report?' asked Rose.

'I am,' said Mrs. Kingi. 'I'm the Treasurer. Well, Co, with Jillq.'

'Do you mean that the Hub Manager is also Co-Treasurer?' asked Rose. 'Do you not understand that the Board employs her, and that if she is on the Executive, she is, in effect employing herself? And as Treasurer, paying herself?'

'But I work here too,' said Mrs. Kingi.

'Do you?' said Rose in surprise.

'Then why are you the Treasurer?'

'Co,' said Mrs. Kingi.

'Who doesn't work here?' asked Rose. Pansy put her hand up. Queenie Marama had failed to show.

'Poor commitment,' Chelsea had hissed to Aljce earlier. Hattie was late. Jillq had been upset, although she had agreed to start when Rose pointed out that they couldn't wait for her all night. If it said 7 o'clock start, they should start considering that it was now half an hour past that.

'As long as we don't vote on anything till Hattie gets here,' she had said.

'If she's here, she can vote,' Rose had said.

Now, Rose was saying, 'This is highly unusual, having employees employ and govern themselves. This will have to be fixed before the next meeting. You will need to co-opt some more people on to the Committee.'

'I've tried,' said Jillq. 'Nobody's committed.'

'Not hard enough, obviously,' said Rose. 'There must be some more people who would step forward.'

'We haven't needed anyone,' said Jillq.

'Highly unusual,' said Rose again. 'However, there doesn't seem to be any other option for now. But as I said, this will all need to be remedied before the next meeting. Still, let's get on with hearing the Financial Report.' Mrs. Kingi gave out a photocopied page full of typed figures. She'd scrawled some notes in the margins. Aljce looked at it and sighed. She always switched off when she saw lists of numbers, particularly if they were part of pages and pages of financial reports.

Rose was squinting at it. 'It doesn't add up,' she said.

'Which part?' said Mrs. Kingi, very quietly.

'Pretty much all of it,' said Rose. 'Who put this together?'

'I did,' said Mrs. Kingi. Everyone looked at the floor, because they all knew that Mrs. Kingi had put it together with Jillq, and that Jillq was the major contributor, with Mrs. Kingi just offering moral support. Aljce looked at the floor with them. If Mrs. Kingi wanted to fling herself under the bus for Jillq, that was her problem.

'You did?' said Rose, her voice getting higher. 'What about the Auditor?'

'We don't have one,' said Mrs. Kingi, her voice getting quieter and quieter.

'Pardon? I thought you said you didn't have an Auditor.'

'We don't,' said Mrs. Kingi, with an air of quiet sacrifice. She couldn't fail to be Jillq's favourite after this.

'I am not,' said Rose, 'comfortable to continue this meeting with Financial Statements in such a mess. I suggest we reschedule for a few months' time to give the Auditors time to look through the books and prepare a report.'

'Good idea,' said Jillq hurriedly. 'There has been some oversight regarding the Auditor. I will make sure that he is aware that he has let us down.'

'I thought you didn't have one.'

'Of course we have an Auditor. He has been most inconvenient.'

'Perhaps we could meet in two weeks' time if he already has your books,' said Rose. 'The Financial Report should be available by then.'

'Your first suggestion of meeting again in a few months' time sounds more compatible,' said Jillq. 'I have my diary with me.' She opened it. 'I have nothing free for at least four months!'

'That's pushing it out quite a way,' said Rose, frowning.

'It's just unfortunate,' said Jillq.

'Has everyone got their diaries with them?'

'I have,' said Aljce. Everyone else shook their head.

'Well, we can't set a date now,' said Jillq. 'No one's got their diaries.'

'We could just set one and then everyone else could put it into their diaries,' suggested Aljce.

'That sounds very inconsiderate,' said Jillq.

'Am I late?' asked Hattie, breezing into the room and collapsing into a chair.

'Very much,' said Jillq. 'We weren't able to have any votes without you.'

'We haven't got past the Financial Report,' said Rose.

'I'll have to let you know when we can meet again,' said Jillq.

'I'll get my staff together with their diaries.'

'Well, I hope I can fit you in,' said Rose. 'My own diary is quite full.'

'We'll be alright if you're busy,' said Jillq breezily. 'I can ask someone else to step in.'

'I'll see you out,' said Aljce to Rose, hoping to have a private word with her. But in the end, Chelsea, Hattie and Marj accompanied them down the dark corridor like a little procession and there was no time. 'Do you have a phone number?' asked Aljce quietly as Rose stepped out the door. The others were fussing around Pansy at Chelsea's desk. Pansy had barely spoken at all during the meeting.

'Oh, ring the Council and ask for it,' said Rose, obviously keen to leave. 'Tell them I said it's fine to give it out! I don't have time to write it down right now. They can ring me and ask me first if they like.'

Aljce felt jubilant as she turned to go back inside. Maybe the tide had turned. Someone else saw right through Jillq and her sham operation.

'I have to go. Babysitter…' she murmured to the others as they swirled around her.

'No one can leave,' said Hattie. 'The whole Hub meeting room needs to be cleaned. Vacuumed. Tables wiped. The toilets will need to be redone.'

'Can't it just be done tomorrow?' asked Aljce.

'Of course not,' said Hattie.

'I hope you're not just standing around Aljce,' said Mrs. Kingi, going past with a bottle of bleach.

'Where's Kat?' said Aljce.

'She didn't have to come,' said Hattie. 'She's a counsellor.' Aljce allowed herself a moment of envy before remembering what a take-down the meeting had been for Jillq. If she'd known, Aljce would have been happy to pay for tickets.

'Give me the vacuum,' she said, snatching it from behind the door of the cleaning cupboard. She would vacuum, and then she would leave. That was a big slice of the tasks to do. They couldn't complain or stop her leaving when she'd done that.

At least that's what she'd thought.

'Leaving already?' said Hattie.

'Yes, I've done all the vacuuming.'

'I've just wiped that table over there. I think you need to go back and vacuum underneath it.' Aljce sighed. Hattie had brushed all the cake and jam doughnut crumbs onto the floor. Possibly on purpose. She got the vacuum out a second time. She hoped that Mamae wasn't going to be pissed off; she had warned her that she might be late. Not that she'd expected that to be because she'd had to clean. Aljce wasn't big on cleaning or housework. She liked moth dust.

She remembered how she had once told Strauss, 'Women will only be freed from the slave drudgery of cleaning and housework and food preparation – I don't mean cooking for fun – when we have robots to do it. The rise of robots, domestic robots will be good for women. It will free them up for creativity, productivity and leisure. There's no way men will ever take to it. Cleaning is an arse job, and no one wants to do it. But it needs to be done. And women are used to doing it. And as more women go into the sciences, they're going to push to develop these things.'

'Bring it on,' Strauss had agreed.

But even if there had been cleaning robots available, no doubt Jillq would have been too cheap to utilise them. In the end, Aljce snuck the vacuum back into the cupboard and edged quietly out the door into the darkness. She could hear the others talking at the other end of the corridor, where Jillq was explaining that perhaps Rose wasn't right for the Therapy Hub if all she wanted to do was find fault. 'She was very rude to you,' Mrs. Kingi was saying. Dulcie laughed her tinkly laugh.

'I don't think she realised,' said Jillq, 'that it was an honour to be asked.'

ALJCE OPENED HER back door to a knock, thinking it was her Mad Neighbour. But it wasn't. A man wearing a SKY TV shirt was on the step. 'You're looking very nice today,' he said, with barely a micro expression to switch him between amused and charming.

'I don't want SKY,' said Aljce.

'Well, I'm not really SKY. I'm more like SKY Santa Claus.'

'You're SKY Santa Claus?' She did her best doubtful look. 'I don't want SKY,' she said again, because it paid to be firm, no matter how much fun they were. This was the first one to be fun anyway, but she didn't want to accidentally find herself signing up because she'd made friends, and then having to pay the subscription every month.

'Well, what don't you like about it?' said the SKY Santa Claus.

'I just don't really have time for it really. I've got stuff I'd rather be doing.' And she thought how writing or dancing gave her so much more pleasure. They were her respite.

'Can I offer you a free trial?' said Santa hopefully, eyeing her fake brown bear fur coat and purple gumboots sideways. Aljce drew herself fully into what she was wearing.

'TV,' she said, 'is the opiate for the masses. People are so busy watching it that they forget to ask what the universe is made of and whether it's real and what its rules are. If people stopped watching TV, they could be learning about the nature of reality. Hypnotised. That's what happens. All those programmes are programmed to make us think in a certain way, to normalise a culture that doesn't think.'

Santa stood his ground.

'I don't want SKY,' she said again. 'But just so that you know, your sales pitch was awesome. I enjoyed it, and there's not much to enjoy lately.' And she realised that it hadn't been so much what the SKY Santa Claus had said, but more his smile, the way he looked amused with his eyes when he saw her, and the way he found the world a big joke. She hoped she had made his world satisfyingly more bizarre. She smiled her most real smile, and closed the door. Not everyone was evil. She needed to remember that. And SKY Santa had offered her a moment of distraction. It was an honour to have been asked.

ALJCE RANG ROSE. 'I'm just wondering if I can talk to you in confidence,' she said. 'As Acting Chair or the Therapy Hub. I need to discuss an employment matter.'

'I'm really sorry,' said Rose, 'but there's no point in telling me anything. I've decided that I can't be associated with an outfit that can put together a Financial Report like that. There's just too much risk to my reputation, and I can't allow it.'

'Oh,' said Aljce.

'Good luck with your employment matter,' said Rose. 'You don't surprise me. There's no accountability at all up there. Try the Employment Court website.'

'Yes,' said Aljce without enthusiasm. Just when she'd thought she might be able to get somewhere. 'Thank you.'

'SO, WE HAVE had the Man from the Ministry with us,' announced Jillq to the room. 'Aljce, I think you met him.'

Aljce had to think. 'The man in the blue suit?'

'Yes. The Man from the Ministry. He has redefined your role. I think it needed to happen.'

'What do you mean, "redefined my role?"'

'You keep talking about how you need to see clients…'

'That is supposed to be a big part of my role, yes.'

'Well, all of that's out the window. From now on, you will see no clients.'

Aljce blinked. Surely not. 'What would the point of my role be then?'

'Exactly. We may have to review it to make sure it's right for us.'

The words 'fuck, fuck, fuck!' lit up green and pink in Aljce's head. If she couldn't clock up client hours, she wouldn't be able to complete her placement and get her counselling qualification. 'I thought he didn't wait around to meet with you,' she said.

'Please don't tell me who I have met with Aljce. Of course we met. He's from the Ministry.'

'Why didn't he meet with me if it's about my role?'

'I thought you said you had met with him Aljce. I'm sure you had ample time to discuss what you needed to discuss.'

'He didn't even ask who I was! I didn't know who he was!'

'And that is the penalty for being so uninformed!' said Jillq. 'If I knew the Man from the Ministry was coming, I would have done research!'

'I didn't know he was coming.'

'That is because you didn't do your research.'

'What's my role now then?'

'As it stands, you will promote positive mental health and violence-free families.'

'To who?'

'Potential clients of course. You will need to do some pamphlets! Some brochures!'

'I don't want to do any more brochures. I had the last one perfect, and someone has gone into my work, which I'd saved on my computer, and changed it.' And that was in fact how she had found it just before the meeting. 'The borders have moved, some of the text has been cut and moved, bits have been added, and there's spelling mistakes in words that I know how to spell. What's the point if someone's going to sabotage what I do?' Jillq frowned. Mrs. Kingi frowned. Marj frowned.

'Why would anyone do that Aljce?'

'I have no idea. Why would anyone do that?'

'Excessive paranoia,' announced Jillq. 'Perhaps you should have counselling yourself Aljce. I'm not sure that you will make a good counsellor. I think you are more suited to being a client.'

'Is it dangerous?' asked Mrs. Kingi. 'Is she safe to practice?'

'Who knows?' said Jillq. 'I think we should be very careful.'

Aljce felt rage rising in her chest, flushing up to her face. She had to hold on. She would bluff this one out, and decide on her strategy later. Chiefly how she would be able to tick off client hours when she was banned from working with clients. All she had to do was concentrate on bluffing this out. 'Perhaps I am mistaken,' she said sweetly. 'Perhaps I'm just not as good at what I was doing as I thought.' Jillq frowned.

'Make sure you correct your spelling,' she said. 'Spelling is very important.'

'I CAN TELL it was her,' Aljce said to Strauss. 'I can spell advocacy. The changes are full of spelling mistakes. I would always correct mine. There's no way I would leave 'avocacy' there. Plus it's spelled the same way several times. There's no way. It's more like avocado. And how did some bits get deleted? And changed so that it's a train wreck?'

'Perhaps she's just trying to help you. Thinks she knows how to spell 'advocacy' better than you.'

'Whatever, cos if that was the way, she'd think it was new and improved, and she wouldn't tell me to correct the mistakes in my work. Although, actually, I don't think she misspelled advocacy on purpose. I think she was just wrecking my stuff in general, and that was a by-product. She probably deleted that bit, and then decided that I'd notice and went to put it back.'

'How would she even get your password?'

'We had to tell Marj what password we wanted so that it could be set up for us when we started. We had to choose a password and tell her.'

'Hope you didn't choose one of your usual passwords? That's what I do.'

'Of course I did. Why not?'

Strauss looked at her.

'Oh fuck. Yes, I did. That's the password for my personal email. Do you think she would look at my browser history and see that I use Yahoo, and then try my work password to get in there?'

'I don't know her. What do you think? Is that something she would do?'

'Fuck yeah, she's been into my documents, hasn't she. Ahh, shit. I'm going to have to change the password to my Yahoo email aren't I?'

'I would. And you might want to watch what you say in your work email too. Cos she's got your password to that.'

'I am. I have always had a bad feeling about doing that. Even when I didn't know she could get in there. Not a specific bad feeling that she'd get in there. More like... just that I can't trust anyone or anything in that place. I'm hyper alert to attack at any time.'

'The whole place is a sham place,' she continued. 'It's not really a therapy hub. It's a pretend therapy hub playground for Jillq to play in. To imagine herself a therapy queen. A psychologist... And she's not even,' she added as an afterthought. 'I don't think...'

'Oh, well, changing your password will help.'

'Yeah, but, I don't wanna change my Yahoo email password. I've, like had it forever. It defines me. I can't let her take that away from me.'

'Yeah, but...'

'What about, if I change my work password? With Marj. Might take her focus off my real password. Before she realises it's the one I always use and thinks of looking at my browser history? She's not that bright. Brighter than Marj. But that's nothing.'

'Good luck with that.'

'Marj, can I change my password please?'

'Why do you want to change your password, Aljce?' said Marj suspiciously. Aljce sighed. Why did they have to make everything so accusing? And so difficult. You are changing your password as part of the battle against them, she reminded herself. They're difficult because they don't want you to win. But then she felt irritated again. Marj wasn't intelligent enough to know what Aljce was doing. She just suspected the worst of Aljce, because she was stupid enough to believe everything Jillq said, rather than experience Aljce for herself. And annoyingly, she just happened to be right to expect the worst in this case. Even though Aljce was ultimately in the right. It sucked that she had to be underhand to protect herself. How could people be so stupid as to take the world at someone else's definition?

'I've forgotten what it was,' she said.

'I'll look it up,' said Marj.

'Too late, obviously, I'm going to get it confused now,' said Aljce, hunting wildly for sensible words.

'Mmm,' said Marj sourly, not onto it enough to know that Aljce was talking rubbish.

'What do you want it to be?'

'Contrariwise,' said Aljce.

'How do you spell that?' said Marj. 'That's not even a word.'

'Contrariwise,' said Aljce, 'it is.'

'You'll have to write it down for me,' said Marj, unable to think of any more arguments or excuses, worn out by the effort that she'd already made. Aljce could tell that she felt vaguely disloyal to Jillq, but couldn't really figure out why, since there was no offence from Aljce that she could personally identify. And that's how it should have been. There was no good reason why she shouldn't change her password. Contrariwise was a brilliant choice. Jillq would be so busy misspelling it that she would never get into Aljce's work before she packed it in due to frustration.

WE'RE ALL MAD HERE

IN HER MAD Neighbour's garden, cactus plants mixed with bright orange railway flowers and long bleached strands of grass about to release their seeds. He was extending his shed; using found natural timber window frames and ornate woodwork that he got from the second chance shop at the dump. Behind him, he had five diagonal rows of three white washing machine agitators, lined up like suburban Storm Troopers ready to attack. His tabby cat, Hello Kitty, smooged around the base of the umbrella. 'Get outside, Dog!' he shouted at Dog.

'Um, we are outside,' Aljce pointed out.

'Haha, so we are,' said her Mad Neighbour. 'Get inside out, Dog!' He turned to Aljce. 'That's better, isn't it?' he said.

'So how was the races?' she asked.

'Oh, I bet like the Queen,' he said. 'So I only lost eight dollars. Not like those people who count themselves lucky if they only lose a couple of hundred. You can really have fun if you only start with twenty dollars, and put a dollar or two on each race.'

'How is that betting like the Queen?

'The Queen only bets two shillings. Two shillings!'

'She doesn't give a fuck whether she wins or not, that's why. Too rich.'

'Oh, she's just there to have fun. If you only have two dollars on a race, you're excited when your horse comes in, but you're not worried that it won't.'

'Perhaps that's what people pay for, that adrenalin rush?'

'Well, they're not there to have fun. I was there to have fun. Just like the Queen.'

'Good to see you keeping up with her,' said Aljce.

'I liked the Queen Mother best. She liked rabbits. And she liked Easter.'

'How do you know?'

'I just do.'

'Psychic, huh? You won't miss her now that she's dead.'

'Oh, but I do. I do miss her, she was such fun.'

'You don't even know her.'

'Oh, yes, I do. I saw her on TV. That's how I know that she likes rabbits and Easter. Because she said so.'

'Holy shit, you don't watch royal documentaries do you? That's just royal propaganda.'

'I do watch them, they're very nice. Did you know that a champagne cork popping sounds like a duchess's fart?'

'That's just the royal machine pumping out stories to turn them all into celebrities for doing nothing. They're just entertainers.'

'The Queen, you know, she's given her whole life in service.'

'That's true. Going from one bizarre encounter to another in a bizarre world.'

'She shakes all those babies' hands.'

'Royals are just people you're never going to get to know. Living some other life. Ordinary people, who have people behind them who know how to work social media, and print media, and how to niche market different royal characters to different generations.'

'I do miss her. I miss the Queen Mother. She was such fun. I really do feel like I'm part of their family.'

'Nice.'

'And I have met the Queen,' he continued. 'She stopped by our town. And she was going along shaking everybody's hand. Till she saw me. And she stopped. And she made some sniffy nose noises to the man behind her, and he whispered to another man. And he came over to me, and he said, "Excuse me sir." Just like that.'

'And then what?'

'He said, "I'm sorry sir, but I'm going to have to ask you to move back behind the barrier and not come any further forward."'

'Oh, so you were too close? She must have thought you were a security risk, haha.'

'Me! A security risk! Do you know what I think happened? She recognised me.'

'Recognised you?'

'Yes.'

Aljce blinked. Sometimes she forgot that he was mad. 'Do you have many conversations about the Queen? Cos you're quite good at this.'

'I'd like to have more conversations about the Queen. Actually, I think this is my first one.'

'You know what you need to do? Follow something more modern. Keep up with the Kardashians.'

'Who are they?'

'You don't know who the Kardashians are?'

'No …'

'Okay, so there's this guy who wins an Olympic gold medal. Called Bruce. And he marries this woman who used to be married to the lawyer who somehow got OJ Simpson off his wife murdering charges. Her last name is Kardashian. And she has three daughters already, who all have names starting with K, even the ones which would usually start with a C. And they are this golden couple. And they have two more daughters together, also with names starting with K. And she sets about marketing her daughters as celebrity commodities, and she is a pioneer of fly-on-the-wall reality shows. And her daughters do everything that all women do; get their periods, have trouble in love, have doubts and insecurities. But they also do this bizarre stuff that people with too much money do: get cars worth more than the debt of a small country for their birthday, get Brazilian waxes in front of global TV audiences, and try bizarre beauty treatments to augment their plastic surgery. So you get that sense of identifying with them while living a fantasy life. You'd really like them.'

'Doesn't sound as if they come from much tradition.'

'No, there are all sorts of non-traditional updates. Bruce is now transgender. Kaitlyn, her name is. Yay. It's the new rich. They get their money for opening up their entire lives to the public. People will pay for that if it's escapist enough. The Queen used to do the same thing in a much more controlled way. Hence the royals trying harder and harder to compete, and needing to open up their own lives. No more buying privacy… We see their intimate dramas now too. And we're coming more and more to depend on other people's lives for entertainment. Hey, do you want to hear my Queen story?'

'What is it? Have you had a run in with her?'

'Ha. We were all lined up down the main street, our whole school, and we had to stand up all day waiting for her, because she was late. And in the afternoon, the tar got hot, and our feet were burning, all of us who hadn't worn shoes, and we were all trying to stand on something, the white line, or a piece of loose clothing. And then someone shouted, "Wave!" and we all waved as three black cars flashed past, and someone said that they got a glimpse of an apricot hat, which was more than everyone else got. And then we all went back to school. And I remember thinking, all that, and she didn't even bother to stop. Totally disappointed.'

'Ahh, well, she wasn't worried about you. You weren't there to see her. You were there as a token of respect from your town, so that she could see you all lining up there to pay your respects. A whole school turned up just to wave when she went past.'

'I don't know if I'm comfortable with that. I'm pretty sure I was there because I really wanted to see a real queen.'

'You might have been, but your school took you out there to show respect.'

'Well, that's my point really. Now they have to compete for viewers. With the Kardashians. Who all go out with rap stars, or basketball players. It's not just the new rich, it's the new royalty. One of them married Kanye West, perhaps because his name starts with K, and, against all expectations, they went in a new direction and called their daughter North. With an N. Which is quite pretty. People laughed, and some disapproved, but that's how much power the Kardashians have. They don't give a fuck. If they do it, soon everyone will want to do it. Like the Queen with her two shillings. She doesn't give a fuck. She's already rich.'

'The Kardashians. What are they on?'

'SKY, that's what they're on. SKY TV.'

'Oh, I meant, what are they on? Like something quite strong. Like something hallucinogenic or something. And you said sky. They're on sky.' He had a laugh to himself.

'Funny,' she agreed with him. 'That's their reality though. Something artificial; constructed entirely of money. A transparent cage that they don't even realise is utterly false. They don't even know that they're in it. What I do like about them is that they're into inter-racial marriage, which was a big no-no in America, land of the free, until they came along. And they are mostly curvy girls, which is cool because they are defining a new sort of beauty, and women don't feel like they have to starve themselves to the clothes sizes of young teenage girls any more. Their power is so big that they can start massive cultural change. And they're sort of interesting, in an ant farm sort of way. Baring your deepest insecurities for you, and showing you that even people who have everything feel unhappy, so there's no need for you to worry about your own situation really. You're just normal. Like them. But without the money and the clothes and the shoes and the walk-in wardrobes.'

'You have to feel sorry for the Queen though. She probably looks like she's got it all, but she probably has a lot of bills. She probably worries about how to pay them all.'

'Bullshit. The Queen gets everything for free. English taxes pay her to do her job. Entertaining the masses. She and her family are the old school Kardashians. And the old Queen is giving way to the new Queens.'

'It's all about stories, isn't it? Life is the stories we tell ourselves.'

TYRES SCREECHED AROUND the corner at the top of the street as she walked down his driveway and out on to the road; ready to turn back up in to her own driveway. She saw her Front Neighbour, and was going to call out, 'Idiots, ay?' But he didn't see her, and spoke to himself first. 'Ooh, here comes trouble,' he said in a voice that suggested that he fully supported it coming. And that made her question her own irritated reading of the situation. The neighbour across the road's teenager's friends took off again, and came back past with their car still in second gear, calling out and laughing to their friends who were still out front in their yard, and Aljce suddenly understood that they were just showing off their happiness and the freedom of their youth. They were not thinking about breaking the rules, or whether they might hurt anyone else. Perhaps it was because she was feeling stressed from work that she'd jumped towards the negative. She needed to stay positive, and not buy in to a negative reality. Life was the stories she told herself.

BUT ALJCE WASN'T always sure who was telling the stories. Time at work maintained its usual slow pace. It was, thought Aljce, simultaneously boring and stressful. Like a hospital, but with more pink. Her thoughts randomly drifted to Lewis as she sat at her desk. He'd taken all her secrets with him. She'd told him all about herself. It had been a wonderful feeling to be able to trust someone, and to talk to someone who was interested in her, who wanted to understand her. Strange how hungry she had been for that. Perhaps she'd thought that if she could show someone her entire world, both internal and external, they wouldn't have been able to help but love her. Not that that had worked out for her.

He could write about me, but I could write about him too, she thought. If he plans to trade in my secrets, he'd better be prepared to release his. Writers were dangerous people.

Dulcie poked her head through the door, interrupting Aljce's trail of thought. 'Hello Aljce,' she said. 'Are you the only one here?'

'I think so,' said Aljce, sorry that she wasn't the only one there anymore.

'So,' said Dulcie, clearly at a loose end without anyone else to chat to, 'how are you liking the job?'

'It's awesome thank you,' said Aljce politely, way too onto it to tell Jillq's daughter what she really thought of the job. 'I love what you're wearing,' she said, changing the subject to something safer. And flattery never hurt.

'Oh, I just got these clothes,' said Dulcie happily, laughing her tinkling laugh. Aljce thought it might possibly be the most beautiful laugh she'd ever heard. Every note was musical and pure and perfect.

Aljce continued on the auto pilot setting of polite attention, commenting on Dulcie's good taste and the bargains she'd got, clothing item by clothing item. Perhaps she could make friends with Dulcie. Perhaps that would change the anti-Aljce dynamic. If Dulcie liked her, she might stand up for her with the others, and maybe her mother would be nicer to Aljce, because Aljce would be an insider rather than an outsider. Dulcie didn't mention her mother at all, happy in the sunshine of Aljce's admiration of her new clothes. This was how it would have been between Aljce and Dulcie if there was no Jillq.

ALJCE THOUGHT ABOUT Dulcie later that night as she drifted off to sleep, into the hazy land where thoughts were free to do as they wished, and she recalled the beauty of her musical laugh. If some representation of a divine creator existed, she thought, then traditionally it was light, blinding in brilliance. But was the divine also at the centre of a pure note of music? In the centre of everything perfect? And if that were true, was the divine also in evil? If it was the perfect representation of evil? And was the divine everywhere? As equal in pain as in pleasure, in destruction as in creation and in sour as it was in sweet?

She grabbed her notebook.

I can't stop, she thought, switching on her light. I'm drunk on words and illusions. Every thought that I have is so beautiful that I have to write it down. I'm so lucky that when I get these raptures, I know that I'm in an altered state, and therefore I can stand outside it without being captured by the delusion. I can just use it.

Perhaps there was divinity in madness.

WORK ALWAYS BROUGHT her back down again. 'Hello,' said Ina. 'Is this where you've gotten to? I didn't know you were working here!' Aljce tried to raise a smile. The intense pink of the reception and hallway area, which had seemed warm on Aljce's first day, had become more than cloying. 'Hey,' said Ina. 'It can't be that bad.'

'It is,' said Aljce, the words rushing out without permission, wondering if she could trust Ina, badly wanting to talk to someone, to have someone understand what was happening to her. 'It can be that bad. I'm being bullied up here. I hate it.'

'It can't be that bad,' said Ina, again. 'Cheer up, Aljce!' And Aljce knew that Ina didn't want to know. Ina was there to do her job, which was to check on the payments from the Ministry of Social Development for the non-existent clients, and not to get involved. She didn't want anything unnecessary getting her off track with that. Come in, tick things off, boom, leave again. The Mystery of Social Development. Aljce wondered whether to tell her about the pencilled list of her own clients, which would have become pen by now. Probably not, since Ina didn't appear to want any rocking of the boat on her watch. 'Cheer up!' she said again to Aljce.

'Sure,' said Aljce, loneliness burning a bright white arc across the inside of her mind.

'AT LEAST YOU know who your real friends are,' said Strauss later. 'You're getting insights into lots of people that you thought were good people. And now you know who will stand up against evil, and who won't.'

'I'm sure I would if it was me,' said Aljce.

'Maybe that's why Jillq doesn't like you,' said Strauss. 'Here's some facts you don't know about her, Aljce. Naturally red haired people need shitloads more anaesthetic than the general population, but also feel pain to a much lesser degree. Except for the cold, they feel the cold. And they get more sunburn. They're just different. I saw it on the net. Did you know it's a recessive gene, and unless they keep marrying each other, it'll die out? Then no more redheads. That'd be a shame. For diversity. You like diversity Aljce.'

'Don't make me feel sorry for her. She's not a bitch cos she's a redhead. It's cos she's a narcissist. And there's plenty of nice redheads.'

'Do you think that she knows she is? A narcissist, I mean.'

'Well, apparently narcissism is only a defence against a strong belief that you're actually an ugly loser, but fuck if you will actually let anyone find that out. Instead, you will destroy the competition. The perceived competition. You will suck them in and manipulate the hell out of them so that they end up feeling like you feel, and then you think, ha, I am better than you, because I am better at the secret personality manipulation game.'

'So what you're saying would mean that they're actually really canny about people's feelings… But they don't care about them?'

'Yeah, that's right, they understand emotions, but only care about their own. Other people's are just academic. They don't understand other people's responses as feelings, only as currency.'

'And what if she's not a narcissist? What if she's just totally fucking selfish?'

'Gotta tell ya, that is exactly how it feels. Could be same diff anyway. But I think that this explains why she needs to hurt me. It's because she needs to make herself feel better, and she has no qualms about harming someone else to do that.'

When her next supervision appointment came around, Aljce led Edyth down to one of the rooms. She was now au fait with the booking sheet, but still nervous that someone might run past her and make a fuss. Surely they must be pleased that she wasn't leaving the building though. 'Thanks for coming,' Aljce said awkwardly, as they sat down.

'You look uncomfortable,' said Edyth.

'I'm scared someone can hear me,' said Aljce.

'Gosh,' said Edyth, 'is it that bad up here? There was an uncomfortable atmosphere when I came in.' Aljce breathed a sigh of relief. Someone was going to understand. Edyth was going to understand. She began to tell Edyth about the things that were happening to her, talking so fast there was no room at all for Edyth to speak. Edyth stayed mostly silent, anyway. Aljce kept her voice low.

'Do you think they're listening now?' asked Edyth in the same low voice, when Aljce paused for a rest from the complexity of the detail of what she was telling Edyth. Every one of those details was sharp and clear and in its place because Aljce went over them repeatedly in her head, trying to make sense of things.

'I don't know,' said Aljce, shrugging. 'I look around the rooms for cameras. Marj's quite techy, which is surprising, considering that she's not that bright. That sounds arrogant, but she's not. She has no imagination for other explanations, and she believes everything that Jillq tells her about me.'

'Why don't you quit?' said Edyth.

'Mortgage and two children,' said Aljce, repeating what kept her there. 'I'd love to quit, but I can't do that till I get another job, because I've got children to feed and I need to keep paying off my house.'

'Are you looking around?' said Edyth.

'Of course. But there's nothing out there.'

'Do you want me to do something?' said Edyth. 'I don't know what I can do.'

'There's nothing you can do,' said Aljce. 'There's nothing anyone can do. She will deny anything she's confronted with, and turn it all back on me. She'll look for ways to make me miserable in revenge, toying with me like she's a cat and I'm a mouse, and then she'll fire me, and I'll have no job, and I need the job. Mortgage and children etc., as I said.' Afterwards, it felt better that she'd talked to Edyth and that Edyth had believed her, but it wasn't going to help.

'I PLANTED THE best seed I had, and I spaced it, and I watered it, and it did no good,' said her Mad Neighbour. 'No good at all. And then this came up, from a handful of rubbish seed that I chucked out the door, to get rid of it. Beautiful plants.' And he indicated the tall cannabis plant near his elbow.

'I guess that really sums up life right there, that little story.'

'I guess it does, doesn't it? The less you try to control things, the better the result.'

'Resistance is futile. Or fertile.'

It was peaceful sitting there in the sunshine from the window. Red net bags of last year's potatoes and onions and carrots hung from the roof, and being taller than her, he had to move between them as he went to his back room. Plants grew in the dirt next to the big windows where the floor wasn't covered with concrete; hungry for the sunshine. Their roots went down into some tank that purified the water for the bathroom. Her Mad Neighbour had reappeared with some scales and some bags in his hand. 'Let me sort out those ounces for you. You will find that I have measured them out beautifully.' He frowned. 'Oh, that weighs twenty now. But the other one is eighteen. That can't be right. I'll swap some from this one to this one.'

'What are you trying to get?'

'Twenty. Sixteen each for the weed, four for the weight of the bag.'

'Well you won't get it from twenty and eighteen. Not if you mean each.'

'I'll go and get some more from the back. I was sure that I measured that out right.' Her Mad Neighbour came back with another handful of weed, and put some in each bag. She wondered if she'd ever seen a madder sight than him taking weed from one bag, casting stray leaves all over the place before moving what remained to the other bag, weighing both of them while muttering numbers to himself, and then moving some of it back the other way. There was weed stuck in his eyebrow, and there was loose weed all over the scales and bench. 'Eighteen, twenty. Twenty, eighteen. Eighteen, twenty…'

'Do you know that you're just moving the same bit back and forwards?' said Aljce.

'No I'm not,' he said. 'I'm just evening them up.' He went to the backroom and came back with another handful, adding it to one of the bags. 'Too much,' he said weighing it.

'Take some out then,' she said. 'I've got to get back. The kids are in the lounge by themselves, and they'll realise I'm not in the house soon.'

'Hang on, hang on,' he said, bending down over the bags and looking perplexed. 'Ahh, I know.' And he moved some from one bag to another. 'That'll be it,' he said. 'Twenty three, twenty three.'

'See, too much,' said Aljce, wishing he'd just hurry up.

'No,' he said, thrusting it at her.

'Some of it's yours,' she said.

'No. Take it, take it,' he said. 'It's doing my head in. It's the universe sending me a message.'

'Thank you. What's the stone like?'

'It's like being so close that you might be knocking on the door of the answer, and the answer's just on the other side.'

'What's the answer?'

'Knowing everything. What it all is.'

'Ahh, yes, I know what you mean. Yip, that's always a good one.'

'I like the last half of the joint best,' she said, changing the subject. 'Like when you save half, and then smoke it. 'Cos the oil has all seeped, yinno. From the hot smoke going through it. And it's all on the paper.'

'True. Is that what it is?' He frowned. 'What were we saying? I'm sure there was something else I discussed with myself. I hope it's not lost...'

'If a thought is lost, it's meant to be lost.'

Her Mad Neighbour nodded. 'No matter how good it was,' he said.

'Can you come here please Aljce?' said Marj. Aljce shrank from the summons. Here was coming misery, and she couldn't avoid it. Show no fear, she thought. She put on a small smile and walked into Marj's office, where Jillq and Marj sat either side of Marj's desk. Aljce waited.

'We've been talking Aljce,' said Jillq. Clearly, thought Aljce, riding out the pause. 'And we've decided,' said Jillq, 'that it would be best for you to have the same external supervisor as everyone else. So you will need to contact Dora and set up an appointment. For next month.'

'What about Edyth?' asked Aljce, trying not to show her dismay. She didn't have a battle plan for this.

'We think it will be best for everyone to see the same person,' said Jillq, avoiding the question.

'But Edyth is the right supervisor for me,' said Aljce.

'I hope you're not going to be difficult Aljce,' said Jillq reprovingly. 'I thought we'd spoken about you being difficult. Our expectations are that you will comply with the rules. I don't think that's unreasonable.'

'Edyth is familiar with my work,' said Aljce, trying to choose her words carefully.

'We are only willing to allow Dora,' said Jillq. 'Isn't that right Marj?' Marj nodded, frowning at Aljce.

'It's more cost effective,' she said. 'Everyone has the same external supervisor.'

'But you're not paying for my supervision. I am.'

'I hope you're not asking for special treatment again Aljce,' said Jillq.

'I don't think it's special treatment,' said Aljce, her heart sinking. She was not going to win this battle.

'That's what it sounds like,' said Jillq. Aljce knew who Dora was; she'd seen her in the Hub. She seemed like a mousy, well-meaning woman who was in Jillq's pocket and completely believed that Jillq was a good person who did worthy work. Dora Locket, in Jillq's pocket. Aljce imagined that confidentiality might not be Dora's strong suit.

'We are yet to have line management ourselves, Aljce,' said Jillq sternly. 'And you have been here for over six weeks. That is unacceptable.' Aljce sighed. 'It is your responsibility as a practitioner to set this up with me,' said Jillq.

'I don't have my diary with me right now,' said Aljce, using the same lie that had worked for her last time, and hoping that Jillq didn't ask her to go and get it. She wanted to put it off as long as possible. She couldn't bear to do line management, which was effectively internal supervision, with Jillq. Not only would Aljce be doing everything wrong, but talking to Jillq about anything to do with her work would leave her incredibly vulnerable, because Jillq would take those things and use them against her. Twist them. Make things more difficult. Jillq would remove the things that were working well for Aljce, because she could. Plus Aljce couldn't bear to be subservient to someone who clearly knew less about counselling, social work and the way people ticked than she did. She didn't want Jillq telling her how to do her work when she clearly had no idea. Luckily for Aljce, Jillq seemed content with her afternoon's work.

AFTER WORK, Aljce bought Pleasance and Liddell a glow stick each as a special treat. She needed to live a positive life. At bedtime, she broke the first one. It was the most beautiful red she had ever seen. True, clear, neon red. 'Pink,' said Pleasance.

'No Baby, it's red, of course. That's the one you chose.'

'Oh, I thought it was pink.'

'No, darling, red.' She laughed to herself. Pink. It was funny what they didn't know. Pleasance had known her colours for a long time. Then she looked at it again. For a moment, it had seemed to be an intensely dark watermelon neon. Watermelon pink. True and clear. Then it looked red again. She concentrated. Could it have been a bright glowing pink? When she thought about it, it was. When she thought about it as red, it was red. Was this how colours worked? Did everyone see the colours that they expected to see? She thought about her hallway, where she had cut tiny sections of print from magazines, and pinned them together in a cluster. There was one quote that said 'the traveller sees what they see, but the tourist sees what they come to see.' Was everyone seeing what they came to see? The label said red, so she expected red, and she saw red. Maybe Pleasance was a traveller who'd seen it for what it really was. Without being manipulated by labels. Perhaps it was a form of the placebo effect, applied to the way people experienced reality. Suggestibility, she supposed it was. Everyone at work seemed to suffer from it. They were just waiting for Jillq to tell them what colours to see.

'You should have made it a necklace,' said Pleasance wistfully. Aljce looked down at the string in her hands. A little piece of paranoia suggested that her daughter could choke on it in her sleep if it was around her neck, anchored to a light stick that could get trapped under her body if she rolled. You never heard of it happening to any other children, but... She leaned down to kiss Pleasance on the forehead.

'I don't need to,' she said. 'It's a sword.' She moved over to her other daughter's bed. 'I swear Liddell, that colour right there in your glowstick was not invented when I was born. Look at that blue glow. Aliens must have invented that. I don't remember any blue that intense. Not even neon.'

'Colours don't get invented mummy.'

'They do. The world is constantly inventing colour. The world changes according to how we perceive it. We create the world.' Liddell was silent as Aljce's words washed straight over her head.

Pleasance was still fighting the dragons concealed in the folds of her bedding. As Aljce snuck out of the room, she could see her swishing her glow stick through the air just above the place where the sheet met her blankets.

It wasn't Pleasance and Liddell's job to love her. It was Aljce's job to love herself. And it was her job as a mother to help her children author their own reality and to create their own self-image. Her job to comfort their insecurities, and to help them find a better narrative about the world, and about themselves. To allow them choose their own colours.

UNEXPECTEDLY, JILLQ LEFT Aljce alone for a few days. She even smiled at Aljce in the hallway. Aljce was puzzled. Could it be that Jillq had just been under stress up until now? Or perhaps she was bipolar, and now she'd reverted back to a nicer version of herself? Were the others aware of it, and just more tolerant than Aljce? Aljce began to feel uncharitable. She hadn't really tried to see the bigger picture with Jillq, and she hadn't tried to figure out what made her tick.

But just when Aljce was breathing a sigh of relief, and wondering if things were going to be okay, and that what had happened up until now would just pass and be forgotten, there it was on her desk: the letter. Ebb and flow again. She had underestimated Jillq by doubting her own experiences. Jillq wasn't a victim. She was a narcissist, who'd been quiet while she planned her next move. As soon as she saw the letter on her desk, she felt sick. She didn't open it at first, but that didn't help, and she decided that it was worse not to know. Perhaps whatever lay inside the envelope with Jillq's handwriting on it wasn't so scary after all. Perhaps it was just further instructions, or some piece of paper that Aljce had left lying around that she was returning. But even that wouldn't be good news. It was surely careless and against all policy to leave anything lying around unattended.

Inside the envelope, the letter was typewritten and formal. The Therapy Hub logo was at the top, on the right, while the date from yesterday was on the left. 'Dear Aljce,' it began. The letter announced itself as a written warning. For bullying the Reporter. They expected more professional behaviour from her, it said. They were disappointed that she had chosen not to take any responsibility for her abusive teasing. This led them to seriously question whether she was able to make any improvement in the future, but this is what they would require. 'Kind regards,' the letter finished itself. Indeed.

Aljce's heart fell out of her ribs. Her breathing felt short. It took her a few seconds, but she found her place in space again, as if she had just come down in a fast lift. Obviously, she had already received a warning for this, although that had just been a piece of paper headed up 'Written Warning,' and it had contained different words. What were they trying to do? Surely they couldn't give her a warning for the same incident twice. Could they be so stupid that they had forgotten the first one, or that they didn't know that you couldn't give the same warning twice and count it as a new warning? Perhaps it was more of a reminder of their power.

Suddenly, she wanted to talk to Lewis, and to tell him all about her work situation, but she knew that wasn't possible right now. Or ever. And this was when she needed him more than she ever had. The paper blurred a little as her hands shook. What the fuck was she going to do? All they had to do was pump another one of these out over some imagined fault, some imagined misdeed, and she would be out of a job. More than two written warnings, and an employee could be legally dismissed. And then what? Not only would they have won, but she would have no income at all other than a very basic benefit. They had so much power, and no matter how hard she tried, another letter like this would come. What was she going to do? All she could do right now was manage the moment and not let them see how big the hit was. Even an empty warning had upset her. She stuffed the letter into her bag. They wouldn't even know whether she'd read it or not yet. Perhaps they would see her with a slight smile on her lips and assume that it was unopened. They would feel a pleasant anticipation that soon she would be broken. Either that, or they would be frustrated that nothing they did could touch her. She hoped it was the second one, although that invited even more abuse.

'Do you know what I associate with Jillq?' she said to Strauss. They were sitting cross legged in front of her black wooden coffee table, and their backs were towards the big glass windows, catching the late morning sun. The girls were outside.

'Roll us a solid stone,' said Strauss.

'She reminds me of that clown on IT, because of her red hair. Something evil masking itself as something fun and happy.'

'Haha, think of Ronald McDonald instead. I'm loving IT.'

'Everyone knows that movie, ay.'

'Yeah, classic.'

'You'd think us being friends, we would have had exactly the same experiences, but no, there's a lot we don't know about each other. Like we don't know what movies the other one has seen. Not necessarily.'

'Not unless we've seen them together. And we can never agree on them.'

'Yeah, you like creepy stuff. Supernatural and horror.'

'And you like that arty shit.'

'Thank you Strauss. I'm improving you. Looking at the images and appreciating the colours is where it's at.'

'I like adrenalin.'

'I can't handle too much of that. I can't bear suspense when it comes to movies. Years ago, when I was watching IT as a kid, I was down behind the couch, trying to hide, and my sister was hissing at me that I was embarrassing her in front of her boyfriend... If they didn't ramp up the freak-you-out-suspense music... I'm pretty sensitive to music induced emotion. And when that clown tried to strangle that kid with the balloons...'

Strauss frowned. 'I don't think that happened. Not on IT. Maybe on that other movie. What was it called?'

'Weird how you can think memory is there, stored in orderly ways, with each piece fitting in to the other super neatly, but when you go back to put the jigsaw together, there's so many missing pieces, and pieces that don't fit at all.'

'Like someone picked your box of pieces up and shook it, and then dropped it with some other boxes, and sort of scooped all the pieces back into whatever box, without really checking them. So you sort of have it roughly, but the organisation is fucked up, and probably some of the bits got lost under chairs and thrown out or vacuumed up.'

'Haha. That's exactly how it is.'

'You think it's all there perfectly, every piece in its place, until you check it.'

Aljce thought how a quote she had come across recently was completely true. You didn't remember what happened. What you remember became what happened.

THE PHONE IN her office rang. Aljce frowned at it. Who would call for her? It was the first time she'd heard it ring.

'Call for you,' called Chelsea brightly from down the hall, happy to have something to do. 'I've just put it through.' There were no direct calls at the Therapy Hub. Everyone had to get through reception first.

'It's a woman. She wouldn't say who she was….' Aljce frowned again. She didn't need unusual occurrences.

'Hello Aljce,' said a voice on the other end of the line.

'Oh, kia ora Hannah,' said Aljce, recognising her voice instantly.

'Just ringing to see how things are going now with the new job at this point,' said Hannah.

Aljce started crying, as quietly as she could, but she was unable to stop herself from sniffling. Luckily Kat was still away, and she had the office to herself.

'Not very good then,' said Hannah. 'I was wondering, because Jillq rang this morning to talk to me. So she said. But mostly what she wanted was to say bad things about you. I told her that we weren't speaking about the same person, because you were the best employee that I've ever had.'

'Thanks Hannah,' said Aljce, swallowing a sob that tried to rise up in her throat.

'Do you know,' said Hannah, 'that she had the cheek to ask me if there was anything I could give her that she could 'use' to assist her in her next conversation with you? And she was making it clear that she wanted to know about any dissatisfactions I had had with you. Anything that you might have done that would show you in a bad light. That is so unprofessional of her. And it's a breach of your privacy.'

'Aren't you my referee though? Isn't she entitled to ask?'

'Not once you've already signed your new employment contract. Permission to contact a referee is only for employee selection purposes. Once you're already employed, her right to contact your referees is over.'

'She has me on a three-month, ninety-day trial,' said Aljce. 'If she can find a reason not to make my job permanent, she will.'

'Let her prove it in Employment Court,' said Hannah. 'We will have her for breach of your privacy.' Aljce gave silent thanks for that 'we.'

'Keep all your emails from her,' continued Hannah. 'Keep a notebook. Document everything. You never know what you might need.'

'I'm just scared she's listening to this phone call,' said Aljce.

'I'll call you on your own phone next time,' said Hannah. 'Take care Aljce. And remember it's not you, it's her.'

THE NEXT WEEK, Kat was back, just as if she'd never been away. 'Oh,' said Aljce, seeing her. Kat was on her phone.

'Do you want to see the photos from my holiday?' she asked Aljce brightly.

'They'd be on Facebook wouldn't they?' said Aljce, looking for an out. 'Where did you go?' Damn, she thought, I shouldn't have given her that last sentence to feed off. But it wasn't as if she was pushed for time anyway. What was a little bit of prattle here, in amongst everything else?

'I thought you didn't have Facebook,' said Kat. Aljce recalled telling Kat that, when Kat had wanted to send a friend request. Aljce did have Facebook, but there was no way she was going to let it get filled up with empty, time-wasting people like Kat. The best way to describe Kat would probably be to say that she had a busy energy, full of minute detail, all of it amounting to nothing. Aljce could suck that up at work, but there was no way she was having that in her private space.

'Um, yeah,' she said. 'Sure, show me now.'

'So,' said Kat, 'here is me in Phuket. And see that lovely young man serving me a Margarita? He thought I was still in my twenties!'

'Mmm,' murmured Aljce, knowing the script. 'I'm not surprised that he thought that. You have lovely skin.' Perhaps she would need Kat one day. But would insincere flattery be enough to buy her? Or did she just expect that as her entitlement; did she give it no gratitude, and therefore assign no loyalty to the person who gave it to her? Or was Jillq giving her more, and better? 'Why are you by the pool?' she asked Kat. 'Were there no beaches there?'

Kat shuddered. 'I didn't want sand sticking to my suntan oil!' she said. 'No one goes to the actual beaches. Why would you when there's sun loungers by the pool?'

'Isn't it just a bit like being at home then, but with hotter sun?'

'Look at that lovely young man,' said Kat. 'You can't find him here at home.'

You probably couldn't pay him enough to put up with your self-centred energy over here, where he could earn actual money, thought Aljce. He probably only gets paid six dollars a day over there, and he's feeding his family on that.

'Did you take all your annual leave at once?' she asked. Kat waved her hand in the air, as if she was brushing something aside.

'I have an arrangement with Jillq,' she said. 'I can take as many holidays as I want, as long as I come back here and work in between times.' Aljce sighed inwardly. She may as well give up on the struggle for Kat's loyalty. She couldn't top a revolving job open at Kat's convenience. Kat could be here one moment, and gone the next. Jillq clearly knew that she needed a counsellor with an actual qualification on board in order to build and maintain her fantasy, where she was the queen of an entire therapy empire.

'What about your clients?' she asked.

'Oh, they're always here when I get back,' said Kat vaguely. 'They never seem to get any better. Look, here's me in the dress I bought at a Sydney boutique. We stopped over for some shopping on the way there. I'll wear it to work sometime to show you. Everyone said it was really my colour.'

'Definitely,' murmured Aljce. It never paid to burn any bridges, even if they were bridges that you didn't think you'd ever need to cross. That was her policy. So much in life was unforeseen.

She wondered if Kat had any idea that other people who worked with her were miserable. Specifically, herself, Aljce; but also people who had come before her. She thought of the woman she'd found crying on the first day she'd arrived. Kat probably wasn't; she was too taken up with herself. Would she care even if someone did tell her? Perhaps she would just wave her hand in the air, and brush it aside, brush it out of the way. Inconvenient. Not something to think about when she had holidays to plan with her Pilot boyfriend. Because that was it. No one here wanted to stand up for anything when they had something to lose themselves. Chelsea had a title, and she got to be Jillq's pet. Little Chelsea Bun. Mrs. Kingi had status, and crumbs of affection. Hattie had the licence to be as mad as she liked. She could ascribe client trauma to their birth experience and ask them to scream and moan as they pushed their way through piles of cushions in order to successfully rebirth. She could suggest that they rearranged the layout of the chairs at their kitchen table to encourage better chi. She could expect that this would help them conquer that fear of rejection, or help them with their meth addiction. Because, apparently, you had to address the root cause, and not the symptom.

'I'M PRETTY MUCH alright when I'm talking to someone,' she said to Strauss. 'It's while I'm by myself that the stress and worry sets in.'

'It's a collision of energies: hers and yours.'

'Yes, it is. Her energy feels like it's ripping me apart. Taking over and filling me with negative feeling.'

'You'll just have to out-energy her.'

'Yeah, that's an interesting idea. But she has real-world power over me.'

'So use your energy subtly.'

'Yeah, that's what I think I'm trying to do.'

'Maybe it's one of those big stories; good versus evil.'

'Strauss, that's why I like you. Although I am not entirely good. And can she even be evil? I don't like to believe in evil.'

'But you do.'

'Well, I wonder if evil is granted entry by those people who are not able to put themselves in someone else's emotional shoes. That absence of empathy. People who do what they choose, as long as it's not going to have any negative impact on them. Because they have big feelings for themselves. Their own feelings fill up all the space in their head that wondering about other people's feelings takes up for us.'

'Yeah, I know those people you mean...'

'Yeah. Jillq's one of them. It's just like she's dead inside when she considers me. There's nothing there, just a cold, solid glassiness. She can't CONNECT with my feelings at all.'

'See?'

'Yeah, I get. She's like a black hole, trying to pull me out of my orbit and into her darkness. She's gonna try to spit me out like gamma rays.' She laughed. 'You should be a counsellor, Strauss.'

'Doesn't seem like the best gig from the sound of it.' There was a pause. 'Actually,' said Strauss, 'there's something I want to talk to YOU about.'

'Why? Because I'm your counsellor in training?'

'No, because me and Jimsy are going to move to Aussie.' The gold to dark ratio in the evening air suddenly changed.

'The FUCK?'

'He's been going to alcohol counselling.'

'Oh. How come?'

'I don't know. He just decided.'

'So nothing happened?'

'No, there was nothing. He just asked me to hook him up. I think it might be to do with his sister having cancer, and, I dunno, maybe just wanting to be healthy.'

'Oh, well, good on him. Yip. But why are you going to Aussie? Is that for a holiday?'

'Maybe. But if we like it, we'll stay. His sister lives there.'

'But you know that means I have to put up with Mamae's Sister on my own.'

'You'll be alright, chick. Talk to Mamae.'

'But I don't like Mamae so much when she's there.'

'Sorry. Talk to yourself.'

'Might have to. I'm trying to be happy for you.'

'I don't even know if I'm happy for me.'

'Can you not go then?'

'See, there's this thing. This man at work. What if I've misjudged myself and I'm not actually that loyal? I have incredible chemistry with this guy.'

'Keep the fuck away from him then.'

'Ya. That's one of the reasons I've agreed to go to Aussie. The chemistry between me and him is so strong. I need to put some distance between our magnetic poles. Jimsy is for life. I don't wanna ruin that. And I feel weak right now.'

FUCK, FUCK, thought Aljce. She had been sitting by her window for a while. The moon was big and golden, and dying slowly, like everything else. If Strauss went to Aussie, she'd probably have to widen her friend circle by at least one. She didn't have a lot of friends, and she couldn't afford to lose one. She wondered if she could be bothered. Less friends versus can't be fucked having friends. You needed friends. It was good to have people to do things with. Fuck. She felt tired at the thought of having to make a friend. Plus there were very, very few Strausses in the world. It would be a long, tiring mission. And maybe a disappointing one. She needed to focus on what she did have. Not what she didn't. You could only control the things that were in your power to change. Everything else had to be let go. Negative karma was not going to help. And she needed her energy for other things. She would have to face everything alone. Especially work.

ALJCE DIDN'T BELIEVE that evil was random, so she usually kept trying out different mental health frameworks; mental health templates, to explain the behaviour of people who did her wrong. Were they traumatised and triggered? ADHD impulsive? On the autistic scale and low in emotional and social skills? She mentally went back to her conversation with Strauss, and the more she thought about it, the more her experience at work was making her think that perhaps it WAS simpler than that. What if evil people were actually just narcissistic people without the right part in the brain to experience empathy? The ones with cold energy? Jillq and people like her.

It was okay to lie and manipulate, to pretend you were someone other than you were, as long as you were fighting evil: to protect yourself or others, Aljce thought, aware that she might be making excuses for herself.

As long as you did it for the cause of good. It was the only way to beat the demons. That's why so many people lost battles. They put their emotions out in front of them, and the emotional vampires said to everyone, 'See, they're crazy!' Feeding off the feelings of others while at the same time making out that normal feelings were a sign of instability. After poking them with a stick to make sure that the feelings came out; and then pretending that they'd never done anything, so that the feelings looked random/unexplained/craaazy. Sucking up people's distress as if it was a power source. The only way to beat evil was to be subversive, to take advantage of its inherent narcissism. The narcissism that led them to believe that they had you nailed. That you didn't see them for who they were. That you were so powerless in the face of their mindfucks, and so full of self-doubt, that all you were thinking about was your own worthlessness. No idea in their minds that you could be so uppity as to be planning their defeat, or so bold as to be acting against them. Jillq was underestimating her.

But Jillq was also ruthless in pursuing detail; micromanaging Aljce to death. Aljce felt as though she could hardly breathe, suffocated by someone else's mediocrity. Blamed for not doing everything Jillq's way, when in reality what Aljce was doing was excellent, but it was clearly Aljce's way, which apparently made it wrong. Aljce could not stand doing things in stupid ways. Had she been more willing to bow, perhaps things would have been different; it could have been someone else being singled out. But could Aljce have stood by and allowed that the way the others did? She didn't think so. And that would have singled her out in itself.

'Aljce. Who has put this poster on the wall?' Jillq had asked.

'Oh. Me.'

'Why?'

'Because it's promoting something that clients might be interested in. It's a march to end the stigma against mental health.'

'Are you suggesting that our clients aren't mentally healthy?'

'I'm suggesting that lots of people experience poor mental health in their lifetimes, and it's likely that that includes our clients as well?'

'I have never experienced poor mental health. People just need to focus on the positive.'

'Well, yip, that can help, but it's hard when your brain chemicals aren't set up for that.'

'Do you have poor mental health, Aljce?'

Aljce had started to speak. Then she stopped. Whatever she said could and would be used against her in a court of Therapy Hub law, and it would be off with her head. I have an excellent grip on both reality and insanity, she had wanted to say. Most people I know only have a hold on one. 'Mental health issues can affect anyone,' she had said instead.

'I have excellent mental health,' Jillq had pronounced, 'so clearly that is incorrect. More importantly, you are not abiding by our rules. No posters on the walls. We don't want the place to look shabby. I have purchased framed prints for the walls. No posters or flyers. That's a rule.'

Aljce had sighed. She found it hard to comprehend why some abstract pictures of dots consuming each other were more important to have on the walls of a place setting itself up as a Therapy Hub than posters with self-help numbers or supportive community events. And given that shabby was the Therapy Hub's middle name, it was hard to see how abstract dots were going to change it. Maybe someone would connect them.

Aljce found herself second guessing everything. What she wrote in the appointment book. How she arranged her desk. The content of her files for non-existent clients. Everything was a potential hazard. Before she did anything, she had to consider it from every angle to see how it could be used against her by the enemy. The secret enemy. And while she did it, she knew it didn't matter how hard she tried to stay ahead of the game. Someone would find some way to hurt her.

ALJCE SAT UP late that night, using the email address that the woman from the conference had given her. She'd been so nice. 'If you ever need any help in your role,' she'd said, 'please come to me.' Aljce needed help now. She couldn't go on like this. It had got to the point where it was affecting her separate, private evening-life space, where no one else should have been able to get in. Her email was long and dense. It detailed every mad, bizarre thing that Jillq had done, and done to Aljce. She proof read it several times, and added things she'd forgotten. It was 4 o'clock before she finished, and even then, she couldn't be sure that she had, because her eyes had started to cloud over, and it was difficult to see the words clearly. She wanted it to be perfect. She wanted it to say everything, because she might never get another chance.

If the woman brought it to Jillq's attention, Jillq would do everything to shut it down and discredit Aljce. 'I would prefer that you didn't speak to Jillq about this,' she wrote. 'What I really want is some advice on what to do, and how to stop what is happening to me.' Was that realistic? Or was she just too scared of Jillq to ask for her to be dealt with? She hesitated before pushing send. Perhaps it was a bad move. And it was a move that, once made, would not be able to be recalled. Perhaps the woman would show Jillq, horrified that Jillq's employee was spreading such slander about someone wonderful who was the loving queen of her own Therapy Hub. Perhaps they would then be a force of two against Aljce. Perhaps the whole thing would backfire into an even bigger nightmare.

Have courage, she told herself. Where in Alice in Wonderland does Alice ever hesitate to act or to take an opportunity once it presents itself? It's not about having no fears. It's about not letting them hold you back.

She pushed send. But she sat there for a long time looking at the computer screen afterwards.

OFF WITH THEIR HEADS

FOR THE NEXT WEEK, she was hopeful. She felt as if something good might happen, as if something might come to her rescue. She felt that she had a secret inside her that no one else knew about, and it kept her happy and resilient. But there was no reply. She checked the email she had sent it to against the email address on the scrap of paper the woman had given her. It would be awful if she'd sent it to someone else by mistake. Aljce didn't know whether to be relieved or annoyed not to have received an answer of some sort. But maybe the woman from the conference was away? The hopeful feeling slowly wore off. On the other hand, there hadn't been any attacks by Jillq either, despite Aljce being constantly alert for them. Perhaps things had settled down. Perhaps it had just been a bad patch. Perhaps she shouldn't have sent that email.

SHE WAS RUDELY awakened from her new hope by Marj. 'I've scheduled a meeting in your diary,' she said.

'Which one?' asked Aljce.

'Your Outlook Calendar. I hope you're using it. Everyone should be using their Outlook Calendar.'

'I just find it difficult to keep track of all the different diaries,' said Aljce, mentally processing the information that there was a meeting while she talked.

'What's the meeting about?'

'Oh, just tidying up some things,' said Marj elusively.

'Who will be there?'

'Myself, Jillq. You.'

Aljce's heart sank. She was clearly the focus then. It wasn't a meeting about somebody or something else where she could just be as silent as possible. It would be another attempt to make things worse for her. Although how it could get worse with everyone at the Therapy Hub hating her, being banned from seeing clients, and expected to have supervision with Jillq and Dora, she didn't know. Perhaps it was going to be where she received her final warning.

She checked her Outlook Calendar. It was Monday and the meeting was on Friday. Several days in which to stress about it then. Because no matter how hard she tried to put it out of her mind, it would always be there at the back of it, worrying her; making things feel unpleasant and sickening. It would spoil everything else. She was sure that Jillq knew this. She employed two techniques: the long, slow anxious wait for the meeting about Aljce, and the surprise meeting about Aljce for which Aljce was unprepared. This one was a return to the first method.

Friday came around, of course. There were no windows in Jillq's office. Aljce thought to herself that if she was the boss, there was no way she'd be in an office with no windows, no matter how opulent it was. She thought of her own desk, where she could see the rabbits eating clover, hopping around without any worldly cares. Even though she was on the wrong side of the glass, she could at least watch another part of the universe unfolding in a stress-free way.

'So,' said Aljce, looking around the walls, and hoping vainly to postpone what would no doubt be unpleasant. Her eye was caught by the bookshelf behind the desk. 'You have some interesting books on your shelf, Jillq,' she said, trying to demonstrate friendly intent; not that that had ever done her any good with Jillq before, but maybe it would soften her somewhat. 'What's that one about?'

'Which one?' said Jillq.

'*The Sleep of Morpheus*. It's an intriguing title.'

'Jillq is an interesting person,' said Marj.

Sounds like a book about a morphine addict, thought Aljce, suddenly curious, and wondering if she dared to lift it off the shelf and look at it.

'You know about the arms of Morpheus, no doubt,' said Jillq.

'Of course,' lied Aljce automatically. Jillq looked at her suspiciously.

She's wondering if I do know, thought Aljce. If she asks me any more questions about it, it will be plain that I don't. But she's probably going to bet that I do know, because I usually actually do. Oh my gosh, I'm so getting like her. Why did I even lie? I should have just said that I have no idea. If it was someone else, I'd back track and say, actually no. I have no clue about the arms of Morpheus. I just don't want this meeting to start. I don't know what will come of it, but it will be horrible for me, no doubt about it. She sighed inwardly. There was no way that Jillq was going to be distracted when she had set the scene and lined up her ammunition. There was no way that Aljce could throw her off track and drift off out of the room without Jillq firing her shots.

Marj held her phone tightly. 'I hope you don't mind, Aljce,' she said, 'but we've decided it's better for everyone if we tape our conversations from now on.'

'Go ahead,' said Aljce. 'I don't feel that I've got anything to hide.' Could be in my favour, she thought. If they talk the shit they usually do. There was a pause while Marj fiddled with the settings.

'I've practised this,' she said. 'I can't figure out why it's not going.'

'See if it recorded you saying that,' said Aljce.

'I've practised this,' said the phone in worried tones.

'See, it's going.'

'So it is. Hang on, I'll start it again.'

What would it be like to have a mind that moved as slowly as Marj's, wondered Aljce. Would she get frustrated with herself, or would she just cruise it; oblivious to higher layers?

'You've been to a Community Meeting, without permission,' said Jillq.

'I thought that was what my role had come down to,' said Aljce. 'Community promotion and information.'

'Did you have express permission to leave the building?'

'I've finished my list of tasks. That means I can get stuck into my role doesn't it?'

'Can I see your notes please?'

'Notes for what?' said Aljce, confused.

'Notes from the meeting.'

'Oh, I didn't take notes.' She felt relieved. It would be hard for Jillq to find fault with notes that didn't exist.

'NO NOTES?'

Aljce realised that she may have made a technical mistake. She belatedly remembered Jillq's fondness for notes. Perhaps she should have taken notes. But she would have been damned if she did and damned if she didn't. She hadn't thought about taking notes. She never took notes because she never needed to.

'How do we know you were even there? If you haven't taken notes, you could have been anywhere.'

'I can tell you what we talked about. I don't need to rely on notes.'

'It's not professional,' sniffed Mrs. Kingi, who had come into the room, quietly closing the door behind her. No doubt worrying that Jillq might need moral support. Immoral support, thought Aljce.

'If I'm at a meeting, I always take notes,' went on Mrs. Kingi. 'I wouldn't remember what was discussed otherwise.'

'That's you,' said Aljce. 'I've got a good verbal memory. I don't need to take notes. There's no point.'

'Always trying to make yourself superior to others,' said Jillq disapprovingly. 'I hardly think you need to place yourself above Mrs. Kingi.'

'It's not that at all. I'm sure she has talents that I don't have, but remembering what was said is one of mine.'

'Sounds nasty and gossipy,' said Jillq. 'And if you are representing us, you will take notes.' All ways are my ways, thought Aljce.

'I think you want me to be somebody I'm not,' said Aljce. 'But I can only be myself. I can't be Mrs. Kingi. I know I'm not perfect. But I think I'm fine. I'm kind and I'm friendly and I work hard. Nobody's perfect. See that poem you've got on the wall? About how you can try as hard as you like to be that perfect plum, but if you're a peach, you'll never be a good plum, and it's better to try to be the best peach you can be? I'm a peach, and that's all I can ever be.'

'Always twisting things,' said Jillq. 'That metaphor doesn't apply to you.'

'Why not? That's silly. Surely it applies to everyone.'

'Aljce!' said Mrs. Kingi in horror. 'I hope you didn't call Jillq silly!'

'And that is the bullying we are talking about Aljce!' said Jillq. 'It doesn't matter what sort of fruit you are if you're a bully.'

'What are your qualifications?' asked Aljce, knowing that it sounded random, but invested in the answer. Not that she could necessarily expect the truth.

'I am a therapist,' said Jillq, looking annoyed.

'What sort of therapist? Where did you train?'

'I shouldn't have to be subjected to an inquisition,' said Jillq, looking around for support. 'It's not me under the microscope being called into question here.'

'You need to listen to Jillq, Aljce,' said Marj. 'She has a lot of training and experience. She knows about these things. All you need to do is listen to her. She's trying to help you.'

'Not that she should bother,' said Mrs. Kingi. 'Not if you're going to be ungrateful.'

'Oh, I'm always grateful for kindness,' said Aljce elusively, not referring to Jillq or anyone to do with the Therapy Hub.

'Jillq has been very patient with you,' said Marj. Aljce sighed. Marj still might not be like the others. There was still a good chance that she was just so stupid that she believed everything Jillq said, and who knew what she might have said to Marj about Aljce. Marj's Jillq wasn't Aljce's Jillq.

Jillq began to detail her version of Aljce at length.

'So…' said Aljce, attempting to clarify.

'You're interrupting again, Aljce.' Jillq had been talking for the last five minutes. 'Sometimes,' said Jillq, appropriating a popular internet quote for her own purposes, 'I feel that you aren't listening to understand, you're just waiting for the opportunity to put your bit in.'

Outwardly, Aljce tried to be prim. She was indeed waiting, having understood the meaning of Jillq's communication several minutes ago. But she put her trying to listen to understand face on, even though her inner self was screaming that conversation was meant to be shared. Disagreeing about whether she interrupted or not would just be another thing to be used against her.

'I find you quite passive aggressive actually,' said Jillq. Aljce raised her eyebrows. Not interrupting was getting harder and harder. 'So this has been yet another challenging conversation,' concluded Jillq.

It has indeed thought Aljce, wondering how on Earth she herself was managing to put up with such high levels of frustration and injustice. 'Well,' said Aljce, mindful of the phone lying on the table. 'I value my job and I will be trying hard to be a great plum. Let's hope it all works out for all of us.'

'I'm not so sure about that Aljce,' said Jillq.

'Not sure about what?'

'Not sure that I want it to work out.'

Aljce tried to keep a poker face. 'I'm sure if we all work together in good faith…' she said.

'I'm not sure where I sit with that. I don't think I can warm to you,' said Jillq. 'I'm not sure I want to try.'

'That's a shame Jillq,' said Aljce.

'I think we should stop it there,' said Marj. 'I'm not sure how much I can record at one time.'

'I think it just goes until you stop it,' said Aljce, but Marj had already stopped it.

'I'm pretty sure we were finished anyway,' said Aljce.

'I determine when we stop and finish,' said Jillq.

'Okay, what else do you want to talk about?'

'I was just going to say that the meeting is over. Marj has stopped recording.'

'So I can go?' said Aljce. Things had become so bizarre that she was more astonished than upset by the process she'd just taken part in. Although nothing should astonish her anymore. She should be used to hearing nonsense and having to participate in it.

ALJCE TRIED TO breathe the serenity prayer as she went back to her office. Somewhere along, she'd gotten the lines mixed up, but she left it like that because she liked it her way. Give me the courage to change the things I can, the serenity to accept the things I can't, and the wisdom to know the difference. She could not control these people, or any people. They lived by some laws known only unto themselves. She hadn't been able to stop Lewis leaving, and she knew it would be pointless to try and stop Strauss going. Not to mention selfish. All she could do was choose how she wanted to respond to the things that happened to her. That was what she was in control of. Everything else needed to be shelved under serenity, or at least acceptance, which was more realistic.

It wouldn't have been so bad if she had an ally. Someone she could talk to at work, to say, 'You're not going to believe this …' to. But MaryAnn was head down, bum up, as she liked to say. She didn't want anything to disturb her own safe space. Not even to help a friend. And Kat was totally engrossed in anyone who professed their love for her. There were several men waiting in the wings, but the Pilot was keen, and because he flew to and from Paris, there was the possibility that he might take her there, she said. 'The city of love,' she giggled to Aljce. Maybe he would propose. She said something in French which Aljce didn't catch. From Kat's giggling it might have been a sexual reference.

If she'd still had Lewis to talk to, that would have been a safe place to go...

When she got up to go to the toilet, she found Jillq lurking in the corridor outside her door. Aljce felt as if she had conjured her up. She had been wondering whether Jillq was in fact a narcissist, or just a crazy self-centred bitch, as Strauss had suggested. Mamae's Sister was a self-centred bitch, and Aljce had been trying to compare them.

Jillq startled when she realised Aljce was in the corridor as well. 'Aljce. I didn't know you were so close,' she said with obvious irritation.

'So close to what?' asked Aljce, eyeing the walls.

'So near at hand.' Jillq sounded as if Aljce had personally offended her by somehow avoiding detection, as if Aljce should have shown up on some sort of radar.

'Um,' said Aljce.

'Um is not a word,' said Jillq. 'Be professional at all times please.'

'Sure,' said Aljce.

Jillq melted away, but reappeared again shortly. 'We are short of golf balls,' she said. 'People are not being mindful.'

'I've had to come in after hours to trace them,' said Marj. 'We need to know whose office they are being hit into the cracks from.'

'Everybody's,' said Mrs. Kingi cheerfully. Marj looked cross.

'I was here all evening crawling around under the building. I put a lot of extra hours into this place.'

'So where were they coming from?' asked Chelsea. She can blame anyone, though Aljce. It doesn't matter if they came from her station or her corridor, because she can just say it was someone else.

'Several came from Aljce's office,' said Jillq.

'Oh, that was probably me,' said Kat. 'I sometimes hit a few while I'm waiting for my Pilot to reply.' Thank you Kat, thought Aljce. Jillq sniffed.

'We all just need to be mindful,' she said. 'Especially Aljce.'

The others had clearly not known that it was an opportunity to slate the blame for something onto Aljce. Perhaps that required pre-priming.

'Why don't we all go outside and collect the ones that are out there?' said Chelsea, no doubt thinking about the sunshine outside.

'Great idea,' said Jillq. 'We can all contribute.'

'Oh, I'm busy,' said Kat.

'I didn't mean you Kat,' soothed Jillq hurriedly. 'I meant everyone else. Of course you are busy.'

'I'm expecting a call,' said Kat.

'Your Pilot?' asked Aljce.

'Oh, no. Although he does like to call me to talk any time he's free. I'm trying to get an appointment at my tanning centre. The woman has made a huge mistake with my booking. She knows it's my usual, and she's double booked.'

'After lunch, the rest of us will meet at the front door,' said Jillq with the air of someone organising a picnic. It's not like there's anything else to do, though Aljce. It's all unrushed fake work here. We probably all get paid from what Kat earns with her counselling. And maybe from what Hattie earns. No wonder Jillq treats them well. She needs them to keep her fake Therapy Hub functioning. But it's really not a therapy hub at all. It's a kingdom for Jillq to rule over. A queendom. Where she can be in charge of excursions. And making pronouncements on other people's character.

AFTER LUNCH, the weather no longer seemed auspicious, and Chelsea's hope of a walk in the sunshine was clearly not going to come to pass. 'Shall we put it off?' asked Mrs. Kingi, peering outside where clouds as thick and dark and dense as new bruises were gathering.

'Rubbish,' said Jillq. 'It's still bright in here.' Of course it is, thought Aljce. It's bright pink. The vibe is cheerful in here. Even though the energy is rotten.

'It'll be fine,' said Dulcie breezily.

'Of course it will,' said Jillq.

'Just saying,' said Mrs. Kingi sulkily. She didn't like anyone agreeing with Jillq more than she did, even if it was Jillq's daughter.

'Where's MaryAnn?' asked Dulcie. 'I thought she was here today.'

'Clearing her office,' said Jillq. MaryAnn's boss had had her moved into an office of her own further down the corridor. 'We no longer have a place for her role. Freeing up room space!' Aljce blinked. She'd talked to MaryAnn earlier, and MaryAnn hadn't mentioned leaving.

'Do we have the buckets?' asked Jillq. 'Marj, where are the buckets?'

'They're here somewhere,' said Marj, looking around as if she had no idea where the buckets were.

'They might be in the cleaning cupboard,' said Chelsea.

'That's excellent thinking,' said Jillq. 'Well done, Bun!' Chelsea smirked.

'She probably put them there,' said Hattie in an undertone to Aljce. She was currently rocking the same shade of red hair as Jillq. Aljce pretended she hadn't heard. She wasn't going to get involved in anyone's squabbles. It was her who would be hung out to dry in the end, with the other two uniting against her; besties again.

'I'll pair up with you Jillq,' said Mrs. Kingi.

'I was going to!' said Hattie.

'First in!' said Mrs. Kingi. 'You can go with Aljce.'

'Let's just go as a group,' said Jillq. 'One bucket between two! Fan out in diamond formation!'

They went outside, with Jillq in the centre of the group, like a queen bee surrounded by her workers. The wind was starting to rise, and it gusted off them, lifting their hair into the air so that it got into their mouths and flicked at their cheeks. Chelsea had a hat on, and almost immediately, she had to run across the paddock to chase it. 'Take a bucket!' shouted Marj, hastening after her with one. Aljce drifted away after them. Better them than Jillq's group.

'Eyes down,' shouted Jillq.

'I can see one!' shouted Hattie, off to the side. Aljce walked in the opposite direction to the white, dimpled ball that Hattie was pointing at. The clouds were low and thick and seemed to shudder as if they were pure energy vibrating at very fast speeds. She could sense a prickling in her spine. The air was as liquid as water, and she felt as if she was swimming. Looking for the balls reminded her of when she was younger, and she'd gone out looking for mushrooms on the farms near where she'd lived. Eyes peeled, waiting for that flash of bright white. That had brought her a lot of pleasure. She didn't know why, but right now she felt quite agitated. That's what this job had done to her.

The atmosphere was tingling now, and even though Aljce couldn't physically see the air in front of her, she knew it was thick with electricity. The cicadas had quietened, and there were no longer any bees on the clover. It was as if nature had evacuated. The only noise Aljce could hear was some rumbling from trucks in the distance, going about their business with no reference to her at all. Thank goodness there's no metal out here, though Aljce. I'd be getting little shocks in all directions. She looked around nervously. She could hear thunder in the distance, chiming in with the distant engines. The stomach of the sky is grumbling, she thought, even though she knew it was the electrical charges in the clouds colliding with each other. She vaguely remembered that lightning strikes were caused by the electrical charge on the ground arcing up and meeting the charge in the clouds. Thunder meant lightning. She did not want to be out here. I've gotten so paranoid, she thought.

She turned to go back in, her bucket empty. She could see the others, separated from each other as if they were all picking strawberries and had their own patch. Only Mrs. Kingi was still at Jillq's elbow, hovering like a butterfly waiting for a flower. Every now and then, one of them bent over, presumably to pick up a ball. The light was receding, like water going down a drain. Surely they won't mind if I go inside, she thought. They probably won't even miss me.

She took a wide curve, so that she would end up around the back of the building. She could go in again without anyone seeing, given that they had already gotten some distance away. She looked guiltily at her bucket. It was still empty. This was clearly not the direction in which the balls came. What a pity that she didn't know Jillq's computer password. It would have been a great opportunity to go in and see what she had in there in relation to Aljce. If Aljce had dared… But never mind, it would be good to just go in and sit in the building by herself, without any of them near her.

She was only just inside the door when she heard the first fat, wet splotches of rain hit the grass outside. The others were still far across the field, but they'd be coming in now too. It was lucky that she didn't know Jillq's password after all. It would have been too risky to use it, and she might have gotten caught. She thanked the universe for keeping her safe. Perhaps there would have been nothing to find anyway: Jillq wasn't known for her good record keeping. Had Aljce been this secretive, deceiving person before she'd come to work here? She laughed to herself. She could have fixed Jillq's spelling mistakes and let her fret about whether anyone had been through HER documents. It was the only way to fight fire. With fire. Without letting the fire know it was being fought. Because the fire expected her to fight it with water, and it was ready for that. She sighed. Things were complicated.

'Heard you were moving somewhere else,' she said, popping her head around MaryAnn's door. MaryAnn was on the floor sorting through papers. She looked guilty.

'Yes; boomers. Closer to town. And my boss didn't want me up here any longer. I find it a bit strange here. They're not keen on me going to meetings, and they keep wanting me to do more brochures. I've got a few up my sleeve now. Keen to get on with the real work!'

'Lucky you,' said Aljce. 'I'd like to do that too.'

'Why don't you move offices as well?'

'If only. Jillq is my direct boss, and I can't see her moving me anywhere. Except perhaps to fire me.'

'She can't do that,' said MaryAnn.

'She can. I'm still in the ninety-day trial period.'

'Why would she?'

'Uh, we haven't gotten on the best. I've been told that I can't see clients. All I can do is network and promote family violence intervention. And that's your role. Even if you're going to be based elsewhere, that's what you'll be doing. It's covered.'

'Funny lady, Jillq,' said MaryAnn. 'Glad to be out of here. But you'll be okay.'

'Lucky you!' said Aljce again.

'Yeah, I'm looking forward to it,' said MaryAnn. She didn't seem to give any thought to leaving Aljce behind, only to her own good fortune to be leaving. But it wouldn't have been good karma for Aljce to be resentful.

'You'll be okay,' repeated MaryAnn.

'I don't think so,' said Aljce. 'I feel like I'm being bullied pretty badly.'

'What do you mean?'

'Oh, always meetings about me, and everything I do is twisted around to make me look bad. Apparently nobody likes me.'

'Really? You've hidden that well! I thought things were hunky dory.'

'Oh,' said Aljce, 'you're hardly ever here. You might have missed it.'

'My boss doesn't like me being here,' said MaryAnn. 'I'm part time and I'm already doing most of my work outside of the office, but Jillq wanted to stop that. That's why I'm moving.'

Aljce was silent. She would have loved to be MaryAnn. With someone in her corner; getting her out of there. 'I'm sure you'll be fine if you just put your best foot forward,' said MaryAnn. 'That's probably all they want really. Funny people though.' It was clear to Aljce that MaryAnn didn't realise how bad things were for her. Would she even comprehend it, or believe it if Aljce was to tell her what was happening in detail? She didn't have the resources to do anything about it, and it didn't affect her, so she wouldn't see it. Aljce hoped she would never be like that. She remembered that she had told MaryAnn what was happening when things had first started going wrong. And MaryAnn had shown no interest in knowing. She didn't like what was happening to her on a much more minor level, but was happy to ignore what was happening to Aljce. It was funny how people who were supposed to be community champions against bullying and violence could be so determined to ignore it when it was under their noses.

'The whole place is a bit tense,' MaryAnn had said. 'I'll be glad to be out of here.' Which was not how Jillq had presented things earlier. She'd made it sound as if it was her decision to get rid of MaryAnn. Free up room space? They had empty rooms with nothing in them except severed electrical cords extending from the walls and crumbling plaster falling like snow from roof to floor. Perhaps everyone shared offices so that everyone was observed by someone else.

WHEN THE OTHERS came in, the rain had saturated their hair so that it stuck to their skulls. 'I said we shouldn't go out,' said Jillq. 'And I have been proven right.' Her beautiful red ringlets sprung out at odd angles.

'You did,' said Mrs. Kingi loyally.

'At least,' said Jillq, 'we have recovered some of the golf balls.'

'How many have you got Aljce?' asked Chelsea sweetly. Aljce ignored her.

'How many HAVE you got?' said Jillq.

'There were none over my way,' said Aljce.

'If you'd had your eyes down you would have seen them,' said Jillq. 'Frankly, I'm not sure how much you contribute.' Aljce rolled her eyes internally. She would not be water. She would not react.

'It seems very narcissistic of you to have just thought of yourself and run from the rain, Aljce,' said Jillq.

Words failed Aljce. She might not have been water, but there was plenty outside. There was a crash, and then a crack over and above of the sound of the rain, which already sounded as if someone was relent-lessly pouring nails down onto the corrugated iron roof. Suddenly, the corridor lit up, as if a nuclear bomb had been detonated; yellow and white and orange, throwing shadows on people's faces. It's okay, thought Aljce. If that was a bomb, I'd already be gone. The corridor had faded quickly back into dimness, although there was still some orange flicker-ing. 'Keep calm!' shouted Jillq. 'Evacuate! Let me past!'

'What the fuck?' said Dulcie.

'Lightning strike,' said Marj matter of factly. MaryAnn popped out of her office.

'Did you see that?' she said. 'Lightning's hit that big tree outside. My gosh. It's blazing!' They all rushed to her window. Aljce thanked the universe that she wasn't outside. That electricity would have found her. What a shame that it had found the beautiful old oak tree.

THE TREE WAS well ablaze, and they all lingered by their office windows, pretending to work, while the fire engine arrived, and the fire officers poured out of it in their yellow raincoats. 'Oh, my gosh, hot!' sighed Chelsea.

'Literally,' said Aljce, referencing the fire. Chelsea glanced at her blankly, not understanding the joke. The fire fighter's puffy white hoses reminded Aljce of huhu grubs. Or fat caterpillars. There was lots of to-ing and fro-ing with not a lot happening, and eventually the tree burned itself down to a smoky stump, by which time the fire officers set upon it with their hoses. Most of the trunk had been taken out by the lightning strike itself.

The older fire officer came to talk with Jillq about why the fire hydrant cover had been left to grow over. 'That was the responsibility of the newer employees,' said Jillq. Aljce had never heard about it.

'Gosh, MaryAnn,' she said sarcastically as they went up the corridor together. 'Lazy! Working when you should have been out weeding!'

'Your job now,' said MaryAnn. 'I'm out of here. Last boxes!' And five minutes later, she was gone without a backwards glance.

'At least we've found the source of the rabbits!' said Marj.

'Mummy and daddy rabbits?' asked Aljce. What she said to Marj was very rarely twisted around on her, mainly because half of it went over Marj's head, and the other half was easily forgotten.

'They've been making a home under that tree. There's a huge rabbit warren under there. The main hole goes so deep that it may just go all the way to China.'

'Oh,' said Aljce, thinking of the rabbits, and how they'd need to rebuild. 'Chinese rabbits.'

'We can poison them now,' said Marj.

'Why would you want to?' asked Aljce, shocked all over again. 'I love watching them flop around on the field while I'm sitting at my office.'

'Aljce,' sighed Marj. 'You should be working. I'm flat out all the time. No time for watching rabbits!' The fact that Marj had no time to watch them didn't seem like a reason to murder them. In fact, the main reason seemed to be that Jillq was keen to do so, and Jillq always knew what was best.

ALJCE WATCHED AS Marj and Jillq went out to the tree. Marj had a box, Jillq had the spade. There wasn't much Aljce could do. Run, little rabbits! she thought. The women wandered around the patch of scorched grass, circumnavigating the trunk. Jillq bent down to try to see what lay in the dark hole. If only I could push her in, thought Aljce. And if only the rabbits ate her alive when I did. Ooh, that's not good for my karma... It was hard to think of Jillq as a person. She was more like a human husk, filled with evil energy. But when it came down to it, she had either been born with a dysfunctional brain, or she had learned to be the way she was, without feeling for others. Something had gone wrong with the part of her which should have been able to feel empathy. Perhaps she had experienced childhood trauma. Perhaps she really had been psychologically abused by her mother when she was young. Perhaps she had an invisible neural disability. A birth defect. Perhaps the appropriate emotion when thinking of Jillq was compassion. Although that was hard when there was nothing there inside her to be compassionate towards. And it was dangerous too. To feel compassion for someone so determined to destroy her would make her vulnerable.

PAINTING THE ROSES RED

OUTSIDE, THE SKY was morning-promise blue. Her Front Neighbour was in his garden. 'Hey,' she said. He looked up, poised with a spade under his foot, surrounded by fresh soil and new potatoes.

'Bit of a Saturday,' he said.

'Yeah,' she agreed. 'Yeah.'

Aljce went to her shed. It's hard to understand how one person can spoil everything, she thought. Everything is beautiful: the smell of coffee from somewhere, the morning sunlight spilling on to the garage floor concrete. And I'm stoned. But I can't be happy, because Jillq is just spoiling it. She's causing a stain over everything. Things would be great, if it wasn't for her. Well, there was Lewis... that was another unhappiness. She caught herself. There was no room for unproductive thinking.

THERE WAS A party on that night. 'Come,' said Mamae. 'It'll be fun, Aljce. You haven't been much fun lately. You haven't done anything with us.'

'Yeah,' said Aljce. 'I suppose. Work getting me down.'

'Forget about work. I'll pick you up. Get a baby sitter.'

When they got there, Aljce regretted putting the effort in. There was no one there she really wanted to talk to, and Mamae was drinking and almost immediately saw an old friend from school that Aljce didn't know. She knew that she should turn to the person next to her and make small talk, but somehow she just couldn't be bothered. It was as if her brain was frozen numb. She wondered how long it was till she could go home. It was the kind of unhappiness that you didn't even realise you had until you did. 'Alright Aljce?' said Mamae.

'Sure,' said Aljce, aware that she was being boring. She felt as if she was observing herself. Watching herself not fit in. She began to peel the label off her discarded beer bottle with a bottle cap.

'You know what they say...' said someone.

'What do they say?' said Aljce.

'That's a sign of sexual frustration.'

'Uh,' said Aljce. Now she was lonely and unwanted as well. Her old self would have made a joke. But she couldn't be arsed right now.

'You wanna analyse that Aljce? Analyse it for us,' said Mamae's Sister. And she sat forward and cupped her chin in her two hands, mocking Aljce. Perhaps Mamae's Sister was drunk. That was when people showed you their true colours. Or perhaps it was Aljce's own fault that she felt so pissed off. She didn't really like alcohol in excess. She hardly ever drank. Perhaps she was just being paranoid, getting those feelings of doom that drinking could bring. That's why she didn't like it. It felt like a bad drug. Plus the fact that you spent an hour or two trying to get to that happy place, and then you were there for like, oh, ten minutes, and then you overshot, and next minute you were a fool, talking too loud, and to the wrong people, and spewing in the garden. Walking home because you'd spent your taxi money, while the orange orbs of the street lights were all double; split into lower and upper. Everything feeling empty. And you didn't remember your last stumbles home, but you did remember the bed spinning, and feeling motion-sick all the way to sleep, but there was nothing you could do, you were trapped. The next day it was a competition between the pain in your head, and how fucking nauseous you felt; plus the thought that somehow everything had been disappointing, and you had somehow fucked up, although exactly how eluded you; you couldn't put your finger on it.

'I'm on a day off,' said Aljce. 'You analyse it.' It fucked her off that she didn't know whether it was Mamae's Sister being a bitch, or whether it was her. She'd prefer it to be the later, but she suspected it was the former. Mamae's Sister's tone had felt malicious. She tried to tell herself that how other people reacted to her said more about them than it said about her. That if Mamae's Sister had a problem with her training for an interesting career, that was about her, and the fact that she was sick of being stuck working at the drycleaners, but didn't have either the talent or the motivation to make a change. Now Aljce was the one being a bitch, even if she didn't say it out loud. Even if it was the truth. But that didn't make it any more pleasant for Aljce. She didn't like people not liking her or people being mean to her, because it made her feel like they thought she was beneath them. Why else would they believe that they could treat her that way? She didn't like to think that they didn't think she was good enough. She sighed. She really was having a blah time. She hoped Mamae's Sister would fuck off. She felt ill equipped to cope tonight. Perhaps this was low level depression. Fuck work. It was sucking her joy.

'Where's Strauss?' she asked.

'Who?' said Mamae.

Aljce turned to the person next to her at the table. She knew that she really should be saying something, but she somehow couldn't be bothered at all. Even though it was socially essential. And she wondered what the fuck was wrong with her, because she was usually really good at making meaningless small talk, and even had the skill to make it interesting and unique without the person she was talking to being alerted to the possibility that she was intelligent. Quirky, unusual, that was her territory. That piece of the set that never fitted, but which people didn't mind keeping, because it was so much fun, even though they really shouldn't have because it wasn't really their style. At the moment, Aljce felt so detached, she could have been an alien from another planet watching herself from some nearby piece of space. Not outer space, but not her inner self either. Somewhere nearby, and slightly higher than her body. Perhaps the fold in space-time where her colours were located.

'I might catch a taxi home,' she said to Mamae.

'Are you okay?' asked Mamae, too drunk to really take it in.

'Yeah, I'm fine. I just have a sore stomach.'

'Sure,' said Mamae. 'Text me when you get home safe.'

'Sure,' said Aljce, echoing Mamae. 'Sorry to be a stink friend.'

Bella was just coming in as Aljce left. She had a new boyfriend in another town and Aljce had hardly seen her lately. 'Whoa. Where are you going?' she asked.

'I'm a bit tired,' said Aljce. 'I haven't been sleeping properly.'

'Tired people sleep all night.'

'What, so don't worry if I'm not sleeping, because I mustn't be tired enough?'

'Yeah, why don't you try just laxing out and letting your thoughts drift?'

'I do. So how come I want to go to sleep when it's nearly time to get up, so I fall asleep briefly, and I'm fucked up when the alarm goes? Tired after work, but not in the middle of the night.'

'What you need is a bitta chill. Stay and party.'

'What I need not to do is to think about work in the middle of the night,' said Aljce. 'It's not healthy.'

'Sure you won't stay?'

'Yeah, nah. But you'll be good. Mamae's here.'

WHEN ALJCE GOT home, she knew it was the right choice. Nobody to talk to. No one to have to pretend to. The girls were still at her neighbours across the road; being looked after by their teenage daughter. All night, as arranged. I'm a bad friend, she thought, because I take up such a lot of my own time.

Her bed was waiting for her like a refuge. Once upon a time, she would have gone on to Facebook, but now she didn't really even have that, because it was marked by the absence of Lewis. Well, not his absence technically; she could still see him posting things, but his profile pic wasn't on the side of her page, just the gap where it used to be. She remembered how she would wait for it to show that he'd messaged her, checking every few minutes. She felt funny to post some things, especially quotes, because he would be able to see what she'd posted. And she didn't want him to know how her feelings were processing, that he'd hurt her, or that she cared. She didn't know what she had to be ashamed of; it was just the way things were. She never re-posted anything of his, but she didn't feel ready to block him completely. She just didn't take the same pleasure in Facebook anymore. It couldn't distract her from being unhappy – about a lot of things. And even in bed, she couldn't think happy thoughts. All she did was replay her Jillq situation, trying to find a way out.

The Therapy Hub was some sort of weird, bizarre world where Aljce had to exist. She had to exist there while she was at work, and now that world was coming with her after work, and she was immersed in it at home too. Home and work: the boundaries were being eroded and everything was merging.

MORNING CAME AS it always did. Her Mad Neighbour was convinced his brother had stolen one of his plants. 'He's a common thief!' he said angrily.

'You don't even know that it was him. He's just one possibility.'

'Let me have a bit of fun, thinking it's my brother…'

'No, cos then you will both be sad and angry and resentful and fight, and I will have to listen to it. Again.' How much, she thought, how much is he aware of his own madness? He carefully cut up some weed for her with small silver nail scissors rendered blunt by the residue of gummy dark green oil on their blades.

'So this one's called Sugar Leaf.'

'Such pretty names they have for the different strains now. White Widow. AK47. That's supposed to be good for calming anxiety, haha.'

'Even the different types. Kush and Indica. The first one reminds me of a Middle Eastern cushion.'

'And the other one sounds like Indian indigo.'

'But anyway, there's a story behind the sugar leaf thing. It produces all these sugary crystals that end up coating the leaves. That's why it's a bit sticky, even though it isn't head.'

'Well, damn it that I'm giving up sugar.'

'You won't give this up.'

'No, I'm going to need it …'

'ALJCE, ALJCE,' shrieked Jillq. 'Where is Aljce?'

'Here I am,' said Aljce, looking down the hallway in surprise. Jillq was sitting on the floor.

'Were you last to walk down this corridor?' demanded Jillq.

'Last?' said Aljce, confused.

'The last person to walk down here!'

'Apart from you?'

'Yes, last before me!'

'I don't know,' said Aljce. 'I've been busy working.'

'Too busy to straighten the carpet that you've left askew, clearly,' said Jillq. 'Perhaps you have left it like this on purpose.' Aljce tried to take a deep breath, but the adrenalin was kicking in and making her stomach feel sick. Other people had come to their doors. 'I need witnesses,' said Jillq. 'Who else has walked along this corridor this afternoon? After Aljce?' No one said anything. 'There you go!' said Jillq. 'Once again Aljce, you have failed in your duty. Do you know how high this could push our insurance premiums? I am going to have to fill out an accident and incident report now. Pages and pages of it! I will make a note of your lack of responsibility, if not calculated misconduct, with this carpet. Marj, help me up! I am the Manager, the Executive Manager! Of the whole organisation! I can't sit on the floor. What would visitors think? Did you even think of that Aljce? What the visitors would think?'

LATER THE SAME MORNING, Jillq poked her head in the door of Aljce's office. What now? thought Aljce. A written warning about the mat? Nothing good ever came from Jillq. 'Aljce. Would you like a coffee?' asked Jillq, solicitously.

'Umm,' said Aljce. 'I actually don't drink coffee. I just have hot water.'
'Don't drink coffee? Why not?'
'It makes me nauseous.'
'I already have the coffee in the cup, Aljce.'
'I'm sorry.'
'This is a waste of coffee, Aljce.'
'I'm sorry.'
'You should have thought first. We all need to be mindful. Coffee doesn't grow on trees you know.' Aljce bit her tongue. 'There is a budget we have to keep to here at the Therapy Hub,' Jillq continued. Aljce wondered why Jillq was so keen to offer her coffee, and so annoyed when she had declined. Perhaps Jillq was trying to poison her. Surely unlikely, she thought. But everything else here was so out the gate that she couldn't really wonder that she might think that way. Jillq didn't seem like a well person. And just the fact that she was being helpful was suspicious. But it might be as small as Jillq needing to be able to evidence that she was in fact kind to Aljce. 'I offered to make you a coffee,' she would say. 'So please don't try to say that you're being bullied.' Not that Aljce had accused her of bullying, although that's what it was. And surely they both knew it, not just Aljce. Surely.

ALJCE HAD BEEN checking her personal emails daily. She hadn't given them much attention for months, but she was still holding out hope that she might receive a reply from the woman from the conference. Nothing came. Perhaps she WAS away on leave? Aljce even went as far as checking her sent box to make sure that it had sent, and checking her spam to make sure that the reply hadn't gone there by mistake. It had been a very long email. Aljce had detailed every instance of bullying and bizarre behaviour by Jillq that she'd experienced, and even though she hadn't been employed long, it had made for an extremely lengthy email. Surely the woman couldn't miss it.

But it wasn't until she'd stopped her obsessive email checking and given up on getting a reply at all that one came, and today was the day.

It was brief. 'I'm sorry you are finding things difficult,' wrote the woman. 'However, I'm sure you appreciate how tricky my position is. Jillq has a very good reputation with my organisation, and especially with Wally and Pen. My role is really only supporting the Family Harm Child Buddies with the role description, with the actual work that they do. I suggest that you contact the Employment Relations Department. They may be able to help you. I wish you the best. King regards.'

Aljce looked at the reply for a long time. Who would help her if the person whose job it was to support her didn't have the courage to? She found it difficult to understand how the woman could consider the delicate politics of her 'position' more important than supporting someone who was being mistreated. And now she had to worry that the woman might say something to Wally or Pen, who were friends of Jillq. They had no idea what Jillq said about them behind their back. Aljce had gotten absolutely nothing from all the hours she had spent composing that email, other than to make herself vulnerable. Why didn't anyone have courage?

SHE LOOKED AT her reflection in the toilet mirror later. There was no doubt about it; her hair was definitely finer than it had been. And even Mamae's Sister had mentioned it. It was like ghost hair. It wasn't falling out, just getting more and more translucent. That couldn't be possible. The light in the Therapy Hub toilets was low, and there were no windows, so she couldn't blame the light. She pulled a handful up to her face. Breaking. It was breaking off around the level of her jawline, leaving the remaining strands of already fine hair with more space in between each one. If this continued, you would be able to see right through her hair as if it wasn't there. Perhaps it's just that I'm getting a little bit older, she thought. Is this what happens? Surely stress couldn't do this.

She contemplated her fractured and nearly doused energy. How had they done it? She had not buckled, but they had hurt her anyway. The constant wearing away of her self-belief. Her positivity had been what had created her energy. Every time they'd come at her, they'd smudged a tiny bit more of her off. Instead of being positive, she was becoming enveloped in the echoes of her old self-hatred. She didn't want to go back to that, but was finding it hard to escape. And it was also hard to escape from the source of negative energy. A welfare benefit wouldn't pay her mortgage. But a real second written warning couldn't be far away. Aljce had no idea why it hadn't come already. Surely one was brewing about the carpet. Or perhaps Jillq wanted to keep toying with her until she had a replacement person to bully the way in which she bullied Aljce. Perhaps Aljce served a purpose for Jillq. Perhaps she kept the current work dynamic functioning. She remembered that Hannah had said that she wasn't the first.

THERE WAS NO rest for either the wicked or the good. 'Have you filled in that form yet, Aljce?'

'Which one?' said Aljce. Marj had left one on her desk that morning, but Aljce was confused.

'The form where you list your qualifications,' said Marj.

'Oh,' said Aljce. 'What is that actually for? Haven't I done it already? For Mrs. Kingi?'

'That was for a brochure. This is for the Hub portfolio, of course,' said Marj. 'I'm updating it. Since you and MaryAnn are new.'

'But I thought MaryAnn had left?'

'Jillq says we should include her anyway.'

Aljce sighed. More pretending. 'Perhaps you could show me the old portfolio,' she said. 'So I can get an idea.' She was interested to see what other people's qualifications were.

'It's on my desk,' said Marj. 'I'll get it, and then you can fill out your form this morning. I'm only waiting on you.'

A few minutes later, a portfolio was placed on her desk. Aljce sighed. How hard could it be for people to align their margins and use readable fonts? And she didn't want to relist her qualifications. She knew it would cause trouble when they were reminded again that she had a university degree. They would all feel as if she had personally threatened them. She flicked through it. Mrs. Kingi. Social worker. Qualification: three-day Certificate in Working With People. Good on her, but hardly enough to consider yourself a social worker. No wonder she was so grateful to Jillq.

There weren't many places where you could be given the title of social worker with so little learning in that field.

Jillq apparently had a degree in psychology, not psychotherapy. A three-year qualification from a Learning Institute. Aljce frowned. Why did Jillq have so little knowledge of theory and practice then? And could you qualify in psychology with only three years of study? At a Learning Institute? Surely you had to attend a university. Aljce felt that something was in the wrong place, that the pieces weren't fitting properly. Jillq could barely spell. Could she have gotten a qualification in psychology? Perhaps spell check was that good.

She felt the urge to investigate, but she wasn't sure how she could.

She reluctantly handed her completed form back to Marj. No doubt they would just make MaryAnn's contribution up. 'Thank you Aljce,' said Marj. 'I'm glad to see you have a qualification. Mrs. Kingi has queried whether you do in fact have one, and whether you should be in your role.' Aljce nearly choked. She had filled out a similar form for Mrs. Kingi, where she had clearly listed her degree in the qualifications section.

'Is that because she has a three-day qualification in People Care or whatever?' she asked sarcastically.

'Mrs. Kingi is qualified, yes,' said Marj. 'Her qualification is listed in the portfolio.'

'I wouldn't have thought that was enough to be a social worker. Don't you have to be registered?' said Aljce, although she regretted the words as soon as they came out of her mouth. No doubt they would be held against her in the future. Undermining the team. Not respecting her colleagues. Arrogance. But maybe Marj would fail to see what a valuable card Aljce's words would be for Jillq.

'She's a Whanau Social Worker,' said Marj. Aljce failed to see how that changed anything.

'What happens to the portfolio?' she asked.

'We use it for publicity,' said Marj. 'When we need to. People like to know we're qualified.' Aljce raised her eyebrows.

No wonder Jillq was good to Kat and Hattie. They had actual qualifications relevant to therapy. Everyone else was doing nothing. Hence Marj and Mrs. Kingi doing near identical tasks in collecting qualification information.

'MARJ THINKS SHE works so hard,' said Mrs. Kingi to Aljce later. 'She has no idea how hard Jillq and I work. We quite often get together on the phone to discuss things. I ring Jillq every day. Several times a day when we're not here at work. Jillq says she doesn't know where she'd be without my support. I don't know why Marj thinks she's Jillq's right-hand man.'

'Right-hand woman,' said Aljce absently, reminding herself how dangerous Mrs. Kingi was, even though she was an idiot, given that she had private conversations with Jillq every day.

'She's not even that bright,' said Mrs. Kingi. Aljce raised her eyebrows. It was intended to convey a naive neutrality. Perhaps surprise – as if she had never considered the matter before. Never mind the fact that it was unavoidable. It was tempting to agree with Mrs. Kingi, despite the irony that Mrs. Kingi wasn't that bright either. Jillq clearly didn't like to surround herself with anyone brighter than she was.

But the last thing Aljce wanted to do was to get caught up in back-stabbing between Jillq's hench people. That could only lead to her own blood being spilled on the floor. Somehow the three of them would end up on one team against Aljce, who would clearly be in the wrong.

HANNAH RANG. 'I just wondered how you're doing at the moment,' she said.

'Badly,' said Aljce.

'Oh?'

Aljce told her about some of the things that had happened to her recently.

'Unacceptable,' said Hannah. 'What you need to do is to prepare a personal grievance.'

'What's that?'

'You write a letter to your employer, telling them what's wrong, and what they need to do to remedy it. If you quit your job, you have a certain amount of days to do it in from the date you leave, and you have to show that it was untenable for you to continue. Then your employer has a set time in which to respond to you, and to fix any genuine griev-ances. If they don't do this, you can go to Employment Court.' Aljce told Hannah about the email from the woman from the conference.

'Yes, you do need to talk to Employment New Zealand. They have a good website too.'

'But wouldn't I have to give the letter to Jillq?'

'That is the whole point, yes.'

'I think I'm too scared to do that. The only thing that protects me right now is that I haven't acknowledged her bullying, and she doesn't know that I'm trying to take action against it.'

'Has that worked for you so far?'

'Not really, no. There's not one person who's willing to stand up for me and even confirm what I say, let alone support me. And there's no one above Jillq to go to. She's the Manager of the Hub, and she's the Chair of the Board. She's the supreme queen of everything in this little world.'

'And that's why you need to break out of her world. Take it out into the real world. You can't stay there Aljce. Write the letter. Post it as you leave. We will go for constructive dismissal.'

'What about my placement? What about my mortgage?' asked Aljce, tasting the salt of her own tears in the corners of her mouth.

'Trust the universe,' said Hannah. 'Hopefully, she will have to pay you out.'

'Is that what can happen?'

'Yes. Sometimes people get reinstated too.'

'I could never go back,' said Aljce. 'It would be just the same, except that she would be super careful. She would tidy up the trail behind her so that it would seem as if she was beyond reproach. There'd be no footprints in the dust.'

HER MAD NEIGHBOUR messaged her. His texting had improved, although his phone was nearly obsolete now that he'd learned. 'Go outside and look at the moon.' She walked outside. He was in his yard.

'Oh, my gosh, that's amazing! Oh goodness,' she said. 'What do you think does that?'

'Ice crystals in the atmosphere?' he mused. 'Perhaps it's a rainbow on the moon.'

'It's a big fucking halo. A glowing white halo. Look how big it is! It's a mile fucking wide. And it's got the same white haze as an angel's wings.'

They looked at it for a while, but it gave her a sore neck so she couldn't keep her head turned upwards for too long. 'I've heard that rainbows look doughnut shape from above when pilots fly over them, and we could be above the moon, rather than it being above us,' she said. 'So maybe if we were standing on the moon, we'd see a white rainbow.'

'What a shame there's no one there. It's being wasted…'

'It looks like Saturn's rings. Like a ring of ice.'

'I've seen this before, with bigger rings around the outside.' She looked up again.

'Oh, I think I can see another one, way out wider.'

'Yes! We're in the centre of a blessing! We're blessed. Very blessed!'

She wondered if a rainbow on the moon would really be wasted if no one was to see it. Or was its very existence in the symphony of the universe, its integral beauty, reason enough? Her Mad Neighbour was still craning his neck upwards. His neck was clearly stronger than hers.

'Mmm,' he said vaguely. Had Aljce spoken her thought out loud?

'Nothing really exists anyway,' she mused. 'It's only because something's observing it that it's been conjured up.'

'Let's just enjoy it,' he said. 'You don't always have to talk.' And in the midst of the beauty, suddenly she was reminded of Jillq, and what she needed to do.

SHE SPENT THE next morning preparing her personal grievance letter. She didn't want to do it at home, because she was trying desperately to keep that space for positive thinking. Not only was she nervous about doing it in work time, and someone potentially reading what she was typing over her shoulder; she was also nervous about the whole process. Disclosing her hand to her opposing player. There would be no going back after that. She needed to word it perfectly. Out the window, she could see Jillq and Marj, once more perambulating around the lightening stroked tree and peering into the hole. She fantasised again about pushing Jillq into the hole. It was becoming her favourite daytime dream. Perhaps the hole would take Jillq all the way down to Wonderland, and she would never climb back out. If the hole narrowed at any point, perhaps she would remain stuck there, jammed head down, starving to death. But if she went without food for long enough, she might come loose, and tumble the rest of the way to the bottom. Aljce tried to word her letter so that it was objective, not subjective. Stating facts, without muddying them with her opinion. Not to mention that if she gave her opinion, it would be a very long letter indeed. And she was careful to put nothing in there about how what had happened had made her feel. She re-read it and altered it again a million times. Maybe Jillq really would just trip and fall down the hole. Maybe she would trip over a rabbit. Maybe there would be no bottom, and she would fall forever.

She managed to get the letter down to three pages. But how was she going to print it at this intensely stifling time, when it seemed as if Jillq was holding a magnifying glass over Aljce? And was it safe on her work computer? She had changed her password, but who knew? When Jillq found the old one didn't work, she would probably just ask Marj for the new one. What she needed to do was print it, email it to herself so that she had an electronic copy, and then delete it. All this subterfuge. She felt like a spy in an enemy country.

Aljce put her head out into the corridor. No one was there. Goodness knows where they all were, although obviously Jillq and Marj were outside. She checked out the window. Jillq was leaning over the edge of the hole. It was too much to ask for. Instead, Aljce hurriedly clicked print times three, and rushed into Marj's office. The paper took its time to glide out of the printer, each sheet taking forever. If I had no concept of eternity before, I do now, thought Aljce. Please, please, paper, come out before they come back inside.

She was hardly able to believe her luck when the pages did pop out. And then she found a missing comma, which altered the whole meaning of one of her sentences. She chose to repeat the whole process. What the fuck? I can't believe I'm this stupid that I'm taking this extra risk over a missing comma, she thought. But it had to be perfect. Amazingly, her luck held, with Jillq and Marj only returning as Aljce walked down the corridor to her own office. 'I hope that you had nothing to do with that hole, Aljce,' said Jillq.

'Nothing at all,' promised Aljce, with the printed side of the letter pressed towards her own chest. She realised suddenly that Jillq's eyes were like big, blue soft-boiled eggs; slightly protruding from her eye sockets. Not quite cooked, or perhaps overcooked.

LATER IN THE DAY, Aljce printed off copies of the warning letters Jillq had sent her. She also took a copy of the qualifications portfolio. The adrenalin in her stomach made her feel sick, but she was proud of her strength.

Sometimes people mistook her compliance for submission. Which was a mistake. She was just more chilled out than them, and more slow to move to anger. It was confusing for them when she was incredibly compliant while she worked to undermine them. It wasn't safe to confront a narcissist head on, because all they did was focus their full attention on your destruction, instead of just a little part of it. Little did they know she was very chill indeed until she felt strongly about something, and then she had the ability to shed her submissiveness and show a strength that surprised anyone who hadn't seen it before. After that, they weren't sure how they could have missed it. Perhaps she'd learned how to be subtle and submissive at a young age.

AT HOME, Aljce always turned straight to the situations vacant page in the free local newspaper that came on Tuesdays, Thursdays and Fridays. Apply for everything, she thought, although she was unsure how she would complete her counselling placement at some of the jobs that she emailed out applications for. Things like helping disabled people to get employment or coordinating rest home visitations. At work, during the dead time when she was not allowed to see clients any more, she perused the notifications from the SEEK job website; hastily minimising her screen when she heard footsteps in the hall. She had to do something to fill in her time. Most of the notifications were a waste of time; days away from where she lived, outside her areas of interest, or needing less or more skills than what she had. There were limits to her apply-for-everything policy. Apply for everything within reason, she corrected herself. Anything is better than this. But something inside of herself was stubborn. She needed to be able to do her Counselling Placement. She wasn't going to let Jillq take that away from her. That would be letting Jillq win. While Jillq might think that Aljce was rolling over, Aljce was in battle mode, but it was better that her enemy didn't know, so they'd be less guarded, less careful, and Aljce would have a better chance of achieving her goals.

HER MAD NEIGHBOUR was in battle mode as well. He'd found out that the Neighbour on his other side was the one who had taken the plants. He'd tried to lift another one and left a trail of leaves. 'Hope you've got the rest in,' said Aljce. 'Else being fully ripped off is just an accident waiting to happen.'
    'Of course I have. I went over and saw her,' he said.
    'His partner?'

'He wasn't there of course. I told her to tell her hubby that if he'd wanted a smoke, he should have just come and asked me for one. No need to rip one of my plants off.'

'Takes all sorts to make a world. Perhaps he has no idea that you would be that generous.'

'Well, he does now.'

'I guess. But he probably doesn't believe it. People can only see you as they are themselves.'

'He was thinking about what he wanted, what he could get for free. Young people. All they think about is the future, whereas middle-aged people like me, we think about the present; we try to hold onto it, make it last. Wander around and smell the flowers. And old people, I suppose they look back at the past. Past glories, that sort of thing. Starting to appreciate it, and what it was, because it's nearly gone. I think we should all look at the present moment. But I would say that, wouldn't I? I'm middle aged.' And he cackled to himself. 'Ask me again when I'm old.'

'So,' SAID THE woman at the garage where Aljce's car was getting a Warrant of Fitness. 'What are you doing with yourself now?'

'I'm a Family Harm Child Buddy,' said Aljce.

'Oh. How's that going?'

'Not well, really. I hate where I'm working.' Now she was telling anyone who would listen, she thought to herself.

'Really, where are you?'

'At the Therapy Hub. Jillq runs it. Do you know her?'

'Is that the mother of Deidra and Dulcie?'

'Yeah, that's the one. Do you know her?' She cursed herself. This woman was probably a friend of theirs. She prepared herself for damage control. She needed to be more careful.

'Not personally,' said the woman, multitasking as she prepared customer invoices. 'We've had the daughters in here though. We won't have them back again. Compulsive liars. And then the mother rang up and got stuck in. How dare we say that her daughters are liars?'

'Oh,' said Aljce, startled. It wasn't often that someone concurred with her own experience of Jillq and her daughters. Perhaps it was because this woman was outside the universe within the universe that was the Therapy Hub. 'What did they actually do?'

'Can't remember exactly,' said the woman. 'It was their mother ringing up and making threats that sticks in my mind. I think it was something to do with one them saying that we'd broken something on their car, and wanting us to fix it for free, when it was just normal wear and tear. And the other one saying she'd paid me when she hadn't. I remember that incident, actually. I told her to bring in her invoice with the paid stamp on it.'

'And she couldn't?'

'Oh, yes she could. It's coming back to me now. She bought it in stamped with a paid stamp that was different to our one. Totally different. And it didn't have my signature next to it. I said she was a liar. And that's when her mother rang up. How dare I accuse her daughter like that?'

'Haha,' said Aljce. 'Yes, that's how I find them too.'

'Stay well clear of them,' said the woman. 'The mother is barking.'

'I'd love to,' said Aljce, 'but I can't. I work with them.'

'My advice would be to look for a new job.'

'I am,' said Aljce with a sigh.

'ALJCE, YOU SHOULD be packing up. Are you packing up? We need to leave for the venue.'

'Venue?'

'For our staff Xmas lunch of course!' There was no way that Aljce had planned to go to the staff Xmas lunch, and she had paid no attention to the details of where and when. All she had cared about was that today was the last day before the summer break. But now, faced with focused peer pressure, she considered whether she needed to. It was expected of her. She had grown used to trying hard to give off the energy of nothing being wrong, so that she wasn't suspected of fighting so hard covertly. She really, really didn't want to go, she didn't want to be near any of their false energies, all secretly hoping to harm her, while pretending to be nice people. If they could do it, so could she. Like needed to be fought with like.

This IS a story about the battle between good and evil, just like Strauss said it was, she thought. I am good, but in order to beat evil, I need to take on some of its weapons. Like deceit. I can't win this by being open and honest. And Jillq, she will use some of the weapons of good, like

239

pretending to help others, and putting herself out as some sort of saint. Painting herself with saint paint, painting over what's underneath. And then there's me. I'm using manipulation; trying to move other players onto new squares; squares that are beneficial to my next move. Perhaps I'm just fooling myself. Maybe each side perceives itself to be good. Maybe Jillq's story of justification is just as powerful to her as mine is to me. Maybe she doesn't know she's evil. Maybe she thinks I am. It was a scary thought.

No, she corrected herself. Her actions are about harming others, and that is evil. Mine are about protection, of myself, and that is reasonable justification. But did Jillq somehow feel that Aljce was trying to harm her; by being better and cleverer, and threatening her façade; the illusion of herself that she'd worked so hard on? Did she feel justified in protecting her position, her castle in the air?

That was why Aljce hadn't liked studying history at school. Great waves of people killing each other, in big and little ways. The coldness and lack of empathy of those who ordered the wars, the trapped obedience of the individual people carrying out the orders. Although sometimes they were cold and cruel too. Jillq was one of the cold and cruel rulers of minions. Empathy was the way forward for the human race, Aljce thought. Empathy prevented people from creating hell and pain for other people. Not everyone had empathy. Some people only cared for themselves. It was a specialised skill, the same way that some people knew how to fix phones, and other people could sing. Nobody knew everything, or had every capability. And yet empathy was essential to peace and happiness. Gosh, she thought. That sounds like Christmas card bullshit.

She couldn't avoid the idea that the universe was backing two horses; one evolving people with high empathy who could feel other people's pain, who could help and heal and nurture, and one evolving people with no empathy or understanding of others, but who could do brilliant calculations which would eventually take the human race to the stars. Because their brains were low on empathy, they had more room for logic and maths. Poor Jillq, who lacked empathy, but who was also essentially stupid. A stupid person with power which she had achieved through hype and lies which had influenced others to believe in her. Because some people were too gullible to evaluate other people for themselves.

They took other people on their own self judgements. If someone hated themselves, the world hated them too. How could they be worth loving, if they couldn't even love themselves? If someone believed they were a shining light, and told everyone so, people believed them, because they wouldn't dare to project such a thing if they weren't would they? They would be embarrassed to do so. Surely.

Was Aljce ungrateful? What if I'd been born a cow? she mused, somewhat randomly. How much more limited my life would be. I'd walk the same path in the evenings, with all the other black and white cows, past the green pond, which, while pretty, would be so normal to me that I would hardly glance at it unless I was thirsty. Everything I knew would be confined to a few paddocks. And whether I lived or died would be in the hands of another species. And here I am, fretting about a woman who is horrible, to be sure, but look at all the advantages and opportunities I have that cows don't have. Because I'm blessed to be a person. And all I'm doing is feeling bad about that. I need to let go of my hatreds and scorns and distresses.

She contemplated that. Letting things go is possibly one of my struggles, she thought. Letting too much go. Am I too soft, and am I letting people off too lightly? I don't wanna let people mistreat me. But when I set boundaries, I feel like a bitch, like I'm being too hard on people, too self-serving. I don't even know who I am any more. I don't know which sort of person I am, or which narrative is reliable.

She returned to her earlier thoughts. I like to think I'm a good person, but am I? Maybe I'm deluding myself. Maybe I'm just as flawed as everyone else. Maybe all those people acting selfishly, meanly, have constructed narratives to allow themselves to do so while still seeing themselves as good people who are justified in their actions. Maybe those fucked up people dreaming up plans to harm others within their reach believed themselves to be the good people. Like wars between countries, where each country believes that they are the righteous one, and that the other is evil. Each creating and believing their own propaganda. Narratives that concentrated on selected, self-serving information. Disseminated by governments and the media. One's own country is always in the right, because we are so accustomed to that way of thinking that we never query it. It's the doubters who are good people. The ones who wonder at their own motives. The ones who question their own narratives. Ironically, it's the ones who wonder if they are in fact, not good people, who are the better people.

'Leaving shortly,' said Mrs. Kingi brightly. 'I'm looking forward to this.' She spoke as if she and Aljce were friends as well as workmates. What planet are you on, thought Aljce, because it's not the same planet as me. Are you the same Mrs. Kingi who so happily backs Jillq up in meetings about how black my energy is, and how no one could like me?

'Are you packed up Aljce?' asked Marj.

'Oh,' said Aljce, 'I can't really leave yet. I've still got work to do before we shut down for Xmas.'

'It should all be done by now,' said Marj. Aljce didn't roll her eyes, but she wanted to. As if there was ever any actual work to do anyway.

'I really want to get it done,' she said. 'I'll be there half an hour after you.'

'What are you working on?' said Marj suspiciously.

'My pamphlet,' said Aljce. Marj thought. She was clearly torn between wanting to leave and be at the Xmas do, and her need to supervise Aljce and make her come.

'We'll be waiting for you,' she said. 'You know where it is, don't you?'

'Yes,' lied Aljce.

As soon as the last car left, she swept the contents of her desk drawers into a plastic bag, along with the photos of Pleasance and Liddell that she had kept on surface of the desk. She was actually packing up.

When the air had cleared of the others, and she thought about it again, she realised that there was no way she was going to spend an afternoon of her life with those two-faced people when she could avoid it instead. Plus she was scared that they would see in her face that she had decided never to come back again. And she wanted that to be a surprise. She would text Marj later and tell her that she was sick and couldn't make it.

SHE ENDED UP leaving it as long as possible to text Marj. In fact, Aljce had gone home by the time she got around to it. The last pay of the year would have gone into her bank. And she was entitled to be sick. So why did she feel so guilty about not being sick, about being home, when she should be at a staff do with a nest of people who hated her and who would do anything they could to harm her, all the while smiling brightly and blaming Aljce? Still, Marj left it even longer to get back to her.

Clearly a good time was being had by all, and no one was missing Aljce. Very late in the afternoon, she received a reply from Marj: she was sorry that she hadn't texted back earlier, and she hoped that Aljce felt better soon, and to have a good holidays; they would see each other next year. It felt genuine. Aljce was good at reading the feelings behind flat words. Written words. Perhaps Marj was hoping for a fresh start with difficult Aljce. Perhaps she hoped a holiday would help Aljce mend her ways.

Out of all of them, Marj bought into the difficult Aljce story because she was thick, whereas the others allowed it to pass, knowing it wasn't true, because it was convenient for them, and it placed them where they wanted to be. They participated in the story and helped to create it. Then there were the ones like Kat, who couldn't see outside their own mirrors. And the ones who just didn't want the trouble; like MaryAnn and the woman she'd emailed. That was more about avoiding disadvantage than securing advantage. Anyway, the whole thing would been an unpaid afternoon, where everyone was expected to buy their own lunch and drinks. Better to be having an unpaid half day sickie at home. Although it was probably too late to deduct it. And Aljce had decided to completely give up alcohol. Which would have made it cheaper, but there was no way she could have gotten through a Xmas work lunch if she was straight. And there would certainly have been no hope of going stoned. She could never give Jillq any ammunition to use against her. If Jillq knew Aljce smoked weed, it would be game, set and match to Jillq. Weed was still illegal, sadly.

SHE REMEMBERED A night she'd spent with Strauss. Not the last one they'd spent together, but close to it. 'What doing?' Aljce had messaged her. '…Because I'm smoking roaches.'

'Sounds good, but I've got some actual weed. As yet untouched. Come over here.'

'Can't. You'll have to bring it over; the girls are in bed.'

It had taken Strauss a long time to come, and Aljce couldn't wait for her to arrive. She really needed to be as stoned as possible. 'Sorry,' said Strauss. 'I was having an out of it moment. Eventually, after I looked under all my cushions on the couch for it, and down the side of the bed, I realised that I had actually lost my phone and not misplaced it. So I got Jimsy's phone to ring myself with, and I went out to the car, cos I thought I might have dropped it in there. And I COULD hear it ringing, so I got in the car to hear where abouts the noise was coming from exactly. But it was confusing me, because no matter where in the car I moved, it seemed to be coming from somewhere different. And then, duh, I realised it was in my pocket of my coat. Big, furry pockets, they sort of muffled the noise. So that sort of took me a while, before I figured it out.'

'Fuck it Strauss, most people just say they got caught in road works when they're late.'

'Between my house and your house? Probably not. Needed something else.'

'Haha. It was a good one. I like it.'

'That happened, Aljce. And that's why I didn't text you to say I was going to be late. Cos I didn't find the phone till I got to the car, and by then, texting back would have slowed me down.'

'Hope you gave Jimsy's phone back.'

'Oh, shit, I didn't. I'll text him. Or maybe, no.'

'He won't need it.'

'True. I'll put it under the bed when I get home, and in the morning, I'll let him ring it with my phone and find it.'

'Gees, who'd want to be married to you?'

'We're not married Aljce. I'm waiting for Lenny.'

Careful what you wish for Strauss. The universe might provide, and then shit, he turns out to be an arsehole and you want Jimsy back.'

'Exactly, Aljce. I know that.'

Strauss had pulled a bud out of her bag and sniffed it. 'We've got the herb, Eliza.'

'Such a druggy sentence. And one herb is better than eleven different herbs and spices.'

'Weird,' said Strauss. 'You're so fucking weird.'

'Good,' said Aljce. 'Look, I'm getting oil on my fingers.'

'Don't you steal my tin,' said Strauss.

'Looks like that tin I loaned you a couple of months ago. It's my favourite too. Yeah, it's the one with the Indian snake charmer on it. And that snake swaying with pleasure. All ecstatic with the smoke and the music.'

'Fuck off, that's mine.'

'Short memories. Plus a lack of gratitude really.'

'Oh, well, you can have it back if you want,' said Strauss a lit bit apologetic, but mainly miffed because she liked the tin herself.

'Nah, I don't need it, I'm just teasing you.'

'Hope you're not bullying me.'

'Ha. Hope you're not mocking me. And I'm happy just to visit my tin every now and then when you bring it around. Not that I will be able to for much longer...'

'You're to blame for my addiction you know, Strauss,' she continued. 'You've encouraged me. I didn't smoke nearly so much before I met you. It's not that I can't do without it, it's more that my body and brain have come to be expected to be gratified by it on a daily. I can do without it, but why would I? If I don't have to?'

'You should thank me, then. Several good years under your belt that you wouldn't have otherwise had.'

'Yeah, wouldn't that have been a shame. Life wouldn't have been nearly so good. We are the lucky ones who get to die, because we have been born,' she said randomly.

'Yeah, think of all those gazillions of wasted sperm, and all those eggs that never got fertilised...'

'And the potential for the sperm that met our egg to get together out of all the infinite combinations of other sperm or eggs they could have got together with to create someone else. Mindfucking that we're here really.'

'What will I do without you?'

'Smoke it up.'

Aljce sniffed her fingers. 'Man, ain't that a beautiful smell. After smoke musky sweet grass smell. Best perfume ever, except that people judge you. Judge you good or judge you bad.'

'Yeah, and the people who judge you good are the keepers. The cool ones that you wanna know.'

'Yeah, that is true. Hardly ever meet a bad stoner. Keep 'em all. It's like a bond.'

'And it's a good scent for a man or a woman. Turns me on if a man smells like weed.'

'Yeah, and it makes women beautiful.'

'If only the money makers knew, they'd bottle it.'

'So do you reckon that for a person's energy to become more positive, they would need to get rid of self-hatred?' asked Aljce, unable to stop herself getting caught up in mental riddles about herself in relation to Jillq, and even Lewis.

'Totally. Yeah, you've got to love yourself to be confident, and being confident is what being positive's about.'

'You're more confident that me really.'

'No, fuck off, you're more confident than me.'

'Hell no. Do you ever get scared though?'

'Oh, fuck yeah. I still get scared. But I know I can push on through, and while I'm pushing on through, I forget I'm scared and suddenly I'm having fun.'

'Do you reckon everyone gets scared?'

'Yeah. Fuck yeah. They must do.'

'You stoned?'

'Yeah.'

'Deeply and completely.'

'I don't know what we just smoked, cos I've got little bits of all sorts from a lot of different places lying around, but I am totally. And utterly. Wasted.'

'I'm so stoned that I almost hope it will drop off into something more mellow. Like everything is almost too much of a too muchness, and I worry that I'm not going to be able to cope with all the intensity; that it's too big for me, and it makes my head ache. Not the universe. Life. What if I can't keep the vibration steady? What if I've mistaken reality? Very hard to explain. I'm doing a shit job.'

'Haha. Sounds sensible. Perhaps it is. Too much of a muchness.'

'Who can tell?'

'Do you ever wonder how other people think of you?' asked Strauss. 'If they had to sum you up in one word.'

'Well, if you were asking the people at work, they'd say nasty or hard. But I hope that most people would be searching between independent and individual,' said Aljce. 'Definitely under I. They're so surprised that I find it more important to disagree with them about something, because that's who I am, than to agree with everything they say. Because to them, that's how you belong, and by all saying the same thing, you fit it. But I can't agree with shit like you can't be a vegetarian because you've got Type O blood. I've got Type O blood, and I'm a vegetarian, so that proves it's shit right there. I shouldn't even have had to say anything once she found that out.'

'Who said that? Someone at work?'

'No. Mamae's Sister of course.'

'Why do we hang out with her?'

'Because she's Mamae's Sister. And she's not totally evil.'

'That's a great criteria for having a friend Aljce. Not totally evil.'

'Well, it's not really a criteria. You're evil, and you're my friend.'

'Haha.'

'And the funny thing is,' Aljce continued, 'now I'm really reluctant to make new friends, unless I know they smoke weed. I just really like that golden dungyness in a friend. That time you spend together. That dark, warm energy. But it limits my friendship choices. Not many are worthy.'

'Yeah, I just can't really be bothered being around someone straight.'

'All that uptight shit. And real daylight bright.'

'Dungyness? I think you just invented that one.'

'That would be cool, ay, to invent a word. I want to invent a word. I'm inventing that one. Dungyness.'

'Wow, yeah, dungyness would be a cool one to invent.'

'Mari-ju-a-na,' Strauss said, in a sexy Jamaican accent.

'What a beautiful way to say it. Like crooning.' Aljce thought a bit while Strauss was trying to get a successful suck out of the J. 'Is that shit still wet?'

'It's okay.'

Aljce thought of her Mad Neighbour. 'Hey, do you think it's a tool for making your life anything you want it to be? Because we base our future thinking on the foundation of our thoughts just as much as we base it on any external reality. Whatever that actually is… and who knows? We really are just our perceptions. All of us seeing life differently. And weed is very… positive and lovely, I guess.'

'Hmm. Must be a bit suck for straight people. Missing out. Maybe this is a bit wet.'

'Course they miss out. Or maybe it just wouldn't do the same shit for them. Maybe they're different. I mean, they've got their own perceptions of course. Different to ours.'

ALJCE HADN'T GONE to the airport. 'You'll be back,' she said.

'Maybe. Probably,' said Strauss; as vague as a weather forecast. They both knew that she wouldn't be, but Aljce had enough to deal with.

I miss Strauss, she thought.

WHY IS A RAVEN LIKE A WRITING DESK?

HER FRONT NEIGHBOUR was outside, cooking pineapple on his BBQ while the fine mist from his sprinkler watered his lush garden. Because his fingers were so green, all he needed to do was throw handfuls of poppy seed around in July, and in summer he had these poppies that grew higher than his waist; apricot, strawberry, dark pink and lilac. Pumpkin vines curled their deep golden trumpets around the stems. All wild and casual and perfect. Aljce wished she had his talent for garden artistry.

She knew that he had the same dream as his brother, of being a landscape gardener, and living in a little caravan by the sea. Cooking fish for breakfast. But he'd never do it. He liked to think about it and drink about it and talk about it. If he got it, there'd be nothing left to hope for, nothing left to dream about. She watched him from the shadow of her car. He laughed out loud to himself, and she realised how quiet the neighbourhood was; as empty as a ghost town, except for him and her and her children. That nothing space between Christmas and New Year. It was a beautiful space. Because she'd escaped. She still felt tense. But relieved.

Pleasance and Liddell had jumped onto the trampoline and were trying to out-bounce each other. Her Mad Neighbour had also come out into his yard, and called out to her as she shut her car door. He waved his hands around; his tall figure was silhouetted against the fence line where the sun was setting. Aljce's eyes enjoyed the feast as she looked into his garden – much wilder than his brother's, but just as beautiful; Cannabis plants intermingled with passionfruit hibiscus with dark purple centres, all bending westward to absorbing the golden rays. The air is the colour of honey, she thought. He talked over the fence about the pink bats he'd salvaged that day, and how tomorrow he'd push them into his bedroom roof. He gave her unsolicited advice on how to make glasshouses. He suggested using a table frame and wrapping Gladwrap around and around it. That made her think of some sort of opaque mummy, or perhaps the thick cocoon that some spiders wove to protect their eggs. If she was going to have a glass house, she would want something made of elegant old windows with wooden frames and chipped white paint. A walk in wardrobe of a glasshouse. Where she could grow a Brazilian Plume tree, and some other things she'd wanted to grow for a long time. Green chillies. Lavender hyssop.

'What I have got growing is moonflowers,' she said. 'They'll be awesome when they bloom. Those ones by my back door. Each one of those leaf clusters has a long bud in the middle. When they open, they'll turn to face the moon, and glow a brilliant white.'

'Ooh, I'd like to see that,' he said.

'I'll come over and get you sometime when they're out and so is the moon. They're beautiful when you can see a whole lot together like that, all mixed up with their patch of big green leaves.'

'Ooh, yes, I'd like to see that,' he repeated.

'No point right now, though. Wait for a full moon,' she said.

'So ALJCE, tell us a little bit about yourself,' said the interviewer. It was her third job interview that week. She thought the trick was to tell them what they wanted to hear, rather than to answer the question. Whatever it was that they wanted to hear – and who could be sure? It certainly wasn't an opportunity to lay herself out to be understood or admired. Tell them too much, and they'd be bored. Tell them too little, and she wouldn't stand out. After saying that she was the mother of two, Aljce talked about how passionate she was about counselling, and how thorough her training was. About how she was able to complete her qualification with a five-hundred-hour job placement, and once that was done, she would be able to apply for Provisional Registration. She already had Student Registration, she stressed. She was on track to become a fully-fledged counsellor; all she needed was this job. She was outgoing, bubbly, friendly, a real people person. Yes, she was good with time management. Yes, she was computer literate. Yes, she had good communication skills. She was a hard worker.

Why did she want to leave the job she was in now? Not enough opportunity to build up counselling hours now that the role had been redefined. Could she get references from her employer? Unfortunately her current employer was out of the country, but she hadn't been in that job for very long, and luckily she had been recently employed for many years by someone else who was happy to give her a reference. Aljce said nothing about it feeling as if she'd been in her current job for eternity. And she knew better than to say that she was being bullied. Employers were bound to think it put a question mark over her. Difficult employee. And that's how Jillq would paint it if they went to her and asked her.

'Tell us about a time you had to deal with a workplace conflict, and how you handled it,' intoned the interviewer. Why is a raven like a writing desk? thought Aljce. All she could do was cross her fingers and hope that she had the right answers.

'I went to the person and explained my perspective, and listened to theirs, and we mutually negotiated a way forward,' she said.

'Great,' said the interviewer. 'That sounds very positive.' No one tells the truth in job interviews, she consoled herself.

It all sounded hopeful, but it was weeks before Aljce heard that she'd got one of the jobs, during which time she had wondered how she would pay her mortgage when she didn't go back to the Therapy Hub and her holiday pay stopped. 'It sounds as if you're crying,' said her new employer.

'I'm very excited to be offered the job,' she said, her voice breaking with a sob of relief.

'We don't pay great money,' they warned her.

'Oh, I'm not fussed at all. When can I come in and sign my contract?'

'Next Monday when you start will be fine.'

'I'm really happy to come in and do it before that,' said Aljce, hoping that she didn't sound desperate. Please, she thought, please don't be like Jillq. Don't take your words back after you've said them.

'I spoke to your recent employer,' said her new employer. Aljce's heart leapt into her throat. 'Hannah had nothing but good things to say about you. She said you were the best employee she's ever had. Welcome to our team!' Thank goodness, thought Aljce. It didn't even seem real.

And they were happy for her to do her Placement there.

THE EMPLOYMENT COURT mediation happened a few months later. Some rooms were booked at a local conference Hub. Aljce was in a room by herself, while Jillq and her team were in another. The Mediator went back and forth between them. Aljce showed her the email she'd sent to the woman from the conference. It summarised most things except the few things that had happened after it had been sent, so it seemed the easiest thing to do. The Mediator raised her eyebrows. 'You're saying all this really happened?' she asked.

'Yes,' said Aljce.

'Their story is different, of course,' said the Mediator. 'They've given me a letter, written by an employee, which paints you in quite a different light.'

She showed it to Aljce. It was a long letter, full of complaints about Aljce, and how she wasn't a nice person at all. It was basically all the things they'd said in the meetings: that she was nasty and hard and people didn't like her, that she'd pushed past Hattie and broken confidentiality, that she'd been rude and stubborn with Chelsea over the filing system, that she bullied people by teasing them, that she didn't care about cabbages for poor people, that she'd gone to sleep at the Conference, that she'd been racially offensive about the woman at the conference's taonga. It went on and on, written in the first person.

'Who is this from?' asked Aljce.

'Someone from the Therapy Hub,' said the Mediator. 'I think you should consider carefully that it could be to your advantage to settle this at mediation, given how damning this letter is.'

'Yes, but all of them are part of it. It doesn't prove anything. Jillq is the main instigator, but they all participate. Who is it actually from?' The Mediator glanced at the name at the bottom.

'D. Jones,' she said.

'D. Jones? I don't even know who D. Jones is.'

'Well, they've clearly worked with you. See this part of the sentence here: 'when we were working together..."

'But no one's name starts with D. Except for Dulcie. And she's not a Jones. She's Jillq's daughter. Surely they can't have made up an employee so that Jillq can write her own letter about me?'

'I can check,' said the Mediator. 'Do you want me to check for you?'

'Yes, that would be good.'

The Mediator left the room and came back ten minutes later, looking somewhat annoyed. 'Dulcie Jones,' she said.

'That's Jillq's daughter!' said Aljce. 'That letter isn't worth anything. Of course she's going to support her mother... Why isn't she using the last name she usually uses?'

'Apparently it's her birth father's name,' said the Mediator.

'So why do that? Just to make the letter more official? They can't present a letter from Jillq's daughter and expect it to be credible.'

'I see your point,' said the Mediator. 'However, it's very difficult to win in Employment Court. You have to prove your case. They don't have to prove that they didn't bully you. You have to prove that they did bully you.'

'Well, I want to take it forward. I don't want this to happen to anyone else.'

'I wasn't able to persuade them to offer you any compensation anyway. But keep in mind that if you take the case, it could last for up to five days, and if you lose, you're liable for Employment Court costs.'

'How much are they?'

'Up to a thousand dollars a day.'

'So if I don't prove it, even though I'm in the right, I could owe five thousand dollars?'

'Not including any costs that they might award to the other party.'

'My gosh. The odds are not ever in my favour are they?' said Aljce, suddenly scared. Where would she find that sort of money if she lost? Could she lose her house? But the stubborn part of her didn't give in. 'They're not offering me anything at all, not even an apology,' she said. 'Because they're not sorry at all.' She thought of Dulcie's beautiful, tinkling laugh. How could the person who laughed like that tell such nasty lies about her? 'I'm going to back myself.'

'Up to you,' said the Mediator. 'And I'm not supposed to take sides, but between me and you, good luck. After talking with them, and talking with you, I can see that you're speaking the truth, but not many people go past mediation; it's usually settled here because it's so hard to prove a case. We're instructed to push for settlements at this level.'

'Not many people go past this point because those numbers you just quoted are so scary. But if you believe me, surely a Judge will too.'

'It's not about whether they believe you. It will be about the evidence you can put up. It's a legal forum.'

'Thank you for wishing me luck. I'm going to need it.'

'I'M SUPER STRESSED,' she said to Hannah, telling her what had happened at Mediation.

'Aljce!' said Hannah. 'Why didn't you take me with you?'

'I didn't want to bother you. You would have been working.'

'And I will naturally take time off work to come to the Employment Court with you. Please let me know when you get a date.'

'That would be wonderful. I'm sooooo stressed about the financial aspect if I lose. Plus, I reeeeally don't wanna lose to Jillq. I don't want her to be able to rub my nose in it, and if she knew I was five thousand dollars down, plus, well, if I have to pay her court costs, I'll be just so gutted.'

'Let's not think about that,' said Hannah. 'You're going to need a clear head.'

'I know. But it doesn't really feel like a fair playing field.'

THE LAWYER'S LETTERS started coming. The Therapy Hub had found someone to take their case pro bono, since they were an organisation fighting bullying and violence in the community, and providing therapy to abused people. Aljce realised that the Lawyer probably had a social conscience and didn't want the Therapy Hub coffers to be drained by some rogue employee who was trying to ruin them. She knew that she would have to represent herself. There was no way that she could afford a lawyer. Especially not for up to a week of submissions, let alone for the prep work beforehand.

The first letter was vaguely threatening, and outlined the financial consequences to Aljce if she continued with the case. The Therapy Hub had 'strong evidence' to present. Aljce's Placement papers had been analysed, and Jillq's signature on them had been done in a different pen to the boxes ticked, so it was clear that the signature had been forged. Aljce sat in her car having a panic attack. The Lawyer offered Aljce no legal comeback on herself if she withdrew the case immediately. Fuck you, she thought, when she could breathe again. But she felt so sick in her stomach after opening the first one that she didn't open any subsequent letters that came in the Lawyer's personalised envelopes. It wasn't a great strategy. Not opening the letters made her feel even sicker. What if there were things she should know that she was missing because of her fear of seeing what was inside?

For a while, she couldn't make out why there would be ink from two different pens on the Placement Agreement, and counted it amongst their many lies. And then the coin dropped into the slot while she was turning it relentlessly over and over in her mind with everything else. Of course the signature was in a different pen. Jillq had been so funny about signing it, that she had ticked the boxes on a different day. And now that made Aljce look bad; as if she had committed fraud. She couldn't stop thinking about it: how unfair it was that Jillq's mucking around and signing her Placement Agreement in two different pens meant that she was now able to accuse Aljce of forging Jillq's signature on the Placement Agreement. She wanted to explain it, but it sounded unlikely even to Aljce. Who signed an Agreement in two different pens? If you applied Occam's razor, you would have to believe Jillq, even though Aljce knew Jillq was lying.

HER MAD NEIGHBOUR had replaced the pink flamingos and the loungers with a bedframe with red enamel bedheads. He'd joined the two ends together, and was gluing slats on. 'We need to keep it on the low dose in the winter,' he'd said earlier in the day.

'Did you poke that bible down inside our hedge?' she asked, now.

'Ahh.' He looked confused. 'I might have done, in a state of madness. Yes, I think I did.'

'Why?'

'I don't know. It was a state of madness. A beautiful state of madness. It doesn't have to explain itself.'

'It's still there if you want it,' she said.

She was sitting in his kitchen. It was full of retro kitsch and outsider art and exposed beams from where he'd ripped the inner wall cladding off to put the bats in. There was a red and white gingham table cloth on the turquoise Formica table, and an art work made of old postage stamps. He now had garlic hanging from strings over the bench island which was the home to his self-installed stove and sink.

'So,' he said angrily; as if the tide of his emotions had suddenly changed, 'I've lost a can of CRC somewhere. It was six dollars. A good bargain. I saw a can for eleven dollars fifty somewhere else last week. And I didn't buy it because it was expensive. But those six dollar ones won't be on special any more. So I'm going to have to buy an eleven dollar fifty one. And by the time I've done that, I will have spent seventeen dollars fifty. I should have just bought the eleven dollar fifty one.'

'Where did you leave it last?'

'I remember carrying it to my car, but nothing after that. Maybe I left it on the roof of the car.'

'You should go back. It's probably in the gutter somewhere.'

'Yes, that's right. No one ever picks up rubbish, and if it's in the gutter, that's what they'll think it is. They won't pick it up to see whether it is or it isn't. Nobody does. Not even the sniffers will bother. It wouldn't be in the gutter unless it was an empty can.'

Aljce went home. Weed or not, she could barely be bothered to talk, and his negativity wasn't what she needed. Hearing people put negativity and bitterness into the universe felt like watching her kids eat sugar. Knowing that all that seductive, pretty, sparkly white stuff was bad for their bodies and their brains. In Aljce's mind shitty energy was sugar for the universe. You couldn't persuade people against it, but it was ultimately destructive.

As she went back down her own driveway, she could see that her Front Neighbour's adjacent kitchen windows were pushed diagonally open. The space between them formed an empty triangle down the Hub of his bent head as he sniffed the steam coming off the pot he was stirring on the stove. 'Yum, yum, pig's bum!' he shouted to himself. Not vegetarian, thought Aljce, grimacing. It was hard to stop other peoples' karma from affecting her own. Her head was full of Jillq, and that was another perfect example.

She wondered if she might have smoked herself sober. She loved the act of smoking itself, and it calmed her, but that happy high feeling was eluding her of late. It was as if she'd never smoked that joint with her Mad Neighbour just minutes ago. Perhaps she needed to cut back and decrease her tolerance, but right now didn't feel like a very auspicious time to be doing that.

'How's THINGS GOING with your case?' asked Hannah, ringing again the following week. 'What dates do I need to put in for leave?'

Aljce started crying.

'Hey,' said Hannah. 'It's going to be alright. You're going to beat this. Think positive.'

'I've got such a lot of typing to do, organising what I need to present,' Aljce sobbed. 'Everything I've gotten down in terms of my case notes and arguments is hand written. It's going to take ages, and I don't know if I can get it all done, and prepare my evidence too. I have to be my own lawyer, cos I can't afford one. Jillq doesn't have to worry, because she has a free lawyer. And everything will be typed up for her. What if my lack of legal knowledge trips me up? I don't know anything about precedents or anything. I should be studying that, but there's no time. All I can do is try to win on the merits of my case.'

'Give me your typing to be done,' said Hannah. 'I can do that for you. You concentrate on sorting out your evidence and putting it in a file.'

'Really?' said Aljce, still crying. 'Why would you do that?'

'Because this is not your fault; you're a nice person, and you're trying to do the right thing and put a stop to this nasty behaviour.'

'Oh, my gosh. You're a nice person too, Hannah, and I will be grateful forever,' said Aljce. 'Plus it's just so lovely to hear that someone thinks I'm a nice person and not nasty and hard and unlikeable.'

ALJCE HAD APPROACHED other people that she had recently heard had experienced bullying by Jillq, and left the Hub and found other jobs. Surely if everyone was telling the same story, the Judge would have to believe her. To her disappointment, they declined. 'I'm sorry,' said one, 'but even after all this time, I don't think I could be in the same room with her. It would all come flooding back; that terrible feeling of self-hatred and not being good enough no matter how hard I try.'

'She makes me nervous of her too,' said Aljce.

'It's more a feeling of myself,' said the other person. 'I seem so inadequate when she's around. Hopeless at getting anything right.'

'Surely you know that's because of her and not about you?' But they just shook their head, their eyes focusing on something beyond Aljce.

'Sorry, but I'd have to scratch her eyes out,' said another one.

'I don't really want to get involved,' said a third one. 'I don't want to get a reputation for having Employment Court disputes.'

'But it's not your dispute,' said Aljce.

'Mud sticks. And I'm good where I am now.'

'Don't you worry for other people?'

'Not really. I'm just glad to be out of there.'

Aljce was most in sympathy with the person who said, 'I just don't really ever want to think about it again.'

257

'Is it wrong,' she said to Hannah, 'to be disappointed that those people can't stand up in court, at no risk to themselves, and testify for me? I mean, I'm the one at financial risk. I'm the target. They'd just be decoration. If someone else had asked me, and I wasn't working at the Therapy Hub at the time, I'd definitely have said yes.'

'Not everyone is you,' said Hannah. 'Perhaps they have PTSD.'

'I guess. But saying that they're worried about their reputation? Really? They'd put that ahead of making sure that the bullying stops?'

'Perhaps people have different priorities. And most people's priority is themselves.'

'YIP, YIP, I'll do it,' said MaryAnn's boss. Aljce nearly fell over, it was so unexpected.

'So you mean you will come and tell the Judge what you observed when we met with the Reporter about our roles?'

'Yes, of course, why not? I will just say what I saw and heard, and I didn't see or hear anything from you that deserved a written warning. She's quite insane, that woman. Didn't want MaryAnn leaving the building. Tried to get us to pay extra to what we'd agreed. I got MaryAnn right out of there.'

'So you didn't think I was teasing him?'

'Some friendly banter is what I heard,' said MaryAnn's boss. 'Can you let me know when I will need to be there? Hopefully not longer than an hour. I can't take too much time off.' Well, that's positive, thought Aljce, mentally high fiving herself. She hadn't even bothered asking MaryAnn, because MaryAnn had never wanted to get involved. She was too busy protecting herself. MaryAnn's boss had been a long shot.

ALJCE COULD ATTEND community meetings without issue now. Unfortunately, she saw Hattie at the first one, all flesh and flustle, and there was no way of avoiding her in the small room that they were in. 'Darling!' she said, brushing her kisses past Aljce's cheeks so fast that they slipped off. 'We're missing you. When are you coming back?' Aljce frowned.

'Did you not hear that I've resigned?'

'Oh, Jillq said something,' said Hattie. Aljce kept frowning, trying to process why Hattie would think she was coming back after Jillq had said she'd left.

'I'm taking them to the Employment Court,' she said.

'Oh,' said Hattie. 'I did hear something.'

'I felt really badly bullied while I was working there,' said Aljce. 'I've got a new job now, but I don't want it to happen to anyone else.'

'Oh,' said Hattie for the third time. 'Aljce. You should have come to me. We could have addressed it! I would have supported you.' What planet is she on? thought Aljce.

'Well, no doubt I'll see you in court,' she said.

'What do you mean?'

'They will want you to testify.'

'Aljce! I would never stand up in court and say a word against you. I'm well aware of the problems at the Therapy Hub.'

'Cool,' said Aljce, cautiously. 'I would appreciate that. It's going to be pretty scary for me. I have to prove that I was bullied. They don't have to prove that they didn't bully me. What if they ask you to?'

'I will decline,' said Hattie firmly. 'Jillq has been quite disobliging lately, and I don't see why I should put up with that.'

'Perhaps you are the new target for bullying.'

'She should think twice.'

'Well, cheers anyway,' said Aljce, making moves to carry on, aware that it was Hattie, and she couldn't really trust her and didn't really like her.

ALJCE OPENED HER shower window, and hurriedly closed it again. What the fuck was that on the fence? She opened it a slit again. Was it some sort of recording device? A camera? It looked like a black receiver dish. It could have been at home on a Star Wars movie. And what were those antennae for? Was Jillq spying on her at home? There must be a better explanation. She shut the window, even though she liked the fresh air, and the build-up of steam from the shower made the house damp. What the fuck? But it was so surreal for such a thing to be there that it didn't fit with all the other pieces of her mind, and there was no time to integrate a misfitting piece.

In the rush to get ready for work and get the kids ready for school, and with the brain fog she'd been in lately, she forgot about it until she'd backed down the drive. But she told herself that spyware would only be able to record her if she was home. She would be able to deal with it just as well after work as she could now. She couldn't afford to lose this new job. 'Did you get it?' said her Mad Neighbour later.

'What?' said Aljce.

'The radio thingy I left for the girls on the fence. I can't use it anymore, and I thought that they might like it for a toy. To play with.' He gestured towards the fence, and Aljce remembered the camera recording device. It was lucky that it hadn't been one at all, because she'd done nothing about it. Jillq could have a hundred bits of spy software around, and Aljce wouldn't have a clue. Paranoia. That was what this court battle was doing to her. Seeping her in paranoia and helplessness. How expensive was a hit man? Could Jillq hire one? Surely not, she said to herself. I'm just being dramatic.

Was there ever a time when there wasn't a fly in the ointment of happiness? When she wasn't scared of something upcoming going wrong? Or a time when things weren't actively going wrong, like they were with Jillq at the moment? Life was like a TV soap. When one plot line was ending, another was just about to blow up, with their beginnings and endings overlapping each other. She reminded herself that things that had seemed big and insurmountable in the past had been left in the dust, only partly remembered. So why was it that the present seemed so…inescapable? So oppressive? Was it because she had so little control over it, and therefore could not predict how things would go?

Sometimes she lay awake at night, going over it all in her head. What if I lose my house, she thought. She tried to stop herself. It's like when you start listening for noises in the dark, she told herself reassuringly. Because you're listening for them, you hear them. And then you get scared. But what you forget is that there are always noises in the dark, and the only reason you don't usually hear them is because you're not listening for them. You create your own reality depending on what you give attention to. Naturally though, now that Aljce had thought about noises in the dark, she did indeed start listening to them. Through her open bedroom window, she could hear a burglar alarm going off in the industrial area a few blocks behind her. She wondered if it was her old work building. Nothing was really safe. Especially not her.

THERE WERE SMALL DISTRACTIONS. 'Come and see this,' her Mad Neighbour called, and when she went over, he had an old projector; painted metal grey, with a long, telescopic lens.

'Looks like a small Dalek,' she said. 'Exterminate. Exterminate.'

'But look,' he said delightedly. 'Look!' He plugged it in to a socket hanging from the roof and switched it on before inserting a slide. A small square of light beamed onto an exposed piece of hardboard. 'Curtain,' he called, reaching across her and unhooking it from the wall, so that the room was in darkness.

'I can't stay long,' she said. 'The girls are home alone.' But the small square of light was hypnotic.

'Wait till I get a bit further away,' he said, backing towards her. She stepped aside. The picture got bigger. It was a flower. A buttercup. She could tell by the leaves, but the petals were barely yellow; they were more creamy instead; like a tiny magnolia.

'Wow,' she said. 'Wow. Like those kid's viewfinders. That is really cool. If you ever don't want that, give it to me.'

'I've only got ten slides though,' he said.

'One's enough, you could just play that on your bedroom wall in the dark, when you're lying on your side, trying to get to sleep.'

'I took it outside last night, and played it on the whole side wall of my Brother's house, and it looked magnificent. Especially the flowers with violet tones in them. They really came out well. It was lovely.'

'A small sign of peace then? Since he didn't even take your plant?'

'Oh, no. I only needed his wall.'

'It must be nearly spring again,' he said as he walked her out. 'I've ignored the weeds all winter, but now, look, I can't walk past that buffalo grass and not pluck it out.'

'Yeah, I know what you mean. It's instinctive.'

'IS it buffalo grass?' he called after her as they parted ways. 'Or is it rhino grass? I think it's rhino grass.'

'What do you prefer?' Aljce asked.

'Let's have both!' he called back, cackling at the thought. 'I brought that grass here by mistake when I got some dirt for the garden from down by the river, and now it's jumped the fence to you. Good for feeding our buffalos though.'

'Yes. Well, thanks,' she said drily. She turned to go down the driveway.

'And our rhinos,' he called, staring at the lawn as if they were gathered there in herds. The problem with conversing with a mad man was that they often weren't in on your joke. They were on their own insane joke, and that was what was funny. There wasn't that shared sense of connection over the same thought. They had their thought and you had yours. It was nothing like the connection she'd had with Lewis. Even though she was highly amused by her Mad Neighbour, it wasn't the same. Not to mention the slight sense of guilt she felt at laughing at him as well as with him.

THE EMPLOYMENT COURT hearing was scheduled to be held in the same place as the mediation had been. On the first day, they all filed in; Lawyer first. Jillq, Marj, Mrs. Kingi. Hattie came in last, eyes down, her hair in demure silver ringlets. Aljce raised her eyebrows. Hattie didn't see her, because she was interested in twisting the buttons on her cardigan. The Judge came in and they all stood up and sat back down immediately. She had big exercise books for writing her notes in, and she explained the processes to them. Aljce would make her case. The lawyer would reply. Aljce would bring up anything she needed to bring up to reply to the reply. This would continue till everything had been said. There would be no talking over each other. 'I'm going to have to learn to bite my fingers,' Hannah hissed at her. Aljce would have answered, but she felt too nervous, as if she was overwhelmed by so much emotion that she couldn't cope with it. Perhaps this was how people with anxiety felt all their lives. She was so nervous she could hardly concentrate on what the Judge was saying.

'So Ms. Aljce, just yourself and two witnesses?' asked the Judge. 'I only see one here today?'

'I'm supposed to message the other one and let her know when it's nearly time for her to say her bit. She can't afford to take time off work.'

'What will he or she be testifying about?'

'She'll be just supporting my version of events in relation to one of the things we're in dispute about. My written warning.'

'That's appropriate if she was present,' said the Judge.

'I would have had character references too,' said Aljce, but no one wanted to stand up and be here.'

'What sort of character references?' said the Judge.

'Other people who've been bullied.'

Jillq snorted.

'Not admissible anyway,' said the Judge. Aljce felt scared. There was so much she didn't know about this process, and she felt chastened by the Judge and her own ignorance. 'We will hear your other witness this morning,' said the Judge.

Aljce had to produce all her emails from Jillq, and her personal grievance letter. She also submitted her letter to the woman from the conference. Jillq raised a complaint about it. Aljce was unfairly ruining her reputation with key stakeholders. Aljce was queried about the placement agreement, and explained that Jillq had indeed been hesitant to sign it, paranoid even, and had initially only signed it and left the boxes unticked. When Aljce had realised, she had gone back for the ticks. It had never occurred to her to tick the boxes herself. She had only agreed to employment at the Therapy Hub because she could do her placement there. Why would she have left a wonderful job with Hannah otherwise?

Hannah confirmed that this was the reason Aljce had given for leaving. Aljce asked why she would have forged the placement agreement. If she didn't actually have a placement, her training provider would have found out down the track, and she would have been wasting her time. She would have been better to wait for a job that actually gave her a placement. 'Mmm,' said the Judge, obviously unsure as to where the truth lay. 'So you don't deny that there were two pens used,' she said.

'At first I was confused,' said Aljce. 'I hadn't really thought to book mark in my mind that Jillq had been hesitant to sign, and still hesitant to do the ticks once I got it signed, so I forgot that she had done the ticks later. When I got a letter from her Lawyer saying that two pens had been used, I was puzzled. I had to think hard to remember exactly what happened, but now that I've located it in my memory, I can remember that that's what happened.'

'Fabrication!' snorted Jillq. 'Confabulation!'

But Jillq avoided the eyes of MaryAnn's boss when she arrived. 'So you don't agree that Aljce was teasing the Reporter?' asked the Judge.

'Good natured banter,' said MaryAnn's boss. 'Aljce is actually very funny, and I know the Reporter took it in that spirit. I think he was grateful to have relief from the formality.'

'My client would contend that teasing is bullying,' said the Lawyer.

'I wouldn't call it teasing,' said MaryAnn's boss.

'Aljce has admitted it was teasing,' said the Lawyer.

'That is because my definition of teasing isn't the same as Jillq's,' said Aljce. 'By teasing, I mean good natured ribbing.'

'Not your turn to talk, Aljce,' said Jillq.

'Yes, it was good natured,' said MaryAnn's boss.

'I don't suppose you thought to call the Reporter as a witness,' said the Judge to the Lawyer.

'My client didn't think it was a good idea to involve someone from the media.'

'We have a voice recording we'd like to admit as evidence,' said Marj.

'Who are the parties in the recording?' asked the Judge.

'Myself, Aljce, Jillq and Mrs. Kingi,' said Marj.

'And was everyone aware that they were being recorded, and did they give permission for that to happen?'

'Yes.'

'Ms. Aljce?'

'Yes,' said Aljce, confused. There was nothing on that tape that they could use against her. Unless they had somehow edited the tape. They weren't above anything, given that Jillq could say that she never signed Aljce's Placement Agreement, knowing full well that she had. 'I'm fine with the tape, as long as it hasn't been edited in a way that's unfavourable to me,' she said.

'I think it will be obvious if it has,' said the Judge. Marj brought her phone forward, and pushed the play button. Aljce listened, but couldn't hear anything amiss. 'Is this a true recording?' the Judge asked her.

'I think so,' she said, still unable to hear what Marj was getting at.

'What is your point here?' the Judge asked Jillq and Marj. Ms. Aljce can be clearly heard saying that she hopes to make the employment situation work. It is Ms. Jillq who is saying that she doesn't want it to work out. Good faith is one of the principals of Employment Law.' Hannah rolled her eyes at Aljce. 'It's a wonder your esteemed counsel didn't advise you against entering this recording into evidence,' said the Judge.

'Um, I tried to your honour. Unfortunately my advice wasn't heeded,' said the Lawyer, looking as if something pained him. Aljce raised her eyebrows. It appeared that all ways were still Jillq's ways, and the Lawyer was beginning to see his clients for who they truly were.

At least she hadn't been stupid enough to tell Jillq to go to hell on tape. Thank goodness she had lied right in her face. What she had really wanted was to find another job and leave as soon as she could, because it had been unsafe for her to be anywhere near Jillq.

Marj at least had the grace to look embarrassed. As soon as it was Mrs. Kingi's turn to speak about her experience of Aljce, Aljce could tell that she didn't plan to hold back, and she was right. And later, the Judge had to ask her to be quiet while Aljce was giving her evidence. After that, she contented herself with snorts and rolling her eyes. Aljce ignored her. The Judge could make up her own mind about her. Mrs. Kingi was really only revealing herself.

Jillq was her most super lovely, honey voiced public self. That would be harder to fight. Butter wasn't melting in her mouth, or in Hattie's mouth either, for that matter. But there was no doubt when Hattie spoke that she was there to argue strongly against Aljce, and that, like Mrs. Kingi, she didn't mind indulging in some character assassination. Aljce felt sick while she spoke.

'So Ms. Jillq rang you about Ms. Aljce?' said the Judge to Hannah.

'Yes,' said Hannah. 'She wanted to know if there was anything that I could tell her about Aljce being a difficult employee. I told her that Aljce is the best employee that I've ever had.'

'It's not unreasonable for an employer to do reference checks on a potential employee,' said the Judge.

'After they have already been employed for eight weeks?' asked Hannah. 'When I told her what a high opinion I have of Aljce, she started telling me that Aljce was very unsatisfactory. I couldn't agree.'

'She rang you eight weeks after Ms. Aljce had already been employed at the Therapy Hub? After her new contract was signed?'

'Yes.'

'Did you know she was ringing your previous employer?' the Judge asked Aljce.

'Not at the time.'

'So you didn't give your permission?'

'No.'

'That would seem to be a breach of the Privacy Laws,' said the Judge, frowning.

'Aljce was a very unsatisfactory employee! I needed to take advice! Unfortunately Hannah was no help at all!' said Jillq.

'I suggest you take some advice from your Lawyer,' said the Judge. 'And to that end, we will take a break. We will recommence in thirty minutes.'

There was only one set of toilets, and Aljce met Hattie, unplanned, at the wash basins. 'I thought you weren't going to come,' Aljce said to her.

'Jillq's been really good,' said Hattie, fidgeting nervously. 'She helped me move my father and all his stuff to his new pensioner flat. She organised everyone to spend all Tuesday and Wednesday packing things into boxes, cleaning and things. I mean, she's been really generous. She gave everyone time off work so that they could help. Who else would have done that for me?'

'Sure,' said Aljce. 'Who else could have done that for you? And great team bonding.'

'Exactly,' said Hattie, glad that the point had been accepted, prattling on about how difficult it had been to decide what her father should keep, and what should go to the Salvation Army. As if she hadn't just said untrue things about Aljce in a court of law. Sometimes, Aljce thought, evil is just the lack of will to stand against it.

WHEN THEY FILED back in, the Lawyer spoke. 'Jillq realises that she's made an error in calling Hannah so long after Aljce's employment had commenced,' he said. 'She was unaware that there were any constraints on doing so.'

'Yes,' said the Judge. 'I'm sure that she would like to apologise to Ms. Aljce for doing so.' The Lawyer shifted in his seat.

'I don't have any instructions from my client to that effect,' he said.

'Well,' said the Judge, 'such things have no effect on legal matters anyway.'

'We would like to submit a key piece of evidence,' said the Lawyer.

'Has Ms. Aljce seen it?' asked the Judge. The Lawyer looked at her.

'Um, I'm not sure. It's difficult in that Aljce doesn't have a Lawyer.' Aljce raised her eyebrows. The Lawyer was alluding to her lack of competence.

'In that case, you will need to give a copy of your evidence directly to her.' Aljce almost felt sorry for the Lawyer. He was young, and probably newly qualified, and no doubt well intentioned in taking a case where he had felt he was doing good for the community. But the prospect of new evidence made her nervous.

There was a fluffle while it was organised for it to be photocopied at the front desk for her. She rushed her eyes over it as soon as it was handed to her: notes taken in an exercise book by Jillq when she was meeting Aljce for the first time about doing her placement at the Therapy Hub, and getting the placement agreement signed off. Of course there were notes from the meeting. Jillq was obsessed with notes being taken. Though, naturally, Aljce had never seen these before. Her heart skipped a beat. But not because she was upset. Instead, she was excited. Even though the piece of paper in front of her was a copy, she could tell that what was written on it had been added to at a later time, because some of the notes were written in present tense and some of them were written in past tense. And, in a piece of major irony, the two different tenses were written in two different pens of slightly different blue ink.

'I'd like to comment on this please,' she said, raising her eyes.

'I'm afraid you will have to wait your turn,' said the Judge. Damn, thought Aljce. But she could wait. The Judge turned to the Lawyer. 'I would like you to explain why some of this is in past tense and some of it is in present tense, and why two different pens have been used?'

The Lawyer looked again at the piece of paper.

'See here,' said the Judge. 'Where it says Aljce is showing me her placement agreement? That's present tense. "We are discussing Aljce's hours of work, and are agreeing on thirty hours." That's present tense. And all in the same pen, even if the spelling is somewhat interesting. Then off to the side, in a different colour ink, "It was made clear to Aljce that she could not do a Placement at the Therapy Hub. Aljce was very rude about it." That's past tense. Everything that would support your client's case is written with the second pen, and has clearly been added at a later date. Would you like to consult with your client again?'

Hannah was all but high fiving Aljce. 'Ms. Aljce, before we break, I will allow you to say what it was that you wanted to contribute a few moments ago,' said the Judge to Aljce.

'It's okay,' she said. 'I was only going to make the same points. The additions to those notes are all off to the side or underneath the couple of sentences that form the actual notes, of which there are only a few sentences confirming my employment.'

'Indeed,' said the Judge. Aljce could not believe how happy she was. Her head wanted to explode. Jillq's narcissism had allowed her to go a step too far, and she had showed her true colours to the Judge, who may have been previously unsure of who to believe because Jillq was good at casting a beautiful illusion of herself. No wonder she had accused Aljce of altering a document, it was something that she had no qualms about doing herself. Talk about projection.

It was smooth sailing after that. Aljce lost her nervousness. She was no longer afraid.

'I am the victim here,' said Jillq. 'I've been a victim all my life. My Mother bullied me. I was bullied at school. And now an ex-employee is bullying me, trying to extort money from me in Court.'

'What I believe,' said Aljce, 'is that you have a Narcissistic Personality Disorder, and that you lie and manipulate and bully and abuse others in your quest for power. And now you're being a martyr to get everyone's sympathy because you can't rely on evidence.' The Judge looked interested.

'Move to have that struck out as opinion,' said the Lawyer.

'Of course,' said the Judge, biting her lip.

Afterwards, the Judge explained that it could take a few weeks for her to write up her decision, and that Aljce and the Lawyer would both receive it via email. A decision about Court Costs would be included in the decision. The whole thing had taken less than a day.

ALJCE CHECKED HER email obsessively. When the decision came, it was in her favour, and there was financial recompense for breach of privacy and constructive dismissal. There weren't many things, she thought, that would ever taste so sweet again.

NOTHING BUT A PACK OF CARDS

ALJCE WAS ANXIOUS in her new job for a quite a while, constantly expecting to be in trouble. 'You seem a little bit defensive, Aljce,' said her new employer.

Aljce bit her lip. 'Sorry, but I've been bullied at work before.'

Her new employer laughed. 'Don't worry, mistakes are okay! Sorry that you've had a bad experience, but try to let it go.' You have no idea, thought Aljce.

One of her early clients recognised her from the Therapy Hub. There was some awkwardness until the client explained that they hadn't been happy with the service they'd received from Hattie. Aljce breathed a sigh of relief. She'd thought the client just felt awkward about her, and what she'd probably been told about Aljce. She couldn't have said anything bad about the Therapy Hub until she knew that the client was on the same page.

'I wasn't very impressed either,' she told the client, using understatement because she was still nervous about how Jillq might try to hurt her. Still. And she didn't want to somehow negate her Employment Court settlement.

'Hattie did nothing for me,' said the client. 'I've was sexually abused when I was six, but she didn't want to talk about that, even though I was ready to. I was finally ready to, and my therapist didn't want to hear. She asked to imagine white light, and then invited me to step into it. Like some sort of imaginary party. Invited me. That's not counselling is it?'

'I don't think it is,' said Aljce. 'If that was what someone wanted it might have been the right thing, but because you didn't, it wasn't.'

'That's what I thought,' said the client.

'Tell me about what you were ready to talk about,' said Aljce.

'WHERE'S THE REST of those Zig-Zag papers?' she asked her Mad Neighbour.

'In my pocket. No they're not. Wait here.'

'I have papers inside,' she tried to explain, but he'd already gone. She sat still and contemplated moths and the late afternoon sunshine. They hadn't had sunshine for a while. She reached out to stoke Highsy, but Highsy always sat just out of reach so that she could stroke him, but not in the perfect place. He had no interest in the perfect place. Or in making it available. He wanted to be stroked, but he didn't want to become vulnerable by letting Aljce know that. It wasn't just that the colours of cats were black and ginger or whatever. They all had their own personalities as well.

Her Mad Neighbour returned with papers. And his plan for a multi-dimensional flying machine. With an office in it, so that it could hover as high as her highest tree, and she could kick back in it and smoke weed and write. The view would be to die for. She wanted one. The downside was that her Mad Neighbour thought he would be driving.

He spoke about the speed of light and magnetic fields and frequencies and consciousness. The problem was that it was impossible to tell whether he was talking his truths or talking bullshit, even when she had him up about it. He'd swear that he always told the truth, and then he'd laugh and agree with her before reverting back to performance art. He was like the Mad Hatter: just when you thought you were getting a handle on the conversation, he pretended that he wasn't on the same page as you, making you doubt yourself as he went off in a flow of jumbled words. He was the only person Aljce knew who realised that he was his own observer, and the director, of his own life. He didn't need to draw other people's attention to his life, even though he liked to talk. He didn't need other people to take notice, or to admire him. His reality was what he chose to make it. He was comfortable with whatever came his way. He did what he wanted without being attached to any outcome. I have the good fortune to be smoking with a mad genius in my garage, she thought. Perhaps I have created him with my thoughts; if nothing is real, that is. But perhaps I'm not real either. Even though I feel so.

'I do my healing for nothing but a cup of tea,' her Mad Neighbour said sadly to himself. 'Nothing but a cup of tea, that's what I work for. Nothing but a cup of tea.'

'You're just trying that self-sacrificing healer working amongst the people for little thanks persona on,' she said. 'To see if you like it.' Her Mad Neighbour laughed.

'I am aren't I?' he said, delighted to be caught out.

'At least you're worth talking to,' she said. 'I get bored with people having those cups of tea and talking about small petty concerns; small talk with no content.'

'Oh,' he said, 'I love that. That's where I excel. That's where I take the floor.' Yes, she thought, you would love it. Tapping your teaspoon against the rose china and cutting up a lamington, while flapping your coat sleeves and adding some bizarrity to their lives. Aljce contemplated her fingernails as she held the joint. When she had them short they were new moon nails; like tiny crescents, and sometimes they were as big and pale as whole moons because they'd grown past the tips of her fingers. Right now they were full.

'I'm gonna give you an even better compliment,' she said. 'You're interesting. Not many people are interesting.'

'Oh, I'm interesting,' he said. 'I'm interesting because I'm interested.'

'You're mad as well, of course.' 'Of course I am!' he said laughing delightedly. 'I'm as mad as they come!' Aljce wondered if he'd ever been diagnosed with anything. His formerly negative energy had been replaced by completely positive energy. Not that a diagnosis meant anything. Lots of people had undiagnosed mental illnesses. Some got away with it, and some didn't. Some were in prison, some were on pills, and some ran free. Written off as a little bit different. And some were deliberately casting illusions to enable them to be coldly and ruthlessly mad while passing as normal. Others were passing as happy while they were numb or drowning inside. And what good would a diagnosis do her Mad Neighbour today? He was happy. Happier than she was. Perhaps he was even happy when he was ranting.

And he WAS definitely interesting. Because he was unpredictable. He said and did things outside the normal scope; that no one else would say or do. He liked things that other people wouldn't like. People were generally a dime a dozen; the same old variations on a theme. He was a completely unique theme.

Was he a fool with flashes of genius, or was he a totally self-aware trickster? 'I just can't understand why other people can't see what I can see,' he was saying, but she was too busy thinking to ask him to put that into context.

LATER, SHE WONDERED what he saw. That reality was fake? That every-thing was but the hum of vibration? That he could make his reality anything he chose to make it? Those were all perceptions from different angles: discovery and uncovery, alternate experience and world building. 'If you can see the view to infinity, you will go mad,' he had said.

'Why?' asked Aljce.

'Because it's too big and beautiful for us to comprehend.' And when he spoke like that, she had no idea whether he was barking mad, or a genius. Perhaps it didn't matter. What was important was that infinity was a faint blue, like distance when you looked towards it. Her colours were coming back.

ALJCE WAS AT the garden Hub, picking her way along a path of zen-grey gravel, when she saw Marj approaching towards her down the aisle of trees. Aljce was sure it was her, even though her hair was so thin that Aljce could see right through it. She could see the bright green of the foliage behind the ghostly fine wisps. Red and white camellias were dotted against the big, dense leaves, which were so glossy that they could have been waxed. The woman who looked like Marj approached. Unfortunate-ly, Aljce wasn't mistaken and it was indeed Marj. Aljce looked around, but the walls of camellia were so high that it was as if she was in a branch of a maze, and there was no way out other than to turn and run, or to go past Marj. Aljce sighed. She knew that Marj's level was on a par with the local newspaper and its lead stories about Girl Guides selling Girl Guide cookies. Marj could and would talk about her granddaughter selling cookies for quite a long time, because it was so very interesting. Aljce sighed. There was nowhere to hide, because the carefully clipped camellias rose up in lines along the grey paths of round river stones. She didn't know which would bring the worse karma; thinking bad thoughts about someone, or having to be exposed to their negative energy. And Marj coming towards her meant that she was going to be experiencing both.

If Aljce was really lucky, she'd get an update on the martyr competition on who was working the hardest and doing the most for the Therapy Hub.

Marj fell on her like a long lost friend; as if they had shared nothing but good times together. As they talked, Aljce tried to sidle past her. Once she had successfully repositioned herself, there would be nothing to stop her slowly increasing the distance between them till they really had to go because they had already left. But Marj wasn't able to keep to the rules. She stepped alongside Aljce until Aljce realised that they may as well be walking, because eventually they would get to the entrance. Sighing because she hadn't gotten what she'd come for, and she'd only left Pleasance and Liddell with Mamae for a fixed period of time, Aljce resigned herself to leaving to escape Marj.

The camellias and their glossy leaves gave way to rows on both sides of standard roses; white alternating with red, set in mop-top green bundles on sticks. Like plain and red-rose coloured candyfloss. Sometimes Marj paused by the white ones, sometimes by the red. And Aljce couldn't bring herself to be rude enough not to pause with her. Besides, some parts of her were interested in what Marj was saying. There had been an unexpected development. Marj was being bullied by Jillq. Jillq wouldn't let her into the building by herself. She had accused Marj of stealing some money that had gone missing. Or had it? Jillq had told the others that Marj had been using their passwords to go through their emails and their computers. 'You know I would never do that Aljce,' said Marj. 'I am a very honest person. I thought that I was doing the right thing backing Jillq up about you. But now I see that maybe I was wrong.'

Aljce sighed. 'I'm sorry that this is happening for you, Marj,' she said. There was nothing to be gained except karma.

'It's not what I'd expect from a psychologist,' said Marj, meaning Jillq.

'She's not a psychologist, Marj,' said Aljce. 'I rang up the training provider she said she'd graduated from, and they said she'd flunked the first year papers three times in a row. I'm not sure why they told me, I think they thought I was checking a job application reference or something. But it fits in with her dyslexia.'

'Dyslexia?'

'Haven't you seen anything she's written without spell check?'

'But she's a psychologist. Psychologists don't get dyslexia, do they? Isn't that when you can't spell your words properly?'

'Um,' said Aljce. 'I suppose they could, but she's not a psychologist anyway.'

'She was very angry about all the money she had to pay you,' said Marj. 'I told her that it was a court order, and we'd have to pay it. But she didn't want to.'

'She hasn't,' said Aljce. 'I'm going to have to get another court order to get her to pay my court ordered compensation.'

'If only I'd known…,' said Marj.

'The future is never any clearer than the past, Marj,' said Aljce. 'And what IS the past other than a misremembered collection of information that doesn't fit together properly?' Marj looked at her blankly, but Aljce showed no mercy. She had had to listen to Marj when Marj talked. Now Marj had to listen to her. 'Consciousness is in the moment. It's our gift that we are able to look into the past and the future. Because everything is connected. But both of them are hazy. And too often we neglect to notice what is happening in the current moment, because we're too busy trying to make them out.'

'It's not a very good present then, is it?' said Marj, referencing Aljce's use of the word gift, her reply fitting what Aljce had said better than she knew.

'It's the only present we have, and it's necessary,' said Aljce, 'for connectivity.'

Aljce ran her fingers through her own hair. It was still fine, but thick enough down to her shoulders, below which it was as silky-fine as Marj's. It was growing back. And Spring was here again. Roses and late camellias proved that. What was her hurry? It wasn't as if time actually existed.

On the way home, Amy Winehouse was on her car stereo. 'He walks away, the sun goes down; he takes the day, but I'm grown. And in your way, in this blue shade, my tears dry on their own,' she sang. She thought of Lewis. The hurt and loss was still there, but it was no longer raw. She was a different person now.

There was still a lot of snow on the ranges in the distance. It glowed white and angry; as if it was bright with infection. A bit of snow cloud hovered above it, creating its own little weather system in the distance. She remembered how they'd talked about newborn snow. It seemed appropriate, but it didn't hurt. It was just snow.

She thought about Jillq, and how she was bullying Marj. No one knew who Jillq truly was until they'd gotten too close to her and she had sucked them in and they couldn't escape. She was a black hole, and her in-group was the event horizon. Once you passed them, it was too late. But ultimately, Jillq was an anxious person. One who calmed herself by dominating others and showing her power by hurting them. Who protected herself against the world by surrounding herself with weak people. Jillq had gathered a buffer of people around her, who allowed her awful behaviour. She'd never be confident enough to be her horrible self without that protection. Most people would have been repulsed and amazed by how she behaved. But the group allowed Jillq to make other people doubt themselves so that they didn't blame Jillq for what she did. Jillq was scared all the time, and when she was really scared, she released it as anger against someone else. Particularly anyone who might threaten her world view, where she was the centre of the universe and right about everything. The queen of everything. That was her. Too scared to be able to be wrong, to fail, to be alone, to be vulnerable to life. There was no point in hating Jillq. She wasn't worth it.

'I LIKE THE old fashioned radio,' her Mad Neighbour said. 'I can even get the radio from China. It has a lot of Chinese music.'

'Yeah, of course. But when they talk, what's the point of listening? You don't understand Chinese.'

'Oh,' he said vaguely. 'If I listen long enough, I start to understand it. Everybody's saying the same thing.' That's so bizarre that it possibly makes sense, she thought, and once again, she wasn't quite sure whether he was a madman or a freestyling genius.

Aljce took a drag on their shared joint. 'What do you know about the different strains?' he said.

'I know that Americans are breeding them like rabbits.'

'Oh, Americans. Mucking with tradition. See this one here that we're smoking now? Panama Red. It has red stems topside when you see it growing. Afghan, that's a potent one. Acapulco Gold: that's got a gold shimmer in the leaves.' He shook some seeds from a pill bottle onto the table. 'See that seed? It's got a gold shimmer in it. That might be Acapulco Gold.'

'Does that actually translate like that?'

'In this case it does. Seeds. You've got to have fun with seeds.'

'It'd be all different in America,' she said. 'As much as we can smoke over here probably translates to two puffs over there. We'd have to ac-climatise.'

'You know me,' he said later on in the conversation. 'You know how

I like to exagereet. You have to poet it up a bit, to get something out of life.' And suddenly, she saw him as a performance artist, aware of his own madness and getting something out of it. Maybe he wasn't mad at all; maybe he was just bored with his little life with no people except her and the supermarket checkout people in it, confined to his garden and his handmade house. Maybe he was just furnishing his life with his imagination, making the air around him bloom as if it was exploding with flowers in every direction.

Aljce let the smoke from the joint trail up her arm. She did such a lot of reflection. On other people. On herself. On herself in relation to other people. Hopefully, people who self-reflect achieve personal growth exponentially, she thought. Like compound interest on money. Because they can notice their own faults and plan what they would like to become a better person. By realising how they might have contributed to situations. By being okay with not being perfect and working towards being whoever they wanted to be. You couldn't do that if you thought you were already perfect. Personal growth surely must begat more personal growth as a person came to understand how much further they had to go, and how much they didn't know. The more they saw, the bigger they realised it was. And I have done nothing but grow, she concluded. So who I was last year must be far behind who I am now. I'm not even who I thought I was when I woke up this morning. And I'm definitely a different Aljce to the one who used to even consider being defined by Jillq.

She tuned in again to her Mad Neighbour. 'Those characters in Wonderland,' he was saying. 'The White Rabbit, the Queen of Hearts, it wasn't Wonderland to them. It was reality. And where are we right now? ...Reality. This IS Wonderland.'

EPILOGUE

I GIVE MYSELF VERY GOOD ADVICE,
BUT I VERY SELDOM FOLLOW IT

THERE WAS A blood moon. She remembered there being a blood moon almost exactly three years ago on the night that she read Lewis's last one-line message. Was reality coming full circle? Moments were endlessly repeating themselves. Everything in the universe seemed to be made up of a finite number of patterns, no matter whether it was stars in a galaxy or grains of sand on a beach. Radio waves and microwaves and ocean waves and particle waves. Nebulas like the pupils of an eye. Galaxies connected like the neurons of the brain, or city streets lit up at night, seen from above. Everything was the same. The same thing in the same moment. Reality was incredibly small on the outside, but it was incredibly big in the centre where infinite possibility lay.

She stood outside with her Mad Neighbour. It seemed rude not to give him the other half of the smoke, since it was a blood moon. Definitely something to be stoned for. She bent to stroke Steinie under the chin. Cats needed to be handled. That was what taught them to be affectionate to you: your affection towards them. That's why she liked cats. It wasn't about whether they were attracted to you. It was about them coming to love and trust you based on the way you treated them.

She thought of the book she was nearly finished writing, cued up on her laptop in her bedroom. She really needed to get back to completing it, but getting stoned had never gotten in the way of that. And strange or beautiful experiences never went amiss.

It was a book about her, and her time working for Jillq at the Therapy Hub. Lewis was inescapably in it. Her feelings of emptiness and loss when he'd left her had fed into that time. Perhaps that had made her more vulnerable, although that wasn't his fault. He knew nothing about that. Perhaps he'd just been scared too; like Jillq. There were no guarantees about anything, but she herself would always take the gamble if there was any chance of real love. Because real love, big love, fairy tale love was too rare and too special to miss out on any chance of it. Funny, because she had always thought of herself as quite a risk-averse person. Perhaps practising courage had made her brave without her realising it.

Maybe she should thank him. Because she'd been so comprehensively rejected by him, she now realised that she had no fears of being rejected by anyone in the future. She'd survived. It was their loss if they didn't have the good taste to know what they were passing up. She must have thought the ground would open up and swallow her while the whole world pointed. Or something like that. All it amounted to was that Lewis wasn't wise enough to recognise a good thing when he met it. Everyone was attracted to different people. She wouldn't be bothered if someone had a different taste in paintings or perfume; in fact, she'd just quietly be pleased about her own choices. So why should this be any different? Particularly since he had probably rejected her due to who he was. Being rejected said everything about the person doing the rejecting, and nothing about the person being rejected. Perhaps Lewis had just gotten more and more antsy about commitment, the closer the possibility of it had gotten. Or perhaps he was a narcissist like Jillq, who had just wanted to make her feel loved, only to snatch it away from her, for his own twisted pleasure and superiority. The more she tried to get to grips with what had happened between them, the further the answers drifted from her. But she was sure it was nothing to do with her. She'd just happened to be there.

She thought about her nearly completed book again. Would people know where fantasy left reality; which would be necessary if they weren't to think she was completely mad? And would people understand that much of what might seem like the height of fantasy actually was true? What would Lewis and the other people on whom it was based find harder to forgive? The fiction she had told, or the reality she'd documented?

She didn't care about the others, but would Lewis be angry? Was it wrong to use some of the bits that he co-created? Was that private to him? Surely existing required physical manifestation, and he hadn't, so perhaps he didn't. Although no doubt he observed himself. Was it wrong to filter his filtered perception of himself, the one that he'd presented to her, and mix it with her own perception to make a whole new him? He would definitely see himself differently to the way in which she saw him. That's how perception worked. She tried to listen to the small voice in her head. Not a good idea. To write a book that took anything from him at all.

But for some reason, Aljce had a compulsion, and she couldn't seem to say no to herself. She had a sense that this narrative was meant to be, and that she couldn't change it. It was the equal of predestined; existing simultaneously with all other moments. Reality would dissolve if any part of it changed. She couldn't fight it; it always had been and always would be.

But it was still risky. Even the messages she sent to try to placate him all that time ago hadn't moved him. He was an angry person. Maybe he'd try to harm her. To widely share the things she'd told him about herself. But she had a sense that he wanted to matter, and being the muse for a story might actually suit him; he might be happy about it. She congratulated herself mentally. That was the way forward; the best way to think about it. And it wasn't as if those things she'd told him were about her. They were about some girl she'd been three years ago.

No character was ever completely one person anyway. One person could form a base for a character, but give them a single characteristic from someone else, and the character became a whole different person. No one should recognise themselves in her novel. She wouldn't use his actual messages or messages, or anything he'd actually said to her. Just the idea of him. It wasn't a story about him, just one in which he had intertwined himself, and now she couldn't unmesh him to tell it without him in it. She thought about emailing it to him first. Should she email it to him first? Be respectful, and get his permission, do the decent thing? No, she couldn't do that. He could and would refuse her. But he couldn't complain. He was the one who'd told her never to contact him again.

And if anyone else saw themselves in her characters, it would pay them to remember that to call her on it would be to admit that they recognised themselves and their situation in the awfulness of the people in her book. To make a fuss about it would mean exposing themselves to the world, and she didn't imagine they would be in a hurry to do that. They would have to prove that they were indeed those bullies. Suing her for money could be an incentive, but she was willing to bet reputation beat money. Would suing her be an option? She had no idea. But surely you were allowed to base fiction on actual events. She could wave her Employment Court decision at them.

Probably more to the point was whether people would recognise the bits of her strewn all the way through it, and whether she could live with their judgements. What if they were people who mattered? Would they judge her if they were? Would they still matter if they did? Although they couldn't possibly know which parts were her and which were embellished, diminished, added or subtracted. They could guess, but guessing didn't make anything true. If they guessed wrongly, and people had a skewed picture of her, what did it matter as long as she had a strong picture of herself? Publicly blurred pictures were good for privacy.

If she was creating her own reality, as quantum physics suggested she was, and everything in the universe was connected, as quantum physics also suggested it was, then everything was one universe, one consciousness. In this universe anyway. So there were no true secrets, just different experiences of consciousness. And writing was a way to process that experience, and to be conscious of it.

Her Neighbour passed the joint back. She was mad; the same as he was. But her madness felt like a beautiful symphony of connections sparking together like crazy-coloured psychedelic fireworks crashing against the black walls of her brain. His was more chaotic, with his neurons arriving at unusual destinations and bringing him to random conclusions that could often be amusing or beautiful. She had a sudden flash about her previous realisation about his self-awareness. She needed to stop putting herself above him. She was mad too. People in looking glass houses shouldn't throw stones. Besides, it was a compliment.

'Can we stand on your picnic table? You know. Get closer. Get a better view.'

Aljce raised her eyebrows. It didn't seem likely. But for some reason, standing on her picnic table with her Mad Neighbour, in her back yard, in the dark, under a blood moon, seemed entirely the thing to do. It added to the poignancy of the occasion.

He leaned back slightly, flapping his arms to keep from overbalancing, like a bird attempting to fly backwards. 'I don't think it's a man in the moon,' he said, commenting on the shadows on its surface. 'I think it's a rabbit in the moon. Look at the two ears in the top left. It's a bunny moon.'

The moon had begun as quite milky white, but since then it had taken on a flush of rose that slowly deepened and bled across its surface with the shadow. It was several shades of pink and red, like human body tissue.

Down on the ground below her, the glow made her feel as if she'd strayed into a red light district, and the few overlooked kids' toys on the lawn looked like red toadstools with little flecks of pure light catching some of the corners and edges.

'That's what all my troubles have been about,' said her Mad Neighbour. I'm right in the line of the moon.'

'We're all right in the line of the moon.'

'Yes, but it's a blood moon. Everything is meant to be.'

Well, she thought, at least they could agree on that. She wondered if the world was coming to an end, and whether her Mad Neighbour had been the prophet to decipher reality all along, if only she had listened to him. Had his unspoken message been that it was all too mad to be true, and coincidences were increasing as all moments became the same? And then she thought, hell, I'm as bad as those end-of-the-world prophets who keep rescheduling. It was hard to tell the difference between deep thoughts and superstition.

THE NEXT DAY, she was finished. There it was. The story. Perfect; exactly as she had known it could be. How could she have refused to birth her story when every colour and every shade brought her pleasure?

I write to express all this inner rapture that I have inside me, she thought. I want to share it. Even though I know that only some people will know what it is. Most people won't, because they'll be unable to tell it apart from anything else. People like Marj.

It doesn't really matter whether someone loves me, or whether the universe chooses to flow him my way or not, she thought. I love the life I'm making for myself. I have beautiful karma. She decided that she didn't need to understand everything or even anything about what had happened between herself and Lewis. It was okay to leave the story strewn with possibilities. Untested, unsolved. Unknown. Never known.

She hadn't had a rapture for a while, but somehow, now, as she danced in her bedroom, the air in the world around her was full of flowers: red and purple-pink, flowering on dark bushes while a red sun set behind them, covering them with a deep orange twilight. She couldn't touch them or see them directly, but she knew they were there, as real as if she could see them. In a place that wasn't her mind or her reality. It was a third place altogether. She felt deliriously happy. Life was the stories you told yourself. And she told good stories.

There was no observer yet, but there would be.

ACKNOWLEDGEMENTS

Aljce and Alice would like to thank: Doch and Bran from Lawrence and Gibbs who are amazing to work with and not at all responsible for the decision to use caps over italics and other questionable editing decisions, (that would be her,) all the people who helped in any way with this book, Anna and Laura, Johanna and Paul for editing and design; all her friends; her former partners and lovers for their contributions to her growth; her children, extended children and family; Brian and Robyn Bargh, John Huria, Steve Braunias and Fiona Kidman for their support for her writing over the years; all the people who've brought her karmic lessons; and the universe, for her experience of life as a beautiful thing. But mostly of all: Jake, because he's her White Rabbit. Always.

Colossal rats invade from the town belt! Your rent is up but everyone is calling it a summer of love. Vivid posters incite residents to an evening of mayhem. For many years rats have contented themselves with scraps. But as summer heats up and the cost of living skyrockets, we can no longer ignore that our friends are seeking their own rung on the property ladder.

RAT KING LANDLORD is Murdoch Stephens' first novel under his own name and was described as "last year's surprise literary hit" by *Stuff*.

He has previously published numerous books with Lawrence & Gibson as Richard Meros, including ON THE CONDITIONS AND POSSIBILITIES OF HELEN CLARK TAKING ME AS HER YOUNG LOVER ("The underground publishing hit of the decade" *NZ Listener*). He is also the author of DOING OUR BIT: THE CAMPAIGN TO DOUBLE THE REFUGEE QUOTA (BWB Texts) on the campaign he founded in 2013.

www.lawrenceandgibson.co.nz

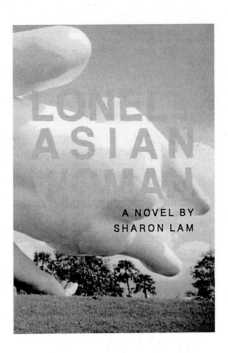

A NOVEL BY
SHARON LAM

LONELY ASIAN WOMAN is the debut novel of Sharon Lam. It ruthlessly skews stereotypes of Asian-New Zealanders at the same time as it offers a fantastical Wellington-centric bildungsroman.

The novel, set in contemporary Wellington, follows Paula, a lazy young woman who is stuck in a rut. Deep in stagnation, the sight of a spam ad for 'lonely Asian women looking for fun' becomes a moment of profound realisation that she, too, is but a lonely Asian woman looking for fun. Paula's new outlook leads her to shoplift a cheesecake-laden supermarket trolley. The trolley contains an unexpected attachment.

LONELY ASIAN WOMAN is not the story of a young woman coming to her responsibilities in the world. Instead, Lam defies the expected and leads the reader and her characters to a deft climax against the grain of the titular lonely Asian woman.

www.lawrenceandgibson.co.nz

It is Saturday afternoon and two boys' schools are locked in battle for college rugby supremacy. Priya – a fifteen year old who barely belongs – watches from the sidelines. Then it is Saturday night and the team is partying. Priya's friends have evaporated and she isn't sure what to do. In the weeks after 'the incident' life seems to go on. But when whispers turn to confrontation, the institutions of wealth and privilege circle the wagons.

SPRIGS is the latest novel from Brannavan Gnanalingam. It was short-listed for the Acorn Foundation prize for best fiction at the Ockham Book Awards in 2021, as was his previous novel SODDEN DOWNSTREAM in 2018. He is the author of four other books published by Lawrence and Gibson.

"It is a scarily contemporary and realistic story ... [part four] is an extraordinary piece of writing, I must say" - Kim Hill, *Radio NZ.*

www.lawrenceandgibson.co.nz